SO YOU CALL
YOURSELF A MAN?

So You Call Yourself a Man?

A Devotional for Ordinary Men With Extraordinary Potential

by T.D. Jakes

Albury Publishing
Tulsa, Oklahoma

Unless otherwise indicated, all Scripture quotations are taken from the *King James Version* of the Bible.

2nd Printing

So You Call Yourself a Man?
A Devotional for Ordinary Men With Extraordinary
Potential

ISBN 1-57778-026-4

Published by ALBURY PUBLISHING
P.O. Box 470406
Tulsa, Oklahoma 74147-0406

TO

my sons who are in the process of becoming
men of integrity.

I, like most parents, am full of hopes and dreams
loaded with rather lofty expectations of grandeur.
Nevertheless, should my sons fall short of my hopes,
I will remain faithful to my call — the call to be their
father. It is not a position to be resigned but a
relationship to be relied upon. It is a call I am glad
to fulfill as with all men who have someone
who believes in them.

The world awaits you!

CONTENTS

Introduction

TIME FOR A NEW LEVEL OF RECONCILIATION AND HEALING!

"And they sung a new song, saying, Thou art worthy . . . for thou wast slain, and hast redeemed us to God by thy blood out of every kindred, and tongue, and people, and nation" (Revelation 5:9).

The church that I pastor is multiracial and multicultural. I believe that is part of God's plan for reconciliation in these last days. I don't believe you can have multiplication if you only have duplication of like elements. Multiplication is born of reconciliation among those with differences.

God loves a multiplicity of people and He blesses people in a multiplicity of ways. We must be willing to accept the different ways in which people receive blessings and then thank God for them. We must be willing to accept different ways of worshiping the Lord Jesus Christ — one may dance, another may bow, yet another may stand and shout. He is One Lord, but He has created many people.

We must never bring people to Christ and then insist to them, "Now, be just like me." We need massive diversity in programming, in our praise, in the expression of our spiritual gifts. In the church, we have divided ourselves in just about as many ways we can be divided. We've divided ourselves by denomination . . .

means of baptism . . .

timetables related to the tribulation . . .

types of services . . .

and meanings for communion. It's time we recognize that the Lord meant what He said when He inspired Paul to write:

- "For we being many are one bread, and one body: for we are all partakers of that one bread" (1 Corinthians 10:17).
- "There is neither Jew nor Greek, there is neither bond nor free, there is neither male nor female: for ye are all one in Christ Jesus" (Galatians 3:28).
- "There is one body, and one Spirit, even as ye are called in one hope of your calling; one Lord, one faith, one baptism, one God and Father of all, who is above all, and through all, and in you all" (Ephesians 4:4-6).

Fads come and go in the church, just as they come and go in society. Prophecy is big right now — people are all looking for the "prophetic word." Some only want to go to services that are labeled "healing services." This one will lay hands on the sick, that one will call out diseases, another one might throw holy water on those with sickness.

The methods and fads don't matter. We serve One Lord. He is faithful to remain the same yesterday, today, and forever. He works through a multiplicity of ways and through all manner of gifts.

It is only when we feel truly free to be ourselves, however, that we allow other people to be truly free to be themselves. The person who enjoys the unique ways in which God has created him, is a person who is likely to appreciate and enjoy the unique way in which God has created others.

Our goal is to preach, teach, and experience truth — not culture.

There's more than one way to skin a cat.
There's more than one way to bake a cake.
There's more than one way to praise the Lord!

It's not just Satan who has bound God's people in their praise. *We* have bound each other in order to promote our own causes, agendas, and preferred styles.

You may not like the way another person expresses his faith in Christ. You may not agree with it fully or choose to adopt it as your means of expression. But you *must* value his right to express his faith in Christ the way he believes the Lord is leading him to express it. And don't waste your time criticizing him and become a prisoner in your own mind . . . heart . . . emotions!

There are many ways to praise the Lord. A person might dance, walk, stand with his arms raised, fall on his knees, lie flat on his face before God. He might sing, shout, talk, cry, laugh. What's important is that a man find a way to open up and express himself to the Lord. There's no "right" position or "right" form of expression for praise — the only thing that must be right before God is a man's heart, humbled to praise Him from the depths of his emotions.

When the world sees Christian men dropping their differences and coming together, the world is going to want what Christians have.

Politicians, educators, economists, scientists, and corporations — they have all tried unsuccessfully to bring the world together and to bridge the gaps that divide nation from nation, tribe from tribe, people from people.

But only God can build that bridge.

And the good news is that God does build that bridge by His outpoured Holy Spirit.

True Pentecost comes when devout men come together from every nation under the one anointing of the Holy Spirit. Regardless of their backgrounds . . .

races . . .

cultures . . .

and denominations. You cannot have a genuine Pentecost outpouring of God's power in the presence of segregation, alienation, or separation among God's people.

When the world sees Christian men coming together under one anointing, it is going to run to our upper room to hear the Gospel.

Yes, indeed. When we are loosed in our hearts of all prejudice . . .

    loosed from our emotional bondage . . .

        loosed in our praise and worship . . .

           and loosed in our ability to love others as God loves them . . .

the world will begin to turn to Christ for forgiveness, deliverance, and healing. It will *run* to the cross.

Loose that man inside you — and let him be free in Christ Jesus!

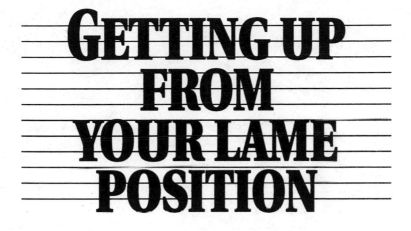

GETTING UP FROM YOUR LAME POSITION

WAITING ON MAN TO GET INTO POSITION

These are the generations of the heavens and of the earth when they were created, in the day that the LORD God made the earth and the heavens, and every plant of the field before it was in the earth, and every herb of the field before it grew: for the LORD God had not caused it to rain upon the earth, and there was not a man to till the ground. (Genesis 2:4-5)

Things must be in place before God will act. The Bible tells us that at the beginning of creation, God had not caused it to rain upon the earth.

This does not mean that the earth was without water. Up to this time, God had caused a mist to come up from the earth to give moisture to the earth. There had been no downpour, however, from the heavenlies.

Why? Because there was not a man to till the ground.

There are some things that God has planned to do, has made provision for doing, and desires to do that He will not do until man is in place to receive what God intends to give.

15

The blessing is there . . . in God's safe keeping.

The need is there . . . insistent, resistant, persistent in its pain and suffering.

But the blessing won't be applied to the need until man's heart is in a position for God to act according to His own laws of redemption, healing, and deliverance.

There are some things that God has in the heavenlies that will not be released to you until you are in the proper position spiritually, relationally, emotionally. Oh, you may be experiencing a "mist" — but in your spirit, you have a restlessness that there must be something more. You have an inner knowing that you aren't fully where you ought to be. You have an uneasiness, a frustration that causes you to say, "Why am I no further than this in my life?"

Rather than blaming your wife, your parents, your boss, or your race . . . you are wise to ask yourself, "Is God waiting on me to be in a different spiritual position before He pours out a blessing on my life?"

When you are in alignment with God and His purposes, He *will* open up the heavens and cause it to RAIN on you! You'll experience such an outpouring of God's blessings that you won't know how to contain them.

———————
———————
———————
———————

Ask God today WHERE He wants you to be spiritually so that you might receive the downpour of His heavenly blessings.

RECOGNIZING THE LAME AT THE GATE

Now Peter and John went up together into the temple at the hour of prayer, being the ninth hour. And a certain man lame from his mother's womb was carried, whom they laid daily at the gate of the temple which is called Beautiful. (Acts 3:1,2)

The lame man who was brought to the Beautiful Gate was incapacitated, and because he was in that condition, he needed special care. While other men walked in and out of the temple area, this man was carried to the temple.

There was nothing wrong with this man in many areas of his body — he could see, hear, touch, and speak. He could move his arms and upper torso. In fact, there was only one thing wrong with this man — his ankles had no strength.

If there is something wrong in only one area of life, however, and that area of weakness is severe enough, a man's entire life can be affected. The "operation" of a man's life — the function, the activity — can be so impacted that it will feel to that man as if *everything* has

17

gone wrong. That was the case with this man. Only one thing was wrong with him, but that one thing created a whole-life problem.

When a man is handicapped, he needs to be carried. He cannot support his own life, pull his own weight, or operate in his own strength. This has nothing to do with whether or not the man is a good man in his heart and motives. It has to do with his having a bad problem.

The lame man's problem had made him dependent upon other people. His problem interfered to a certain extent with their lives — he had to be carried by other men to a place where he could beg, and then carried home at the end of the day. He could not get to where he wanted to be on his own.

This man no doubt felt discouraged and low in self-value. When a man has to be carried about, unable to move about on his own, he feels demeaned. When a man has to beg for a living and is not allowed to participate fully in the activities of other men, he feels diminished.

Not only was this man lame in his ankles, he had a lameness in his emotions and his spirit. One area of weakness had created another in his life. Not only were his ankles lame; he was lame.

Virtually all men are in that position today. We each have a weakness in our lives that keeps us from functioning as a whole person. But what do most of us do? We deny our own lameness. And we pass by others who are lame because we don't have either the courage or the compassion that it takes to stop and help them.

It's time we quit kidding ourselves. We each have a need for God's healing power. Others have needs, and they need for us to help them experience God at work in their lives. Yes, we are all lame at the gate at some point in our lives, in some area of our lives.

The good news is that God sends people to the gate where we sit to help us receive what God has for us to receive. Watch for that person in your life. Look for that person to come. And be very aware that *you* may be the person that God is sending to bring deliverance to a lame man.

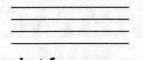

Be on the alert for a person who may be sitting at a gate through which you will pass today.

WHAT ARE YOU EXPECTING?

And a certain man lame from his mother's womb was carried, whom they laid daily at the gate of the temple which is called Beautiful, to ask alms of them that entered into the temple; who seeing Peter and John about to go into the temple asked an alms. (Acts 3:2,3)

What do you want when you go to church? Why are you really there? What is it you are seeking?

Are you present only so that you can tell others that you go to church? Are you there so that you can play a role that you think gives you some kind of status in your community? Are you there just to keep peace in your family and to avoid the nagging and pleading of your wife or your mother or your children?

Jesus once asked a group of people concerning John the Baptist, "Who did you go out into the wilderness to see? A reed shaken with the wind? A man clothed in soft raiment? A prophet?" (See Matthew 11:7-15.)

It's an important question for us to ask ourselves: Who are we going to church to see and hear?

If we are going to church just to hear the choir sing or to hear a preacher speak, we are making the same mistake that the lame man made when he was carried to the Beautiful Gate that day. He was looking for the wrong thing. He was seeking alms. He wasn't expecting healing.

We also need to ask ourselves some serious questions about the way we regard the people we meet on a day-to-day basis: How are we looking at other people? What do we expect from our encounters with them?

So often we approach people the same way this lame man did. We are looking for what they are going to do for us. We are looking for what we can get from them. We aren't looking for what it is that God wants to do in us or through us.

I call this a "get-over" spirit. The person with a get-over spirit is always looking for some one or some thing to help him get over his problem. He's looking for what he can take from others, or what they will give to him freely — which is no different than alms-begging — without any effort or responsibility on his part.

People with a get-over spirit are users. They use people, but don't really love them. They latch onto people and seek to take from them what they desire or lust after — it may be sex, it may be money, it may be fawning adoration. They have little interest in other people apart from what they can get from them that will help them make it from today to tomorrow.

God calls us to see Him when we see other people. He calls us either to give to other people as He would give to them, or to receive from other people as if we are receiving from the Lord Himself.

When we go to church, we are to go with an expectation that *God* is going to speak to our hearts and heal our lameness.

When we encounter other people, we are to regard them with love and compassion — open to receive what good thing they may say to us to encourage us in the Lord, and also open to say and give to them whatever the Lord prompts us to say and give.

In this way we live in freedom — freely receiving and freely giving. (See Matthew 10:8.)

_____

Identify precisely what you are expecting from God today.

WHY ARE YOU WHO YOU ARE?

A certain man lame from his mother's womb. . . . (Acts 3:2)

Have you ever stopped to think about who you are and how you got to be who you are? Have you wondered how it is that you got through all the things you have been through? Have you ever thoroughly considered your own life?

So many men are so busy looking at their lame ankles — their problems, their needs, their area of weakness — that they fail to see the big picture of their own lives. They don't have an awareness of where they are in their lives, primarily because they don't have a clear picture of where they have been.

This man who was carried to the Beautiful Gate had not become crippled as the result of an accident or an illness. He hadn't fallen from a rooftop or been thrown from a horse or been run over by a cart. He had been born lame. He had never known anything other than lameness all of his life. His lameness was not a disease, but a *weakness*. The bones of his feet and ankles simply had never gained strength.

23

This man actually had two advantages that many men do not have today.

First, the lame man knew that he had a problem. His lameness was obvious — not only visible to others, but visible to himself. He had to face his problem; there was no way to avoid it or ignore it.

Many men today haven't faced their lameness. They think that because they can look in the mirror and not see any major flaws, or get through a social event without making any major mistakes, or keep a job without getting fired . . . things must be all right. The fact is, we *each* have an area of lameness in our lives. It's there — even if we refuse to face it, even if it isn't obvious.

Second, the lame man knew the reason for his lameness. He knew the cause of his problem. He knew the "why" for his life being the way it was.

One of the things we each must do about the area of weakness we have in our lives is to trace it back to its origin. We need to ask, "*Why* am I like this? *Why* do I do what I do?"

Until we know why we are so angry . . .

so filled with hate . . .

so resentful and bitter,

we cannot understand fully what it is that we need to do to get beyond our problem.

Why do I come home from church where I've been acting like a saint and leaping about in praise like David . . . only to act like a wild gorilla with my wife and children?

Why don't I know how to communicate? Why am I unwilling to learn how to communicate better?

Why do I feel an inner rage all the time? Why do things often spin out of control?

Why am I not succeeding more at work?

Why do I feel depressed at times?

Why am I not growing more in my spiritual life?

Why am I not further along in my walk with the Lord?

Why am I who I am?

Get your own résumé and read it to yourself. Look back over your life. Face your life. Find out why you have been camping out in a state of lameness for so long.

Taking a look at your own life can be depressing if that's the point where you *end* your search of self. But if you use your new understanding to say, "This is how I got where I am, and here's what I am going to do about it," then your self-exploration can be highly positive.

When we look closely at our lives, we each discover that we need a Savior, we need a Lord, and we need relationships with other Christians who will teach us God's Word and build us up in Christ Jesus. That's one of the greatest discoveries a person can ever make.

There's a reason that you are who you are. But there's an even greater purpose for your life. You may be who you are, but you are not yet who you will be! God has bigger and better things ahead for you. We each are called to be a "partaker of the glory that shall be revealed" (1 Peter 5:1).

Consider today not only your problem and its cause, but your calling in Christ Jesus and its result!

ALIVE AND AVAILABLE

Now is the accepted time; behold, now is the day of salvation. (2 Corinthians 6:2)

Where are you on God's agenda? Do you know?

The Bible doesn't tell us how long the lame man sat at the Beautiful Gate, but I feel certain that being carried to the gate was his daily habit. He had no reason to think that the day he encountered Peter and John was any different from any other day in his life. To him, it was probably "just another day" of begging alms.

Most of us don't know what day it is on "God's calendar." We don't know the day that is *the day* that God has marked on His timetable for us to receive our miracle. We very often aren't aware that God has a life-changing, mind-altering, spirit-redeeming, soul-cleansing miracle for us . . . today.

The challenge to us is to be aware of our miracle moment when it comes. And the only way I know to be aware of that moment is to stay aware always. We must be available *continually* to receive from God *continuously.*

Being ALIVE is the first requirement for being available. The good news is . . . *you ARE alive!*

In spite of the pain and weakness in an area of your life . . .

in spite of not being able to do what other men are doing . . .

in spite of not being able to move about like other men move about, walking and leaping about with full freedom of mobility . . .

the fact is,

you are still here! You have survived to this moment.

No matter how broken

or wounded

or frustrated you may be, you are alive!

And as long as you are alive, a miracle is possible. To receive a miracle of any kind, however, you must be *available* for a miracle.

Miracles happen to those who know they need them and make themselves available to receive them. So the devil would much rather see you so active and busy that you never give God or your life or your weakness a moment's thought. The devil would much rather see a man become completely involved with contracts and opportunities and business trips and too-full schedules than to see a man be brought to a place of being available should a servant of God walk by or should a servant of God come to speak a word from the Lord.

Being available means that we are . . .

• *alert.* We're looking for a miracle.
• *ready.* We have our hands lifted in praise, ready to receive.
• *excited.* We have a sharp, eager anticipation about what God is going to do.

Jesus said to His disciples — including us — "Your time is alway ready" (John 7:6). Let's live with that degree of availability!

———————
———————
———————

Stay available today to receive the miracle that God has on its way.

GUARDING YOUR MOST PRECIOUS SPIRIT

The thief cometh not, but for to steal, and to kill, and to destroy: I am come that they might have life, and that they might have it more abundantly. (John 10:10)

Many people have security systems for their houses, or alarms for their cars. They know they have something of value. And they also know that there are thieves loose in the world who are likely to want the valuable possessions they have.

While this is true for material possessions, so many men do not have a security system for their emotional and spiritual lives. Part of the reason is that they don't know *they* are valuable to God. And another part of the reason is that they don't know that a thief is loose in the world who wants to steal, destroy, and kill everything of value that they possess.

You can put bars on the windows of your house . . .

You can put an alarm system on your car that will cause sirens to sound and lights to flash on and off . . .

You can put video cameras and silent alarms in your store . . .

You can put padlocks on your bicycle or on trunks filled with things you hold to be valuable . . .

You can put your most prized possessions in sealed vaults with highly sophisticated security systems . . .

But are you putting something in and on and around yourself to guard your precious emotional and spiritual life from the ravages of the thief who wants to steal from you your very life?

You were created in the image and likeness of God. That's the only reason the thief needs to want to rob you of *who you are*. He knows that first and foremost you are an offspring of the omnipotent, omniscient, omnipresent, all-loving God.

You are a spirit . . .

that has a soul . . .

and lives in a body that was formed from the dust of the earth. Your spirit comes from God's "is-ness," and therefore you can know God in your spirit.

In your spirit you have God-consciousness. You have an awareness of Him and a desire for Him.

In your soul you have self-consciousness. In your mind, your psyche, your memories, and your emotions you know who you are and what you are supposed to do.

In your body you have world-consciousness. In your body, you know if you are hot or cold, hungry or satisfied, comfortable or uncomfortable.

The thief is after you solely because you have a part of God's eternal Spirit in you.

Guard your spirit. It's not only the most valuable part of you, it's the eternal part of you.

How do we guard our spirits?

First, build your relationship with Jesus. Spend time communicating with Him. Draw your identity from Him.

Second, build yourself up in God's Word. Read your Bible. Study it. Bind the Word of God to your mind.

Third, build up yourself spiritually in praise. Worship the Lord. Serve Him in every way you know.

Stay on guard. The thief never sleeps.

_____

_____

_____

Look for the abundance that is found in Jesus. He has come to RESTORE whatever the thief may already have taken from you.

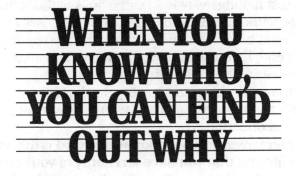

WHEN YOU KNOW WHO, YOU CAN FIND OUT WHY

The spirit of God hath made me, and the breath of the Almighty hath given me life. (Job 33:4)

When God blew from His own breath into the dust body of man, man came alive and knew who he was and Who God was.

Your understanding of yourself and your understanding of God are intricately intertwined. You cannot know fully who you are until you know Who God is. Until you recognize that God is the One Who has given you your life — the One Who has formed and fashioned you with a specific plan and destiny in mind — you cannot find either peace or a sense of purpose. It's time we stopped letting other people breathe on us their plans and start looking close into the face and heart of God for our identity.

Until we allow God to breathe upon us and breathe into us His Spirit, we will be vulnerable to any person and anything that comes along that seeks to define us, and in defining us, manipulates and controls us.

31

There are many men who get up every day "just swinging," just beating the air. They are in a fight, but they don't know what they are fighting about. The person who is just flailing away is a man who is without purpose or goals, without direction or impact. He senses he is in a struggle but he doesn't know who with. The result is that at day's end, he is exhausted, frustrated, and angry. He has virtually no ability to win.

But the man who gets up every day knowing who he is battling is a man who can fight with purpose and intelligence and direction.

In order to win you must know that God is the Source of your life and that you have an enemy of your eternal spirit, and that God your Source will help you *defeat* your enemy. It is only when you come to that awareness that life makes sense.

If you don't know that God is your Source and the devil is your enemy, life can overwhelm you. There are too many issues and situations that just don't make sense, don't connect, don't produce as they should, or don't fit.

Say to yourself today, "The Spirit of God has made me. The breath of God is giving me life."

_____
_____
_____
_____

Don't let anyone breathe his or her identity or plans into you except God.

PLEASING TO THE FATHER

This is my beloved Son, in whom I am well pleased. (Matthew 3:17)

When Jesus stepped down into the Jordan River to be baptized by John the Baptist, He stepped into the fullness of God's purpose for His life. Jesus' step into the Jordan waters was symbolic of His perpetual death and resurrection.

Have you ever stopped to think that by the time Jesus stepped into the waters of the Jordan River that day, they were teeming with the sins of mankind? John the Baptist had baptized countless people in the Jordan, their sins figuratively passing from them into the sea of God's forgiveness, just as the waters of the Jordan River end up in the Dead Sea.

From the shores of spiritual blindness, one might think, "How awful! Jesus was wading into sin." Jesus was doing so, however, to fulfill the purpose of God — redemption from sin. Jesus was *exactly* where God wanted Him to be, doing *precisely* what God wanted Him to do.

As Jesus stood in the very place God desired for Him to stand, God opened up the heavens, the Spirit of God descended upon Him, and a voice spoke from heaven

33

saying, "This is My Son. This is My seed, My Son, Who pleases Me!"

Don't expect God to speak up for you — or to cause others to see you for who you really are — until you are willing to step into the place where God has called you to be. When you step into that place where you are supposed to be, you don't have to speak up for yourself, fight for yourself, or demand anything of others. God will speak for you. He'll command whatever forces are involved to yield to you, give to you, honor you, listen to you, obey you.

Don't expect God to open up the heavens and pour out His Spirit of power and truth and wisdom and righteousness onto your life unless you are where you are supposed to be. When you step into the place God has destined for you, you won't have to take on your own battles, grope about for the right decisions, or wonder if something is right or wrong. God will give you every ability you need. He'll put into your path what you need to have. And you won't have any doubt that it's God Who is providing for you or working in you.

To please the Father . . . obey Him. Even if it means wading into someone else's muddy waters.

Go only where God calls you to go. Once there, do only what He commands you to do. You will be pleasing to Him!

THE ENMITY BETWEEN YOU AND THE DEVIL

And the LORD God said unto the serpent
. . . I will put enmity between thee and the
woman, and between thy seed and her seed;
it shall bruise thy head, and thou shalt bruise
his heel. (Genesis 3:14,15)

Are you fully aware that the devil is after you? Do you
have a keen sense that the devil is on your trail?

Yes, you.

You.

You.

You.

We sometimes think, "Oh, yes, the devil is alive and
lurking about today, but he's not after *me*. I don't have
anything he wants. I'm nobody. I'm not called by God to
do anything spectacular. Why would the devil want me?"

He wants you because you are a potential seed for
producing a harvest for God in this earth!

God prophesied to the serpent that had seduced Eve
into sin that He was going to put enmity between the *seed*
of the woman and the serpent. This word for seed, *zera* in
Hebrew, is also a word used for semen. Women don't have

35

semen. The seed of the woman, therefore, was to be a "man-child" descendant of Eve.

This prophecy was fulfilled in Jesus Christ, but that fulfillment in and through Christ is ongoing in *us* until the day God brings this age to an end. The devil is a defeated foe in the context of eternity, but he has not yet been defeated fully in the context of earthly time. He still has access to men, women, boys, and girls to tempt them into sin. He still has an opportunity to lay a claim on the souls of mankind.

Therefore, there's enmity between you — one of the human seeds born down through the centuries from your great ancestor Eve — and the devil. Paul wrote to the Romans: "The God of peace shall bruise Satan under your feet shortly. The grace of our Lord Jesus Christ be with you" (Romans 16:20). The devil's hate is still raging against you.

Enmity is a state of ill will or hostility. It doesn't come and go. It remains the devil's intent to destroy you no matter what you do. His nature is the nature of a violent murderer who is on the lookout for his next victim. In 1 Peter 5:8 we read, "Be sober, be vigilant; because your adversary the devil, as a roaring lion, walketh about, seeking whom he may devour."

The devil is stalking you. He hates you. He is in a state of perpetual ill will, hostility, and conflict with you whether you know it or not. He is after your self-esteem, your identity, your mind, your emotions, your wife and children, your job or your business, your church, your well-being, your witness, your productivity, your health. He's after everything you value and hold as being good. Ultimately, his goal is the destruction of your eternal spirit.

Throughout the centuries, this warfare of the devil has been aimed primarily at the man-child. The devil's primary battles have been against men. When Pharaoh looked at the Hebrews and determined that they were becoming too numerous and too powerful, he didn't authorize the killing of all the Hebrew babies — no, only the male babies. (See Exodus 1:22.) Pharaoh didn't have an understanding that the Messiah would one day be a man born to an Israelite virgin. The one who knew this fact was the devil; Pharaoh was simply one of his pawns. And therefore, Pharaoh's order was that any time a man-child was born, the midwives were to kill him.

The devil is after you. He wants you. He seeks to kill you.

The devil doesn't mind your coming to church. He just doesn't want church — the Spirit of God — to come into you.

The devil doesn't mind your holding a position. He just doesn't want you to occupy *the* position you're supposed to hold in the kingdom of God.

The devil doesn't mind your having a title. He just doesn't want you to operate in your divine calling.

I have traveled the nation in recent years and have seen the power of God work in marvelous ways. Let me assure you, when men begin to move into the positions that they are called to occupy in the body of Christ, things happen! They happen both individually and in churches.

Are you in the position you are supposed to be in with God?

Being in the right place with God is the only way you can remain secure in the face of the devil's assault against you. To stay alive, stay connected to God as the Source of your life.

To stay alive in your spirit, stay alive in God's Spirit. That's the only way you will defeat the devil every day.

DON'T LET THE DEVIL DESTROY YOU!

Man that is born of a woman is of few days, and full of trouble. He cometh forth like a flower, and is cut down: he fleeth also as a shadow, and continueth not. (Job 14:1,2)

You don't have long on this earth. Even if you live to be a hundred years old, or older, you are going to look back on your life and think, "It's only been a few days that I've been alive."

In some communities and among some groups of people in our nation today, man's days are especially few indeed.

All around us we see man killing man.

Man gunning down his fellowman on the street . . .

Man lying lifeless in crack houses . . .

Man curled up on street corners, homeless but too drunk to do anything about it . . .

Man suffering in a hospital bed, HIV positive, until he breathes his final breath.

All around us we see men killing their seed, their *zera*.

Men making babies and then not having the desire or taking the time to be fathers to them . . .

men impregnating women and then not
marrying them or caring about their *zera*,
encouraging women by their lack of
involvement and provision to get
abortions . . .
    men abandoning their children and
    teenagers, leaving their sons to struggle with finding
    their own identity in a godless world.

If there ever was a mission field in need of a missionary,
it's the mission field of the men in our nation. It's easier to
get ten women to come to church, and then to love and
serve God, than to get one man to do so.

What are we doing to God's seed? How are we
destroying our lives? Wars and plagues don't need to cut
down our men anymore. We are cutting down ourselves!

Who molested our boys and girls?

Who raped our women?

Who beat our toddlers?

Who abandoned our babies?

If the devil can't destroy your seed, he will do his best
to damage your seed — to make it lame in some way, to
make it weak in the ankles, to limit the effectiveness and
strength of the seed.

We've all hurt some people . . .
    betrayed some covenants . . .
        made some mistakes . . .
            blown some money . . .
                missed some opportunities . . .
and sinned against God. But thank God, He is merciful.

The good news — the very BEST news — is that God
forgives.

He forgives the molester . . .

He forgives the abuser . . .

He forgives the addict . . .

He forgives the liar and the thief . . .

He forgives the SINNER.

And He doesn't stop there. He heals the situation that sin created. He restores men to wholeness and changes their circumstances into a blessing.

The devil may be out to defeat you, but God is out to defeat the devil. Stay on God's side. Receive His forgiveness. Walk in His commandments. Praise His holy name. In staying on God's side, you are staying on the winning side.

_____
_____
_____
_____

Make every day you live a day that you CHOOSE God's life over the devil's death.

ARE YOU STUCK AT THE GATE?

A certain man lame from his mother's womb was carried, whom they laid daily at the gate of the temple. (Acts 3:2)

This lame man was laid daily at a gate that was so beautiful it had Beautiful as its name! If a man has an ugly problem, it matters very little that he is in a beautiful place. A person with an ugly problem has very little ability to enjoy beauty or appreciate it.

Not only that, but this man was living in the Promised Land. Yet he had very little ability to receive the fullness of the promises that others were receiving. As a lame man, he was not allowed into the temple. According to the law, his condition made him unworthy to participate in the rituals that able-bodied men kept.

So many men are close to being in the right place, but they aren't yet fully there.

They are just close enough to the church to know what's going on — to know who's who and what's being preached. But they are not all the way into the body of Christ so they can experience the fullness of God's power and provision in their lives.

41

They are stuck at the gate.

Some of them even know when to kneel and when to raise their hands. They know the songs in the hymnal and precisely what time the service should start and end. They've heard more altar calls than they can count. They know all the protocol. They take all the ritual of the church in stride and from a distance . . . but they never get all the way into the place where they can receive God's blessing.

What keeps them stuck at the gate? Their attitude.

They have the same attitude that they have in the world, an attitude that says, "I'm like this because nobody will help me. I'm the way I am because nobody will help me 'get over' to the place of blessing."

They bring their unrenewed minds into the church. They expect the church to change them and do for them in the same way they expect their bosses, or the government, or the neighborhood social worker to change their world and do for them.

Now you don't have to be poor or financially destitute to have a get-over spirit. You can be rich and still blame your problems on somebody else who you believe is failing to do for you what you think they should be doing for you. You may be a very wealthy business owner and still have a get-over attitude, blaming your employees or your competitors for keeping you from the success you think you should have. You can be a church pastor and have a get-over attitude, blaming the members of your church for not appreciating you the way you think you should be appreciated.

The worst attitude in the world is a get-over attitude regarding God — that you are expecting somebody else to provide for you what God alone can provide for you, and then blaming that other person or group of people for failing you and causing you to fail.

Nobody can be your Source but God.

Are You Stuck at the Gate?

And nobody can put you into a right relationship with God but *you.*

_____
_____
_____
_____

If you are stuck at the gate today because of your own bad attitude, repent of that attitude! Go all the way into the place where you can receive God's blessings for YOURSELF . . . DIRECTLY from God. The way to that place is praise and worship.

CREATED FOR WHOLENESS

This is the book of the generations of Adam. In the day that God created man, in the likeness of God made he him; male and female created he them; and blessed them, and called their name Adam, in the day when they were created. (Genesis 5:1,2)

God created man in His own image — whole.

So often we get into a numbers game in the church. We get all wrapped up in determining if God is one or three — a single entity or a committee, a unity or a trinity. The Hebrews didn't have this conflict about God. Moses said, "Hear, O Israel: The LORD our God is one LORD" (Deuteronomy 6:4). The Lord is whole. And that is the only perspective that is necessary. The Lord isn't fragmented or divided. God is full and complete, lacking nothing whatsoever.

God has never faced a question He couldn't answer. He has never faced a need He couldn't supply.

He never had a desire He couldn't fulfill.

He is altogether self-sufficient and perfect.

And God made man in His likeness and image — *whole*. Male and female created He *them*. He called *their* name Adam.

44

This first whole man had dominion over everything. He had a position granted to him by his Creator.

One of the great differences between men and women is rooted in this: Man had position with God before he had a relationship with another human being. Woman was birthed in relationship.

We see today that men are positional and women are relational. Men are concerned about power and status far more than women. Men love titles. Women are concerned about their relationships: their children, their spouses, their friends. When men get together they ask one another, "What do you do for a living?" In the course of the conversation, they expect to find out what position another man holds in his company. When women get together they ask, "Are you married? Do you have children?" In the course of their conversation, they pull out pictures of their family members and give details about every one of them.

Man's first job was naming. If he called a giraffe a giraffe, it was a giraffe! He had dominion over his world. But when man looked around, he didn't find a mate for himself. God said, "This situation isn't good. Man is too much like Me. He's too self-sufficient, too self-contained."

When God made Eve He didn't reach down into the earth again. He reached into man. He said to Adam, "I'm going to reach into you and pull out of you something that I've already placed in you." Man was created with woman inside him. And out of the inner emotional and spiritual womb of man, Eve was created.

Jesus approaches us in the same way today. He says to us, "I've placed My faith and My Spirit and My life in you. I'm going to pull out of you something that I've placed in you. I'm going to bring My desire for your wholeness to a reality that you can fully experience."

Jesus said time and again to those He healed and delivered: "Be thou made whole." He saw people as being whole entities — spirit, mind, emotions, psyche, body, relationships — all linked together so tightly that it was impossible to separate or fragment the elements of man.

Wholeness is God's plan for you. Jesus came to make you whole in His way, His timing, and for His glory. His wholeness for you includes *whole* relationships.

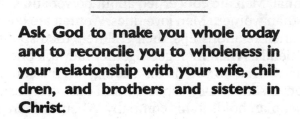

> **Ask God to make you whole today and to reconcile you to wholeness in your relationship with your wife, children, and brothers and sisters in Christ.**

WALKING IN WHOSE LIKENESS?

Adam lived an hundred and thirty years, and begat a son in his own likeness, after his image; and called his name Seth. (Genesis 5:3)

After Adam and Eve had fallen into sin and were expelled from the Garden of Eden, we read that Adam fathered a child, and the boy was just like him. Adam's son was born "in his own likeness" (Genesis 5:3).

Adam had been created in the image of the wholeness of God. Seth was created in the image of his fallen father.

And throughout the generations, we men have been born in the image of fallen men. We bear their sin nature. How many times have we heard it said about ourselves, "He's just like his daddy"? In some cases, we are too much like our daddies. History repeats itself over and over and over again.

Daddy was angry and frustrated ... now look at my temper.

Daddy couldn't stay with Mama ... now look at my string of divorces.

Daddy was an alcoholic ... now look at my drug addiction.

Daddy had girlfriends ... now I'm involved in a relationship I have to hide.

47

Daddy was a workaholic . . . and now I spend fourteen hours a day at work.

Daddy wasn't affectionate with his children . . . and now I don't know how to hug and kiss my children.

We have an interesting and clear example of the way in which sin tendencies are passed along from father to son in the stories of Abraham and Isaac.

> *And Abraham journeyed from thence toward the south country, and dwelled between Kadesh and Shur, and sojourned in Gerar. And Abraham said of Sarah his wife, She is my sister: and Abimelech king of Gerar sent, and took Sarah. (Genesis 20:1,2)*

Sarah looked so fine as an old woman that Abraham knew that when he entered the south country of Gerar, King Abimelech was going to take one look at Sarah and want her as part of his harem. And Abraham was right. Abimelech did come and take Sarah to be his concubine.

Abraham told Sarah, "Tell him you are my sister." Abraham knew that if Abimelech thought Sarah was his sister, he would treat Abraham better. But if Abimelech thought Sarah was his wife, he would kill him so he might have sole right to Sarah. Abraham was willing to tell a half-truth and allow his own wife to be raped by a heathen king in order to save his own skin. And not only that, in the process he was jeopardizing his own future, since Sarah at that time had not yet given birth to Isaac, Abraham's *zera*, his destined seed.

Abraham passed on his tendency toward deceit to his son.

In Genesis 26 we read that Isaac, the son of Abraham and Sarah, faced a famine where Isaac lived, and he went south in search of food. He also went to Abimelech, king of the Philistines, and "Isaac dwelt in Gerar" (Genesis 26:6). History was repeating itself.

In Genesis 26:7 we read:

> *And the men of the place asked him of*
> *his wife; and he said, She is my sister: for*
> *he feared to say, She is my wife; lest, said*
> *he, the men of the place should kill me*
> *for Rebekah; because she was fair to look*
> *upon.*

Isaac wasn't even alive when his father had made the same statement about Sarah. And yet there it was — the sin tendency of his father appearing in his life.

We see the pattern again and again in the Scriptures.

When you receive Jesus as your Savior, you become a son of God. Paul says, "Wherefore thou art no more a servant, but a son; and if a son, then an heir of God through Christ" (Galatians 4:7).

No longer do you need to walk in the likeness of your earthly daddy. Rather, you are called to walk in the likeness of your heavenly Father, your eternal Abba, Daddy God. Determine that you will be more and more like *Him,* day by day!

————————
————————
————————

Choose today to WALK in the image of your ETERNAL Father.

THE IMPORTANCE OF A FATHER'S BLESSING

And it came to pass after these things, that one told Joseph, Behold, thy father is sick: and he took with him his two sons, Manasseh and Ephraim. And one told Jacob, and said, Behold, thy son Joseph cometh unto thee: and Israel strengthened himself, and sat upon the bed. . . . Now the eyes of Israel were dim for age, so that he could not see. And he brought them near unto him; and he kissed them, and embraced them. . . . And Israel stretched out his right hand, and laid it upon Ephraim's head, who was the younger, and his left hand upon Manasseh's head. (Genesis 48:1,2,10,14)

The blessing was passed down from generation to generation among the Israelites when fathers placed their hands upon their sons and spoke God's words over them.

Jacob was on his deathbed when Joseph came to him with his two sons so that Jacob might bless them. In blessing them, Jacob prophesied their identity.

Father to son.
Father to son.
Father to son.

The people of Israel understood who they were largely because individual men learned who they were from their fathers and their grandfathers.

In the last few years as I have traveled this nation ministering in conferences of men, I have encountered literally thousands of men who do not know who they are. They never have had fathers who would lovingly lay their hands upon them and tell them who they were — either in their human family, or in the eyes of God.

A man who grows up without a father grows up not knowing his name, his identity. A boy who doesn't have a father figure after which to pattern his life will run the streets looking for father figures to give him a sense of identity and a name. He'll find one eventually — most likely a gang. He'll take on their name and become a Red or a Blue or a Cryp or a Blood. He'll take on the identity of his "older brothers" in the gang who actually operate in the role of a father to him, telling him who he is and what he is destined to be and do.

If that boy doesn't run into the arms of a gang, he's likely to run into the arms of the corner dope dealer or crime boss. He'll give him a name — Freakin' Freddy or Jumping Jim or Slick Sam.

Every man-child needs a name. He needs an identity. He can't get that from his mother. Mothers are capable of giving great love and encouragement to their sons, but they cannot give them their identity. Only a father can do that.

Jacob refused to die until he could lay his hands on his sons and grandsons and tell them who they were and what they were destined to do.

We must follow his example today. It doesn't matter if our sons are five or fifty years old. We need to put our arms around them and tell them that they are loved by us. We need to tell them who they are in God. We need to quote Scripture over them and tell them —

- *You are a lion's whelp, and your hand shall be in the enemy's neck. (See Genesis 49:8,9.)*
- *You are more than a conqueror. You can do all things through Christ who strengthens you. (See Romans 8:37, Philippians 4:13.)*
- *You are a son of the Most High God. You have been purchased by the shed blood of Jesus Christ on the cross. You are a joint heir with Christ — a prince of the King of kings. There's greatness in your bones and in your bloodline. (See Galatians 4:6,7.)*

One Sunday in our church, I called all of the young boys who had no fathers to come forward so that I might lay hands on them and prophesy over them and tell them who they are in the Lord. I looked up and found that a thirty-year-old man had come forward and fallen at my feet. He said, "Pastor, I know I'm not a boy, but nobody ever told me who I am. Will you lay your hands on me and tell me who I am? I'm hurting because nobody has ever blessed me like that."

Call your sons and your grandsons to you today. Lay your hands upon them and tell them that you love them and that God loves them and has a purpose for their lives. Give them an identity.

If you are a grown man, find someone who can truly be a spiritual father to you. Ask him to bless you and tell you who you are in Christ Jesus.

Give a blessing to your children today. Talk to them about their identity in Christ Jesus. Encourage them with your love and faith.

RELYING ON GOD TO REVEAL YOUR TRUE IDENTITY

And Jacob was left alone; and there wrestled a man with him until the breaking of the day.... And he said, Let me go, for the day breaketh. And he said, I will not let thee go, except thou bless me. And he said unto him, What is thy name? And he said, Jacob. And he said, Thy name shall be called no more Jacob, but Israel: for as a prince hast thou power with God and with men, and hast prevailed. (Genesis 32:24, 26-28)

You are not who the devil or sinful people say you are. You are who God says you are. And sometimes you have to go directly to God to get your real name and your real identity.

That was certainly the case in Jacob's life.

All of his growing-up years, Jacob had been called a supplanter, one who got what wasn't rightfully his. Jacob's very name means "trickster."

Schemer, where's your coat?

Schemer, come into the kitchen.

Schemer, put on your overshoes.

53

Schemer, take out the trash.

Can you imagine as a boy growing up only to hear every time somebody called your name what they believed to be the most negative aspect of your character?

Hey, con man!

Hey, fat boy!

Hey, worthless slob!

Hey, bastard child!

Hey, doper!

Hey, crook!

Hey, unwanted baby!

Hey, crippled man!

Jacob grew up believing what others said about him — that he was a schemer, a plotter, a manipulator, a con man. And Jacob lived true to what was said.

He believed the lie about him until he became the lie. He tricked his father into giving him the blessing and the inheritance that was rightfully his older brother's. He tricked his uncle Laban in his care of Laban's flocks, and he hoped to trick his brother Esau in the way that he returned home to face his family.

And then all alone in the dark of night, Jacob had an encounter with God. He wrestled with God until daybreak and finally cried out to God, "Bless me!"

The Lord asked him, "What is your name?" Jacob replied, "I am who people have said I am. I am Jacob, the trickster, the con man, the schemer."

And God said, "No, you are not. You are Israel. You are a prince, the child of God, and you have power with God."

You may have done what people say you did, but you are not what people say you are.

When you start praising God, He'll tell you who you are. When you get into God's Word and ask God to reveal to you your identity, He'll show you who you are. He'll show you that you are —

The head and not the tail. (See Deuteronomy 28:13.)

Above only, and not beneath. (See Deuteronomy 28:13.)

Chosen for this generation. (See 1 Peter 2:9.)
More than a conqueror. (See Romans 8:37.)
Part of a royal priesthood. (See 1 Peter 2:9.)
A peculiar treasure. (See Exodus 19:5.)
The citizen of a holy nation. (See Exodus 19:6.)

Look to God to reveal your true identity. He alone knows ALL about you.

_____
_____
_____

Who is God saying that you are . . . right now?

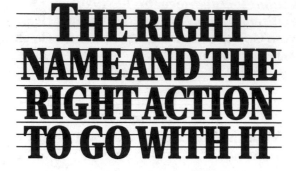

THE RIGHT NAME AND THE RIGHT ACTION TO GO WITH IT

Peter said, Silver and gold have I none; but such as I have give I thee: In the name of Jesus Christ of Nazareth rise up and walk. And he took him by the right hand, and lifted him up. (Acts 3:6,7)

When Peter and John came to the temple at the hour of prayer, they fixed their eyes on the lame man by the Beautiful Gate and Peter said, "Look on us." Peter didn't want this man to be distracted. If a person gets distracted, he can miss what God has for him.

Peter wanted this man to pay close attention to what he was about to do. He wanted him to *really* hear him. I believe he got right down into the face of that man and locked his eyes on that man's eyes so that everything else in that lame man's awareness was shut out. That's the way we need to deal with people who are in pain.

If we are the ones who are suffering, that's the way we need to look at Jesus. We need to get so close to Him, and look so directly into His eyes, that we don't see anybody else, we aren't aware of anybody else, we don't hear anybody else. We only hear and see Jesus.

56

And then Peter spoke to him with a name.

Every one of us needs a name that is stronger than the devil's name. . .

a name that is stronger than your problem . . .

a name that is greater than your need . . .

a name that is more potent than your pain.

That name is the name of Jesus.

Paul wrote, "At the name of Jesus every knee should bow, of things in heaven, and things in earth, and things under the earth; and that every tongue should confess that Jesus Christ is Lord, to the glory of God the Father" (Philippians 2:10,11).

It is the name of Jesus that is higher than any other name. The writer of Hebrews says, He is "holy, harmless, undefiled . . . and made higher than the heavens" (Hebrews 7:26).

There is no other name that can make whole the part of you that is lame. Only the name of Jesus.

But then Peter went beyond words. He did what needed to be done. This lame man by the Beautiful Gate heard what Peter said, but the words themselves had no visible effect on his life. You may hear a sermon and in your mind say amen, and then find that nothing changes in your life. People in great need all around you may hear about the love and mercy of God, the blood of Jesus, and the power of the Holy Spirit, and yet not experience any of it for themselves.

Peter put the name of Jesus into action. He reached down and took this lame man by the right hand and lifted him up. And it was *as* Peter pulled this man to his feet that the lame man's feet and ankle bones received strength. (See Acts 3:7.) This man who had never walked, didn't need any help walking. No, he only needed help getting up on his feet. Instantly, he was standing, walking, and leaping about as he praised God.

There are people around you today who need for you to speak the right name into their lives — the name of

Jesus — and they need for you to help them get to their feet spiritually and emotionally, and in some cases, physically and materially. It is your hand reached out in love and compassion, with genuine help that is not born of sympathy but which is born of faith, that will help them stand. You don't need to be their crutch. You don't need to spend the rest of your life helping them. But you do need to pull them to their feet so that God can heal and strengthen the lameness in their lives.

If you are the one who is being helped to your feet by a Christian brother, then rise up in faith on the inside even as you are helped to rise. Don't place your confidence in the person who is lifting you or praying for you. Put your trust in the name of Jesus. He is the One Who will heal you of your lameness, strengthen you in your weakness, and cause you to walk in boldness. He alone is the One Who can make you whole.

God is desiring to work in you and through you today.

_____
_____
_____

Speak boldly and act boldly when He reveals to you the person you are to help.

DYSFUNCTION IS NO EXCUSE

And Cain talked with Abel his brother: and it came to pass, when they were in the field, that Cain rose up against Abel his brother, and slew him. (Genesis 4:8)

In Genesis, the book of beginnings, we find the first fight in the first family between the first two brothers. We find our first example of dysfunction.

You can hardly turn on a talk show today without hearing people give this justification for their abnormal and often sinful behavior: I came from a dysfunctional family. As if that's supposed to be a legitimate excuse!

Oh, the words sound good and they ring true. The *excuse*, however, is lame. The reason the words ring true to us is because we all have a degree of dysfunction in our lives. The reason for the lameness of the excuse is this: we are *all* from dysfunctional families. *Every* family has an element of dysfunction to it. We are all the descendants of Adam and Eve, our great ancestors who fell from a state of perfect function. So, if *any* person is able to rise above dysfunction, then *all* people are able to rise above dysfunction.

Adam and Eve became the parents in the first dysfunctional family. They gave birth to a dysfunctional son,

Cain. Murder and mayhem broke out among the first two brothers.

That same murdering spirit exists in the world today. We seem perfectly oblivious to the fact that we are all brothers — that we all have the same blood flowing in our veins. We allow ourselves to fall into the same competitive, jealous, angry spirit that Cain first manifested.

People sometimes have a "get him first" killing spirit, while at the same time they give an appearance of being courteous and cooperative.

You must face the reality every day that some of your problems stem from the fact that there is *somebody* who doesn't like your success. International wars have resulted from the jealousy of one man over another man's success or possessions. Is it any wonder that the minor skirmishes we face in the daily battles of our personal lives come from the same root of jealousy?

Your attitude today is something that is totally under your control. You choose. You choose whether you will be prejudiced . . .

    angry . . .

        hateful . . .

            bitter . . .

                resentful. It is in your power to make a decision about what you will think and how you will act.

Don't blame your actions on your dysfunctional family. Base your actions on an attitude born of functional faith. "The grace of our Lord was exceeding abundant with faith and love" (1 Timothy 1:14).

Rather than have a "get him before he gets me" attitude, choose to have a "give to him first" attitude. Such an attitude will be far more beneficial to you . . . not only now, but for all eternity.

———————
———————
———————
———————

Refuse to blame your circumstances on the dysfunction of men. Instead, place your circumstances in the path of the function of the grace and love of Christ.

WE ARE ALL THE CHILDREN OF OPPRESSION

God anointed Jesus of Nazareth with the Holy Ghost and with power: who went about doing good, and healing all that were oppressed of the devil; for God was with him. (Acts 10:38)

Nearly every person who came to America from another nation came to this nation as a wounded person — someone who was oppressed in the land where he or she lived before coming to America. Every group of people has a horror story to tell as part of their personal cultural heritage. The oppression may have had some distinctive qualities, but oppression in general is a common denominator for every group of people who came to America.

Oppressed people readily become oppressors. We know that molested children are the most likely children to become molesters, abused children are the most likely to become abusers, and so forth. Every victim can easily become a victimizer. Those who have had no control in their past are the most likely to seek the most control in their future.

We Are All the Children of Oppression

Oppression is nearly always by "family." When the Jews were sent to the concentration camps, they were sent as families. When the Indians were put on reservations, they were put there as families. Our problem is never ours alone. It is by "family."

As a result, an attitude of oppression is passed down family by family, tribe by tribe, people by people. Just about every "family" thinks it is more oppressed than all other families!

A man can be oppressed but not be able to identify his feelings as being oppression. He only knows that he feels trapped and he's angry about it.

Any time a man thinks that he cannot change things and that he has no options, he becomes filled with rage and becomes abusive or violent . . . or he becomes despondent and depressed.

Some men who are filled with rage are talking encouragement but walking defeat. They try to convince themselves that things can be better, but they only give lip-service to such change. In their hearts, they feel trapped.

The man who feels trapped has no tolerance for people who tell him things that he needs to do or points out to him things that he has left undone. He has no capacity for hearing that the trash needs to be taken out, the children need to be disciplined, or the room needs to be painted.

The fact is, however, if you don't like your circumstances or your situation, you can change it.

Whatever is oppressing you — people, habits, addictions, circumstances — whoever or whatever your slave master happens to be . . . you are mightier with Christ than the thing that is oppressing you!

Jesus came to heal "all that were oppressed of the devil" (Acts 10:38). And that, sir, includes *you.* He came to set you free, and he whom the Son sets free of oppression, is free indeed. (See John 8:36.)

_____
_____
_____
_____

Accept God's healing today. Walk in the freedom that Christ Jesus gives to you!

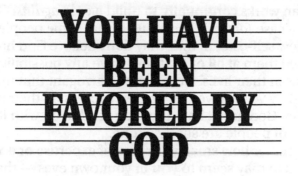

YOU HAVE BEEN FAVORED BY GOD

By this I know that thou favourest me, because mine enemy doth not triumph over me. And as for me, thou upholdest me in mine integrity, and settest me before thy face for ever. (Psalm 41:11,12)

One of the things that Satan wants to keep you from knowing is that the favor of God is upon you and that you have been touched by Him and allowed to become the success that you are. Satan doesn't want you to give any of the credit to God. In fact, he doesn't want you to think that God has ever done anything for you at all.

Satan's lie is that a man has no purpose, power, or potential. The enemy does his utmost to get a man to buy the lie that he is broke . . .

busted . . .

disgusted . . .

oppressed . . .

depressed . . .

and confused.

The enemy will try the race card, and if that doesn't work, he'll try the childhood memories card. And if that doesn't work, he'll dredge up all of your past sins and run them by you. He'll remind a man of broken promises and broken dreams.

Satan works continually to build a case *against* God, never a case *for* God. The result is that some people have such low self-esteem that they don't believe God has touched them at all or that they have any possibility for success in their lives. Others are so arrogant that they think they've achieved all of their success on their own and that God hasn't had anything at all to do with it. Both groups of people are sorely wrong.

No matter how small your area of expertise or accomplishment may seem to you in your own eyes — that degree of success has been made possible because the Lord is on your side. You can't even hold up your own pants without the Lord giving you the strength and knowledge and ability to do so. You certainly can't raise a God-fearing family or contribute your talents to a job without God's assistance.

The irony is that often others are about to stab us to death — emotionally, spiritually, mentally, in our jobs, in our churches — and we don't even know why! We don't know that it's because others are perceiving the favor of the Lord on our lives and are jealous of it. We don't know that we have been blessed by God. We don't know that others are motivated to a great extent to act against us because they are jealous of what they see in us. How sad that they see what we don't see in ourselves!

Refuse to walk in ignorance of your own *God-given* blessings.

_____
_____
_____
_____

Praise God today for His FAVOR shown to you.

THE PROMISED LAND OF YOUR LIFE RIGHT NOW

Be strong and of a good courage: for unto this people shalt thou divide for an inheritance the land, which I sware unto their fathers to give them. (Joshua 1:6)

You can be in the right general area for your success, but until you claim that area and move into it, you cannot possess the fullness of all that God has promised to you.

Are you in your promised land? Are you in your field of dreams?

If you answer no to those questions, it may very well be because you have a false concept of what it means to be in a place that bears the marks of God's favor and blessing.

Many of the old hymns in our churches talk about "Beulah Land," "Canaan Land," or "the promised land" — they all speak of a wonderful land "over there," one that we will experience in the "sweet by and by." Many of these songs came right out of a slavery mind-set, but they have been sung for decades by both white and black people. Even today the idea is deeply engrained in us that we can only experience God's promises and blessings in the future, and very specifically in heaven.

That thinking is erroneous from a Bible standpoint.

When the Israelites went through the wilderness and arrived in the Promised Land, they encountered the Canaanites, the Jebusites, the Amorites, the Hittites, and a whole lot of other "ites" that didn't want them to settle in their area, much less take control over it. The Israelites had to do serious battle in order to *claim* the Promised Land that God had for them — the land to which God had called them, the land God had promised to them, and the land that God was going to help them conquer. The Promised Land wasn't a land they were going to enter after their death. It was a land they were expected to conquer during their life!

When you stepped through the blood of Jesus that flows from the cross, you stepped into your promised land.

Somebody else presently may be occupying the territory that God has for you — they may be in the job that God has destined for you; they may be living in the house that God has planned for you to own; they may be holding the office that God expects you to win in an upcoming election; they may be occupying the store or warehouse that God is going to help you purchase. Nevertheless, you are *in* your promised land. The Lord has led you to the place where He wants you to manifest His power and His greatness.

Keep in mind that you didn't arrive in the promised land of your life today by yourself. Neither did any Israelite man who crossed the Jordan River with Joshua to take claim to the land God had designated for them arrive there on his own. Each man came to that Promised Land with his family — either with his parents or with his wife and children. He came into the land with all of the other Israelites — his tribe and the other eleven tribes, as a whole, his people, his "church community."

The same is true for us today. You don't come into your promised land alone. Your acceptance of Christ involved other people and the claiming of your promised land still involves others. Factor in your family. Move as a whole family to the territory God is calling you to claim.

Take an inventory today of the things that God has promised to you. You'll find those things in the many promises that God has made to His people in the Scriptures. Every promise that is in the Bible is for you and your family *today.* Those promises are not for the hereafter. They are for NOW.

_____
_____
_____

Target and then conquer a portion of your promised land today.

THE WAY WE COME INTO BLESSINGS

The kingdom of heaven suffereth violence, and the violent take it by force. (Matthew 11:12)

Santa Claus isn't going to come and drop large bundles of God's blessings into your life. If you are sitting at the base of your fireplace with a glass of milk in one hand and a plate of cookies in the other just waiting for his arrival, you are going to be sorely disappointed.

Neither does God drop blessings out of nowhere. He doesn't sprinkle them around on the unsuspecting like so much fairy dust.

Receiving God's blessings into your life is a matter of warfare. This is not warfare waged with guns or knives or bombs. It is not warfare that is rooted in jealousy, anger, bitterness, or hatred. It is warfare against the true enemy of your soul — warfare in the spirit realm, warfare that is very real.

So many men are lacking in so many things today — things that must be won first in the spirit realm and then manifested in the natural realm — because they are lazy. I'm not talking about being lazy physically, or being lazy mentally, or being lazy on the job. I'm talking about being lazy spiritually. They don't want to have to *do* anything to bring about God's blessing in their lives. To get what you want you have to want it badly enough that you are willing to fight for it.

In the last several years, I've ministered to large groups of women and to large groups of men, and I've noticed a significant difference in the two groups. Women aren't at all reluctant to get into the trenches of spiritual warfare. I invite women to praise and worship the Lord, and then often I have to tell them when to quit so I can get on with my next point! They have no problem at all crying out to God or weeping unashamedly for the desires of their hearts — even if it means that their eye makeup goes streaming down their faces. They have no problem with raising their voices in prayer or laying hands on their sisters and rebuking the devil off their lives.

But when I invite a group of men to enter into the warfare of praise and worship, sometimes I'm lucky to get a couple of hallelujahs. If some men stand and praise the Lord for longer than thirty seconds, they think they've sacrificed a great deal of time and energy. Even under a strong anointing, some men find it difficult to enter into fierce spiritual battle.

Oh, they feel the anointing. You can't convince me that they don't feel what the Holy Spirit is doing. And they sense the power. You can't convince me that they aren't aware of the power of God or have a knowledge of what it is that God is desiring to do. The difficulty they have lies in their unwillingness to *express* what they feel and in their inability to *yield* their own pride to the power of God.

Unless a man is able to cross this hurdle and humble himself before God and engage in genuine praise and worship, he won't win the battles that are necessary for him to win in the spirit realm. He won't be able to lay claim to his promised land.

_____
_____
_____

Be prepared to fight today in the spirit realm for the territory of blessing that you desire.

GIVING TO GOD WHAT HE WANTS

And the LORD had respect unto Abel and his offering: But unto Cain and to his offering he had not respect. (Genesis 4:4,5)

Have you noticed that Superman is out? Clark Kent is the one everybody wants.

If you are offering Superman results to a woman today, you may attract her attention, but you won't be able to keep her affection. You may as well hang up your cape back in the closet.

If you are choosing to be a stoic, strong superhero to your sons and daughters, you may impress them, but you will not fulfill them. Your children would rather be caressed by you than impressed by you.

The strong, silent type is out. Some of our fathers were so silent they never told our mothers that they loved them . . . they never told us they loved us. Some of them were so strong they never learned how to express themselves except through rage and abuse.

If you use accomplishments and power to replace affection and availability, you are not going to be regarded as a "king" by your wife and children. You are going to be considered as a heartless robot.

Machoism is dead. It's the sensitive and caring and vulnerable and available man who is desired today. If you are still offering machoism to the world, you are offering a product that nobody wants. Including God.

Your machoism placed against the standard of God's holiness and righteousness and compassion is about as impressive to God as a feather on the back of an elephant is impressive to the elephant.

God isn't remotely impressed by our approaching Him and asking, "What's up?" He isn't impressed by your résumé or your fancy suit. He isn't impressed by your expensive new wristwatch or your recitation of church history. He isn't impressed by your degrees or your pedigree. God is responsive only to those men who are willing to fall on their faces before Him, completely yielding everything to Him, and placing themselves in utter reliance upon Him.

An amazing thing happens when we learn how to bless the Lord — how to praise, worship, and exalt His name. We become more willing and able to bless our wives and children! In giving God what He wants, we are better able to give others what they truly need and desire from us.

God accepted Abel's offering because Abel gave God something that God wanted. Are you willing to give God what He wants from you today — a humble, open, loving heart filled with praise and worship?

Give God an ACCEPTABLE offering of praise today. He WILL receive and respect your sacrifice.

MOVING THE HEART OF GOD

And the LORD your God, he shall expel them [your enemies] from before you, and drive them from out of your sight; and ye shall possess their land, as the LORD your God hath promised unto you. (Joshua 23:5)

Until you learn how to move the heart of God, you will never be successful in spiritual warfare, and until you are successful in spiritual warfare, you cannot be completely successful in your life.

You may look like who's who and know what's what, but you will never possess all that God desires for you to have until you move the heart of God to "fight for you" and win the territory for you that He desires for you to have.

The first and foremost step for moving the heart of God is to break down the old man inside you and give him up. We dismantle the old man in us when we say with a genuine heart, "It's not about me, God. It's about You."

You can tell a lot about a man by listening to him pray.

I pray that You will endow us with all such endowments that may matriculate

77

*from Your throne, and cause us to enter
into various dimensions of glory. Even
now as I stand on the crystal shore, I pray
You will lead me into a place* ....

Who are you trying to fool?

God doesn't need or want your egotistical, intellectual-ized image. In fact, He doesn't desire anything that is man-engineered or man-contrived. Including your flat-tery.

If a woman came to you and, measuring you up like a specimen in a lab, said to you, "You are a wonderful example of the male physique, with huge biceps and tight abs and a great smile," you might be impressed that she's impressed with your body. But her objective appraisal of your body is not going to be what would make you want to snatch her and hold onto her for the rest of your life. In your heart of hearts, you want a woman who knows the inner you and loves you anyway. And the same goes for God.

God desires for you to come to Him not with lofty words that express theological and historical facts about what He has done, but with a heart that is *dependent* upon Who He is and what He does and will do in order for you to take your next breath. He wants you to come with a desire to know Him, and with a willingness to lay your entire life bare before Him so He can heal you and restore you and create in you the likeness of His Son, Jesus Christ.

Cain tried to impress God — and Cain failed miserably. Cain gave to God something that he felt he had accom-plished on his own. After all, he had tilled the earth and planted the seed and gathered the harvest. He came proudly to God, saying in his heart, "Look what I've done. Bless me on the basis of what I have accomplished."

Abel came to God and said in his heart, "I didn't do a thing. You caused this lamb to be birthed. You caused it to survive and grow. You provided the water for it to drink and the grass for it to eat. You are the Creator of all life. I'm giving back to You what *You've* done. I trust You with my life."

Ask yourself, "Is God receiving what I am giving to Him?" If you are giving Him a good front or a good line about yourself, He won't receive it. If you are giving Him your heartfelt praise and worship, He will receive your sacrifice of praise and bless you in return.

Look at yourself in the mirror today and say to yourself about your own egotistical pride, "Give it up." And then start praising God for Who He is and who He desires for you to become and who He is making you to be.

WHERE ART THOU... REALLY?

And the LORD God called unto Adam, and said unto him, Where art thou? (Genesis 3:9)

Are you in touch with where you are? How you feel? Can you accept your own progress? Have you faced your faults, and also your great assets?

When God called to Adam in the Garden of Eden, He wasn't trying to find Adam. God knew where Adam was. Nobody and nothing can hide from God. No . . . God wanted for Adam to *admit* where he was. He wanted Adam to recognize fully who he was and what he had done.

One of the most important questions you can ever ask yourself is this: Where am I in my life?

Men get into trouble when they don't know where they are.

So many men I've encountered are in one stage of their lives and acting as if they are in another. They have entered into marriage and fatherhood, and therefore, they have certain responsibilities, but they are still living as if they are boys playing in the park.

Even if you don't tell your wife . . .

Even if you don't tell your children . . .
Even if you don't tell your boss . . .
Even if you don't tell your pastor . . .
At least tell *yourself* where you are in your life!

When we hide, we turn phony. We act out a charade. We put on a "face" and participate in our own masquerade. Only two things are worse than being phony with other people: being phony with yourself and being phony with God.

If you haven't faced up to who you are and what you have done, you will find it very, *very* difficult to enter into praise and worship. Furthermore, you'll find it very difficult to relate to other men, or to their wives and children.

If you are feeling lonely and deprived, in all likelihood you are emotionally intimidated by other people. You can't open yourself up and give them a hug or pay them a compliment or look them in the eye with compassion because you are *afraid* they may look inside your heart and see the real you. Why are you afraid? Because you haven't looked there lately and you are afraid of what you might find if you do!

Until you face up to your flaws and failures — openly admit them to yourself and to God, and accept the fact that you aren't perfect — you'll never be able to allow other people to know, much less accept, your imperfections. If you aren't open to that kind of sharing, you will feel forever cut off, estranged, isolated, lonely, deprived, and alienated from other people.

Many men spend a lot of time and energy asking about the other men around them, "Where are they?"

What does that man have that I don't have to get
that kind of woman?
What does that man do to be able to afford that
kind of car and live in that kind of house?
How is it that HE *has that kind of job and*
authority and power?

These are all variations of asking, Where is *he* at? The answer to that question leads to a dead end. It results in jealousy and competition and hatred and distrust and suspicion . . . all of which result in a murderous attitude.

Instead, ask *yourself*, "Where am *I* at?" That's the question that can lead to life. That's the question that will lead you to repentance before God, to an ability to get close to other people, and to fulfillment and true satisfaction in life.

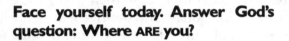

Face yourself today. Answer God's question: Where ARE you?

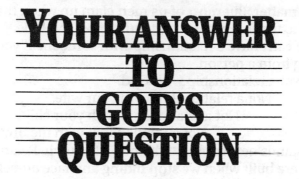

YOUR ANSWER TO GOD'S QUESTION

And he said, I heard thy voice in the garden, and I was afraid, because I was naked; and I hid myself. (Genesis 3:10)

God called to Adam and asked him, "Where art thou?" And here's how the first man answered the first question that God had asked him: "I heard . . . I was afraid . . . I was naked . . . I hid."

Most men don't like open confrontation. I have known some physically big, powerful men who were afraid to go home to their five-foot-two-inch wives because they knew they would be facing a confrontation with her the minute they walked in the door.

In my years of counseling men who had a long history of being physically and emotionally and sexually abusive, I discovered that abusers are among the most fearful men I've ever met. They come across to their victims as being totally unafraid, but the fact is, they are *very* afraid of themselves and of being confronted with who they are. They rarely face themselves — they don't know who they are or where they are at — and they are highly fearful that somebody else might discover the darkness that they secretly know is inside them.

Men tend to talk very easily about things that don't really matter. But most of us men clam up when the talk turns to the things that matter the most. We hide.

You can't have a relationship with someone if you are hiding from a person.

Not a relationship with God.

Not a relationship with your wife.

Not a relationship with your child.

Not a relationship with the brother who stands next to you in the pew at church. Relationships are built when we stop hiding and face ourselves, and then allow ourselves to be vulnerable and open with other people.

A man sometimes acts as if he can't hear, or hasn't heard. The fact is, he heard — he just didn't like what he heard.

He heard his wife when she said she needed more time, attention, or consideration.

He heard his child when he complained that Dad wasn't around very much. He heard his daughter when she said, "I love you, Daddy," and he heard her sigh when Daddy didn't say anything back.

He ran and hid emotionally because he didn't know how to give to other people what they said they needed.

A man who is afraid and doesn't know what to do is a man who feels exposed. He feels undone. He'll go to great lengths to hide himself — to bury himself in his work, to get involved in an affair that doesn't require any vulnerability on his part, to put up a brick-wall facade around his heart to hide his true emotions.

So men end up afraid, frustrated, whimpering inside, locked up, impotent. And all the while, they are doing everything they can to cover up their inner feelings and emotional inadequacies.

Truth requires that you open up and share who you really are. It requires an honest answer to God's question, "Where art thou?" rather than an excuse rooted in your own fear.

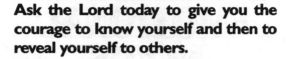

Ask the Lord today to give you the courage to know yourself and then to reveal yourself to others.

ACKNOWLEDGE YOUR EMOTIONAL NEEDS

My heart is like wax; it is melted in the midst
of my bowels. (Psalm 22:14)

What is the harm in keeping your fears and your
emotional needs to yourself?

Because what you use to hide your fears and needs
from others will eventually become a prison to you. It will
lock you up,

freeze you up,

bottle you up . . . and keep you from moving in to
claim all that God has for you in your life.

Some men turn to alcohol or drugs in an effort to hide
themselves from their fears and emotional needs.

Some turn to prostitutes — they won't trust their wives
with their emotions, but they'll trust a total stranger with
their bodies, their potential *zera* (seed), and their reputa-
tions.

Some turn to overwork — putting all of their energy
into the job and burning the midnight oil — in an effort
to avoid the need to relate to people.

Eventually, each of these escapes — and any other
escape — becomes a prison. It traps you even further into
a cycle of silence, because once you are entrapped by

your escape mechanism, you won't want to tell anybody about that trap either. Your fear only grows greater as your silence grows deeper.

The fact is, God created you with emotions. He created you with a need to feel, to touch, to express, to have an emotional outlet and release. Look at a little boy. He's free to express himself, to vent his feelings, to hug and kiss and be hugged and kissed in return. He hasn't learned to hide yet.

What happened to you on your way to becoming a man?

Where art thou?

What caused you to feel that you need to run and hide?
There's another you behind the facade.

You need to be touched just as much as the next guy.
You need to be held.

You need to hear loving words, spoken in a gentle way.
Don't deny your emotional needs.

David wasn't afraid to admit to himself and to God that he was weak, afraid, sorrowful, angry, or in need of love. He even said that his heart melted like wax! (See Psalm 22:14.) In fact, the entire twenty-second psalm is *filled* with emotions. Read it!

The Bible says about Jesus that He was a man "who in the days of his flesh . . . offered up prayers and supplications with strong crying and tears" (Hebrews 5:7.) Jesus was a Man Who knew how to express His emotions.

Tell God you need Him.

Tell Him you love Him.

Tell Him you are in trouble in your life.

Tell Him where you ARE.

_____
_____
_____

**Express your emotions to God today.
He created you to pray with FEELINGS.**

BREAKING THE SILENCE OF THE LAMBS

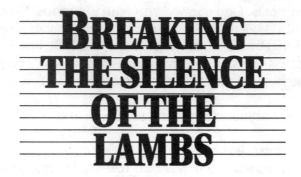

Hear my cry, O God; attend unto my prayer. From the end of the earth will I cry unto thee, when my heart is overwhelmed: Lead me to the rock that is higher than I. For thou hast been a shelter for me, and a strong tower from the enemy. (Psalm 61:1-3)

God knew that Adam not only needed to know where he was at, but that he needed to say so.

Are you a man who turns off the lights at night, only to lie in the darkness of your own bed, unable to say to your wife, "I love you"?

Are you a man who, when your son comes to you, you respond with "Hey, what's happening, man?" instead of putting your arm around your son and giving him the hug that he really desires?

Many of God's men — God's sheep, His beloved lambs — are silent today.

They know who they are and what they have done, but they have lockjaw when it comes to talking about it, even in private confession to God.

They *know* they need to be held, but they'll never *admit* that they need to be held. Instead, they'll come home and say to their wives and children . . .

Why haven't you cleaned the house?

Why aren't you making better grades in school?

Why didn't you catch that fly ball that came your way?

They are scared that they are about to lose their job but they'll never say a word about it. Instead, they'll march around with a chip on their shoulders, as if to say . . .

What are you doing in my way?

Who gave you the right to tell me what to do?

Why are you showing favoritism to everybody but me?

They are afraid that if they tell what they feel, others will lose respect for them or will take advantage of them.

Our fears can erupt in anger and in criticism. But most of the time, they lie just under the surface of our stone-cold silence. As long as they remain there, they will foment and brew . . . unhealed, unchanged, unresolved. We will remain weak on the inside even though we may seem strong on the outside.

David said, "O LORD my God, I cried unto thee, and thou hast healed me" (Psalm 30:2). Hasn't the time come for you to break your silence so God can heal *you*?

———————
———————
———————

Make today the day that you break the "silence of the lamb" in your life. Tell God what you are feeling. Tell your wife and children today how you feel about them. Express to them what you need emotionally — first, that you have emotional needs, and second, what they are. Open yourself up to receiving from them the love they will give you.

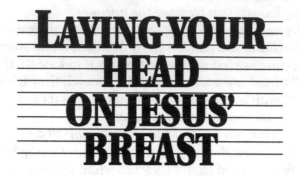

LAYING YOUR HEAD ON JESUS' BREAST

Herein is love, not that we loved God, but that he loved us, and sent his Son to be the propitiation for our sins. Beloved, if God so loved us, we ought also to love one another. (1 John 4:10,11)

During the Last Supper, as Jesus was eating His final meal with His disciples before going to the cross, we read that John was "leaning on Jesus' bosom . . . lying on Jesus' breast" (John 13:23,25). Can you imagine what people would say about a man who did that today? Even if we knew the person was very spiritual, we'd probably raise an eyebrow.

But John had no problem with it. He knew that he was loved by Jesus. In fact, throughout the gospel of John, we find John referring to himself as the "disciple whom Jesus loved." (See John 13:23.)

John was open in his devotion to Jesus. Of all the disciples, only John is mentioned by name as being at the crucifixion. He is the only disciple to whom Jesus spoke directly from the cross. Jesus gave John the responsibility for Jesus' own mother. Jesus no doubt knew that, of all the disciples, John was the one most capable of expressing love to His mother.

I once did a study of the life of John and I discovered that John was the youngest disciple. Peter, James, and the others were probably in their forties at the time of Jesus' ministry, but John was very likely in his early twenties. John hadn't been corrupted yet into denying his emotions. He wasn't hiding. He wasn't afraid.

Love and showing love one to another is the hallmark of John's letters. (See 1 John, 2 John, 3 John.) It is the theme of John's gospel — "For God so loved the world, that he gave his only begotten Son" (John 3:16).

Are you aware that John is the only disciple that we know with certainty died of old age? All of the other disciples, about whose deaths we know, died in martyrdom. But John died peacefully at more than a hundred years of age. I personally believe that was because John had learned how to love people and how to express his faith with loving words backed up by loving actions.

If you want to live a long life and die in peace, I suggest that you lay your machoism down and lay your head on Jesus' breast.

———————
———————
———————

Voice your love to God today. Then swallow your pride and fear and say to your wife, your children, and your friends, "I love you."

THE DOMINO EFFECT OF YOUR PRAISE

[I] will yet praise thee more and more.
(Psalm 71:14)

There's a domino effect that starts to manifest itself when you praise and worship God.

When you open up yourself to tell God how wonderful He is and how much you love Him and enjoy spending time with Him . . . you are very likely to find that your wife starts telling you how wonderful *you* are and how much she loves you and enjoys being with you.

When your wife starts talking to you like that, your children are going to overhear her at some point . . . and very likely they are going to start telling you what a great dad you are and how much they love you and enjoy spending time with you.

What happens to you in the process?

Your loneliness — that ache in your inner man that feels alone and isolated and hurting — is going to be healed. You're going to feel more courage and strength than you've felt before.

As you continue to go to God in open, free-to-be-yourself vulnerability and continue to praise and worship Him

with your entire being, your love for Him is going to grow
. . .

your love from and for your wife is going to grow, your
love from and for your children is going to grow, and
your love for *yourself* is going to grow so that you can
appreciate the good things that God is doing for you
and in you and through you.

But as long as you starve God of the praises due Him,
you are going to be starving yourself of the praises that
you need. You'll find yourself living in an emotional
wasteland, without love and deep appreciation from the
very people with whom you *should* have the most loving
relationships.

David said, "O magnify the LORD with me, and let us
exalt his name together" (Psalm 34:3). The end result of
your magnifying and praising the Lord is that your entire
family is going to want to join you in magnifying and
praising Him, and as they do, they will magnify and
praise one another so that your home will become a
haven of peace, rest, and emotional strength.

It's time we start saying to the Lord —
You are wonderful. There's nothing You can't fix.
There's nothing You can't do. There's no problem
You can't solve. There's no need You can't meet.
There's no issue too great for You. I'm casting all of
my care upon You. I'm giving it all to You. I'm giving
all of ME to You. I'm laying my head upon Your breast,
Lord. I know You love me and I'm relying
upon You to provide for me everything I need!
I'm not going to have this depression. I'm not going
to stress out. I'm not going to have this nervous break-
down. I'm going to trust You to defeat my enemies for
Your glory. I'm trusting You to break down the doors that
are locked and to wax great on my behalf. I'm relying
upon You to win the victory!

When we praise the Lord, He opens up the gates of His
kingdom and sends forth His warriors to fight and win

the spiritual battle you are facing. They ride on the wings of our praise.

It's time to break the silence!

_____

_____

_____

Give voice to your feelings, to your needs, and to your praise. Lay your head on Jesus' breast today!

REFUSE TO PLAY THE BLAME GAME

And the man said, The woman whom thou gavest to be with me, she gave me of the tree, and I did eat. (Genesis 3:12)

God asked Adam, "Who told you that you were naked? Have you eaten of the tree whereof I commanded you not to eat?" (See Genesis 3:11.)

Adam didn't answer either question. Oh, that he would have! Oh, that he could have been honest enough with himself to cry to God, "I have sinned. Have mercy on me!"

Instead, Adam tried to justify what he had done by blaming someone else. He said to God, "It's the fault of the woman you gave to be with me. She gave me of the tree, and I ate of it." (See Genesis 3:12.)

How many men try that same line today?

I'd be a better husband, Lord, if my wife would just . . .

I could be a good father, Lord, but my wife . . .

I'd be further along in my life and in my career, Lord, if only my wife would . . .

I wouldn't get so angry and lash out with so much

hatred, Lord, if my wife . . .

And if it isn't his wife who gets the blame, he might try to lay it on someone else.

I'd be more honest in my business dealings if my partner . . .

I'd have better control of my temper if my boss would just . . .

I wouldn't be like this if my parents . . .

I wouldn't have all these troubles if the people in the government . . .

The "blame line" didn't work for Adam, and it won't work for you. The situation in your life is not the *fault* of someone else. It's *your* responsibility.

Deal with yourself. And you'll probably find that those you have been blaming are not nearly the problem they were!

Come before God today and with an honest heart admit, "God, the problem is with me. Fix ME, Lord. Show me what it is that I must do in order to be forgiven and healed by You and to be free to forgive others and to heal my relationships with my wife, my children, my friends, and my coworkers."

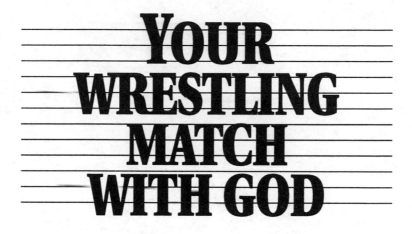

THE ENEMY IN-A-ME

And even as they did not like to retain God in their knowledge, God gave them over to a reprobate mind ... being filled with all unrighteousness, fornication, wickedness, covetousness, maliciousness; full of envy, murder, debate, deceit, malignity. (Romans 1:28,29)

In any group of men, I know in my heart that every kind of problem is present ...

every kind of need ...

every kind of weaknesses ...

every kind of struggle.

I also know that *today* is the time when we need to confront those problems, needs, weaknesses, and struggles.

It's time that we begin to challenge and confront ourselves about what we hold within ourselves.

I am not too concerned about the witches or witchcraft, or about demons, demonology, sorcery, or astrology. As bad as crime is, I'm not too concerned about the mugger, the rapist, or the con artist. What I am concerned about, however, every day of my life is *the enemy in-a-me*. If there's anyone you need to confront continually, it's yourself.

When a man ignores the commandments of God and refuses to turn to God and acknowledge Him as Lord, the worst punishment God gives to that man on this earth is to turn him over to himself — to give him over to his own reprobate mind.

A popular advertising slogan in recent years had as part of its slogan — "have it your way." The problem is that when we seek to have it our own way, we literally self-destruct.

I am always amazed at how a man can look at another man and arrogantly say, "I'm better than that person." I'm not talking about racial or social distinctions here — I'm talking about the distinctions that we make about another person's sinfulness. When we make a claim that we aren't as sinful as the next person, we are, in effect, claiming that one type of sin — and in particular, *our* type of sin — isn't as bad as another type of sin. The man that draws such a conclusion doesn't know his Bible. The Bible says, "All have sinned, and come short of the glory of God" (Romans 3:23).

The fact is, the capacity for *every* type of sin resides in each one of us. We may not have done it, but chances are, we've thought about it! We each know that there are lots of things in our imaginations that we don't talk about. And if we haven't thought about it *yet*, given the right situation and circumstance, we *will* think about it and possibly even do it.

If you were pressed . . . or under certain stresses . . . or faced with certain alternatives, you'd have no problem at all in committing every sin in the book.

If a murderer entered your house and was heading for your child's room, would you have any second thoughts about stopping that man no matter what it took to do so?

If you and your family were starving and you came across a cart filled with food, would you have any hesitation about becoming a thief?

If you were told that you had to have sex with a certain person in order for your baby's life to be spared, would you say no?

In our human nature, we are totally depraved. We have an equal capacity to sin. And we each must face that capacity within us. We must confront our sin nature.

Thank God today that He has not turned you over to your own self, but that in His great mercy, He is still present in your life.

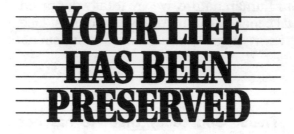

YOUR LIFE HAS BEEN PRESERVED

And Jacob called the name of the place Peniel: for I have seen God face to face, and my life is preserved. (Genesis 32:30)

God isn't finished with you yet. You haven't arrived. There's still more to be done by you, and therefore, still more that needs to be done in you. God still needs to work on each one of us.

That truth doesn't scare me in the least. I'm just grateful that He's kept me alive long enough so that He *can* work in me! I'm grateful that He's poured into me what He's already poured into me, and I'm looking for anything else that He wants to pour into me because what He pours is always good!

We each know, if we're honest with ourselves, that the Lord has protected us or we wouldn't be at the point we're at today. We have to admit that His hand was on us long before we were saved.

When you were driving around drunk, an accident just waiting to happen . . .

When you were slapping your wife around and she was on the verge of calling the police . . .

When you were lying to that girlfriend to get her to do what you wanted her to do . . .

God was there. Even then. He had you in His grasp.

If God hadn't been merciful to us when we were sinners, we'd all be dead!

So often I see men who have been through so much in their lives that I am amazed they are still alive.

Anybody else would have self-destructed.

Some of their school classmates died.

Some of their teenage friends were murdered.

Some of their adult friends overdosed on drugs.

Through all of their troubles, they are still alive!

The devil has tried to take me out on numerous occasions, through one means and another, but I'm still here. And before I'll let him take me out completely, I'll tie a rag around my head and put a knife in my teeth and wait for him in the bushes! I'm prepared to do battle with the devil.

Some people get depressed too easily.

They become discouraged too easily.

They become suicidal too easily.

You've got to have a little Rambo in you!

I'm not giving up. I'm going to FIGHT. I'm going to HOLD ON. That's what Paul wrote to Timothy when he said, "Fight the good fight of faith, lay hold on eternal life, whereunto thou art also called" (1 Timothy 6:12). I refuse to give in!

Thank God today that He is still at work in you. Refuse to give in to the devil. Fight him every step of the way.

REFUSE TO REMAIN A WELL-MARKED TARGET

He was manifested to take away our sins.
(I John 3:5)

If you don't confront your own frailties and your own capacity for sin, you remain a well-marked target for the devil. If you don't admit that you are vulnerable to committing sin in a certain area, you remain vulnerable in that area. Why? Because in being so sure that you'd never commit the sin in question, you take no safeguards against it. And without safeguards, you are wide open to the devil's attack.

You never thought you could get that angry.
You never thought you could be that hostile.
You never thought you could have an affair.
You never thought you could be that weak.
You never thought you could cheat in your finances.
You never thought you could leave your family.

And because you never thought you could . . . you did.

Look at yourself in the mirror and admit, I *could* commit every sin. I'm capable of it in my human flesh.

People may be saying to you, "You're going to have to deal with your problem." They see your problem as being drugs, or alcohol, or an affair. They may see your problem as being your temper, your hatred, your prejudice, your bitterness.

But I'm telling you, "There's a problem *behind* your problem" And that REAL problem is sin.

What is it that makes a thirty-five-year-old married man try to act like he's seventeen and single?

What makes a man want to drown his troubles in alcohol or use drugs to give himself a high?

Why does a man feel a need to prove himself by doing daredevil stunts?

The bottom-line answer is this: man's sin nature.

Your sin nature is your tendency to want to do what the devil tells you to do, more than you want to do what God tells you to do. It is your sin nature that is changed when you believe in Jesus Christ and accept Him as Savior, and then follow Him as Lord. John wrote, "He that committeth sin is of the devil; for the devil sinneth from the beginning. For this purpose the Son of God was manifested, that he might destroy the works of the devil" (1 John 3:8).

If you have never asked God to forgive you of your sins and change your sin nature, do so right now! God stands ready to forgive you. As 1 John 1:9 promises, "If we confess our sins, he is faithful and just to forgive us our sins, and to cleanse us from all unrighteousness."

Face your own sin capacity and then accept God's capacity to forgive you and transform you.

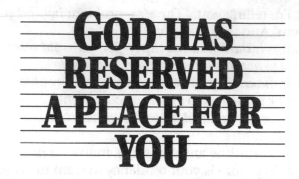

GOD HAS RESERVED A PLACE FOR YOU

God, who quickeneth the dead . . . calleth those things which be not as though they were. (Romans 4:17)

A re you aware that God has made a statement about you in eternity?

God exists in eternity. We exist in time. When God says something, He says it in the context of eternity. That means that it *will* happen and it *will* last forever.

What has God said about you? God has taken a chair and placed it in the midst of His angels in eternity. Then, pointing directly at you, He has said to them, "This chair belongs to that man. I'm going to bring him right here for an encounter with Me. I'm going to do My best to love him until he receives My love and My forgiveness. I am going to make him into one of the jewels in My crown."

And when God speaks, He doesn't listen to any of the arguments that oppose His will.

But that man is a liar.

God says, "A liar is a bad thing to be, but it doesn't stop Me from loving him. I'm going to bring him into My presence. This chair has his name on it."

But he's a thief.

God says, "That's not good, but it doesn't stop Me from reaching out to him. I'm going to bring him into My presence. I love him and I want him here."

But he's a molester.

God says, "That's a very hurtful thing to be, but nevertheless, I'm going to bring him into My presence so I can tell him I love him and desire to forgive him."

Murderer . . . homosexual . . . rapist . . . drug dealer. God says, "I've got a chair with his name on it in My presence. I've got a plan for bringing him here to Me so I can love him and forgive him and live with him forever."

But he's a man who is violent emotionally and physically to everybody he meets.

"Yes," says God, "but when *I'm* finished with him, he's not going to be that way. In fact, he's going to be a deacon in his local church and he's going to be sharing the Gospel with men who are violent emotionally and physically."

I know men today who, ten years ago, would never dreamed of attending one of my conferences, much less praising and dancing and shouting before the Lord.

God calls those things which were not as though they were, because He knows He has the power to make them become what He says they will be. God does not have any doubts about His own ability to save, redeem, deliver, or transform a human life.

Furthermore, the seat that God is holding for you is *your* seat and nobody is going to sit in it but you. You don't have to worry about someone else getting your gifts or taking your place or earning your rewards.

Your enemies never thought you'd be there.

Some of your friends never thought you'd be there.

There were moments that even *you* thought you'd never be there. But the time came when you sat down in God's presence and He sat down with you, and you had an encounter with God and it changed your life.

His right hand and holy arm pulled you out of the place you were and placed you where you are. He has done, is doing . . . and *will do* . . . *ALL* that He has planned and purposed for you.

That's why God can call a person holy, blameless, and righteous while they are still confused, in trouble, in turmoil, and tied up. He knows His plan and His power. He knows that He *will* accomplish His purposes.

Thank God today for holding a seat for you — for making you an advanced reservation in His kingdom. Trust Him to do in you all that He has planned.

GOD WRESTLES WITH YOU ... ALONE

And Jacob was left alone. (Genesis 32:24)

God maneuvers each one of us into a place where He can deal with us directly. He calls us to a state of "aloneness." He doesn't deal with us in the context of other people. Cliques, clubs, groups, and all sorts of entanglements, societies, and mentalities can keep us from hearing God as much as they can help us to hear from God. When God gets you to the point of dealing with the deep issues of your life, He does so one-on-one. Just you and God. Just me and God. Just each one of us alone with God.

Who are you really?

When nobody's looking . . .

   when you aren't "prepared" . . .

      when all the camouflage has been removed . . .

         when you don't have an ego to

           defend or anything to prove . . .

              when you aren't bogged down in
              imitations or concerned about
              status?

Who are you?

Anytime you are surrounded by people who don't know the real you . . .

Anytime you are in a situation where you can't fully be yourself . . .

109

Anytime you have to camouflage who you really are to be accepted . . .

You are alone. You will feel isolated, as if you are watching people through a glass wall.

When God is ready to do His divine surgery on you, He brings you to an "alone" place. Nobody invites guests into an operating room. Neither does God. His work on you is private.

When God begins to move in on your life and starts setting up His one-on-one appointment with you, you may feel very uncomfortable. In fact, I believe the first response of nearly all of us at that time is to try to surround ourselves with more and more people. We feel restless, frustrated, lonely in our spirits. We feel a greater need to have somebody with us, to protect us, shield us, wrap their arms around us, join us, walk with us. We soon discover that the presence of other people doesn't meet the need. The loneliness and restlessness we are feeling in our spirits is God's call to us. He is reeling us in to our one-on-one encounter with Him.

You can be surrounded by people . . . and still be alone.

You can have intimate relations with your wife . . . and still be alone.

You can have dozens of close friends . . . and still be alone.

It's when we admit that we are lonely and need something that people can't supply — we need Someone to fulfill a part of us that nobody else seems to be able to fulfill — that's when God steps in.

When you say that you are left alone, it means that somebody that you thought you could count on for protection has disappeared. You feel isolated, separated, apart. Alone.

When we feel left alone, therefore, our hope is usually that someone will come along and comfort us. In fact, we expect from our human standpoint that "comfort" is what a loving God would do to a man who is left alone. God says, however, that He is not coming to comfort, but to *confront*.

God came to challenge Jacob, to wrestle with him.

Jacob's first reaction was, no doubt, "Oh, no, not You too!"

Everybody is wrestling me.
My wife is wrestling with me.
My children are wrestling with me.
My boss is wrestling with me.
My creditors are wrestling with me.
My coworkers are wrestling with me.
My church is wrestling with me.
My own mind is a wrestling match.
And now, You, too, God?

The Bible says, "Faithful are the wounds of a friend" (Proverbs 27:6). A true friend is one who "wounds" you for a good reason. What he says may hurt you, but in the end, it helps you. What he does may seem painful to you, but in the end, you'll thank him for doing it because it was for your good.

A really good friend doesn't agree with you all the time. No matter how brutally you roar, a good friend will stand right up in your face and say, "You're still wrong."

You don't have real help until you have someone who will confront you about what needs to be changed in your life.

God comes to each one of us . . .

To stand up to us, and to force us to face our sin.

To confront us about our lies.

To make us uncomfortable about our bad habits.

To move us away from mediocrity.

To challenge us to excellence.

———————
———————
———————

Are you ready today for your private appointment with God?

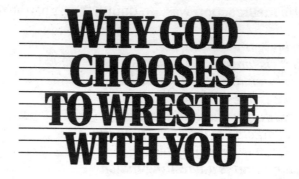

WHY GOD CHOOSES TO WRESTLE WITH YOU

Seek, and ye shall find. (Matthew 7:7)

God wrestles with you so that you will discover what you are made of. He already knows what He created you to be and He knows what you've done with His creation. He's waiting for you to discover who you are. He wrestles with you so you will know His power and your weakness, His wisdom and your error, His strength and your frailty.

God wrestles with you to make you realize that you are wasting your life . . .

that you are mistreating your wife . . .

that you aren't the "greatest" or the center of the universe . . .

that you aren't the "least" and unworthy of anything good.

God wrestles with you to make you see that you need to keep this job and not quit it like you did the last three jobs . . .

you need to stay involved with this church and not back away from it like you did the last three times you say that you "got religion" . . .

112

you need to stay in your marriage and not
wander off like you did the last time.

God wrestles with you until you face the facts of your
life. He doesn't sugarcoat anything. He gives it to you
straight. He wrestles with you until you admit . . .

Yes, I'm unstable.

Yes, I'm making excuses.

Yes, I was wrong.

God also wrestles with you so that you will start
searching for Him and hunting for what He wants you to
find.

Man is a hunter by nature. God's commands to man at
his creation were to "be fruitful, and multiply, and
replenish the earth, and subdue it: and have dominion
. . . over every living thing that moveth upon the earth"
(Genesis 1:28).

To subdue means to conquer, to have dominion means
to maintain one's conquest. Somewhere as part of the
masculine nature is the need to subdue, the need to
conquer, the need to track down and bring something
into dominion. There's a hunter inside every man.

We may be hunting for a contract or business deal.

We may be on the hunt for a woman.

We may be hunting for the perfect new car.

Sometimes we don't even really want what we are after,
we are just hunting because it is our nature to hunt. Fish-
ermen often catch fish, unhook them, and throw them
right back. They say, "Look what I caught." And then they
toss that fish back into the lake. That doesn't make the
man any less a fisherman. It means that he is merely
fishing for the sport of it, not for dinner. He is "hunting."

Unless we allow God to step in and give us the right
goals and guide our "hunting" instinct, we can spend our
entire life hunting for the wrong things.

Jesus said, "Seek ye *first* the kingdom of God" (Matthew
6:33). And He promised that if you seek for it, you'll find
it. (See Matthew 7:7.)

_____
_____
_____

Wrestle with God today until the night ends, the dawn breaks, and you can see His face, feel His love, and know His purpose.

THE URGENCY OF GOD'S PURPOSE

Return ye now every man from his evil way, and amend your doings, and go not after other gods to serve them, and ye shall dwell in the land which I have given to you. (Jeremiah 35:15)

Return NOW.

There is always an urgency in God's call for us to repent of our sin and to return to Him.

There is also a persistence in God's wrestling with us. People will sometimes tell us what they think, but then they abandon us. God doesn't give up. He wrestles with us *until*. He isn't swayed from His purpose.

There's an appointed time for the wrestling match in your life to end. God wrestled with Jacob "until the breaking of the day" (Genesis 32:24). God wrestled with urgency, with insistency, with greater and greater strength. He knew that if Jacob didn't confront who he was in that night, he was going to miss the prime opportunity to become who he was destined to be.

You may be running out of time, too.

A lot of things you perhaps could get away with in times past . . . you no longer can get away with. A lot of excuses you've used in the past . . . you no longer will be allowed to use.

God's urgency must not be ignored. He knows something about your life and your encounter with Him that you don't know. He knows when Satan's assassins have been launched against you for your demise. He knows when the death angel is allowed to do his work. He knows when He is returning again.

Before you lose your life . . .
Before you lose your integrity . . .
Before you lose your wife . . .
Before you lose your son or daughter . . .
Before you lose your future blessing . . .
Before you lose what God has given to you . . .
God's urgency is for a *purpose.* Don't ignore Him.
You don't have time to fool around.
You don't have time for detours.
You don't have time for childish things.
You don't have time for your rebellion.
You don't have time to play games.
You don't have time for an affair.
You don't have time for meetings and committees that aren't important.

If you're going to experience the place God has reserved for you, you are probably going to have to cut off some relationships . . .

give up some things . . .

dig deeper into God's Word . . .

learn how to pray for yourself . . .

and truly become the priest of your home.

If people ask you why you can't do what you've done in the past, tell them, "I don't have time. I'm going someplace and I've got to get there."

116

Look at your watch right now and say to yourself, "Now is the appointed time for me to serve God so I can dwell in the land He has prepared for me!"

THE REALITY OF THE SPIRIT REALM

We wrestle not against flesh and blood, but against principalities, against powers, against the rulers of the darkness of this world, against spiritual wickedness in high places. (Ephesians 6:12)

There is a world about which many of us are unconscious, or unaware. It is real nonetheless. In fact, it is more real than the world we can see, touch, taste, hear, or feel. It is the realm of the spirit.

The most real part of you is your spirit. You *are* a spirit. Many men seem to think the real part of them is their body, but no matter how much you build it up, manicure it, dress it, or feed it, you are not first and foremost a body. You *have* a body. You live in a body. It is a temporary home.

You also have a soul. The soulish area of man is where most of the problems occur; this is the area of the mind, the emotions, memories, appetites, desires. The mind of man, including the mind of the Christian, is often trapped between the physical and the spiritual — flashbacks to memories of the former life in the flesh can fill the mind. The result can be a tremendous wrestling match, with each force, spirit and flesh, trying to dominate the other. In fact, it is only when a man receives the Word of God and engrafts it to his mind that he is able to save his mind from the clutches of the flesh.

Demons are disembodied spirits. They don't have a body, and they don't have a soul — they have no mind of their own or will of their own. Their will is totally subjected to Satan. They are vessels and carriers of Satan's nature. They are filled with his desires, his lusts, his passions, and his unclean thoughts.

Because demons don't have bodies, they are seeking one. They are seeking a vehicle through which they can express their lusts and passions for evil.

Jesus once said to Simon Peter, "Simon, Simon, behold, Satan hath desired to *have* you, that he may sift you as wheat" (Luke 22:31). He was saying to Peter, "Satan desires to possess you, to have you, to dominate you." Men know what it means to lust after a woman in order to *have* her. That's the way Satan looked at Peter. He lusted after him, that he might completely *take* Peter's mind and body — to satisfy his cravings through him.

Satan's demons desire the same thing today regarding you —

To use your body, your temper, your lust, your passions.

To work through the broken places of your childhood to fulfill their ravenous desires.

To possess you so that he might sift you.

Before Satan makes a move to have you, he studies you. He learns all he can about you — your moods,
your attitudes,
your background,
your past hurts and
painful memories,
your desires.

He has stalked you. He has put you under surveillance, watching always for an opportunity to move in to take you. He *longs* to possess,
> dominate,
>> control,
>>> rule over,
>>>> and act through you.

That's the reason you must walk *closely* by the side of Jesus. Cling to Him. Never for a moment believe Satan's lie that you can go it alone or make it on your own strength. David — one of the bravest and most capable men who ever lived — cried out to God, "Hide me under the shadow of your wings." (See Psalm 17:8.) Tucked under the wings of God . . . that's the only place you will ever feel fully secure.

Trust in the Lord today. Ask Him to give you the courage and faith to withstand Satan's sifting.

WHO IS IN CONTROL?

Lead us not into temptation, but deliver us from evil. (Matthew 6:13)

Every act of your life is motivated by a spiritual force.

Who is controlling you?
What is motivating you?
What spirit is being satisfied through your body?

If it is Satan's spirit that you are allowing to work in you — manifest through his demons — then you are grieving the Holy Spirit. Any time you allow the enemy to work his will through your mind or body, you grieve the Holy Spirit.

The Holy Spirit also desires to use you. But He wants to use you for God's glory and God's service. You will feel satisfied and have great joy when you live for God's glory. The Holy Spirit's purpose is not to dominate you or crush you, but to fulfill you.

Satan desires to use you for his own purpose, as a pawn in his hand to laugh in God's face. He desires to use you, abuse you, and then refuse you. You are in a state of living death when you succumb to the devil's purpose. He defies God as he works in you through his demons, saying in effect, "Is this someone You wanted, God? Well,

124

I'm here first and I'm not moving. You called this man Your son? Look who's really in charge of his life. Look what I am making Your son do."

Temptation is Satan's tool for getting you to do things that you really don't want to do. Deep inside your spirit, you know that what he is tempting you to do is wrong. The worst and most hardened criminals in our world today know they have done wrong — they may blame others for their actions, they may act as if they don't care about the fact that they've done wrong, been caught, or are facing serious consequences — but deep inside, they know. They knew when they were doing wrong that what they were doing was wrong.

Satan's lie is that you have a *right* to do wrong.

Society is at fault. You have a right to get even with society.

Your daddy is at fault. You have a right to rebel against him.

Your boss is at fault. You have a right to steal from him or cheat him.

God is at fault. He made you this way. You have a right to act the way you do because He made you with this temper, this anger, this lust, this desire.

God's Word says that you have a right to choose. Joshua said to the Israelites, "Choose you this day whom ye will serve . . . as for me and my house, we will serve the LORD" (Joshua 24:15). You have a right to choose, a free will, a mind that can make a decision. But you have no right to sin.

Make sure today that you are yielding the control of your life *only* to God.

Make it your prayer today: "Deliver me from evil!"

DON'T LET SATAN DIVIDE AND CONQUER YOU

If we say that we have no sin, we deceive ourselves, and the truth is not in us. (1 John 1:8)

One of Satan's foremost tactics is the tactic of "divide and conquer." When Jesus encountered the man with an unclean spirit, He found him dwelling among the tombs. He was outside the city, away from family and friends. He had been "divided," and then conquered.

Satan always and relentlessly will attempt to move you away from community, family, and ministry. He will do anything in his power to convince you to break away, because he can conquer you more easily if you are isolated.

The enemy will move you to break away from others by feeding you lies, some of which are that . . .

You're exceptional. You're not really LIKE these people. You are better than they are.
Your situation is different. You grew up in conditions that weren't like those of anybody else's. Your childhood has molded you in certain ways that cannot be altered.

126

Don't Let Satan Divide and Conquer You

Your problem is unique. Nobody can relate to your problem because nobody has had it as bad as you had it. They can't relate to how you feel.

These lies become your excuses. They become your false premise for your taking license to act or speak in ways that are contrary to God's commandments. If you think that you aren't like other people, then it's only one step further for you to come to the conclusion that you don't have to abide by the same rules as other people.

If you find yourself saying . . .

I wouldn't be like this if my mother hadn't given me away . . .

> *if I'd had a different father . . .*
>> *if I had a more loving wife . . .*
>>> *if I had a better job . . .*
>>>> *if I had not faced so much opposition*
>>>>> *. . .*

. . . wake up! You are giving yourself a passport to failure, a visa to flunk. You are hardening your attitude so that no matter who preaches to you, you whip out your yeah-but card and say, "This is why your message won't work for me."

If you adopt an attitude that you are "different," then you mentally and emotionally begin to separate yourself from other people. You disconnect from your foundation and from the fundamentals of truth. There's grave danger in that, especially if you are disconnecting from people who truly know God and are serving Him.

Once you are disconnected mentally and emotionally, you are also disconnected in other areas of your life whether you intended to be or not. You'll find it impossible to keep a job . . .

> hold a marriage together . . .
>> relate in good ways to your children . . .
>>> or make any long-term commitment that requires self-discipline.

The reason that you offer to others is always a *good* reason. It makes sense to you. It may even make sense to other people. It just doesn't fly with God.

Your excuse may keep you from being disgraced. But it will also keep you from being convicted and from changing.

Don't buy into Satan's lies. Don't give yourself license to lay in the cesspool of sin. Get rid of your excuses!

Refuse to be separated from God's people, God's plan for righteousness, or God's purpose for your life.

When Satan comes around with his lies, confront him with God's truth.

BEWARE: MAN OUT OF CONTROL

There met him out of the tombs a man with an unclean spirit ... no man could bind him, no, not with chains. (Mark 5:2,3)

One of the indications that a person is bound by Satan's influence is that "no man could bind him, no, not with chains."

The issue is one of control.

Now, I'm not talking about whether this man was possessed or oppressed. In either case, a person is being controlled by Satan. Even a Christian can be so oppressed that he operates under Satan's control.

A little boy might be sitting on his daddy's shoulders, pulling at his left ear and saying, "Daddy, go this way," and then pulling at his right ear and saying, "Daddy, go that way." And in play, the daddy does what the little boy demands. This little boy isn't *in* his father, but he is *controlling* his father's actions. And that's the way demons operate. They seek to fuel our desires and direct our passions, and in so doing, exert such tremendous influence on our behavior that it's almost as if we no longer have a will of our own.

129

You can be so oppressed that you might as well be possessed. The result is that you are a lascivious man.

Lasciviousness is unrestrained action. It is being "out of control." No limitations. Whatever flesh says, flesh gets.

If you are angry, you tear up everything in the house.

If you are lustful, you'll even try to date your sister-in-law.

If you are filled with hate, you'll break every stick of furniture in sight.

The man who is lascivious might as well wear a sign around his neck, "Man out of control." He does things he may not even like to do solely because they are *possible* to do. He can't be trusted. He can't fulfill responsibility.

The lascivious man can't be bound. He doesn't pay any attention to the restraints of others or to the normal conventions of society or to the normal restraints of his own conscience. He certainly doesn't pay any attention to the commandments of God.

Domestic violence is "man out of control." It's a man beating what he ought to be protecting, it's a man beating his own body.

Sexual and physical abuse is "man out of control." It's a man turning on his own *zera*, his seed, so that his own children can't feel comfortable sitting on his lap.

Lasciviousness knows no boundaries. It infects every race, every culture, every nation. Rich and poor. Educated and uneducated. It doesn't care if a man is wearing a pin-stripe suit with a red paisley tie or a plaid flannel shirt and jeans or a torn T-shirt and baggy pants.

Nobody tries to get close to a man out of control. They want to, but they are afraid to.

Daddy's drinking.

Papa's high.

Father's in a bad mood tonight.

Honey's not at home and it's midnight.

It's not a matter of temptation. All men are tempted. It's a matter of self-control and self-discipline. Can God trust you to control your own *self*, to put boundaries on yourself?

One of the indications that this man had an unclean spirit was that nobody could get him to stop doing what he was doing. And what is it that he was doing? He was "crying, and cutting himself with stones." He was hurting *himself.*

The Bible says this man "had been often bound with fetters and chains, and the chains had been plucked asunder by him, and the fetters broken in pieces: neither could any man tame him" (Mark 5:4).

This man had been caught in the past, but he got away. He had made New Year's resolutions, but he broke his commitment to himself before January was over. He had been to the altar before and told God, "never again," but he had lied to God. He had done the very thing he had vowed never to do again. And you know, once a person has lied to God, he has no trouble at all lying to his wife, his children, his pastor, his friend, his boss.

Oh, you're so slick. You can slip past anybody if you want to. You can get away with anything.

Oh, you're so discreet. You're just sitting idly by, hunting with your eyes. Nobody knows what you're thinking, nobody knows the fantasies that you are living out in your mind.

Oh, you're so clever. You have a justification for everything, an excuse for every action, an alibi for every hour.

The reality is, you are hurting yourself when you break through all barriers. You are cutting short your own potential. You are breaking chains that were in place for your own good.

Is there an area of your life today that is out of control? Ask God to bind it up — and to give you restraint by the power of the Holy Spirit.

Say no to your flesh today and say yes
to the Spirit of God.

STOP LIVING IN THE TOMBS

And always, night and day, he was in the mountains, and in the tombs. (Mark 5:5)

The fact is, we're killing ourselves. Countless men are living in the "tombs."

I'm not talking about murder in the streets. That's there, and it's real, but that's the "outer world." I'm talking about the "inner world," the world that's just behind the facade that you put on.

You can kill a person with your words, your attitude, your absence. You can kill a relationship without any other weapon than your tongue. You can murder an association or a relationship without exploding any bomb; you can destroy it by neglect.

We are a people living out in the tombs. We're surrounded by death, and much of it is death that we have inflicted upon ourselves.

How many aborted babies were yours, and you didn't even know it because you weren't *around* to know it?

How many of those boys in the 'hood are running in gangs because you refused to be a father to them, and perhaps didn't even know you *were* their father?

133

How many women are in counseling offices every week because of what you said you'd do that you didn't do, or because of what you said you didn't do that you did do?

How many chains have you broken?

How many people are bleeding from wounds that you inflicted?

How many of your children are going to need serious pastoral counseling?

How many people are suicidal or messed up in their minds because of the lies you told?

How much death and destruction have you caused in your life? What tombs are you living in?

Jesus said, "I am the way, the truth, and the life" (John 14:6). Turn to Jesus today and ask Him to forgive you for all the deaths you have caused. Ask Him to lead you into the FULLNESS of His life.

———————
———————
———————
———————

Today can be your resurrection day in Christ Jesus!

THE VICTIMS OF SPIRITUAL AIDS

This poor man cried, and the LORD heard him, and saved him out of all his troubles. (Psalm 34:6)

AIDS.

It's a deadly disease.

But there's something even worse than acquired immune deficiency syndrome and it's this: "Spiritual AIDS."

A spiritually acquired immune deficiency syndrome has some of the same hallmarks as AIDS:

- It is *acquired.* You get it, catch it, or buy it. You become infected with it. You pick it up and it stays in you.
- Its presence in you is related to the broken-down barriers in your life. Just as your immune system keeps you from becoming sick from every germ or virus or bug that comes close to you, so your *spiritual immune system* keeps you from falling prey to every trick and temptation of the enemy. When your immune system breaks down, you get sick. When your spiritual immune system breaks down, you are an easy target for the devil.

135

- It is a *deficiency.* You are lacking the spiritual immune system you are supposed to have. The barriers that once kept you from sin have been torn down in your mind. You know, people sometimes say they are scared to be around people with AIDS. The reality is, people with AIDS should be a lot more scared of you, a person without AIDS, than you should ever be of them. Why? Because you have immunity and they do not. You are carrying germs and viruses in your body that aren't affecting you because of your healthy immune system, but those germs and viruses can be deadly to them.

The person with spiritual AIDS catches everything that passes by him. The Bible says, "He that hath no rule over his own spirit is like a city that is broken down, and without walls." (Proverbs 25:28) Without immunity, without defense, without walls.

- It is a *syndrome.* Spiritual AIDS becomes a habit. It sets itself up in the spirit and it becomes a man's identity.

The man with an unclean spirit had a spiritual disease that was out of control, and it was killing him. He was already living in the tombs. He wasn't far from death himself.

The man with AIDS is a man who is living with a time bomb in his body. Death is stalking him. The man with spiritual AIDS is also living in a state of death — and his state is much worse because it is a state of *eternal* death.

The cure for spiritual AIDS is found in Psalm 34:14,17 — "Depart from evil, and do good; seek peace, and pursue it. . . . The righteous cry, and the LORD heareth, and delivereth them out of all their troubles."

————————
————————
————————
————————

Ask God to give a boost to your spiritual immune system today.

136

HUNGERING FOR RIGHTEOUSNESS

Blessed are they which do hunger and thirst after righteousness: for they shall be filled. (Matthew 5:6)

The man with an unclean spirit looked strong. He caused fear in others. Nobody wanted to get close to him because they were afraid of his strength that could "pluck asunder" fetters and leave chains in pieces.

But when this man was alone, he was anything but strong. He was crying. (See Mark 5:4,5.)

Countless men are crying today because deep down inside their hearts, they have become something they didn't *want* to become.

Not wanting to be who you are is the key to your deliverance. It's not what you've *done* that makes you a candidate for God's forgiveness; it's how you *feel* about what you have done and how you *feel* about what you want to be.

Jesus did not cross the Sea of Galilee on a stormy night to meet this man simply because he had an unclean spirit. No doubt there were people with an unclean spirit on the shore where Jesus was. No . . . Jesus was led by God to this man because this man was in the tombs

137

"crying." He didn't want to be the man he had become. He didn't want his future to be the same as his past.

Thank goodness, Jesus didn't say, "Blessed is he who *is* righteousness." That would eliminate all of us from God's blessing! Thank goodness, Jesus said, "Blessed is he who still wants to be righteous — who still has an appetite for doing the right thing, who still thirsts to be a better person, who still wants to be whole even though he knows he isn't whole . . .

who still wants to be the good husband he knows he isn't . . .

who still wants to be the father he believes he can be but isn't right now . . .

who still wants to change and grow,

who still desires to be holy."

Deliverance begins with desire, a PASSION in you that challenges the PROBLEM in you.

I do not want to live like this anymore.

I do not want to be like this.

I do not want to act like this.

I do not want to be a drunk, a drug addict, a homosexual.

I do not want to be this angry, this critical, this cold, this indifferent, this destructive, this lazy, this trite.

I do not want to be jealous, suspicious, or distant.

What is it that you *don't* want to BE anymore?

What is it that you *don't* want to DO anymore?

What is your cry to God?

God can and does hear you when you cry. He doesn't condemn you for crying out to Him. Rather, He moves toward you when you cry. He comes to you with deliverance and forgiveness.

Cry out to God today for the changes you want in YOUR life.

STOP
CUTTING
YOURSELF
DOWN

He was ... in the tombs ... cutting himself
with stones. (Mark 5:5)

This man with an unclean spirit is a classic example of
a man with extremely low self-esteem. He didn't
value himself. He was cutting his own flesh with stones.

Countless men today are "cutting themselves" in their
own minds. They may put on a brave front to the outside
world, but when they are alone, they wound themselves
and bleed — they dissipate their own energy, their own
life force.

They are insecure about themselves, hating themselves. The man who hates himself cannot love another
person. How can you give to another person what you
can't even give to yourself? It's not possible. The man with
low self-esteem can't build up other people — not his
wife, or his children, or his employees, or those he is
asked to supervise at work.

Self-image is the most important thing in the world
that you need to have next to your faith in God. It doesn't
matter what others think of you. It matters only what *you*
think of you based upon what *God* thinks of you.

139

When you start cutting and gnashing at yourself, you become preoccupied with self-hatred.

We each treat other people out of our own reservoir of self-dignity and self-respect. If you don't have respect for yourself, you won't have genuine respect for other people. Jesus taught, "Love thy neighbour as thyself" (Matthew 19:19). If you don't love yourself, you can't love your neighbor.

The Bible also says that a man should love his own wife as he loves himself. (See Ephesians 5:28.) If you don't like yourself, you can't love your wife.

Most men who abuse their wives are self-haters. It is out of their own anger and frustration that they lash out at their wives. They aren't overflowing with hatred for their wives, but for them*selves.* If you truly want to know how you feel about your*self,* look at how you treat your wife. She is your body, one with you. She is "bone of your bone and flesh of your flesh" — the feminine expression of your masculinity. The way you treat your wife is the way you treat your*self.*

If you are physically, sexually, emotionally, or verbally abusing your wife, you are abusing yourself.

You are denying,
 screaming at,
  lashing out at,
   ignoring in your silence,
    cutting to the core of . . .
     your very own self.

You cannot receive the esteem of your son or daughter if you do not esteem yourself.

The man with an unclean spirit was cutting himself, doing far more damage to himself than any other person had ever been able to do to him. The same holds true for us. We do far more damage to ourselves than others do.

Self-esteem has to come from self. You won't believe the good things that anybody else says about you unless you first believe those things about yourself.

I like me. I'm glad if other people like me, but I don't do what I do *so* that other people will like me. I'm not dependent upon whether other people like me or not.

If I come across anybody who doesn't like me, I am very happy to say to them, "I disagree with you." I don't give in to the way they feel about me and like myself less. I simply disagree with their opinion. I like me! I have a right to my own opinion.

I know all about me . . . and I still like me. I know all my faults, but I still like me.

I like me in part because I'm still here — I've survived. I've lost some friends, some jobs, some cars, some things . . . but I'm here. If you have no other reason to like yourself other than the fact that you are a survivor of life's problems, like yourself for that reason.

Be who you are and be proud of it.

Not a lot of blacks live in West Virginia, especially in the rural areas. Sometimes when I am out in the remote regions, I encounter little white children who have never seen a black man. I recall this one little boy who just stared at me, aghast. He had never seen anything like me in his life. He said, "Lord, mister. Are you that color all over?"

His mother almost turned purple in embarrassment. I said to him, "Yes, I think I am. Everywhere I can see and everywhere I can see in the mirror, I'm this color. It seems to be all over me."

I'm not at all ashamed of being a black man. That's who God made me to be!

Start believing in the *you* that God made *you* to be. He loves you and that's all the reason you need for loving yourself.

Compliment God today on the fine job He did when He made you.

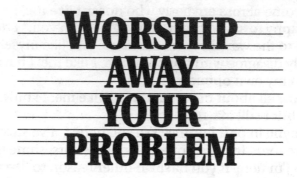

WORSHIP AWAY YOUR PROBLEM

When he saw Jesus afar off, he ran and worshipped him. (Mark 5:6)

This man with an unclean spirit saw Jesus from afar off and his response was to worship Him.

I want you to note that this man didn't get delivered first and then worship Jesus. He worshiped Jesus and *then* was delivered by Jesus.

Some men today aren't delivered from the oppression they are experiencing from the devil because they haven't learned how to *worship away their problems.*

Even the devil has to bow down and acknowledge that Jesus is Lord of all. The Bible tells us that *every* knee must bow to Him: "of things in heaven, and things in earth, and things under the earth; and that every tongue should confess that Jesus Christ is Lord, to the glory of God the Father"(Philippians 2:10,11). Every system, government, and society must bow to the Lord of lords and King of kings.

Every hex, every curse, every evil work must BOW to the name of Jesus. That includes every satanic power and generational curse. "No weapon that is formed against

142

thee shall prosper; and every tongue that shall rise against thee in judgment thou shalt condemn. This is the heritage of the servants of the LORD, and their righteousness is of me, saith the LORD" (Isaiah 54:17).

Your childhood hurts . . .

    your painful memories . . .

        your addiction . . .

           your past sins . . .

                must BOW to the name of Jesus.

You must condemn anything that rises up in you to destroy you and your ministry — your lust, your anger, your hate, your bitterness, your rebellious spirit, your job-quitting, church-hopping spirit — and say to it, "*Bow* to the name of Jesus."

Bow in worship.

When this man began to worship Jesus, the demons in him cried out, "What have I to do with thee, Jesus, thou Son of the most high God? I adjure thee by God, that thou torment me not" (Mark 5:7).

The fact is, demons have NOTHING to do with Jesus. They have nothing in common with Him, no association with Him, no alliance with Him. And Jesus has NOTHING to do with them except to cast them out. The very presence of Jesus torments demons.

If you are in a truly anointed worship service, demons scream out and flee from people who are calling out to the name of Jesus. Nobody has to touch a person or pray a long prayer over a person with unclean spirits. The very atmosphere of worship is a torment to demon powers.

Worship is the key to your deliverance.

Run to Jesus today and worship Him!

BREAKING THE DEVIL'S STRONGHOLD

Deride every strong hold. (Habakkuk 1:10)

David was a good man. He was creative, strong, coura-geous. He was a man of musical and songwriting talent. He was a natural leader. But he had a generational curse on his life — a lust problem that cropped up from time to time.

Everybody around David apparently knew he had this problem. In fact, the Bible says that when David was an old man and he could not get warm, his servants brought a young virgin to lie in his bosom, that "the king may get heat." (See 1 Kings 1:1,2.) His servants said, in effect, "If being with this young woman can't get David's circulation going, nothing can! He probably *is* dying if he doesn't feel anything when he's with her."

The generational sin in David was passed on to Amnon, who had a lustful spirit for his sister, Tamar. He lured her to his bed and raped her. The Bible tells us that when David heard what Amnon had done to Tamar, he was very angry . . . but he didn't say or do anything to Amnon. What could he say? His son was just like him. His own spirit of lust had passed on to his son. (See 2 Samuel 13.)

Lust is not a craving,
    a fancy,

or a whim. It's sin.

When a pattern of evil passes from generation to generation, it becomes what the Bible calls a spiritual "stronghold." A spirit of evil is passed from generation to generation until it truly has a *strong hold* on a man's life. He can't get free of it simply because he wishes to be free or hopes to be free. Only Jesus can set that man free.

Many men can look back at their family history and see a bad spirit at work in their family, generation after generation.

Daddy drank too much . . . and granddaddy drank too much . . . and great-granddaddy drank too much.

Dad cheated on Mom, and Grandpa cheated on Grandma, and Great-Grandpa wasn't even around to cheat on Great-Grandma.

Father had a bad temper . . . and so did grandfather . . . and so did great-grandfather.

Sometimes a man can look and see a pattern of abuse and sin and evil coming at him from both sides of his family tree. It isn't only his grandpa on his father's side who was filled with anger, but his grandpa on his mother's side. Or, a man may know nothing about his grandparents or great-grandparents — and perhaps not even his father's behavior — but he may see a particular pattern of behavior rampant among his brothers, uncles, and cousins. His *family* has been infected with a bad spirit.

When Jesus commanded the demon who afflicted the man in the tombs to tell Him his name, the demon replied, "Legion: for we are many" (Mark 5:9).

Very often, the demonic oppression on our lives has many facets — it has many names, simultaneously. The spirit is not just one of lust, but of anger. It is one of emotional deprivation and one of poverty. When you combine various types of demonic oppression they multiply in their hold on a person's life.

A spiritual stronghold is not something that you can drink out of your life . . .
    smoke out of your life . . .
        curse out of your life . . .
           argue out of your life . . .
                or plead out of your life. BUT you can CAST it out of your life!

Before you go to the judge . . .

Before you go to the rehab center . . .

Before you go to the counselor . . .

Go to God.

Get to the altar and ask God to break that stronghold from your life. You may still need help to learn *how* to express yourself, but first and foremost, you need God's help in breaking the spiritual oppression that has you in its clutches.

If you don't break the spiritual strongholds on your life, your own sons and daughters will be victims of it. Lay your hand on your son and your daughter and say . . .

Don't let the same things that infected me, infect another generation.

Don't let the same abuse be passed on to my children.

You could be a great husband.

You could be a great father.

You could be an outstanding employee.

You could be a very effective witness.

What keeps you from it? Name that stronghold and ask God to break it off your life.

———————————
———————————
———————————
———————————

Make Jesus the Lord of anything that is lording it over you.

BREAKING THE CURSE OF POVERTY OFF YOUR LIFE

Bring ye all the tithes into the storehouse, that there may be meat in mine house, and prove me now herewith, saith the LORD of hosts, if I will not open you the windows of heaven, and pour you out a blessing, that there shall not be room enough to receive it. And I will rebuke the devourer for your sakes, and he shall not destroy the fruits of your ground; neither shall your vine cast her fruit before the time in the field, saith the LORD of hosts. (Malachi 3:10,11)

Just recently I heard a report about a young child who went to school wearing a $400 pair of shoes. This child was the son of a woman who was selling drugs. I thought to myself, if that woman can trust the devil and his demons to clothe her baby like that, how is it that Christian men refuse to trust God to take care of them and their families.

And yet I see it all the time: Christian men jealous of other men. Mostly they are jealous of their *stuff*. They are jealous of their house, or their car, or their wristwatch, or their clothes, or their gold jewelry, or some other possession they have.

Then, to compound matters, they try to cover up and justify their jealousy by saying, "We shouldn't have nice things or own the best that is available to purchase." They turn their jealousy into a stingy, angry spirit. They complain about the kind of car their pastor drives, although when they were in sin, they never once complained about the gold jewelry and big diamond rings and fancy cars that were owned by the man who ran the local bar or the corner pool hall.

I refuse to give in to the jealousy of other people. I want to say to any person who might be jealous of something I own, "I paid for what I have, and I paid first of all in the spirit realm."

God said that He would bless me if I brought my tithes into His storehouse. He said He would open up the windows of heaven and pour out a blessing on me and my family that was so great I wouldn't have room enough to receive it. He said He would rebuke the devourer from my family. He would cause us to be fruitful in every area and that others would see our blessing and call us "delightsome." (See Malachi 3:12.)

I broke the spirit of poverty over my house by giving my tithes and giving my offerings. I beat the devil out of my checkbook and pleaded the blood over my finances. I scraped and crawled my way up out of poverty and into God's prosperity by doing what God said to do! And you can, too.

I refuse to listen to those who have spent the money that should have been their tithe and offering to God, who are bound up in a spirit of poverty and stinginess toward the things of God, and then complain that I shouldn't receive or enjoy God's blessings. The simple fact is, I have done what God has said to do. They haven't.

Do what God says to do in His Word. And then . . .

Let God bless you! Enjoy what He gives to you!

_____
_____
_____

Take authority over your finances today. Rebuke the devil from your finances in the name of Jesus, give your tithes and offerings — as the man and priest of your house, and then look for God's blessings to be poured out from heaven on you.

CASTING THE DEVIL OUT OF YOUR FAMILY

[Jesus] said unto him, Come out of the man, thou unclean spirit. (Mark 5:8)

Jesus' response to the man who was living in the tombs was to speak to the evil spirit in him, "Come out of him." (See Mark 5:8.) Jesus didn't condemn the man. He condemned the evil spirit that had attached itself to the man.

This was a good man who had a very bad spirit in him. The bad spirit needed to be pulled out of him, the power of the evil spirit broken in his life.

When Jesus rebuked the devil in this man's life, the demon started pleading. He didn't plead about leaving the man, but about leaving the "neighborhood." It was as if he was saying to Jesus, "I've been assigned to this territory. Don't make me leave my post."

The devil may not mind your being free. But he will mind being cast out of your family. He may say, "If I can't have you, at least let me have your son." The devil will do his best to drive a wedge between you and your son so you can't communicate and so that he will come to a conclusion that you don't love him.

The devil may say, "Fine, if I can't have you. Let me have your brother, your cousin, your neighbor." He wants to stay in your neighborhood.

Your answer to his compromise must always be NO!

Shout it at him. Refuse to give an inch. No to his having your son. No to his having your daughter. No to his having your brother or sister. No to his having your neighbor. Shout it *LOUD*.

There was so much demonic power in this one man that when Jesus commanded the power to leave, He sent it into an entire herd of swine. They broke their natural instinctual tendency and leaped into the sea.

If the devil can't have you, he will make a bid for your family. Don't allow it.

Pray that the blood of Jesus will cover your entire family today. Claim your wife, your children, your brothers and sisters, your nieces and nephews, and your grandchildren for God.

DIRECTING YOUR DELIVERANCE BACK HOME

And when he was come into the ship, he that had been possessed with the devil prayed him that he might be with him. Howbeit Jesus suffered him not, but saith unto him, Go home to thy friends, and tell them how great things the Lord hath done for thee, and hath had compassion on thee. And he departed, and began to publish in Decapolis how great things Jesus had done for him: and all men did marvel. (Mark 5:18-20)

When a man is truly delivered by Jesus, everybody can tell. You can't keep it a secret.

When the man with an unclean spirit named Legion was delivered, everybody in both the city and the surrounding countryside knew it. They all went out to see what had happened.

When you are delivered by God . . .

Your old girlfriends are going to know it.

So are your old running buddies.

And your old drinking buddies.

And your coworkers.

152

The people in your old neighborhood are going to hear about it.

And for some of you, the people in your church will be able to see a difference!

Don't be ashamed to be a witness!

Be happy about what God has done for you.

If all God wanted was your salvation, He would have heard your pleas for forgiveness, saved you, and then killed you. No! God wants you to be His witness.

Where?

First, to those who are right where you are.

This man wanted to go with Jesus as He departed by boat to go to the other side of the lake, but Jesus said no. Why? He intended for this man to be a witness *to the people who knew him best.*

His ministry wasn't to be in the tombs or in the mountains where he had withdrawn in his torment. It was to be in the cities of the Decapolis, the place no doubt where this man had first become oppressed by evil.

God never intends for us to live apart from the world, but to be witnesses *to* the world.

Have you ever been to a meeting or a conference that was so wonderful, you never wanted it to end? Have you ever been on a retreat in a place so beautiful that you never wanted to go home?

That's the way the unclean man felt after Jesus had delivered him from the demon power that was oppressing him. He didn't want to leave Jesus' presence.

God frequently gives us "mountaintop" spiritual experiences — leading us to times and places where we can experience a powerful anointing of His presence — but then the time comes when He says to us, just as Jesus said to this man, "Go home."

Ask God today where He wants you to witness for Him. It very likely will be the place you know best.

_____
_____
_____

Today, tell somebody who is CLOSE to you about the love and power of God.

GETTING BACK INTO YOUR RIGHT MIND

[T]hey saw him] that was possessed with the devil, and had the legion, sitting, and clothed, and in his right mind... (Mark 5:15)

When God does a work in your life, He does it in calmness. He brings about a peace in your life. All hell may be breaking out against you, but you can sit back and whistle.

This man with an unclean spirit sat calmly at Jesus' feet after his deliverance. He had been ranting and raving, roaming through the mountains and tombs — restless in his outward actions, just as he was forever restless in his inner spirit. After his deliverance by Jesus, he knew the peace that only God can give.

This man was clothed, where he once had been naked. The Bible tells us that those who overcome the enemy shall "be clothed in white raiment" — they will be in God's eyes as if they have never sinned. Peter tells us that we are to be "clothed with humility," completely submissive to God so that we will hear what God wants us to hear, see what God wants us to see, and then say and do what God wants us to say and do. (See Revelation 3:5 and 1 Peter 5:5.)

155

Have you thought about the fact that once this man had been delivered and forgiven by Jesus, it was as if he had *never* been under the influence of a demon power named Legion? It was as if he had never walked around with torn chains hanging from his arms and legs, slashing himself with stones and living in the tombs. He was *clothed* with righteousness. God saw him only as *forgiven.* He had no "past" with God, only a bright future.

The assurance of forgiveness is what gives a man peace. When you truly know you are forgiven, you feel a calmness born of trust, a peace born of assurance. Paul described it for the Philippians as a peace that "passeth all understanding" (Philippians 4:7).

Every man I know needs this kind of peace.

You cannot be the head of your house and be hysterical at the same time. You can't fall apart just because your wife has fallen apart. You can't lose your cool just because your kids have lost theirs. Somebody has to keep their wits about them and say, "We're going to come out of this." As priest of your home, you are called to be a stabilizing, protecting force in your home. When you walk in the front door of your house, everybody in your family should feel safer. You are called by God to have a "right mind." "Let this mind be in you, which was also in Christ Jesus" (Philippians 2:5).

Having a right mind means being aware of your responsibilities and accepting them.

I know many men who let their wives deal with all the stress of the family, including anxiety over the family finances, worries over the spiritual life of each family member, and concerns over family provision. That's not her role. You and your wife must share the responsibility for your children and work together to make a plan for your family. It's a cop-out for a man to say to his children every time they ask for a decision, "Go ask your mama."

Can you answer these questions about your children?

Where are your children?

What time do they go to school?
What time do they get home?
Where are they in the evenings?
What time will they be back?
You should know!

Having a right mind means being responsible in providing for your family.

I see absolutely no excuse today for a man not to have a job. If there isn't a job available in your community that's suited to your educational level, find a job that's lower than your educational level and fill it until a better job opens up. If it's not illegal, and it's not sin, go for it! Pick up a shovel and dig a ditch if you have to. You may say, "Bishop, have you ever done that?" I certainly have. I have dug ditches until my hands were bleeding in order to get $100 to buy groceries to feed the children for another week. As long as I am in my house, I am responsible for providing for my household.

If you can't provide everything you *want* to provide for your family, do what you *can* do. You may not know everything, but you can find people who can teach your children the things necessary for them to know. You may not understand the Bible fully, but you can get your children to church and Sunday school and to youth group programs where they can learn the Bible, experience the power of God, and learn how to apply the truth of God to their lives. You may not know everything about prayer, but you can pray for your children with a humility of heart and a love that speaks volumes.

Ask the Lord to transform you by the renewing of your mind. (See Romans 12:2.) The Lord Jesus Christ *is* your sanity.

———————————
———————————
———————————

**Ask God to give you a clear, pure, right
mind today.**

GUARD, GIRD, AND GUIDE

For this God is our God for ever and ever: he will be our guide. (Psalm 48:14)

As husband and father, your role is threefold:
• *to guard your family*, which includes practical safety, but also spiritually guarding against evil.
• *to gird your family*, which means to provide for your family the support it needs — including food, shelter, clothing, and general well-being.
• *to guide your family*, which includes having a plan and direction for your family — setting goals, developing your family's witness and outreach efforts, and guiding your family into a greater understanding of God's truth.

Guarding means that if there's a strange noise in the night, *you* get up. If your child is having serious trouble in school, *you* go there. If somebody comes to the door, *you* answer it. Guarding sometimes means simply showing up. For you to be there when your child needs you, you need to be sensitive to their needs.

Girding means that your children have shoes on their feet and clothes on their back. It means making sure your wife has what she needs. I do everything in my power to make sure my wife looks good. She's a reflection on me! I do everything I can to make sure that she's happy and content. She's my best sermon! In fact, I expect to live in such a way with my wife that if I die before she does and she remarries, her next husband will *hate* me. He'll have to work overtime to do for her as much as I have done — including writing songs and poetry just for her, blowing kisses to her across the room, buying her nice things, giving her the compliments she deserves. He's going to get very tired taking care of her in the way that she is accustomed to.

Guiding means having a plan. For example, as you face your family's finances, do so with a plan. Then, share that plan with your family. Make it an all-family effort. Say to your wife and children, "Things are tight right now, but here's what we are going to do. In three months, this is where we should be. In a year, this is our goal. In three years, we should have our finances fully under control." Give your children a future to anticipate with hope. They can't have hope if you haven't spelled out a plan and set a direction toward a circumstance that will be better than what they know today.

Have an agenda for your family's spiritual growth. Plan with your wife what you are going to do together to raise your children up to know and love God, His Word, and His church.

Guard.
Gird.
Guide.
Make that your motto!

Even as you choose to guard, gird, and guide your family, trust God to guard, gird, and guide YOU.

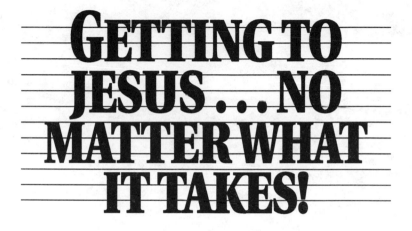
GETTING TO JESUS . . . NO MATTER WHAT IT TAKES!

THE UNTAPPED POWER OF CHRIST

For thine is the kingdom, and the power, and the glory, for ever. (Matthew 6:13)

One of the things that needs to be better understood within the body of Christ is the power of Christ. In many cases, the church needs to understand this as much as the world does. Christ is not a weak, impotent, unresponsive force. Our God is a God of power — He impacts every situation and circumstance He is allowed to enter with revolutionary, life-changing power.

One Christian can chase a thousand, and two can chase ten thousand because our God allows it to be so. (See Deuteronomy 32:30.) The church bears all the power necessary to heal marriages and to heal those who are sick — physically, emotionally, mentally, and spiritually. The real psychologist's couch resides in the Word of God. The church can impact every community — its families, its economy, its health.

When Jesus came to a city, the magistrates and all of the city leaders knew it. He worked in such a way that everybody knew He was there. He *changed* things.

It's time that more of us in the body of Christ be noisier about the power of Christ — to be movers and shakers who will go into the enemy's camp and take back what he has stolen from us.

We have the answer to domestic violence,
racial tension,
immorality. His name is Jesus. We don't need to look to the White House, but to the church house. We don't need to take over the ballot box; we need to kneel before the altar.

This is not to say that the church today is so perfect that it couldn't be amended or improved. But what is wrong with the church is of man, not Christ. His power is absolute, unchanging, and perfect.

The power of Christ can be criticized . . . but not contained. It can be frustrated or thwarted . . . but not stopped. It can be hindered . . . but not quenched. If God is behind even the smallest thing, it becomes mighty, effective, and powerful to the tearing down of all types of strongholds.

It's time we used the name of Jesus to declare that the enemy no longer has any authority over our own lives, or the lives of our families. We must force the issue with the enemy. We must be radical enough to "make" him loose us and let us go.

Say to the enemy today, "In the name of Jesus, loose me. Loose my family. We belong to God and to Him alone!"

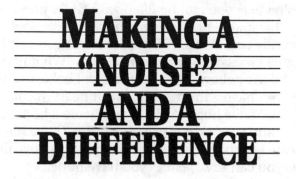

MAKING A "NOISE" AND A DIFFERENCE

And again he entered into Capernaum ...
and it was noised that he was in the house.
(Mark 2:1)

When Jesus arrived in Capernaum, He turned the city upside down.

Whatever you enter today ...
Whatever you belong to ...
Whatever you participate in ...
Whatever you are in ...

Your presence ought to be felt.

If you're on the usher board, every usher ought to be blessed because you're on the board.

If you're on a neighborhood committee, every other person on the committee and every person your committee touches ought to be blessed because you are there.

If you're on the job, your boss, your coworkers, your customers and clients, your vendors and suppliers, your employees ... everybody with whom you do business ought to be blessed. You are God's agent for making a difference for *good*.

165

Your presence also ought to provoke change. Wherever God is present, change happens. Things grow. People's attitudes are altered. Situations are turned around. There's no way you can be filled with God's presence and then be incapable of altering your circumstances.

I recently was asked, "Bishop, what do you think about the hopelessness in our nation?" I said, "What hopelessness?" I don't believe in hopelessness. I believe that as long as you have a thumping of your heart in your chest, you should have hope. As long as you are a blip on a monitor and your skin is warm you *must* have hope! I don't care how bad you blew it or what you have done, as long as you can say, "Jesus," you have hope.

You have hope because you serve a God Who has the power to change things, and to call into being things that are not.

Make some noise today about Who God is and what God does. Do it by your love in action as much as by your words of hope!

———————————
———————————
———————————

Be God's agent for change wherever you go today.

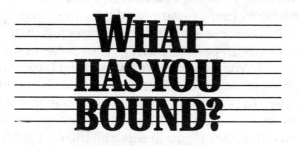

WHAT HAS YOU BOUND?

Bringing one sick of the palsy. (Mark 2:3)

This man who was sick of the palsy was in an immobile state. Palsy is a term that was applied to a number of diseases at the time of Jesus. It was used to describe the condition of any person who was unable to command movement in an area of his body. This man apparently was incapable of commanding movement that enabled him to walk.

In palsy of this type, the muscles, tissues, blood vessels, bones, nerves, and every other physical attribute necessary for movement are present. But for some reason, flesh rebels against command.

I should be able to move from where I am, but I can't. I'm stuck.

I want to move on, but I can't. I'm stuck in this place.

I don't want to live like I'm living, but I can't seem to change. I'm stuck in this condition.

I want a better life for my family, but I can't seem to make it happen. I'm stuck where I am.

Men get angry when they feel "stuck." They feel as if everybody else is moving and free. They have all of the physical, mental, and emotional attributes necessary for change and growth — they can still think, still feel. They

167

still have talents and skills. They still have opportunities and possibilities. But their inner spirit does not respond to command. They are in a state of inner rebellion.

Stress turns into pressure, and pressure into rage, and constant rage creates a state of weariness. Webster defines weary, in part, as having "your sense of pleasure exhausted." When you are weary, nothing is exciting. Everything seems bland. You become numb, unable to act or even to believe for change. Every day seems like the day before.

It doesn't matter if you live in a ghetto or a penthouse, if you are not liberated in your mind and encouraged in your spirit, you will feel as if you are in a jail cell. You will feel stress.

Stress, anger, and prejudice are not linked to any one race or level of income. They infect nearly every person. And if they become severe enough, they bring a person to a state of weariness, of numbness, of immobility.

Such a person is sick of inner palsy.

A man can get stuck in childhood memories.

He can get stuck in teenage issues.

He can get stuck in an adult problem.

While one type of palsy leaves a person "frozen," incapable of movement, another type of palsy leaves a person with spastic motions — the person can't coordinate his movements, or hold onto objects he desires to hold.

Some men can't hold a job.

They can't hold a relationship together.

They can't seem to hold onto their finances or save money.

They can't keep their word.

A part of their lives is out of control.

Lust out of control . . .

   rage out of control . . .

         bitterness out of control. The man with this type of palsy knows something is wrong with him, but he can't seem to do anything about it.

168

A third type of palsy comes from sheer muscle exhaustion. A man's muscles become so worn out he can't move. The mind, the emotions, and the spirit also can become exhausted.

If you have everyone around you drawing from you, you can quickly become depleted unless you have another means of making deposits into your life. That's true in your finances, your emotions, your ministry, your health. If you don't give something back to yourself, you will soon have nothing to give out. It simply isn't possible to be a continual encouragement to others, and not become discouraged, drained, or depleted in the process. You must avail yourself of conferences, meetings, seminars, and retreats that will build you up and give something back to your spirit.

Whatever the cause of this man's palsy — frozen muscles, spastic muscles, or exhausted muscles — Jesus was his Great Physician! Whatever your palsied state today, Jesus holds the key to your vibrancy, freedom, healing, and an abundant life.

The Bible tells us that when David's family was taken captive at Ziklag and David was "greatly distressed," he "encouraged himself in the LORD his God" (1 Samuel 30:6). Jude speaks of our "building up" ourselves on our most holy faith. How? By praying in the Holy Ghost and by keeping ourselves in the love of God, looking for the mercy of our Lord Jesus Christ unto eternal life. (See Jude 20,21.) Build yourself up in Jesus!

Refuse to live in a frozen, out of control, or exhausted state. Ask Jesus to impart to you His LIFE.

BE PREPARED FOR A HEAVY LOAD

They come unto him, bringing one sick of the palsy, which was borne of four. (Mark 2:3)

Let me assure you of this, if you ever decide to carry another person, you will discover that he is heavy. It took four men to carry the man with palsy to Jesus and he no doubt was a heavy load for even four men to carry.

Anytime you pick up the weight — the problem, the need — of another person, you'll likely find that it is a heavy load. Don't ever be duped into thinking that ministry is easy. Genuine and effective ministry to another person is always a great challenge.

First, you must be sensitive to a person's need to be carried. In any church service you are in, there's somebody close to you who is lying on a "stretcher" on the inside. He may act as if he has his life together, but he knows he's putting on a facade. He knows he has a need, but he may have trouble telling you about it. He's hurting . . . he's out of control . . . he's paralyzed in some way . . . and he knows it. In all likelihood, his wife and children know. You will have to be very sensitive to the Holy Spirit if you are to know it, too.

Don't be fooled by the prayers he prays when others are listening. When he's alone, he's praying a different way.

He's mumbling and groaning and crying into his pillow. He's crying out, "Lord, if You don't help me, I'm going to lose everything I have."

Don't be fooled by his fancy clothes or big smile. On the inside he's crying, "Help!"

Don't be fooled by his race, his denomination, or his status in society.

Black man . . . gotta get to Jesus.

White man . . . gotta get to Jesus.

Brown man . . . gotta get to Jesus.

Red man . . . gotta get to Jesus.

Baptist man . . . gotta get to Jesus.

Pentecostal man . . . gotta get to Jesus.

Rich man . . . gotta get to Jesus.

Poor man . . . gotta get to Jesus.

Big-shot executive . . . gotta get to Jesus.

Down-and-outer . . . gotta get to Jesus.

Don't be put off by his "dirty" reputation or by his sin.

Man on crack . . . get him to Jesus.

Man abusing his wife . . . get him to Jesus.

Man abandoning his family . . . get him to Jesus.

Don't pick up another person only to drop him. If you commit to helping another person come to Christ, make sure you bring him all the way to Jesus, no matter what it takes.

Many times we only want people delivered if it's easy on us. We don't want to have to sacrifice to see the deliverance or healing of another person.

Hold him steady.

Hold him tight.

Hold him until Jesus touches him with His power.

As you carry him, reassure him . . .

You have an appointment with a miracle. God has set a time for you to experience a complete makeover . . .

a massive turnaround . . .

a total reconstruction. You may not be able to help where you have been, but you can do something about where you are going. God has something better for you than anything you've known to this point!

Once you get a man to Jesus, you no longer have to carry him. Make sure you get him there, but once you have him in Jesus' presence, leave the work to Jesus. David said, "In thy presence is fulness of joy; at thy right hand there are pleasures for evermore" (Psalm 16:11).

If a person who is hurting is brought to Jesus, he isn't bashful about asking for what he needs. He knows that he may be experiencing his last chance to cry out to God and be heard. David cried out, "Lead me to the rock that is higher than I" (Psalm 61:2). The hurting man WANTS you to take him to the One Who can meet his needs.

Helping another man get to Jesus is the greatest thing you can do in this world. Be a lifesaver, a soulwinner, a family-healer, a community-changer. It will happen as you get those with palsied spirits to Jesus, the Healer and Deliverer.

_____
_____
_____

Join with a Christian friend today in praying and believing for a man who needs to be healed by Jesus. Be sensitive to what God tells you to do for him and say to him.

BRINGING THE NEED TO JESUS

And they come unto him....And when they could not come nigh unto him for the press, they uncovered the roof where he was: and when they had broken it up, they let down the bed wherein the sick of the palsy lay. (Mark 2:3,4)

These friends of the man with palsy brought him to Jesus. They didn't bring him to church — not to the bureaucratic power structure of the church or to a cold, dead church service. They brought him to the direct power of Jesus.

They brought him to the One Who could heal him. They brought him on a stretcher because he couldn't walk on his own power.

Every time I hold a men's conference, I know that there are some who come because they want to be "seen" at the conference . . .

others come because their friends are coming and they don't want to be left out . . .

some come simply because they have a new suit and they are looking for a place to wear it . . .

still others come because they say they don't have anything better to do . . .

but there are also those who come on a stretcher. They may be brought by others who saw a need in their lives. They may be bringing their own needs into the conference as if bringing their inner man on a stretcher.

Those who have spiritual palsy — paralyzed in their need or sick with needs that are out of control — are the ones who get the most help. You see, they don't care if their names are called or who sits next to them. They are present to receive from Jesus all that He has for them. They need help . . . and they know it. They aren't embarrassed to reach out and receive all the help Jesus offers to them.

One of the things every person has to do in coming to Jesus is to get through the "press."

So many men come into the church today and they can't get to Jesus for the "press" — the press of all the church politics and the press of all the she-say, he-say, they-say hearsay. So many people are in their way, they can't see Jesus, even though He's the One they came to see and the One they need to see the most.

Some people have become so "professional" in their approach to church, they've forgotten why they are in the church. They've forgotten how they once felt, who they once were. They've lost sight of Jesus for the "press" of knowing who's hot and who's not. They've been around so long they've lost the pure motive of worship — of humbling and casting themselves before Jesus in total submission.

Don't let anything or anyone stand in the way of your bringing your need to Jesus.

Don't think about what other people might think of you . . . or what they might say to you. Don't worry about how you look . . . or about how you sound. The thing that matters is that you express yourself to God. Tell Him what you need. Praise Him for His provision.

No matter what effort it may take, get to Jesus today!

EXPECT TO RECEIVE

When Jesus saw their faith . . . (Mark 2:5)

The men who brought their palsied friend to Jesus were men of faith. They didn't just have faith. They had an active, alive, relentless faith. They had faith in action.

I have to admit, I really LIKE the four men who were carrying the man with palsy to Jesus. They were not ordinary believers. They were *radical*. They weren't about to let anything get in the way of their receiving from Jesus what they wanted to receive. They had come to get a blessing and they weren't going home until they got it.

When you go to church, make a commitment to yourself that you aren't going to go home until you have received from God what you need and want to receive from Him. Say to yourself . . .

I'm not going home until I come out of the bondage I'm in.
I'm not going home until I'm delivered from the pressure I feel.
I'm not going home until I get the blessing I need.
I'm not going home until I release the unforgiveness, discouragement, anger, or resentment I feel.

176

Expect to Receive

Open yourself up to every bit of the power of Christ that is present.

Draw out the power of Christ that's in the singing.

In the preaching.

In the teaching.

In the praying.

In the communion.

In the giving.

In the loving.

Don't shut yourself off to any of the power of Christ that is flowing toward you.

And if there's no *power* of Christ Jesus in your church, get to a place where His power *is* flowing freely.

I have no use for dead churches. I have too many things that I'm fighting to come into a sophisticated arena where everybody is acting like intellectual, spiritual elitists and Holy Ghost yuppies. I need the power of God to be at work in my life every day!

I want to be in such powerful services that if I have any demons whatsoever trying to cling to me, the very power of praise and worship will shake them off. I want to be under the anointed preaching of God so that as the Word of God goes forth, it will deal with any issues in my heart that need to be changed. I need to be in the presence of an anointed ministry that will cause tears to well up in my eyes and confront me with the hard issues that I have been refusing to face, but need to face, so I can truly be set free of all influences of evil that are aimed at my destruction.

Go to where the power of God is being manifest. Open yourself to receive God's power and presence. Expect with your faith that God *will* fill you to overflowing.

Put your faith into action today. Go to God and expect to receive from Him.

TEAR AWAY ALL HINDRANCES

They uncovered the roof where he was: and when they had broken it up, they let down the bed wherein the sick of the palsy lay. (Mark 2:4)

When the four men who were carrying the palsied man arrived at the house where Jesus was preaching, they couldn't get in. They went up on the roof, but there was no opening there. They had to uncover the roof — peeling away the roofing material to create their own "door" through which they could let down their friend. Nothing about bringing this man to Jesus was easy. They had to make it happen.

The roof was a hindrance to them, but they didn't let a mere roof stop them.

What is hindering you today from getting to Jesus?

It might be your temper . . .

It might be your loneliness . . .

It might be your frustration . . .

It might be your childhood.

Tear the roof off! Get to Jesus — whatever it takes.

Who told you that you couldn't get a job?

Who told you that you couldn't have a good marriage?

Who told you that you couldn't get free of drugs?

Tear the roof off! Believe God can do it.

If you are bringing another man to Jesus, you are going to run into all kinds of hindrances.

He hasn't been to church in twenty years. He won't go with you.

He is too strung out on dope to know what's going on. He's not in a condition to go with you.

He's too angry to hear your invitation. Don't try talking to him now.

He's too involved with crime to give it up. Don't endanger yourself.

Tear the roof off! Don't let fear or pride stand in your way. Get that man to Jesus.

I don't know what "roof" separates you or someone you love from Jesus. Whatever it is, it *can* be removed. It can be torn away.

As these men were working on the roof, they were only a matter of feet away from Jesus. They were very close to their miracle. They were not about to be denied.

You are close to your miracle today. Get to Jesus no matter what it takes. Don't let anything stop you.

Don't give up. Jesus has a miracle for you and for those you love. Get to Jesus. His power is sufficient for every need.

GIVING A NAME TO THE FATHERLESS

He said unto the sick of the palsy, Son . . .
(Mark 2:5)

The Bible doesn't give us the name of the man with palsy. In many Bible stories, we not only have the man's name, but we have his father's name. For example, we know that the blind man in Jericho was Bartimaeus, son of Timaeus. (See Mark 10:46.) When a person's name and father's name are given, the implication is that the person is important. This palsied man was a no-name boy. We don't know his name. We don't know his father. For that matter, he may not have known his own father.

Fathers in the Bible give their sons status, a place in the society. They give them their identity. Today — as then — if a boy doesn't have a father, he doesn't have full status. He doesn't have a full identity.

When I look at our society today, I see thousands upon thousands of young men who are fatherless. They group themselves together because they don't belong to a group called family that is led by a leader called father. When I was a boy, my friends and I were afraid to walk into a group of men who might be standing on a street corner.

180

We'd give them a wide berth. Now I see grown men who are afraid to walk into a group of boys. They go out of their way to avoid them.

Fatherless boys are very often called by their problem, not their names. They are labeled just as this man was labeled — "sick of the palsy." He was identified by his condition.

Troublemaker.

Dope-head.

Gang-banger.

Homosexual.

Convict.

Rapist.

Fatherless boys become known for their condition, their predicament, their past actions.

We, as Christians, must go get these fatherless boys. It may take four of us to reach one boy, but we must go get them and bring them to Jesus.

And what did Jesus call this man who was called by everyone else as the one who was "sick of the palsy"? Jesus called him "son." He saw beyond this man's problem and looked into his person. He spoke to him, giving him a name that gave him a relationship. Jesus gave this man an identity, even before He forgave his sins and healed his body!

In calling this man "son," Jesus was taking upon Himself the role of "father." We must do the same.

We must not wait until the fatherless boys we encounter are cleaned up, singing in the choir, or leading the Bible study. Jesus called this young man "son" while he was still sick. He didn't condemn him for what had caused his palsy. He didn't say to this man . . .

You shouldn't have dated that girl.

You shouldn't have hooked up with that gang.

You shouldn't have taken that first drink.

You shouldn't have smoked that first joint.

You shouldn't have gone into that pool hall.

You shouldn't have . . .

No. Jesus loved him as he was. He entered into a relationship with him while he was still sick and in sin.

Neither did Jesus put any qualifications upon His relationship with this man. He didn't say to him . . .

If you'll clean up your life . . .

If you'll agree to do things my way . . .

If you'll stop . . .

If you'll start . . .

No. Jesus loved him without qualification, without condition.

We are called to do the same.

I tell my sons, "You are strong . . . handsome . . . vibrant . . . able . . . resourceful . . . intelligent *men,* not wimps. You are able to take a licking and keep on ticking. You are *somebody!* As God's child, you don't ever have to be lonely, destitute, desperate, or empty. You never have to be jealous of anybody. You are rich soil and fertile ground for a great harvest of blessing."

I have told my daughters repeatedly that I am their first date. I am the one who takes them out to nice places and buys them pretty dresses and shows them a good time. I'm the one who shows them the example of how a man should treat a woman with courtesy and manners. I'm the one who tells them that they are special, beautiful, and lovely in spirit. When they get to be dating age, their dates are going to have a tough act to follow. My daughters are accustomed to affection and praise and kindness; a young man would have a very tough time slapping my daughter and then trying to convince her that she deserved it. She'd likely say to him without any hesitation whatsoever, "I don't *think* so. My daddy told me otherwise."

Tell your children who they are to you, and who they are to God. Do the same for your spiritual sons and daughters.

Giving a Name to the Fatherless

Every child needs an identity. Every child needs a daddy.

Identify a boy or young man today whom you can love and help as a spiritual son. Bring that young man to Christ. Don't put qualifications, conditions, or condemnation on him. Love him as Jesus loves him. Call him "son."

FROM THE INSIDE OUT

[Jesus said], Why reason ye these things in your hearts? Whether is it easier to say to the sick of the palsy, Thy sins be forgiven thee; or to say, Arise, and take up thy bed, and walk? But that ye may know that the Son of man hath power on earth to forgive sins . . . I say unto thee, Arise, and take up thy bed, and go thy way into thine house. (Mark 2:8-11)

Jesus first healed this young palsied man on the inside — down deep where nobody could see any manifestation whatsoever that he had been healed.

So often, we bring a man to Jesus and then we say to ourselves, "Nothing happened." We are looking for signs on the outside. We don't know what Jesus is doing on the inside of that man, or what Jesus has already done to heal him where he hurts the most.

We say, "He doesn't really know Jesus. He's not really saved. If he was saved, he'd . . . ."

We say, "He didn't get delivered. If he was delivered, his life would be cleaned up."

The reality, however, is that God may very well have accomplished a definitive work on the inside of that man. In *God's own timing*, He will also do the outer work.

God heals the man . . . and then He heals the man's marriage.

God saves the soul . . . and then He deals with the man's addiction.

God delivers the man . . . and then He addresses the issue of the man's finances.

God deals with the inner man . . . and then He gives the promise, delivers the gift, and creates the new identity and reputation.

God doesn't heal our circumstances until He first heals us so we don't destroy the new circumstances He creates!

Believe that God is at work in the ones for whom you are praying . . .

to whom you are witnessing . . .

for whom you are believing . . .

and with whom you are ministering.

Believe for both an inner healing and an outer restoration.

———————————
———————————
———————————

Never dismiss or discount God's ability to work in ways that may remain a mystery to you.

PICKING UP YOUR SICKBED

And immediately he arose, took up the bed, and went forth before them all; insomuch that they were all amazed, and glorified God. (Mark 2:12)

Once the Lord has established Himself as Lord over your spirit, He seeks to establish Himself as the Lord over your life. He anoints you, calls you, and leads you into service. He gives you the strength and energy and ability to carry the very thing that once was the mark of your sickness.

Once Jesus had healed this man and raised him up from his sickbed, this man raised up his sickbed and carried it away.

When this palsied man was forgiven and healed by Jesus, he had a bed — but the bed no longer had him.

True deliverance is when you have control over the thing that once controlled you.

You can control your temper, when once your temper ruled you.

You can control your spending habits, when once your lust for things had control over you.

186

You can control the wandering eye that once was always looking for a new woman to conquer.

Your problem may remain, but it isn't bossing you. It isn't in control of you. You are in control of it.

And to whom does the Lord often call you to minister?

To a person who is in the very condition you were in before you were brought to Jesus! It is to that person that your witness is the most effective because you can say with authority, "I once was lost just like you. But now I am found. I once was blind. But now I see. I once was lying paralyzed and out of control in a sick condition just like you, but now I am healed. Jesus made the difference for me. And He can and will make the difference for you."

———————————
———————————
———————————

From what has God delivered you? To whom, then, is He calling you?

LIFT UP YOUR HANDS

Thus will I bless thee while I live: I will lift up my hands in thy name. (Psalm 63:4)

I have a young son and when he was learning to walk, he didn't walk with his hands down by his side, but with his hands raised straight up. That position apparently gave him a sense of balance he didn't feel when he had his hands down.

When we raise our hands in praise, we find a new balance for our spiritual lives. We are better able to walk, regardless of the circumstances that may be in our way or which direction our path takes us.

No matter how tired I might have been when I got home at night, if my young son came toward me, toddling along with his hands raised up in the air, I couldn't help but pick him up. Even if he was stinky, if he grinned at me with that cute grin of his, I had to pick him up. I'm his father. He's my son. I couldn't help but pick him up and hold him close.

The same for our heavenly Father. He responds to our uplifted hands of praise. He picks us up. He carries us through the places that are too hard for us to walk through. He holds us close and whispers in our ear how much He loves us.

No matter how stinky we may be in our sin, if we will only look toward Him, He picks us up and forgives us. He calls us "son."

You may be wounded . . . but you're still His son.

You may be hurt . . . but you're still His son.

You may be in sin . . . but you're still His son.

He wants to lift you up and heal you so that you can lift up whatever it was that once held you down.

Praise Him today. Lift up your heart, your voice, and your hands to Him.

Reach up today to the One Who is already reaching down to you — your heavenly Father.

ABOUT THE AUTHOR

Born and raised in Charleston, West Virginia, T.D. Jakes has been ministering the Gospel of Jesus Christ for twenty years. In Charleston, he served for sixteen years as Founder and Senior Pastor of Temple of Faith Ministries. In July 1996 Bishop Jakes relocated T.D. Jakes Ministries to Dallas, Texas. There, he is Senior Pastor of The Potter's House, one of the fastest growing churches in the country.

Bishop Jakes' ministry is noted for deep inner healing and practical application of Christian principles amidst the tragedies of life. He is a highly celebrated author of six books including *Woman, Thou Art Loosed!* and *Loose That Man and Let Him Go!*

Bishop Jakes' weekly television program, "Get Ready With T.D. Jakes," airs three times each week on Trinity Broadcasting Network and Black Entertainment Television. The international broadcast reaches numerous countries including the Caribbean, South Africa, and Zimbabwe.

Bishop Jakes resides in Dallas, Texas, with his wife Serita and five children — Jermaine, Jamar, Sara, Cora, and T.D. Jr.

BOOKS BY T.D. JAKES

So You Call Yourself a Man!
Woman, Thou Art Loosed! (Hard Cover)
Loose That Man & Let Him Go! (Hard Cover)
Loose That Man & Let Him Go! (Soft Cover)
Loose That Man & Let Him Go! (Workbook)
T.D. Jakes Speaks to Men!
T.D. Jakes Speaks to Women!
Woman, Thou Art Loosed! (Spanish)
Loose That Man & Let Him Go! (Spanish)
T.D. Jakes Speaks to Men! (Spanish)
T.D. Jakes Speaks to Women! (Spanish)

Here's what critics
Leslie Langtr

"I laughed so hard I cried on multiple occasions while reading MARSHMALLOW S'MORE MURDER! Girl Scouts, the CIA, and the Yakuza... what could possibly go wrong?"
—*Fresh Fiction*

"Darkly funny and wildly over the top, this mystery answers the burning question, 'Do assassin skills and Girl Scout merit badges mix…' one truly original and wacky novel!"
—*RT BOOK REVIEWS*

"Those who like dark humor will enjoy a look into the deadliest female assassin and PTA mom's life."
—*Parkersburg News*

"Mixing a deadly sense of humor and plenty of sexy sizzle, Leslie Langtry creates a brilliantly original, laughter-rich mix of contemporary romance and suspense in *'Scuse Me While I Kill This Guy.*"
—*Chicago Tribune*

"The beleaguered soccer mom assassin concept is a winner, and Langtry gets the fun started from page one with a myriad of clever details."
—*Publisher's Weekly*

BOOKS BY LESLIE LANGTRY

Merry Wrath Mysteries:
Merit Badge Murder
Mint Cookie Murder
Scout Camp Murder
(short story in the Killer
Beach Reads collection)
Marshmallow S'More
Murder
Movie Night Murder
Mud Run Murder
Fishing Badge Murder
(short story in the Pushing
Up Daisies collection)
Motto for Murder
Map Skills Murder
Mean Girl Murder
Marriage Vow Murder
Mystery Night Murder
Meerkats and Murder
Make Believe Murder
Maltese Vulture Murder
Musket Ball Murder
Macho Man Murder
Mad Money Murder

Greatest Hits Mysteries:
'Scuse Me While I Kill
This Guy
Guns Will Keep Us
Together
Stand By Your Hitman
I Shot You Babe
Paradise By The Rifle
Sights
Snuff the Magic Dragon
My Heroes Have Always
Been Hitmen
Greatest Hits mysteries
Holiday Bundle

Aloha Lagoon Mysteries:
Ukulele Murder
Ukulele Deadly

Other Works:
Sex, Lies, & Family
Vacations

MERIT BADGE MURDER

a Merry Wrath mystery

Leslie Langtry

This book is dedicated to my most awesome critique partners; Janene Murphy, Susan Carroll, Ella March Chase and Bob Bradley. I couldn't have done this without you guys! Thank you!

CHAPTER ONE

It's not every day you find al-Qaeda's number four operative dead in a Girl Scout camp in Iowa.

The body was twisted unnaturally in the rope course's spiderweb element that consisted of a large wood frame crisscrossed with elastic bungee cords. Sadly, it was my troop's favorite thing to do at camp. Now I had to disappoint them. I hated disappointing them.

A man hung there. He *had been* in his twenties and of Middle Eastern descent. The neck was clearly broken before he'd been placed into the ropes at Camp Singing Bird. He looked surprised to find himself here. I'm sure the irony would be lost on him that in death, he really was surrounded by seventy-two virgins. Did it matter that they were grade-schoolers, I wondered? Maybe that was just splitting hairs.

I would've been surprised too, had I not been through this kind of thing before. But I'd seen this stuff in Syria and Uzbekistan—not in the placid, wooded hills of eastern Iowa.

And my second grade troop was due at any minute. I was pretty sure I couldn't pass this off as something adorable—like I had with the bats in Tinder Trails Cabin or the mice in the latrines. Troop Leader's Helpful Hint Number One—if your Girl Scouts freak out upon meeting a bat/mouse/wolf spider for the first time—tell them it's just a *baby* bat/mouse/wolf spider. Little girls are suckers for that, and soon what was scary is *adorbs!*—whatever that means.

I bent to take his pulse, just to make sure. Yup. He was dead. His glassy eyes were opened wide, and his mouth hung open. Dammit. I needed this like I needed wet work in the slums of Rio.

The sounds of giggles and singing came from the trees just around the corner. Any minute the fourteen seven- and eight-year-old girls who called me their leader would appear. I was pretty sure I couldn't convince them that this dead terrorist was a cute, dead *baby* terrorist. I pulled the parachute I was going to use for games later out of my backpack and threw it over the spiderweb.

"Mrs. Wrath!" The girls squealed in unison before tackling me in a sticky group hug. Kelly, my co-leader, smirked at me. She could get away with smirking at me because she's known me since *we* were six-year-old Scouts.

"Girls!" I gently pushed them away. "How many times do I need to tell you—it's *Ms.* Wrath. I'm not married." Of course, I knew the answer to this question. Ad infinitum. Meaning, they'd always call me *Mrs.* Any woman over the age of twenty-one in Iowa was *Mrs. Clearly* it was *me* who didn't get it.

"Mrs. Wrath?" the third Katelynn asked. Or was it Kaitlin the Fourth? They all looked the same to me. And each one of them spelled her name a completely different way. Spy work had *not* prepared me for that.

"It's *Ms.* Wrath, Katelynn," I said with a smile. Troop Leader's Helpful Hint Number Two—when talking to little girls, always smile. They cry if you don't. I'm not kidding. You don't know real terror until you've stared at the watery eyes and rubbery bottom lip of a cute kid.

The second-grader looked confused for a moment, which was to be expected. "Okay. Mrs. Wrath?" she asked again.

I sighed. "Yes, Katelynn?"

"Why is the parachute over the spiderweb? And why is it all lumpy?"

Kelly squinted at the parachute, eyebrows knit together. She'd probably figure it out, being a nurse and all.

"The spiderweb is out of commission, girls," I announced, stepping between them and the dead man.

A chorus of complaints came from the little girls, and I held up my right hand in the universal Girl Scout symbol for silence. They quieted down immediately. I once

again really wished I'd known about this trick when I was surrounded by FARC rebels in Colombia.

"Head on over to the Peanut Butter Pass—I think you're old enough for that one now," I said in a nice save worthy of someone of my caliber.

"Yay!" The girls exploded in shrieks and raced off to that element, leaving me in the dust.

Kelly narrowed her eyes. "They aren't old enough for the Peanut Butter Pass."

"You'd better get after them before they start scaling the rope, then. I'll be there in a second." I shoved her in the direction of the squealing herd before she could respond. "We can't leave them alone for a minute, you know."

Kelly gave me a weird look but took off after the troop. I turned back to the dead man in the parachute. It kind of looked like he was cocooned in the web—as if a giant spider had caught him, poisoned him, and wrapped him to save for later. If only that was what had really happened. No way I could get that lucky.

With a heavy sigh, I took out my cell phone to call the ranger. This was going to suck. You think the CIA is bad with paperwork? Langley (CIA headquarters near DC) has *nothing* on the Girl Scouts of the USA when it comes to filling out forms and accident reports in triplicate. Nothing.

My name is Fionnaghuala Merrygold Wrath Czrygy. And I'm a Girl Scout leader. Well, I used to be a covert operative in the CIA—a career that has remarkably prepared me well to lead Troop 0348. (And yes, you have to have a zero at the beginning—it's very important for some reason that no one can explain.) I was a CIA agent, that is, until I was unceremoniously and allegedly "mistakenly" outed by the vice president of the United States' chief of staff.

That's right. I was outed. My name and photo were leaked to *The New York Times* "inadvertently." This is a fancy way to say that the vice president was pissed off at my father, who was the head of the Senate Committee on Foreign Relations, because he didn't back the veep's reelection campaign (a fact even more curious because the VP was a Republican, and my dad was a Democrat). So, my

name got leaked, and the chief of staff took the fall and was fired the next day just before going to prison (and of course, pardoned later by the president).

I, however, was not in a cozy corner office in the White House with a nice view, like he was when my name and face were broadcast live worldwide. I happened to be in Chechnya where—to my surprise—the rebels in the bar I frequented had internet and were devoted followers of *The New York Times'* online edition. (They also read *Cosmo,* but that's a story for another day.) It took me forty-two hours, two gunfights, a strange encounter with an armed chicken, calling in fifteen favors that I'd been saving, and a rather dicey drive to Estonia in the back of a jeep with no shocks to get out of that mess.

Back in DC I testified before Congress, got a nice fat check from my boss at the CIA, along with a short letter explaining why I couldn't work there anymore, and just like that, I was out of a job and internationally infamous.

It was Dad's idea for me to change my appearance, use my middle name, take on my mother's maiden name, and move to my hometown in Iowa. Dad's name was Czrygy. So brunette, brown-eyed Finella (the true pronunciation of my name) Czrygy became blonde, blue-eyed (you have to love what they do with contact lenses these days) Merry Wrath.

The sheriff and a few deputies arrived at camp half an hour after I'd called. I'd managed to get my troop back to the cabins without them seeing the dead guy, staunching their protests with promises that Kelly would make them endless s'mores in the middle of the day—something that would probably bite me in the ass later. The ranger—Bob Williamson—sat with me as we waited. He wasn't very happy to find a dead man tangled in his newly refurbished ropes course. That meant a lot of paperwork for him too.

"Huh," the sheriff said as he poked the dead body with his finger. He stood up and tried to tug his belt up over his beer belly with little success.

"So, what happened here?" he asked Bob.

I tried not to roll my eyes. We'd already told the sheriff that I'd been the one to find the body. But this old, redneck sheriff was only interested in what a man had to say.

Bob pointed at me. "Ask her. She found it."

I once again told the sheriff about how I'd found the body. I once again suggested that they comb the camp for whoever did this, since they were probably still around. And once again, the sheriff looked to Bob for answers.

"Is that right?" he asked.

"Yes," I said. "And now, if you'll excuse me, I have my troop to get back to." I left before I could see their responses. If the sheriff was going to write me off, I was done with him. Besides, this wasn't my problem anymore. I couldn't care less what happened to the dead guy. I was off the clock permanently these days.

Back at our campsite, fourteen girls were bouncing off the walls after mainlining a *lot* of sugar. Kelly gave me a glare that said I owed her big time.

With the possibility of a murderer running around camp, I decided our trip was over. Kelly and I packed up and called the other moms to help us carpool the thirty minute drive back home. The girls were too keyed up to even notice it was over until we arrived in my driveway. But by then, they had parents there ready to wrangle them into waiting cars.

Kelly and I watched and let out a very visible breath as the last girl was picked up.

"So, what the hell was that all about?" Kelly said as she led the way into my little house. Once inside, my friend and co-leader helped herself to a glass of wine and sat at my tiny breakfast bar.

"Dead guy," I muttered as I made a peanut butter and jelly sandwich. We had tons of the stuff left over since we'd cut the camping trip short. Little girls love peanut butter. I had to admit— they really had something there.

Kelly nodded, "Yeah, I got that part. But *why* was there a dead guy?"

I shrugged, my mouth glued shut. "Don't know."
Only it came out like, "nnnt no" due to the aforementioned
peanut butter. I really shouldn't talk with my mouth full.

"You don't think it's a little odd that you retire from
the CIA and a dead Middle Easterner shows up at Girl Scout
Camp the same weekend you are there?" Kelly crossed her
arms. I should never have told her, in that drunken haze,
about my past. She waited. I'd have no chance to stall with
another bite of sandwich.

I swallowed. "Yes. I think it's odd. But it might just
be a coincidence." That was a lie. There was no way it was a
coincidence. I mean seriously, al-Qaeda's number four? In
Iowa? And me being former CIA? Not a chance.

Kelly studied me. "Are you going to be alright?"

I nodded. "I'll be fine. Don't worry about me." After
all, I'd handled things like this before, on my own, and in a
Third World country. No sweat. And this wasn't my problem
anyway. Let the authorities take care of it. I didn't do that
anymore.

Kelly drained her glass and walked to the door. She
paused and looked around my little, beige living room.

"When are you going to get some drapes?" she
asked, looking at the sheets I'd had hung in the windows.
They had Dora the Explorer on them because I got them on
sale. It had really seemed like a good idea at the time. I'd
always thought Dora was undercover CIA, recruiting kids to
be double agents.

I shrugged. "Soon? I just moved in, remember."

She laughed. "Yeah, one year ago. It's time you had
drapes." And with that she was gone.

I leaned against the door and looked around my
house. She was right. I didn't have any drapes. I had very
little furniture. After being recruited by the CIA right out of
college, I'd never really had a place with things like furniture
and curtains. I kept a very sparse apartment in DC but spent
most of my time in dingy hotel rooms and safe houses all
over the world.

When I was "retired," I moved back to the small city
my dad grew up in and bought the first house I looked at.

This house. The realtor told me it was something called a "craftsman." It was small and quiet and had a nice little fenced in yard in back. I bought a little car to put in the little, attached garage. I bought groceries and paid the utilities. But furnishing it was completely out of my wheelhouse.

Instead, there was a green couch in the living room that I'd bought at a consignment store on impulse. A flat screen TV sat on the floor. The kitchen had a built-in breakfast bar, so I didn't think I really needed a table and chairs. I did buy an expensive queen-sized bed with a mattress made of something called "memory foam." Years of sleeping on floors and crappy mattresses got old quickly when I finally stayed in a five star hotel in DC while visiting Mom and Dad.

I knew I needed furniture and drapes and stuff. I just didn't know how to do it. Do you just go to a store and ask for drapes? Do you need measurements? Where do you measure from? And should they be beige like the walls and carpet or green like the couch?

Every time I thought about these things, I needed to go and lay down. But today was the day. Today, I'd think about getting drapes. I wandered over to the large, picture window and started examining it. Which is when I noticed the moving van across the street.

Huh. I didn't know my crazy-old-lady-cougar-neighbor had moved out. A U-Haul was backed up into her driveway, and men were unloading furniture. There was a lot of it too—tables, chairs, a desk, various lamps of various sizes, rugs, you name it—they had it. Must be a family or something.

I found myself strangely fascinated watching this whole bizarre process. For a brief second, I ran into my bedroom and got a pen and pad of paper. I needed to take notes on this. Maybe I could learn something.

Oooh! A potted tree! I liked that idea! I should do that. I made note of the stuff with great glee. The desk and desk chair were nice. I just used a laptop so I worked on the couch or in bed. But maybe it was time I put together an office.

Not that I had anything to do in it. I didn't have a job. I didn't need one. The settlement from the Agency would take care of me for at least the next ten years. The only thing I had was the Girl Scout troop that met every other week. Huh. I wondered if that was weird. Maybe I should have a job or a hobby or something. It seemed to be what normal people who hadn't previously been CIA operatives did.

A car pulled up in front of crazy-old-lady-cougar-neighbor's house but didn't pull into the driveway. I drew back into the shadows behind Dora and her monkey (who was clearly her case officer) and realized that curtains really might be a good idea after all. I'd have to get on it. But first I needed to check out the new people. Slouching behind the cover of the sheets, it kind of felt like the old days, spying on that politician in Spain or that drug runner in Colombia.

Whoever was in the car across the street wasn't in a hurry to step out. When I'd first moved into the neighborhood, I noticed people mowing their lawns, walking their kids to school, or walking their dogs, just doing normal things. Until day two. That's when I first saw *her*.

The woman had to be in her seventies, with bleached blonde hair up in a ponytail and a ton of makeup on. It was sixty-five degrees, and she was out mowing her lawn. In a bikini. I watched open-mouthed as she worked her way up and down the lawn, smiling and waving at any men who were out and about. She did not wave at the women. I also noticed that about halfway through the yard, she let both shoulder straps "accidentally" fall to her elbows.

She was in pretty good shape for an old lady. But the saggy skin and varicose veins were enough to make me want to go back undercover. For the first few weeks, I was fascinated. After a month, I wanted to burn the image from my brain. Forever. It was worse than some of the things I'd seen in the field. And that's saying something.

The black SUV with tinted windows finally moved forward up into the driveway. This was it—the big reveal. I slid back even farther into the Dora sheet/curtain. The driver-side door opened, and a man, maybe in his early thirties,

stepped out. He stretched for a moment, then looked at the house.

Oh yeah, and he was GORGEOUS. Short, black hair, athletic build, handsome, boy-next-door face, and lean muscles in all the right places. He wore a fitted, black T-shirt and blue jeans. Was this my new neighbor? If so, the view just got a lot better.

I stared as he walked around to the passenger side and opened the door. He reached in and pulled out a large duffle bag. Slinging it oh-so-casually over his shoulder, he closed the door to the SUV and went into the house. His house. My new neighbor's and the possibly future Mr. Wrath's house.

The doorbell rang, and I jumped backward, tripping over my own feet and crashing into the green couch. What the hell? How did I miss someone coming to my own door? That was just bad spy craft, retired or not. I stumbled across the living room and looked out the window next to the door. Oh, my God.

"Hello Riley," I said as I opened the door, trying to act as if it was totally normal that my previous boss and handler was standing on my doorstep.

"Hey Wrath." Riley smiled lopsidedly. He was a very attractive man in his late thirties, with wavy, blond hair and deep blue eyes. I always thought he looked more like a surfer than a CIA case manager. I motioned for him to enter and followed him into my house.

He was standing in the entryway, staring at my living room. "Did you just move in here?" Riley frowned. "I thought you'd had this address for a while, but maybe I'm wrong." He knew he wasn't wrong. Riley was a notorious fact checker. He double-checked everything before he did anything. We called him "Nerd OCD Boy" behind his back.

I scowled. "No. I just haven't gotten around to decorating yet." Riley pissed me off. He always did. Even when he wasn't speaking, he usually irritated me. Still, he was a good guy to have in your corner when the chips were down and the Russians were fully armed outside your door.

Riley shrugged. He just stood there looking at me. Oh right. This was one of those host thingies that I had no experience with. I rarely had guests in my tenement in La Paz or my yurt in Mongolia.

"Come into the kitchen. Can I get you some coffee?" I didn't really have coffee. Never touched the stuff. I was more of a tea drinker. Ninety-percent of the world drank tea—well, at least the places I'd been stationed in did. So I drank tea.

Riley followed me into the kitchen and climbed up on one of the breakfast barstools. "Nothing for me, thanks." He grinned at me, and I felt my hackles rise. "Although I must admit—it is interesting to see you being so…" He waved his arms around. "Domestic."

"*You*, Riley. What are you doing here?" I asked as I got out the bottle of wine Kelly had opened earlier and poured myself a glass. CIA case officers never checked up on retirees. Something was up.

"Dead Ahmed," he answered. "Found in your neighborhood. What's up with that?"

Riley rarely messed around. He always got right to the point. Of course he'd notice a dead terrorist showing up where I was in Iowa. Any good employee of "The Company" would.

"Oh right," I said, looking off into space as if I just remembered the dead al-Qaeda operative at Girl Scout camp. "Him."

Riley nodded, "Right. Him. Ahmed Maloof. Why was he there?"

I shrugged, "Don't know, and don't care. Not my problem. Not anymore, at least." I took a gulp of wine and pointed at him. "I don't work for you guys. I'm retired. Remember?"

Riley smiled his easy, surfer smile. He really was cute, if you liked that California golden boy look, that is. "You can't be surprised I'm here, Finn." He said.

"Actually, I am." That wasn't entirely true. It was only a matter of time before he or someone like him showed

up. "I had nothing to do with it. And don't call me Finn. I'm *Merry* now."

I started working with Riley ten years ago. Our first assignment together was in China. I'd thought he was cute back then. But then I discovered that Riley was a serial lady-killer. I think I found him in bed with women more than a dozen times. The attraction wore thin after that.

My former boss held my gaze for a moment. He was reading me. Trying to figure me out. Riley had the reputation of being a sort of mind reader. He was very good at it.

"Actually," he said slowly, "we think you did have something to do with it. I've been sent to investigate."

I slapped the breakfast bar hard. "Are you serious? You think I was involved? Why in hell would I do that? I got kicked out of Langley. Or did you forget that?"

"I didn't forget that, Finn," Riley answered, ignoring my request for him to call me Merry, "and personally, I don't think you killed Ahmed. But I do think there's a connection."

"There's no connection, Riley. I've been out of the agency for a year now. And I haven't worked the Middle East in a long, long time. I barely knew the guy." Uh-oh. I'd slipped up there. Maybe I should quit with the wine.

Riley grinned, "That's right. You barely knew him. But you did know him. And that makes you a person of interest."

Dammit! You make one mistake with a terrorist years ago, and nobody lets you forget it, ever! How the hell was I supposed to know my driver in Kabul was Ahmed's brother? The Kabul Office should've known that before they hired him. Anyway, I was a professional, and I was retired. Enough of this crap.

"You need to leave now, Riley, before I get mad and get my ice pick. Remember how good I am with an ice pick?" My voice dripped with fury. And the ice pick thing was just thrown in to aggravate him. I was hell on Earth with an ice pick, and he'd once seen the results of my work. I was also good with a shotgun, and throwing knives, and once I did this thing with a didgeridoo that would probably be

classified as a serious violation of the Geneva Convention—but that's another story for another time.

Riley rose to his feet, placing his hands defensively in front of him. "Fine. I'll go." He reached into his suit jacket and pulled out a piece of paper with only a phone number on it. A local number. Damn it.

"I'll be staying at the Radisson. Call me when you want to talk like a normal person." He set the slip of paper on the breakfast bar before heading for the front door. He turned in the doorway and looked at me.

"You know, Finn, you really should get some drapes." Then with the flash of his oh-too-white smile, he left, closing the door behind him.

Perfect.

CHAPTER TWO

———

So the agency thought I was involved in Ahmed's death. That could mean I was being framed. I had no idea that bastard was even in the country, let alone in the Midwest. Was someone out to get me? That would totally suck.

The drapes would have to wait. I pulled out the laptop and did some research. You might be surprised to know that most CIA intel comes from research. No kidding. In the internet age—you could get more info online than you could in the field half the time. I kind of resented the fact that I'd missed cold war espionage by a decade. I'd be willing to bet it was way more fun than what I had to deal with.

Ahmed turned up on Al Jazeera's website. Just a few mentions about him hiding out in Pakistan. Who didn't hide out there? I couldn't find much and toyed with hacking into the CIA's mainframe. But I didn't want to deal with the hassle if I was found out. And it might make me look guilty. I closed the laptop and shoved it aside in disgust.

I didn't have any access to agency resources anymore. If I was going to find out what happened before another dead body turned up, I'd have to do it on my own. And I was pretty sure that there would be another body, because if someone wanted to frame me, they'd have to do a lot more than this.

So, who hated me enough? I got my pad of paper and made a list. After I got to thirty five, I called it quits. Spies have lots of enemies in lots of places. It wasn't unusual. And I had been PNGed out of the agency. Even with my blonde hair and blue eyes now, if someone really wanted to find me, they probably could.

Which pissed me off. I was mostly off the grid now. I had zero presence on social media and an unlisted cell phone number. Kelly knew about me, but she wouldn't tell anyone because I'd threatened her with some blackmail I had from the ninth grade. Considering that her parents never did find out who burned down the garage because a certain *someone* was smoking *something*, I was fairly confident she didn't want that to get out.

My parents wouldn't tell anyone. They tended to be a tad protective of me after what I'd gone through. So who knew I was here? It was frustrating. Oh, I know it takes time to find these things out, and I used to have patience in the field. But since "retiring" I was a bit less so. Okay, I was completely impatient. Two people in front of me at the grocery store usually set me off these days. When I want my Oreos—I want them NOW.

Great. Now I wanted Oreos. I grabbed my purse and keys and headed for the store. In all honesty—I wasn't a great shopper. Kelly told me she goes to the store once a week. I go every other day. I'm not very good about stocking up on stuff. I guess that comes from living on the fly and picking up a baguette here or candy bar there. (By the way—*never, ever* buy a candy bar in Uruguay.) I should probably learn how to cook and shop and that kind of thing. It wasn't like I didn't have time.

This time I bought TWO packages of Oreos. On the drive home I was congratulating myself on my foresight and thinking how this might lead to some day buying a whole quart of milk, when I ran over a man.

That's right, I hit a man. With my car. My driving skills aren't bad. I've driven in some real shit-holes, usually in crappy, stick shift only cars. So watching a man roll off my hood and onto the street in front of my car caught me by surprise.

I slammed on the brakes and shifted into park as I got out and ran toward the man I'd hit. *Please don't be dead...please!* A middle-aged Latino man clawed at the air, gasping for breath. His eyes paused on mine for a second before he collapsed to the pavement, dead.

The police were there immediately. I was in a fog as they shoved me aside and started CPR on the dead guy. Another cop grabbed me by the arm and pulled me over to his car. He started asking me what happened.

"I don't know," I answered, never taking my eyes off the dead man. "I didn't see him. He just ran out in front of my car."

I looked around, checking my surroundings. A group of witnesses were being questioned. I listened to hear them say the same thing. The man wasn't there, and then he was. Apparently to them, he also just appeared in the middle of the street.

"Do you know him?" the officer asked me.

"No," I lied. "Never seen him before." I was good at being interrogated. Graduated at the top of my class at The Farm. That's the CIA finishing school in the middle of nowhere, by the way. Anyway, I could take almost any kind of abuse. Except water boarding. I hated water boarding. I had this thing about my face getting wet.

The officer nodded and asked for my license and registration. I went through the motions of handing them to him. My brain was racing, trying to sort everything out. How did *he* get here? And why did he jump in front of my car? And what the hell was going on?

These questions played like a broken record over and over as I watched an ambulance take the body away. There was a huge, bloody puddle on the ground in front of my car. I'd seen bloodstains before. Hell, I'd even caused them a time or two. But this was different…more sinister.

"Thanks, Ms. Wrath," the officer said. I would've told him how much I appreciated him using the proper title and not calling me *Mrs.*, but then I'd have to explain, and it wasn't worth the effort. "We'll send a detective over to see you in a few hours. You can go."

Without a word, I took back my license and registration, got into my car, and drove the remaining four blocks back to my house. Once inside, I locked all the doors and drew the Dora sheet across the length of the window. I

paced the kitchen while eating an entire package of Oreos. Thank God I'd bought two.

I picked up the cell phone and dialed.

He answered on the first ring. "Finn?"

"You'd better come over. I just ran over Carlos the Armadillo. He's dead."

There was a measured silence on the other end before he replied, "I'll be there in five minutes."

CHAPTER THREE

———

Riley made it to my house in three minutes. I opened the door before he even rang the doorbell, and he followed me into the kitchen. He looked at the empty Oreo carton, then at me.

"What happened?"

I told him the whole story. How I'd been driving, minding my own business, when Carlos the Armadillo—the Columbian drug lord—ran out in front of my car. How he'd died there. How the police seemed to believe me.

Riley listened patiently until I finished. I'd always liked that about him. He never interrupted or argued with you. He listened. Not many field agents did that.

"They'll send a detective over soon. It's only a matter of time before they discover who he is. You did the right thing, calling me." His voice was reassuring, and I nodded.

"Why is this happening?" I asked, knowing he had no answers. "I was undercover in Carlos' operation for four months, three years ago. Why are these bad guys from my past turning up here...now?"

Riley shook his head. "I have no idea. It looks like someone is setting you up on an international scale. This is pretty big—whoever it is. Somehow they managed to smuggle two Watch List terrorists into the U.S. and kill them on your territory."

I nodded. "That's exactly what's happening. But why? I'm out of service. Is it revenge?"

Riley ran his hands through his blonde hair. He did that when he was nervous. It was his only tell. "Maybe it *is* revenge. You were a spy and a damn good one. You'd have a

lot of enemies. Trying to narrow down the suspects will be tough. We might have to get the Feds involved."

I slumped onto the stool next to him. I didn't want to do this cloak and dagger stuff anymore. I was starting to get used to this lifestyle. I was even going to commit to drapes and furniture soon.

"You did the right thing in calling me," Riley said softly. "I can help. We'll figure this out." He reached out and put his hand on my shoulder. That made me feel a little better.

"What's the agency's position going to be on this? Will they want to investigate?" I asked.

Riley shrugged. "How could they not? Two international terrorists got into this country unnoticed. They'll be all over it." Still, in his eyes I saw a shred of doubt, and I wondered. Did he really think the CIA would get involved? Or did he think I was doing this? I filed that information away mentally.

The doorbell rang. I looked out the window to see who it was and was stunned to see my gorgeous new neighbor standing there. What was he doing here? This wasn't exactly the best time to introduce himself. And wasn't *I* supposed to be the one to welcome *him* to the neighborhood? At least someone was worse at domesticity than me. That was a plus.

I opened the door and smiled. "Hi! I'm Merry!" And then I felt like an idiot. That wasn't how you were supposed to answer the door. You asked *can I help you* or something like that. Or maybe I should've opened with *will you marry me?*

The man smiled and held out his hand. I shook it. "I'm Rex. Your new neighbor."

"Great!" I answered, still holding onto his hand. Feeling ridiculous, I dropped it like it was on fire. "Um, would you like to come in?" I stood off to the side, making a sweeping motion with my hand (that I'd seen once on TV) to invite him inside.

"I should probably explain..." he said, still standing on the porch. "I'm not really here to introduce myself as your new neighbor."

I looked at him in surprise. "No?" Well, maybe that meant he was here to ask me out. He must've seen me drive up in the dented, bloodstained car, my face covered in crumbled Oreos and thought—*now that's a woman I need to get to know!*

"No. Actually, I'm Detective Rex Ferguson. They called me up on my day off to handle this investigation. Especially since you live across the street from me."

"Oh," I said, feeling deflated. "Okay. Well you might as well come in."

Riley was standing in the hallway, waiting. I watched them as they sized each other up. Then Riley held out his hand.

"Detective. I'm Riley Andrews. Ms. Wrath's cousin." Riley flashed his surfer grin at Rex. Rex shook his hand, looking at Riley thoughtfully. I didn't think he was buying his story, which was unusual. Riley was very convincing with his cover stories. I once saw him convince a tribe of Bedouins that he was Japanese.

"Let's go into the kitchen." I interrupted the testosterone fest. Yes, I now mostly entertained in my kitchen. I didn't want Rex to see my Dora sheets in the living room because then he might think I was a weirdo and might not want to marry me. The two men took seats at the breakfast bar, and I stood on the other side because there were no chairs left.

"Tea?" I offered. Both men shook their heads. They really were alike, I thought, as I made myself a nice, soothing cup of oolong. Both alpha males, both attractive, both used to being in charge. I could only assume Rex was intelligent because that's what I wanted Mr. Wrath to be. He *had* to be smart. Who ever heard of a stupid detective?

"Ms. Wrath," Rex started as he pulled a notebook out of his back pocket and laid it on the table in front of him. "I know you've given the officers at the scene your statement. But could you tell me again what happened?"

I took a drink of tea to stall and glanced at Riley. The look in his eyes said *don't mention CIA or Carlos the Armadillo.* Or maybe they said *make sure you mention the CIA and Carlos the Armadillo.* My radar wasn't as good as it used to be.

"I was driving home from the store when this man jumped out in front of my car. I stopped as soon as it happened. He was alive for a few seconds. Then he died." It's always good to just give the basic facts when dealing with the police in any country. Too little information and they'll believe you're guilty. Too much and they can twist your words into seeming guilty. Believe me, I've been there. It isn't pleasant.

Rex nodded and didn't speak for a moment. It's a common intimidation ploy. People get nervous when an authority figure says nothing, so they talk to pick up the slack. And they usually screw up and say way too much when they do that.

Because I was so smart and knew this, I said nothing.

The detective sighed, "Ms. Wrath, did you know you ran over a known Columbian drug lord?"

Wow. How did he find out so fast? Did Columbian drug lords now carry ID and business cards that stated their profession? Unlikely.

I put on my best *ohmygosh* face. "What? No! That can't be right! What would a Columbian drug lord be doing here?" I widened my eyes for effect. Out of the corner of my eye I saw a flicker of amusement on Riley's face.

"You're joking, right Officer?" Riley said, mirroring my shock. "This is a joke, right?"

Rex looked from Riley to me. "No, I'm afraid not. He is known as Carlos the Armadillo." He cocked his head to one side. "They say he got that name by being a tough guy, impervious to pain."

Nope. I was one of the few people who knew how Carlos had gotten that name. The first time he was busted for drugs, as a teenager, Carlos was so freaked out that he jumped straight up in the air. It looked so ridiculous the

DEA gave him the nickname because armadillos jump about three feet in the air when afraid. An embarrassed Carlos turned it into some story about having thick skin and being a tough guy. He wasn't.

I shook my head. "I don't believe it! How did he get here? And why?"

Rex shook his head. "We have no idea. But the DEA and FBI have all called me so I think it's a big deal, Ms. Wrath." He rose to his feet and held out his hand to Riley, who shook it.

"Sorry we had to meet like this," Rex said then grasped my hand firmly. "Seems like a nice neighborhood."

I led him to the door and saw him out while babbling about how we ought to get a block party together or something. After closing the door behind him, I went back into the kitchen and poured yet another glass of wine.

"You did good, Finn." Riley grinned.

I tipped the glass toward him. "You need to stop calling me Finn. I'm Merry now."

He laughed. "I didn't call you Finn in front of the good detective. I'm not an idiot. I've done this before." He looked at the door for a moment. "I'm a little suspicious that a detective has just moved across the street from a former CIA operative."

I rolled my eyes. "Oh come on! I've been here a year now. It's a total coincidence." A yummy, yummy coincidence.

"I don't know..." Riley said. "I mean, the guy shows up right after the whole Ahmed thing? I'm going to have to look into your neighbor."

"So are we out of the woods with the Feds and DEA investigating?" I asked hopefully, in an attempt to change the subject. I liked my new neighbor. I understood Riley's suspicions, and in my old life I might've felt that way too, but my life was supposed to be normal now. I was kind of into normal. Not good at it—but definitely into it.

Riley shook his head. "I think that might make it worse. I'm sure they've found out about Ahmed by now. I was hoping we could solve this and wrap it before the other

agencies found out. But now with Carlos involved, it'll be hard to keep it out of the papers and away from the Feds. It's a pretty juicy carrot to dangle in front of them."

"So let the Feds and the locals duke it out. That'll delay things. They'll be so busy fighting each other that maybe I'll slip off the radar," I said.

"Or..." Riley looked me in the eyes. "They'll each go overboard investigating you in an attempt to outdo the other, and you'll have two agencies studying your life with an electron microscope."

My stomach sunk. I hadn't thought of that. "My cover will be blown." I looked in the direction of Rex's house across the street. "And I was just starting to like this place."

Riley stood. "I'll see what I can do. I'll try to convince the other agencies that we have an undercover agent here. Maybe they'll keep quiet. But if the police know about Carlos, you can bet the media do too."

I nodded. "I'll leave it to you then. I am retired, after all." I said it but I didn't believe it. Two international badasses turned up on my doorstep. I was pretty sure there'd be more before Riley figured this out.

"I'm heading back to the hotel." Riley stretched his long, lean body, and I couldn't help but admire it. I was pissed at myself for even looking at him that way. I walked him to the door and promised I'd call if anything else turned up. The way it was going, I'd probably be calling him soon.

I spent the rest of the day googling Carlos and Ahmed, looking in vain for some sort of Midwest connection. I didn't find any. It was just so bizarre. I was pretty sure Carlos had never been farther north than Texas, and I knew Ahmed had never crossed over the Atlantic. So why were they both in the same place tens of thousands of miles from home base?

Maybe they were lured here. But why? What would make them come to Iowa? It would have to be something very, very big. Ahmed Maloof was al-Qaeda and a terrorist who declared jihad on the U.S. Carlos the Armadillo was a cartel leader who ran drugs from South America to the U.S.

They had very different missions. Ahmed wanted to destroy us, but Carlos needed us as paying customers for his drug trade.

There was no common ground here. And as far as I knew, they didn't know each other. So why these two? I'd pissed off a lot of people in other countries—especially when I was outted. But of all of them, I never would've thought Carlos and Ahmed would've come after me.

Was that it? They'd come to kill me and somehow were killed themselves? No, that didn't make any sense. These guys were big players. They would've sent assassins. They wouldn't have done it on their own.

My brain was spinning. Probably from the wine and Oreos. Pulling back the Dora sheet, I saw it was dark outside. I'd been at this a while. I made my rounds, locking doors and getting ready for bed. Before I fell asleep, I wondered if Rex would still be interested in me if he knew the things I'd done. In my imagination—he loved it.

CHAPTER FOUR

_____

I was just having this dream where Riley and Rex had taken me surfing and both were rubbing lotion on my back when I was rudely interrupted by someone pounding at the door. I instinctively reached for the pistol that was not under my pillow. Old habits die hard. Instead, I got up, and after wrapping a robe around my Dora the Explorer pajamas (Seriously, I could relate to her.) I made my way to the front door.

I looked through the Dora curtains at the front stoop. I really need to get a security camera, I decided. All I could see was the back of a very hot woman shoe-horned into a dress that seemed to be painted onto her. A thick cascade of wavy, blonde hair tumbled down her back. I hated her, whoever she was.

Opening the door, I hated her even more.

"What the hell are you doing here, Svetlana?" I was pissed. Twice in twenty-four hours I'd been visited by people I didn't want to be visited by. And in this particular case, I'd rather have the dead terrorists.

Svetlana Babikova gave me a dazzling grin before pushing past me into the house. I sighed and shut the door behind her. The woman standing in front of me was a former Russian operative I'd turned to spying for the U.S. back in the early '00s. I hated her then, and I hated her now. Question was—what was she doing at my house? I'd have preferred her showing up respectfully dead, like the other two had.

The drop-dead gorgeous woman winked at me and then made her way to my kitchen where she pulled a bottle of vodka out of the freezer and poured herself a shot. Blasted

Russians. Well, former Russian, technically. But it didn't matter.

"It's Lana, now, Finn." She drained the shot smoothly and poured another. Why did I even keep vodka in the freezer? In the house? It only encouraged them.

"Your American accent is getting better, *Lana*," I said as I pulled up a stool and sat at the breakfast bar. I really needed to get better furniture in my living room. If I didn't, the kitchen needed more comfortable stuff. I wondered if they made barstools that reclined.

"Thank you!" Lana's bright blue eyes grew wide, and she pouted her full, sensuous, red lips.

"Stop flirting, Lana," I growled. "It never worked on me."

Lana nodded and drained another shot before coming around and sitting on the stool beside me. The skin-tight dress didn't have so much as a wrinkle and barely covered her crotch as she sat down. I won't even mention the high heels. They were ridiculous.

We sat there looking at each other, me in jammies without any makeup on, her made up as if she was doing a floor show for Mötley Crüe. Svetlana…er…Lana was one of the operatives I'd turned. Formerly a Russian spy, she went double agent for me for a couple of Beyoncé CDs and a pair of Louboutin pumps. The very ones she was wearing now.

Lana had been a decent agent. She'd scored lots of info for me over the two years we'd worked together. I think she'd always wanted to come to America and be a Playboy Bunny. I used that to my advantage. I might have hinted that I had Hugh Hefner on speed dial once or twice. Not really my bad—Eastern Europeans were convinced that every American had powerful Americans on their cells. They really misunderstood that whole Six Degrees of Kevin Bacon thing.

"What are you doing here, Lana?" *Alive*, I added mentally.

She giggled and looked around the kitchen. "You know, I could really get used to this place! You have running water?"

I picked up my cell and dialed. Riley answered on the first ring.

"Hey Merry," he started.

"Tell me this isn't what I think it is," I said with a growl in my voice.

"What *what* is?" Riley asked with a poor façade of innocence.

I held up the phone to Lana. She giggled and squealed. I took the phone back and waited.

"Oh," Riley said.

"You have three minutes to get over here or I'm shooting her," I said as I hung up.

"Oh Finny!" Lana touched my arm seductively. "You are so funny!"

"It's Merry, not Finn and NEVER Finny," I snarled at the blonde.

The doorbell rang right on time. I let Riley in and dragged him into the living room.

"She is NOT living here!" I whispered angrily. Have you ever done that? It's far less menacing than you'd think.

Riley held his hands up in front of him defensively. He should do that. I might hit him. I had a mean right cross, and he'd had some experience with that.

"We don't have a choice. The agency thinks she's safer here, hiding out with you. At least until everything blows over in Kiev."

"Oh, they did, did they?" My eyes narrowed. It was a good look—a look that has gotten me way more confessions than I'd deserved. "Well I don't work for the agency anymore, remember? And I'm not *hiding out* here—I live here now!"

Riley nodded. He'd accurately assessed that I wasn't going to get violent with him just yet. "Hear me out."

I folded my arms over my chest in the universal sign for *you'd better make this quick and you'd better get this right.*

He sighed. "Lana needs constant supervision. You don't work. And we'll pay you. Sort of like a consultant." He

gave me that big, stupid surfer grin that I was beginning to hate.

"I don't work because I am between things at the moment. And consultancies are usually voluntary. And I didn't volunteer for this." I pointed to the wall separating us from the buxom blonde who was probably three more shots into the vodka at this point.

"Besides," Riley continued as if I hadn't just said anything. "I'd feel better having someone around you 24/7 with these new situations popping up. And Lana was a trained FSB agent—she could be helpful." FSB were just newer initials for the KGB. It wasn't a lot different than the old, Cold War secret police, but I guess they thought they felt they needed a shiny new name for the same old tactics. Go figure.

"Only if I need to seduce a Russian general— something there's a bit of a noticeable lack of here in the middle of nowhere," I grumbled.

"Rileeeeeeeeeeeeeeeeeeeeeeeeeeeeeeeeey!" Lana launched herself into the room and into Riley's arms. She buried her face in his neck and pressed her body so close to his I thought maybe they'd melted together. For some strange reason I felt a little prickle of jealousy. Now why did I feel that way?

Riley pried the blonde off of him and held her at arm's length. "You can't do that here, Lana," he admonished gently. "Americans like their personal space. Remember?"

She put her index finger on the corner of her mouth, and her eyes grew impossibly huge. I had to admit—the girl was good.

"I am so sorry, Riley! I am just so excited to be Finny's roommate!"

I was about to tear her throat out when Riley stepped between us.

"Use contractions, Lana. Americans never say *I am*—they say *I'm.*

"Well, I guess she won't blend in. You'll just have to take her back to Langley and put her in a cage..." I said as I

tried to shove them both toward the front door. They didn't move, dammit.

Lana looked at me and pouted. Her eyes got all sad, and somehow she was able to dilate her pupils till they were huge. How did she do that?

"Finny doesn't want Lana?" Her lower lip quavered. Oh no. This was not happening. Not here. Not now.

I steeled myself. "That's right, Lana. Finny doesn't want Lana here. It's no good. It wouldn't work out."

Lana burst into tears. Giant teardrops poured from the corners of her eyes, somehow not dislodging the makeup there. She dropped to the couch, and since it was lower than her knees, her black lace panties made a rather disturbing appearance.

"First Putee throws Lana out. Then Russia throws Lana out. Now Finny, my only friend in the world does not want me!" She wailed in a voice that somehow made it seem like I was strangling kittens in front of school children.

Riley looked at me. "See what you did?" He motioned to the couch.

Not having the faintest clue what to do next, I sat down next to the wailing Russian and tried to calm her.

"Now, Lana. It's not that I don't want you. It's just a bad time right now. I can't look after you. I've got...*stuff* going on." What stuff I didn't know, but I did know it didn't include this knockout blonde bimbo.

She looked at me. How did she manage to cry and still look beautiful? Seriously, her eyes weren't red, and her makeup wasn't smeary.

"It is just...just that I miss Putee. He threw me out!" She went back to wailing.

"Putee" was a certain Russian president she was working over for me. She did a good job. But women like Lana always put a little too much of their hearts into their playacting. And it hurt when they got turned out. Which is why I'd never resorted to seduction as a tool in my tradecraft kit.

"I'm sorry," I said as I awkwardly patted her arm. Damn, her skin was firm and soft at the same time.

Lana looked at me. The tears stopped. Just like that. Then she threw her arms around me, strangling me with her firm/soft arms.

"Oh yes! Finny says I can stay! Thank you, Finny! You really are my best friend!"

I was trapped. And Riley knew it as he grinned smugly above us. *The day you retire, buddy, I'll be in the shadows with a baseball bat.*

CHAPTER FIVE

———

"So," I said to Lana once Riley had gone, "where's your luggage?" Not that the luggage mattered really. I was still reeling from the news that I now had a roommate.

Lana shook her head sadly. "This is it. They extracted me before I could pack anything."

I had to admit—she looked uncomfortable. "Okay, well, we'll go shopping then, because you can't run around here dressed like that."

"Did you know you have a large dent in the front of your car?" Lana said as she squeezed herself into my tiny vehicle. While I scrubbed off the blood.

I nodded. "Yes. I ran over Carlos the Armadillo earlier. Now behave yourself, or that's what will happen to you."

Lana nodded solemnly as she put on her seatbelt. I tossed the bloody towel and got in, starting the car and heading for the mall. We'd have to get her clothes and toiletries. It looked like I'd have to pay for everything, but since I was now a *consultant*, I could put it on the bill I'd send the agency. The very large, impossibly padded, possibly outright bullshit bill. This was going to cost Riley.

Have you ever taken a knockout blonde shopping? Me neither. It was a fiasco. Apparently malls are the domain of teenagers. And teenage boys are gawkers. I had a pack of them following us around. There's nothing like being followed by a group of pimply adolescent boys who didn't speak and for some reason always had their hands in their pockets. It was disturbing to say the least.

Lana didn't seem to notice them. She was gleefully skipping from one store to the next, grabbing tube tops and

tiny shorts. At one point, she held up what looked like a sock but turned out to be a dress. Three of the boys behind us fainted.

"No," I said firmly. "You have to blend in. I'm not buying you clothes that would usually be seen circling a stripper pole in Vegas." Behind me, a couple of the boys growled as menacingly as they could with squeaky voices that hadn't changed yet.

I turned around and glared at them. "Really?" I asked.

The boys turned as one unit and were suddenly fascinated by the pink and glittery princess display outside the Disney Store.

Lana pouted as I dragged her to The Gap and made her try on khakis, capri pants, and shorts befitting a Midwestern woman. I threw in some light sweaters, T-shirts, and button down shirts. Lana didn't argue, and she even came out to show me what she was trying on. Unfortunately, with her huge boobs and slim frame, everything looked like it was molded to her body.

We hit the shoe store and got her a pair of ballet flats, some tennis shoes, and something called wedges. At the department store I had her fitted for bras, picked up panties and socks, and finally we were out the door. As we walked out, I thought I heard the boys behind us weeping.

After spending a fortune at the drug store and even more at the grocery store, Lana and I managed to make it home without killing anybody or each other. I'd picked up an inflatable mattress and a pump along with some cheap sheets and a pillow. I set her up in what was supposed to be my office. There was no dresser or closet in there. I'd have to pick something up so she could organize stuff.

Lana spent the rest of the day in her room. I heard the air compressor for a little while as she blew up the bed. I took the time to put the groceries away.

It was hard to believe that a woman with a figure like that could eat only junk food. But that's what she'd wanted. Maybe they didn't have Twinkies in Russia. At any rate, my kitchen was, for the first time, fully stocked with

what could technically be called food. There was a little satisfaction in that.

I was walking down the hallway to check on Lana when a blast of music made me jump. It sounded like pop music, and it was screaming from Lana's room. I wasn't a fan. I liked peace and quiet. Spend one month stationed in Germany undercover in a techno pop bar, and you'll agree with me.

"Lana!" I shouted while banging on the door. "Lana! Turn that down!"

Nothing happened. I put my hand on the doorknob but changed my mind. I didn't want to see her naked. Nothing would scar me more than seeing the perfection I could never achieve.

Instead, I stepped into the bathroom to find a cyclone had gone through it. Five wet towels covered the floor, and the steam was enough to make me choke. Who needed five towels after a shower? Wait...I owned five towels? I bent to pick them up when I saw that the counter was covered to the point you couldn't see granite. I'd never seen so many beauty products, and I didn't remember buying most of them. I picked up a jar of face cream and stared at it. There were three more—all different brands and sizes.

Was I missing something? I just basically used soap on my face, and a little lotion when it got dry. I stared at myself in the mirror. Sure, I used makeup—well, a little mascara and ChapStick. I wasn't a total loser. But maybe I was screwing up by not using alphahydrox...something. And what was a CC cream?

There were bottles of hairspray, leave-in conditioner, mousse, gel, and other stuff I couldn't identify. Again I looked in the mirror. I was lucky to have naturally curly hair, and I wore it short. It was basically drip dry. The most maintenance I did was to dye it over the sink once a month to maintain my blonde cover. Should I be using this gunk? Lana really did have amazing hair. I stared at my unruly, curly bob. It always seemed okay to me. But what if it didn't look that way to anyone else?

And my clothes—basically T-shirts and jeans or shorts. In the winter I wore one of three wool cardigan sweaters over the T-shirts. I looked at my feet. I was wearing moccasins. They were comfortable.

I wasn't a total waste case. I had a dress and ballet flats in my closet for special occasions. Mom had bought the dress for me. Okay, so I'd never had any reason to wear it…but it was there if I needed it.

Huh. Before Lana moved in I'd only been insecure about my lack of window coverings. Now I was second-guessing my appearance too. I didn't like it. I spent so long looking in the mirror that I didn't notice that Lana had turned off her radio.

"Merry!" Lana stood in the doorway. She looked amazing in a polo shirt and capri pants. I didn't look that amazing.

"Riley is on the phone." She held my cell up to me. "He says it is important." She shrugged.

"Fantastic." I took my cell from her and put it to my ear.

"Wrath," Riley said, "tell me you haven't been outside in the last half hour."

I brushed past Lana and made my way to the living room. My front yard, which had been wonderfully peaceful and quiet before, now was filled with people and news trucks. CNN, NBC, ABC, CBS, FOX, and what seemed like a million others stood there, staring at my house.

"What the hell, Riley!" I shouted into the cell. "I thought you were going to keep this from happening!"

"Oooooh! Television cameras!" Lana squealed beside me. She started for the door, but I yanked her back.

"What do I do?" I asked Riley.

"Don't go outside. Don't appear in any windows. I'm going to try to give them a red herring to make them leave you alone."

I frowned. "And just how are you going to do that?" This whole thing gave me the willies. I liked anonymity. In spy work, you wanted to be ignored. Any attention was bad.

That rule carried through to my new life. I was two seconds away from a meltdown.

"I'm holding a press conference at the hotel tonight to give them a different direction. With any luck, they'll leave you alone and believe this is just all a coincidence."

"You'd better make it work," I growled into the cell as I ended the call. Immediately the cell rang.

"Hi Kelly," I said weakly.

"What the hell Merry? Your house is on every news network! And did you run over an armadillo? They're not native to Iowa."

"No. This one wasn't either." I recalled Carlos' face plastered against my windshield.

"Do you need me to come over?" Kelly asked.

"No. You'd better stay there. This is all just a mistake. It'll blow over soon," I said, not very confidently.

"Okay. I'll sneak a casserole over later." That was the Midwest answer to anything uncomfortable. Bring a casserole. It was the ultimate *I'm so sorry/congrats on the new baby/I have no idea what to say, but I can bake* thing.

"I'll use the back door," Kelly said as she hung up.

Lana was once again making her way to the door. I dragged her back to the couch and made her sit there. Then I drew the Dora curtains shut.

"We can't go out there," I said. "Riley wants us to stay put and stay away from windows and doors."

Lana nodded. "Good thing we got all that food."

I switched on the TV and turned it to CNN. Kelly was right. There was my house, behind Wolf Blitzer. Wow. I warranted Wolf Blitzer. I kind of had a little fangirl moment in spite of myself.

"I'm coming to you live in front of the home of Merry Wrath. For some reason, we can't find any photos of her, and she's not answering her phone or door," Wolf said.

As if on cue, my cell phone erupted. How did they get my number? I was unlisted, dammit! I didn't recognize the caller, so I turned it to vibrate and set it down.

"Merry Wrath has had the dubious honor of finding Ahmed Maloof, al-Qaeda's number four, dead on the ropes

course where she and her Girl Scout troop were camping. Shortly after that, Ms. Wrath ran over and killed Carlos the Armadillo—a Columbian drug lord, right here, blocks from where she lives. What connects Ms. Wrath to these two known terrorists? Stay tuned to CNN. We'll give you instant updates as more facts come to light."

Damn, damn, damn, damn.

"Merry?" Lana asked. I sat down next to her on the couch, completely freaked out.

"Are you alright?" Lana asked.

"Probably not," I answered, unable to take my eyes off the screen.

My cell vibrated. It was my Dad. I picked it up. "Dad, are you watching TV?"

"I am, Pumpkin. I can be there in a couple of hours." His voice was deep and comforting. But the last thing I needed was for Wolf to make the connection between me and Dad.

"No. Don't do that. If they see you here, they'll know who I really am."

"It's only a matter of time," Dad said gently.

"It'll be okay, Dad. The Agency is working on it. They're going to have a press conference later to try to get the heat off of me. I'll be fine." I was pretty sure I wasn't going to be fine. But he didn't need to know that.

Dad didn't sound convinced. "I don't know, I think I should be there…"

"I'm good. Really, Dad. I've had to handle much worse—believe me." That was true. And at least the media didn't have assault rifles—not that I couldn't get out of it if they did. I convinced Dad I was fine and made him promise not to come out here before hanging up.

"Twinkies will make this better!" Lana shouted, jumped to her feet, and raced to the kitchen. I got up and followed her to make sure she didn't run out the back door. I stopped just short of her in the kitchen. Lying on the floor, in a puddle of blood, was Midori Ito. A heavyweight in the Japanese Yakuza.

Lana stared at the body for a moment, then checked the back door. It was locked. She drew the shades on the door and window before kneeling to take Midori's pulse. She looked up at me and shook her head.

CHAPTER SIX

I'd always wanted to be a spy, even when I was little. When the other kids played capture the flag, I spied on them and gave misleading information to both sides, selling them out for M&M's, quarters, and the occasional kitten.

The CIA recruited me my junior year in college. I was an International Studies major and spoke fluent Spanish and Russian and because of a two-year relationship with a hot foreign student named Adolf, I could pass somewhat in German. The day after I graduated, I flew to Langley for the interview. My interview consisted of one question: "You and your informant are talking in a hotel room when suddenly the local police are beating down the door. What do you do?"

I thought about it for just a second. "We'd start making out. Make them think we were having an affair and that's why we're hiding out."

"What if it's another woman?" the interviewer asked.

I shrugged, "Same thing works there too, I guess." I got the job. By the way, the wrong answer to that question is: "Who? Oh right, this guy. He's the Minister of Defense, and I'm CIA." The interviewer told me someone actually said that once. They put him on the No-Fly List because they didn't want an idiot like that ever leaving the country. It's not just smart folks we're afraid of, people.

I loved the training and graduated from the Farm at the top of my class, mainly because all I did was train. And when I say *train*, I mean all I did was get to play with guns, evade capture, and learn how to mix a mean batch of cyanide. (Hint—don't ever eat cupcakes offered to you by a

spook.) One month later, I was in Buenos Aires. When I discovered that making out with a stranger, when la policia are beating down your door, works. I also discovered that you should carry breath mints at all times, just in case.

To say I was crushed when my career ended would be a severe understatement. I loved turning spies, recruiting new ones, and even the occasional shoot-out. I picked up some other languages along the way...Japanese, Arabic, and a smattering of Portuguese—which only really works in two countries, but Lisbon can be very nice in the spring.

I'll admit, I still missed it—all the cloak and dagger stuff. Who wouldn't? But I was starting to get used to my new life. I really wanted to make a go of it. And someone wasn't letting me retire quietly. Whoever it was, if I ever found them, was going to die. Probably by cyanide cupcakes.

"You have to call Riley," Lana said quietly. The bimbo giggle act was gone, and it was eerie. Nothing is creepier than a serious Russian accent. For a moment, I liked her better as a shallow blonde.

I nodded and dialed. No point in actually saying out loud that Lana was right. Riley picked up on the first ring. I guess this was becoming old hat to him; Dead Terrorist = Wrath. Not a great equation.

"Midori Ito is dead in my kitchen," I said.

"You are kidding me!" Riley exploded. "What the hell, Wrath? I told you not to do anything!"

"I didn't kill her! I don't know how she got here!" I snapped back. "I didn't want any of this to happen!"

A long, slow sigh came through the phone. "Alright. Sorry. I'm just pissed that this is happening to my favorite agent."

What did he say? His favorite agent?

There was a knock at the kitchen window. Lana jumped into a defensive stance as I looked out and saw Kelly standing there with a casserole. She motioned that she was coming in through the garage. Wait, the back door to the garage was unlocked? So that's how Midori got in here.

I ran out to the garage. "Get in here!" I hissed as I opened the door and pulled her in, locking it behind her. We stepped into the kitchen where Lana was waiting for us. I locked that door too. You can't be too careful with terrorists falling all over themselves to die in front of you.

Kelly stared at the dead Japanese woman on the floor, then stared at Lana, who was still hovering over the corpse. I'm not sure which one freaked her out more.

Her nursing training took over, and she set the casserole on the breakfast bar and knelt down beside the body. After checking her pulse, Kelly started looking the corpse over. She didn't say anything. It's nice to have friends who aren't so judgy.

"Wrath? Wrath! Are you there?" Riley shouted in my ear.

"Yeah yeah," I said as I watched Kelly. "Someone just dropped off a casserole."

"Tuna noodle," Kelly said as she examined Midori's head, "your favorite."

"It's tuna noodle," I said to Riley.

"You let someone in the house? How do you know the food isn't drugged?" Riley shouted. I ignored him.

Lana and I stared as Kelly turned the head gently to one side. It wobbled easily. Too easily.

"Broken neck," Kelly said.

"Where's the blood coming from?" I asked.

"Where's what blood coming from?" Riley asked. "Dammit Wrath! Answer me."

"Shhhh," I shushed, "Kelly's working."

"*Who* is Kelly?" Riley was screaming now. I was pretty sure he was annoying his neighbors in the hotel rooms on either side of him. That wasn't very nice.

"There's a wound on the back of her neck." Kelly looked up at us. "I'd say she was hit at the base of the skull with something like a baseball bat. It broke her neck and caused the bleeding." She stood up and reached for a dishtowel to wipe the blood off of her hands. I was surprised to realize that I owned dishtowels.

"What's going on, Merry? And who is this?" She pointed at Lana.

The buxom Russian took this as her cue and turned the perkiness up one hundred fifty percent. "I'm Lana! I'm Finny's best friend!" Her huge eyes blinked, and her full, juicy-looking lips curled into a beguiling smile.

Kelly folded her arms over her chest and frowned. "I'm *Merry's* best friend. And don't you forget it." She looked back at me. "What's this?"

"Wrath! I'm coming over!" Riley stormed.

"Come in through the back. There's a door to the garage," I said before ending the call. Great. Now I had to go and unlock the garage door. I grumbled as I did it and returned to the kitchen.

The aroma of fresh-baked tuna noodle casserole started to get the best of me as I realized I hadn't eaten in a while.

"Let's eat," I said as I pulled four plates and forks and served up four huge servings. Lana and Kelly glared at each other. Did Kelly actually believe she'd been usurped? That was ridiculous. She should know better.

"We should cover that up first," Lana said, pointing at the corpse. "I can't eat with a body in the room." She ran off down the hallway and emerged with a comforter. *My* comforter. From *my* room. Off of *my* bed. I was about to protest as my stomach growled.

I threw the blanket over Midori. Kelly and Lana sat at the breakfast bar, so once again, I was standing. I didn't care. Kelly's cooking was totally worth it. That woman really knew her way around a kitchen. Too bad she was married. If she was *my* roommate, I wouldn't have room for Lana.

The kitchen door swung open, and a furious Riley stormed in. I thought I'd locked that door. But then, Riley was good with locks. He stomped up to the counter next to me and saw that there was a plate for him. My mouth was full of food, so I motioned for him to eat. He glared at me for a moment, but the aroma of home cooking got the better of him. Riley's face changed from anger to hunger in a few seconds. It was kind of awesome to see.

"Tuna noodle casserole, didn't you say?" he said, licking his lips. "Smells good. What's in it?"

Oh right. Riley was kind of a health food nut.

"If I tell you," I said, "you wouldn't eat it."

"Fair enough," he said as he tasted it. A huge smile lit up his face. He liked it. "Is this organic?" he asked.

I kicked him under the breakfast bar, and he shut up. Kelly looked like she was about to murder him. He'd have to get in line because I was pretty sure she was going to do in Lana first. Maybe I should've brought her in from the beginning.

We ate the entire casserole. Murder makes people hungry.

Riley wiped his mouth on a napkin, reminding me, to my surprise once again, that I have napkins, and nodded to Kelly. "My compliments. That was perfect."

Kelly started to melt a little as she introduced herself. Riley's looks and manner would do that to anyone.

"Kelly's been my best friend since we were little," I said with a little glare at Lana. "She knows about my past, and she's a nurse. She thinks Midori was hit at the base of the skull with something. It broke her neck."

Riley walked over to the blanket and lifted it, exposing Midori, who'd started to turn a little gray.

"Shit," he said. "Now the Yakuza's involved? What the hell is going on?"

"No idea," I said. I was clueless with this one. I'd never worked with Midori. Never even got close. Not that I hadn't tried. I did a brief stint in Tokyo, but I couldn't turn anyone in her organization. She was just too terrifying.

Midori Ito was the Yakuza's first lady. Her husband was the kingpin, but she was the one who really called the shots. She was very short and wore a chin-length bob that people said was conditioned with the tears of infants. And she had a thing for torture, especially torture including sharp pieces of origami that she could jam into soft places on your body. She enjoyed hurting people. The CIA had her on their radar for some time, but we just couldn't break the organization. No one would talk.

Whoever killed Midori was good. Rumor was the woman was half-ninja, half-robot. She'd killed literally dozens of men who'd betrayed the organization. After that—no one would even think about screwing her over. There wasn't enough Hello Kitty crap in the world to bribe someone to do that.

"Japanese organized crime...Colombian drug cartel...and al-Qaeda. All here, all at the same time. What does it mean?" I asked.

"Will someone please tell me what's going on?" Kelly asked as she started washing dishes. She was just awesome like that. Riley looked at me, and I nodded. He filled Kelly in as I stared at the body, trying to make sense of it all. I briefly filled her in, punctuating my language with extreme pantomime. The way she rolled her eyes told me she thought that was a bit over the top.

As for the explanation of how this was being pulled off...I couldn't come up with anything. None of these organizations collaborated with each other. As far as I knew, none of the dead bad guys had ever even met. It made no sense whatsoever. And talk about effort. Getting these three together *alive* seemed impossible.

"They all died here," I said.

"What's that?" Riley looked at me.

"They all died here. They were all brought here, or came here on their own, alive. Now what would make something that epic happen?"

No one spoke. We had nothing. No ideas. There was no way to know without doing some investigating. But the media on the front lawn made that impossible to do.

"Shouldn't you call the police or something?" Kelly asked, pointing to the dead Japanese mobster.

I looked at Riley. "What are we going to do about that? We can't just get rid of her. But if we call in the police, my house becomes a crime scene."

"We'll have to move it," Riley said, rubbing his chin. "Dump her somewhere else to draw the attention away from Merry."

I nodded. It sounded like a fairly good idea. "Where are you going to take her, and how are you going to get her out without being spotted?"

Kelly spoke up. "I could take her to the hospital."

"That's still too close," I said. "Anywhere in the same state is going to set off alarms."

"Well how far away do you want to go so it's not too close?" Kelly asked.

"Japan," I suggested.

Riley shook his head. "That's not going to happen. I think I'll take her to Chicago and dump her in Chinatown."

"She's not Chinese, Riley," I said.

"Hey!" Kelly grinned. "There's that huge Japanese supermarket in the suburbs! You could take her there!" Kelly would know that. She loved taking trips to Chicago for ingredients you couldn't find here. I usually went with her for the free samples.

I thought about Midori's body being found in a grocery store. "How would they explain it? That she got hungry for edamame she could only get in Chicago?"

Riley said, "Who cares? It becomes the Chicago PD's problem, not ours. The FBI will probably get involved too. Then it becomes a circus. *Their* circus."

"I'm going with you." I couldn't stay in this house one more minute, and going out the front door wasn't going to work.

"No way," Riley disagreed. "If we got busted with the body and you in the same car, this would only get worse. Much worse."

"I think she should go," Kelly said. We turned and looked at her. "She's got to get out of here before they break down the door. They don't know what she looks like, but if they take her picture it'll be broadcast all over the world." She pointed at my hair. "And even with different hair and eye color, someone would figure out who she really is."

Lana nodded. She'd been quiet this whole time. No *look at me* this, or *I'm a hottie* that. I wondered what had gotten into her.

"We can't just leave Lana here alone," Riley said. I smiled. He'd agreed I could go. That was a small victory.

We looked at the Russian bombshell. No, leaving her alone meant too much temptation for her to burst out the front door asking for directions to Hugh Hefner's Playboy mansion. Lana was a powder keg of unpredictability. I looked at Kelly meaningfully.

She shook her head and waved us off. "No way. I'm not bringing *that* home to my husband. Especially since I have to work the night shift tonight." Kelly didn't really have anything to worry about. Her husband, Robert, adored her. But that might not stop him from staring. And there was much to stare at.

"She has to go with us," Riley said finally. Lana's face lit up like a Christmas tree as if Riley had just proposed, overthrown her beloved Putee, and given her Russia for a present.

"I don't think that's a good idea. She has to stay here," I said, suddenly smiling. "Now, where did you park your car? Because I have an idea."

CHAPTER SEVEN

———

"This is never going to work," Riley said for the thirtieth time. We ignored him like we had the previous twenty-nine times he'd said it.

"If two CIA operatives, one Russian spy, and a nurse can't make this happen," I said, "no one can."

"One CIA officer, one ex-CIA agent, and one ex-Russian spy," Riley corrected. "Although I do have absolute faith in the nurse."

Kelly blushed, and I wanted to smack her. She had no idea how Riley could use his charms. But he was right, I was pretty sure of all of us, she really was the competent one.

Lana giggled and bounced up and down, which meant that other parts of her also bounced up and down. She'd changed back into her skin-tight dress and Louboutin heels. I had no doubt she could pull this off. Lana lived for acting. That's why she'd been good at what she did.

Riley zipped up the suitcase and nodded. It was time to go. We opened up the door, and Lana slipped through the doorway. Five seconds later, Kelly followed, nodding solemnly at me as she headed out. Ten minutes later, Riley and I left. I locked the door behind me as Riley wrestled with the old, beat up case. Hopefully, anyone watching would think I was splitting with a packed suitcase, never suspecting that a diminutive and rotting Japanese gangster was folded up inside.

Riley had parked in the alley behind my house. Only the neighbors knew it was there—and they didn't care really because it was technically mine and I never used it. Weeds and seven-foot-tall bushes obscured the entrance because I

thought it looked rustic that way (which really means I was very lazy). It was overgrown and out of sight. Outsiders wouldn't think there was an alley because I had a driveway in front of the house. Unfortunately, there was only one way out of the alley, and it was so close to my house we would definitely be noticed leaving if the media was overflowing around the corner.

He popped the hatch of the SUV that screamed *HELLO, MY NAME IS: Government Agency* and shoved the suitcase in. The hatch slammed shut, and we climbed aboard. I glanced back at the suitcase. I'd hauled one or two dead bodies in my career, but it still unnerved me. It was worse now. But maybe that was because this was the third dead body in a couple of days. I never had that kind of body count in this short of a time before. And I was pretty sure no one else in the CIA had either.

Once in the driver's seat, Riley pulled a tablet out of the glove compartment and turned it on. After a few touches, the screen was filled with an image of my house, Wolf Blitzer out front. I looked around us but didn't see anything suspicious.

Wolf was once again reporting that they had no idea who I was, what I looked like, nor could they get hold of me. I was impressed with the number of media on my front lawn. As we'd suspected, the reporters were spilling around the corner. Every network seemed to be there, including The Travel Channel and Animal Planet.

"Why is Animal Planet here?" I asked, my eyes locked on the screen. I hoped it was Jackson Galaxy, the host of *My Cat from Hell*, even though I couldn't think of a single reason why they'd have him covering dead terrorists. But then, some of those cats were evil geniuses. I liked evil geniuses.

"Maybe I should get a cat?" I asked. Riley gave me a look that said I should shut up now. Clearly, he didn't watch the show.

"Look." He pointed at the left side of the screen. Off camera, something was going on. I smiled. The cameras

started turning away from my house as these newsmen turned into slack-jawed, lobotomized basset hounds.

Lana finally appeared on screen coming down the sidewalk toward my house, giggling, jiggling, and waving at the reporters. She even blew a few kisses, which I thought was slightly over the top. Anyone holding a camera suddenly forgot they were recording. All eyes were on the Russian knockout as she walked down the sidewalk.

It really was a sight to see. You know those slow-motion shots they show on TV of gorgeous women walking toward you? It was like that here. Apparently Lana controlled time and space too.

Lana walked down the sidewalk in her tight dress and ridiculously high heels. She really worked it like a runway at a desperate singles meet and greet. She winked and smiled, causing a few guys to actually drop their cameras on the sidewalk.

"Ma'am!" Wolf Blitzer shouted, running toward her. "Are you one of the neighbors here?"

It was like watching a badly written sitcom. Slowly, it dawned on the reporters that they might have an excuse to ogle the giggly blonde for their story. You could see their faces change as the gears inside turned. They swarmed her like diabetic bumblebees to sugar-coated honeycombs.

Riley saw his opening and pulled out of the alley onto the street. No one was there to see us. He made it to the interstate, and soon we were crossing the Mississippi River. I turned my attention back to the tablet.

We'd told Lana not to speak. If they heard her Russian accent, the reporters really would have an angle. But we knew they'd ask questions, and she'd need to do something to make sure she held their attention.

She fainted. Dropped right there on the sidewalk. I couldn't see her because of all the reporters. There were shouts of, *I'll give her CPR! She needs chest compressions!* The reporters were starting to fight over who would get to touch this heavenly creature.

"OUT OF MY WAY!" Kelly appeared, advancing through the crowd. "I'm a nurse!" She shouted.

All of the men surrounding the fake-unconscious Russian turned to frown at Kelly as she pushed her way through to Lana. From the looks on their faces I think some of them actually contemplated murder. The way Kelly ignored them was impressive. Maybe she should consider acting. She shoved men aside until she got to where Lana lay.

"We have a development!" Wolf turned toward the camera, smiling for the first time. "A neighbor of Merry Wrath was coming up to us to make a statement when she fainted! A nurse from the area is with her now. Stay tuned as we bring you the latest. This is CNN."

"Huh," I said. "I knew they'd come up with an angle, but to make up that she was a neighbor who wanted to confide in them? Seriously?"

"They had to have some excuse for turning the cameras on a beautiful woman," Riley said as he took the exit for Chicago.

My stomach lurched. Riley thought Lana was pretty? I scowled. Of course he did. A blind man would be dazzled by her looks. And hey, why did this upset me?

"So you think Lana's beautiful," I said before I could stop my stupid, stupid mouth.

"Are you serious, Wrath?" Riley chuckled. "Of course she is. That woman is very well put together. It's what made her so useful to us, remember?"

I answered with a laugh that I hope implied that I didn't care what Riley thought of Lana. "Of course! Duh!" I looked back down at the tablet.

Kelly had helped a dazed Lana to her feet and started walking her toward her own house. The press looked like they wanted to lynch her for taking their sexy, exclusive story away. I watched as the two women exited the screen and turned the tablet off.

"It really was a good plan," Riley murmured. "The fainting was a nice touch."

I shrugged. "We couldn't have her talking. They'd hear that thick accent and know something was up. And you can't count on Lana not to say anything. That girl might've

thought this was her big acting break and blown the whole thing." Of course, Kelly was not thrilled that she'd have to take Lana to her house. Robert would thank me, though. I really owed her one. With the Girl Scout abandonment at camp, I owed her two…and maybe including the casserole, it was three now. I'd have to buy her a new car if this kept up.

"Yes, well, it was a great idea, and it worked." My former handler grinned as he drove, his eyes on the road. "You were a good agent, Wrath. I'm sorry we had to get rid of you."

I snorted, "I was a GREAT agent." I had to admit— I'd missed the adrenaline rush from a mission. Stupid Vice President of the United States.

"You were *good,*" Riley corrected. "Don't get any ideas."

I leaned back into the leather seat. This car had all the bells and whistles. I turned on the seat warmers and then the air conditioner to counter it. Pure bliss. Maybe I should get one of these. I thought about my little car with the huge, terrorist shaped dent in it.

"So, we have a few hours," I said. "We should try to figure out what's going on."

Riley turned to look at me, flashing me an undies-melting grin. "It's kind of fun having you back. Even if it *is* temporary."

I swallowed hard. I'd been immune to his charms once. I could do it again.

"So what's Kelly's story?" he asked

"She's married." I blurted out. Where had that come from? Was I jealous? No. Clearly this was from being alone for the past year. I needed to get this case cleared up so Detective Handsome across the street could ask me out.

I took a deep breath. "We've been friends forever. I totally trust her. And she was with me when I found Ahmed."

Riley nodded. "And that's where it all began. With Ahmed Maloof. That's where we need to start."

"You have access to the CIA files. You'd have more information than me. Didn't you find anything on him? When he disappeared? Travel records? Anything?"

"He was on the No-Fly List. He shouldn't have been able to enter the country without us knowing." Riley frowned.

"So someone brought him here…smuggled him in. It's not that unusual. I've been smuggled into lots of places." The worst was Canada. Do *not* allow yourself to be smuggled into Canada.

"This is different. I can only assume that Ahmed, Carlos, and Midori were brought here by force. I don't think they would've come on their own."

"What if they wanted to come here? What if they were lured here for the promise of something?" I asked.

"Like what? What would each of them want that would bring them to Iowa?" Riley shook his head. "The only thing we do know is that they were all killed here."

I studied him. We were on our way to some Japanese grocery store near Chicago to dump a body. We were working CIA tradecraft in our own country. Why?

"Why were you assigned to this case?" I asked.

Riley looked at me, then back at the road. "I volunteered."

I sat there, stunned. "You volunteered? For this? I was your biggest pain in the ass. Why would you want to help me?" That wasn't like Riley. He wasn't the kind of guy who'd just step up and take on a seemingly impossible case.

"That's right. You were my biggest pain in the ass. You were also one of my best operatives. And I felt guilty about you losing your career."

There was that knot in my stomach again. I'd always assumed Riley barely tolerated me when we worked together.

"You felt guilty? You didn't do anything. In fact, it wasn't even about me. It was about Dad."

He nodded. "I know. But still. It wasn't right. Part of me hopes the Vice President opts out of Secret Service coverage when his term is up."

Riley wanted to avenge me? "Aw shucks Riley. Didn't know you cared."

"I don't. I just want this to be over." His voice went back to all-business again. I'd lost him, that weird, sentimental guy I'd just caught a glimpse of. Maybe he was bi-polar or something.

I settled back into the warming car seat and closed my eyes. Screw Riley. He could figure this out himself. I fell asleep thinking of ways to torment my former boss.

* * *

"Yeah. Okay. You too." Riley's voice woke me up, and I sat straight in the seat to find him talking on his cell phone. It was dark out and the car was moving slower now. We must be close.

"Who was that?" I said as I rubbed my eyes.

"Kelly," Riley said.

I stared at him. "*My* Kelly? You were talking to *my* Kelly?"

"She gave me her number," he answered.

"Kelly gave you her *number*?" I asked.

Riley turned to look at me. "You're repeating yourself. You know that?"

"Okay," I conceded grudgingly, "what did she say?"

"Half of the media pulled out of the neighborhood. Including your friend Blitzer. She thinks the story is winding down somewhat."

I frowned. "That happened fast. I wonder why they lost interest so quickly. Did your red herrings work?"

He shook his head. "Never got time to employ them." He squinted at a sign for the grocery store. We were really close.

"Did she say anything else?"

"Apparently she's had it with Lana. Our little Russian friend kept snuggling up to her husband. So Kelly took her to work."

My jaw dropped. "What? Kelly took Lana to the hospital?" Wow. It had to be bad if Kelly took her to work.

How could Lana be so stupid as to flirt with Robert? I was going to have a chat with her when we got back. And by *chat*, I really meant something involving thumbscrews.

Riley shrugged. "We're here." He pulled into an empty parking lot. Although it was dark, all the lights in the lot were on. This wasn't going to be easy.

We drove around back and found a series of Dumpsters. Rats and roaches scattered the minute our headlights caught them. The smell was horrible—mostly rotting fish and probably sushi that had seen better days. I never liked sushi. I couldn't understand the appeal. Raw fish on fish eggs wrapped in seaweed just seemed like a bad dare some drunk in Japan had come up with in the eighteenth century for his wasted friends.

"Camera." I pointed at a mounted camera near the Dumpsters. We weren't in its range yet. My guess was they'd had other people trying to dump stuff here. People were so possessive of their trash bins. I once watched two of my neighbors get into a screaming match over one woman putting her bags in the other's bin. It came to blows. Both mother and daughter had to go to the hospital for stitches. No one should live next door to their mom.

Riley maneuvered the SUV out of the camera's range and around the Dumpsters to the other side. Now this area showed more promise. A dark, narrow area on the far side, hemmed in by a high, cement retaining wall. Up and over the wall were trees—some sort of little woodland area. No cameras. The only problem would be getting out. Only one car could fit so you went backward or forward. If another car came in, that exit would be blocked.

On the plus side, there were no cameras, but there were no odors—something I didn't think was good because the stink would cover the smell of a rotting corpse. Still we didn't really have any other options. I nodded at Riley, and he shut off the engine, and we stepped out of the car.

I pointed up above the wall. Riley studied it for a moment, then nodded. Putting Midori on the pavement meant she would be found as soon as people came to work. But stuffing her up over the wall and into the woods meant it

would be days, possibly weeks, before she was found.
Maybe years. It didn't look like anyone ever went up there.

I climbed the wall and hopped over it. Oh yeah. This
was perfect. There was at least an acre here. Lots of heavy
ground vegetation meant no one ever traveled through this
place. There were no beer bottles, condoms, or trash of any
kind. Most likely, people didn't even know this little forest
existed.

I looked down at Riley and nodded again. We didn't
speak. There's no point in doing so if you can communicate
nonverbally. If anything was monitored, they'd only have
visual. We weren't about to volunteer information that the
authorities didn't need. Riley had done a good job removing
the plates from the SUV sometime before I woke up. He had
standard issue black stocking caps in the glove compartment.
We all carried those on a mission to avoid leaving hair at a
site, and they were quite useful when it was cold outside.

Riley dragged the suitcase over to the wall and
gripping the handle, began to spin in a circle. As he turned,
the case lifted off the ground. It was heavy. He was going to
hurl it up here, like those hammer-tossers at Scottish
Highland Games.

He was pretty strong. I noticed his biceps bulging as
he spun. That man had a nice body. If he wasn't such a
douche, I'd...

The suitcase came flying through the air and hit me
in the stomach. I fell backwards onto the grass, the case on
top of me. It started to slide down, but I grabbed it before it
fell back down the wall, and hoisted it and myself up into the
woods. I lay there gasping like a fish for a few minutes. The
case hadn't knocked the wind out of me, but it did knock me
down.

"Hey!" I whispered to Riley as he joined me. "That
really hurt!"

"Sorry. You really should pay more attention to what
I'm doing." The wicked grin on his face told me he'd seen me
checking him out. My face grew hot.

"That's not...I wasn't...and you know it!" I
stammered.

Riley winked at me, then scrambled up to the suitcase. I followed him as he dragged it a little farther into the trees and then watched as he wiped it down completely with a rag to remove our fingerprints. I found a branch with leaves on it, and as we headed back to the wall, I brushed our footprints and the drag marks away.

Back in the car, Riley drove out of the parking lot and up the street. About two miles away, he stopped at a closed gas station and put the plates back on the car. I handed him my shoes, and he took off his boots. We drove a few more miles before dumping our muddy footwear in a random Dumpster.

"That went better than I thought it would," Riley muttered as we cruised back toward the interstate.

"Except for you hitting me with the bag, yes." I was a little pissed about that.

"You need to learn to get out of the way." Riley chuckled. "You didn't used to be so distracted." I noticed he'd put an emphasis on *distracted.*

There was no way I was giving him the satisfaction of thinking I was staring at him. "I was just trying to figure out what our next move should be."

"Right." Riley arched an eyebrow. "*That's* what you were thinking."

The bastard. I showed him by not talking at all on the way home.

CHAPTER EIGHT

We arrived back at my house a few hours later. Riley pulled into the hidden alley. He stopped the car and looked at me. I was furious with him and his pretty blue eyes. For him to imply that I was checking him out was…was…totally true—but he didn't need to know that.

Stupid, smug, gorgeous man.

"That was fun," he said with a smile. "Let's never do it again."

I laughed out loud—which made me mad at myself. Great, now he thought that I thought he was funny too. And I needed that like I needed a gunshot to the shoulder. I touched the scar on my right shoulder to remind myself.

Riley reached up and cupped my chin in his hand. I stopped breathing. His skin was warm and sent little shockwaves of heat through my body. What was he doing? He leaned closer, and I could smell his cologne. It was subtle—masculine and clean. The scent went well with his surfer looks—it reminded me of an ocean breeze.

His eyes locked onto mine. He really was hot. I closed my eyes automatically, and then I felt his lips brush…my cheek.

"Good job kiddo." My eyes flew open as he leaned back in his seat. He looked amused. I felt totally exposed.

Anger flared inside of me. I struggled to open the door—my fingers seemed to stop working correctly. I shook the handle, but it didn't budge, so I started swearing. The more I jiggled and failed, the louder and more creative my swearing got. Finally I got it open and, because I wasn't expecting the door to open, fell sideways out onto the gravel. It took a few seconds to get back on my feet.

"Just search the agency records on these guys!" I hissed as I slammed the door and turned on my heel to walk away. For a second, I thought I heard him chuckling. I kept on walking, never looking back until I got to the back, kitchen door. I fumbled with my keys until I finally got the door opened, then closed it behind me and leaned back against it.

I was a wreck. I was shaking. I was furious. And I had gravel in my shorts.

"Finny!" A familiar female squeal caused me to open my eyes. Lana sat at the breakfast bar. To my surprise, she'd changed out of her slutty clothes and into khakis and a T-shirt. Her voluminous, shiny hair was swept up into a pony tail, and I could swear she wasn't wearing any makeup (although she still was stunning, damn her).

"Lana." I stared at her. "How did you get back in?" I'd forgotten to give her a key.

Lana waved me off and got up, walking to the fridge. She pulled out the bottle of wine and poured two glasses, handing one to me. I took it gratefully and slumped onto one of the stools. I downed it like a shot. If I was going to drink wine like that, I needed to buy cheaper wine. There was no point in slamming the good stuff. Not that I knew what the good stuff was.

"I'm good with locks, Finny." Lana grinned and poured me another glass.

I nodded. "That's right. I remember that. By the way, nice job with the media assholes." I meant it too. For as much as she drove me crazy most of the time, she'd done well, and I wanted to praise her. It kind of felt like praising a dog. As if she could read my mind, Lana grinned and wiggled her butt with happiness. I struggled to control my gag reflex.

"It was so much fun! And then I got to meet Robert and go to the hospital with Kelleeee!" She giggled. "She had me go around with magazines for the patients. They were all so happy to see me!"

I'll bet. "Well thank you anyway."

She raised her eyebrows as she drank her wine. "Did you take care of the problem?"

I nodded. "Yup. All done. Where we put her, she won't be found for a long, long time. That gives us some room to figure things out."

"Midori was a beeeeetch. I hated her." Lana's usual one million watt smile was gone.

I straightened up, alert. "*You* knew Midori?" I guess that was possible. I mean, Japan was pretty close to Russia, and there'd been rumors for years that the Yakuza and Russian mob worked together now and then.

Lana nodded. "She haaaaaaaaaaaaaaaated me. I think Kelleeee hates me too." She set her glass on the counter and gave me her full attention. It was like staring into the sun. A blinding, bright sun with a 34 DD cup.

"Why do women hate me, Finny?" she asked, her lips in an adorable pout.

Hmmm…what to do here. I decided, perhaps a little meanly, on the truth. "Well, you fling yourself at every man around. You're more beautiful than any Hollywood starlet, and you dress like a tramp."

Lana stared at me for a long, terrifying moment. I thought I could see the synapses connecting in her brain. Did she really not know this? Did she really have no idea how she affected people? Had I gone too far?

"Do *you* hate me Finny?" Her eyes with the impossibly huge pupils searched my face.

"No." I slammed the other glass of wine and set the glass back on the table. "I'm getting used to you. But if you don't start calling me Merry, we might have a problem."

Lana responded by hurling herself into my arms. I stood there, stunned for a moment, before wrapping my arms around her and hugging her awkwardly. I guess this was better…

She pulled back but kept her hands on my arms. She grinned like she'd just invaded the Crimea and they made a postage stamp in her likeness. "I knew you and I would be best friends!" Lana squealed. Then she hugged me. Again.

I gently extricated myself from her grip. "I'll be your best friend forever if you can help me get out of this mess," I said jokingly.

Lana's eyes grew wide, and her mouth opened into a charming O. "You mean it? I will help you! I will solve this, and we will be best of friends forever!" She smiled like I'd never seen her smile before. This smile was…more genuine? It wasn't the smile she gave corrupt Russian politicians or even the media horde in front of my house. This was the real thing. I couldn't help falling for it. It reminded me of bunnies and freshly baked cookies.

As she bounced off down the hallway to go to bed, I wondered. Had Lana ever really had a friend before? And then I realized, besides Kelly, I didn't have other friends. Being a spy is a very lonely business. Are we so starved for attention that we'll do anything for any kind relationship?

My mind went back to Riley in the car—how I thought he was going to kiss me. Kiss me *romantically*. Was I that desperate and lonely that I'd let his charms overwhelm me? I felt a rush of humiliation at the idea.

I recycled the empty bottle of wine (Yes, I'm that awesome.) and washed the two glasses (And I'm domestic—how am I not a total catch?). It was nearly two in the morning. I needed to get some sleep.

My phone buzzed in my pocket, and I pulled it out. Kelly was ending her shift at the hospital and had left me a message. I pulled it out of my pocket and checked it out. What I read made me more terrified than when I found out I'd accidentally eaten the wrong part of the blowfish.

Don't forget we have a Girl Scout meeting tomorrow!

Damn.

The troop was meeting at the state park about ten minutes away. We were going to work on knots and making fires. A month ago, this had seemed like a terrific idea. We'd planned for a full afternoon in the great outdoors. I'd even been looking forward to it.

But now…

It was too late to call Kelly or the girls to cancel. I'd have to go through with it. And worse yet, I'd have to bring Lana. What else could I do with her? Riley wanted me to keep an eye on the blonde bimbo.

This was going to be a disaster. Lana would be useful only if we were working on a *How To Sleep Your Way Through The Kremlin* merit badge, and I was pretty sure the Girl Scouts didn't have one of those. I imagined all sorts of scenarios—Lana screaming at the sight of a daddy longlegs spider…Lana breaking a nail just looking at the outdoors…Lana getting poison ivy on her… Well, I guess it wasn't all bad. I'd just have to make her stay out of the way. It was going to be hard enough as it was with the fire and knots and any dads in the area standing there like brain-dead mouth breathers.

Damn it. Instead of being an afternoon of awkward quality time with my girls, it was now going to be a tense babysitting session with me trying to keep Lana out of trouble while trying to teach something I was terrible at. I was angry and worried, which meant I wasn't getting any beauty sleep tonight. Sigh.

* * *

I woke up early and stumbled through the shower. After digging out my rope supplies from the garage, I got Lana up and dressed without killing her. The park was only twenty minutes away, so we didn't have far to go. Lana and I snuck out the back and using the back yards of my neighbors, made it to Kelly's house unnoticed by the slowly dissipating media mob. I knocked on her sliding glass door at 12:30pm. She did not look happy to see us.

"What's *she* doing here?" Kelly folded her arms across her chest.

Lana piped up cheerfully, ignoring the insult. "I was Girl Scout back in Russia! Fifteen years!"

What? Lana had been a scout? I imagined the blonde as a Brownie with long, lustrous hair and huge boobs. I'd bet

she sold more cookies than anyone. If they sold cookies, that was. What else would they sell? Vodka and borscht?

I gave Kelly a weak smile. "Come on. We're doing knots and making fires. We'll need all the help we can get." It was an okay argument. Not my best, but I just needed Kelly to buy it. Fourteen second-graders were about to be dropped off in a park, and we had to make sure to send them home without third-degree burns or partially strangled by rope.

Kelly narrowed her eyes and studied Lana. I'd dressed my roomie carefully—T-shirt, khakis, tennis shoes, and a baseball hat with her hair in a ponytail behind it. I didn't even let her wear makeup. She still looked like a super model, but it was the best I could do.

"Fine," Kelly said finally, "she can help." She turned and went into her house, and we followed meekly. My argument had worked. It had taken all my talents as a persuasive spy to convince my best friend. I was exhausted.

The drive was agonizing. Kelly didn't speak to me, not once. I could feel her hostility with every bump in the road. In fact, I was pretty sure she was hitting every bump in the road just to get back at me.

I had a tiny, fragile sense of hope that maybe Lana would be okay. I didn't know what Russian Girl Scouts did—maybe just evaded wolves or wrestled bears or sent Boy Scouts to gulags—but there had to be a shred of skill there, right? Maybe it would be kind of okay. And by that I meant that maybe I could keep Kelly from killing her.

My fears and concerns—the ones that kept me up all night, I might add—dissolved the minute we arrived. At the campsite we'd rented for the afternoon, Lana jumped into action. She met each car as it drove up and dazzled the parents, men and women alike, before shepherding their daughters to Kelly and me. The girls looked at Lana as if she was a living Barbie/Fairy Princess. They were hypnotized. Lana apparently *liked* kids.

"I've got to admit," Kelly grumbled, "she's pretty good at this part."

I nodded. Usually parents just dumped their kids and left, sometimes complaining that this was inconvenient for them. I was pretty sure the parents hated us most of the time. But now, many of them parked and came back to join us. Of course, almost all of them were men...

I started to talk to the girls as they sat on the ground, waiting. But Lana interrupted me.

"We need tinder, kindling, and fuel!" She bubbled enthusiastically as she held up examples of the three that were so perfect I had a hard time believing those twigs actually existed in nature.

"And we need a lot of all three of them. Who wants to help me gather the tinder, kindling, and fuel?" Lana asked.

Every single hand shot up into the air. And that included the parents who were with us. For a second, I thought I saw Kelly's hand twitching. I put my hand on her arm to keep it down, just in case.

Lana divided the girls into teams, each with strict orders to bring back one of the three kinds of sticks. Then she marched them into the woods with storm trooper precision and led them off to collect the wood. I was not surprised to see the dads following her.

"Who's that?" One of the Kaitlyn's moms asked. Her eyes were glazed, and she was certainly in Lana's thrall. No real shock there. Lana had that effect on women, if they didn't have their men around, that is. I tried to remember this mom's name, but to be honest, I really didn't interact with the parents much.

"Her name is Lana." I looked at Kelly and she shrugged. "She's with WAGGS—the World Association of Girl Guides." Which wasn't totally a lie, necessarily. "She's in the U.S. to work with different scout troops."

The mom nodded, her eyes still trained on the woods. "That's nice. Gives the girls access to someone from another country..." she said absently.

I nodded, making the lie true. The mom stood there, gazing at the woods while Kelly and I set up the ropes for knot tying. To be fair, it was kind of nice having an extra pair of hands even if they were Lana's. Kelly and I usually

felt like we were in over our heads. Fourteen girls was a lot to work with. Maybe between the three of us, we could actually get through a whole meeting minus the usual chaos and bleeding.

"Come on girls!" Lana shouted cheerfully. She emerged from the woods, followed by the girls in two perfect lines, each carrying a load of wood.

My jaw dropped open. The girls weren't chattering. They weren't goofing off and trying to hit each other. They didn't try to eat the sticks. They were *listening*. What alternate universe was this? Lana didn't even have to use the universal quiet sign. Not even once!

We stared in awe as the girls followed Lana to the fire pit and unloaded their wood into three neat piles—one for each size stick. Then she selected two of the Kaitlins to fetch a bucket of water and find a rake. I noticed the mom next to me was grinning with pride that her daughter had been selected for this seemingly amazing honor.

Lana somehow *wordlessly* got the girls to surround the fire pit in a perfect circle. No girl was left out. Every girl was spaced completely evenly. And none of them spoke. It was like watching a Soviet propaganda movie on manners.

We watched in gaping silence, Kelly, the mom, the random dads, and me were all hypnotized by Lana's performance.

"She's really good," the mom murmured to me.

On a cue that I didn't see (or that happened under some sort of collective group mind control), every girl picked up in an *orderly* manner, a handful of tinder, kindling, and logs and took them to her spot in the circle. Each girl then knelt down and under Lana's instructions, built a perfect teepee-framed base.

Kelly and I looked at each other in shock. We couldn't even speak.

Lana reviewed fire safety with the girls as if she was Smokey the freakin' Bear. The girls listened in a way second grade girls *never* listen, and I wondered for a moment if they'd been secretly replaced with Russian little people. I've seen a lot of bizarre things throughout my career as a spy,

from a man being killed by his own elbow to an otter that delivered secret messages, but I'd never seen anything like this.

"Okay girls! Now we start the fire! Katelynn! You first!" Lana enthused. She knew the girls' names already! She even *pronounced* the kaitlins in a way that somehow reflected how you'd spell their names. I don't know how she did it, but it was completely obvious that she did.

One by one, the girls came forward as she called on them to help build the main fire. Then each girl lit a match without setting her clothes on fire and held it to the tinder. It was like watching a surreal movie that you knew couldn't be true, even though you were watching it with your own eyes. I expected that George Lucas would walk in at any moment and yell, "Cut!"

A small part of me was jealous. I'll admit that. But a large part of me watched in wonder that something like this could actually happen. And another part of me was ridiculously happy that Lana was here with my troop.

I had no idea what Kelly was thinking. I could only guess she thought the same thing. At least I hoped she was thinking the same thing.

"Great job girls!" Lana praised, and the girls almost fainted under the glow. "Who wants to make s'mores?" she asked, and every hand shot up, including the five dads. Lana laughed and clapped her hands. It was obvious she was having fun.

Kelly took charge and called for the girls to come over to her. The girls blinked at each other, then looked to Lana. Lana nodded, and the girls broke loose, racing over to us in loud, chattering chaos. We were swarmed as we put marshmallows on sticks and handed them out. When the last one was handed out, Kelly and I exhaled.

"Did you see how they descended into complete chaos when we asked them to do something?" Kelly whispered.

"Yeah. I think we should have Lana run everything from now on." I was covered with sticky marshmallow goo—and they hadn't even melted the marshmallows yet.

"Agreed," Kelly said as she tore the wrappers off the Hershey bars and I opened the graham crackers.

It started up again as the girls crowded us with their burned and squishy marshmallows. We somehow managed to scrape each one off the stick onto the chocolate and graham crackers. When the last girl walked away, I noticed Kelly had bits of graham cracker in her hair, and I had a huge smear of chocolate down one leg.

"You know," the mom spoke up, "you really should have had Lana handle that."

Kelly and I looked at each other and nodded. She was right. We really should have.

Lana took over for clean up. Once again, the girls snapped to silent attention, and in brigades worthy of a military parade on Red Square, erased all evidence of the mess they'd created and put out the fire.

And no one got hurt. No one.

When they were finished, Lana got the girls to sit in their circle around the fire pit again. I noticed with amazement that each girl was sitting exactly where they'd stood during the fire lesson. They were replaced with robot girls. I was dealing with Stepford Scouts.

Kelly and I gave each girl two twelve-inch pieces of rope. Lana jumped in and proceeded to lead them through a knot tying lesson the likes of which has never been experienced on this Earth. Never. She put every seasoned sailor to shame. If any of them would've been with us, they would've wept.

I'd never been good at knots. I'd been preparing for this since we arranged this meeting. But no matter how much I practiced, I couldn't grasp it. The square knot was hopeless. The bow-line hitch was out of the question. Thank God I'd never had to hang anyone because the guy would just drop harmlessly to the ground, watch the ropes tumble around his toes uselessly, and then he'd run off. I hated knots.

Kelly had some experience — being a nurse made her something of a natural. But between the two of us, we'd been very worried about how we were going to pull this off.

If I couldn't master a knot, how could I possibly teach fourteen girls to do it?

"Right over left," Lana was singing, "and left over right, makes a square knot that's sturdy and tight!" She held up her square knot, and as if on cue, all fourteen girls did the same. And each and every knot was perfect.

"Who *is* she?" Kelly asked.

I shook my head. "I'm starting to think that I really don't know."

Thirty minutes later we were done. The girls had learned to make about ten different (and in my opinion, scientifically impossible) knots.

"Okay girls! That's it!" Lana said.

A chorus of horrified *no!s* broke out, and the girls swarmed around Lana, hugging her. Two of the Kaitlins burst into tears.

Lana hugged each and every one of them and immediately after each hug, each girl had a blissed-out look on her face as if she'd been hugged by a pink and glittery princess unicorn.

"Please stay!"

"I don't want to go home!"

"I love you Miss Lana!"

This was ridiculous. And embarrassing. The girls acted as if being parted from the Russian spy was like being sentenced to cleaning their rooms with their tongues. Kelly and I were faced with sobbing second-graders. No way I wanted their parents picking them up like this. Some of the dads were openly sobbing.

"How about a game then?" Lana asked. As if by magic, the tears dried up, and quivering lips were replaced by huge smiles.

"She knows games too?" Kelly whispered. I just shrugged. I hoped she knew more games than The Slutty Nurse and the Naughty Russian Prime Minister.

Lana organized the girls into what I can only think of as the ultimately safe Red Rover. The girls formed two rows facing each other, their hands in front of them, palms

up. One side huddled with Lana, giggling and whispering. They broke up and resumed their line.

"Red Rover, Red Rover, send Ava right over!" They broke out in a chorus. Ava ran over and walked up and down the line, gently slapping their hands in a sort of flat, double high-five. At the end of the row, she reversed her hands and slapped up against Hannah's hands and ran for it. Hannah gleefully chased Ava to her line but didn't catch her. She joined Ava's side.

Lana then huddled with Ava's team. More giggling and whispering. They chose Emily to come over. This went on and on until the parents arrived.

I can only describe the pickup as the saddest thing I'd ever seen. Yup. Those are the words I'd choose. *The saddest thing I'd ever seen.* Even for the dads. Maybe especially for the dads. More than one of them had to be chased off. As the last girl was dragged kicking and screaming away, I collapsed onto a picnic table. Kelly plunked down next to me, exhausted.

Lana, on the other hand, was bouncing around like a balloon filled with Red Bull and zapped with electricity.

"That was so fun! Wasn't that fun? When do we get to do it again?" she asked all in one stream of words.

"You're not tired?" I asked. "We've been here four hours. How could you not be tired?"

Lana just shook her head. Her ponytail bobbed seductively. "No! I love being with the girls! I miss it!"

Kelly stared at her. "How did do you do that?"

Lana stopped bouncing and bit her lower lip. "Do what?"

"That!" Kelly swept her arms around her. "This! How do you make people so happy?" She left off *and make women like me so miserable,* but it was there, hanging in the air like a small, toxic cloud.

Lana didn't get her meaning. "I don't know. I just figure, why not be happy all the time. The alternative is to be sad. And I don't like being sad."

"What experience do *you* have with sadness?" I asked. It was a legitimate question. I'd only ever seen Lana happy.

Lana sat down next to Kelly. She took a deep breath, then started her story. "I grew up in a Russian orphanage. It was very sad there. I was able to go to school and be a Girl Scout, but every night I went back to the orphanage. When I turned sixteen, the director gave me fifty rubles and a blanket and sent me out onto the streets. That was my whole life until I met you, Merry." Then she looked up and smiled. "This life is better! Much better!"

Kelly, my snarky, sarcastic Kelly, the one who never ever lets me get away with anything and who calls me on my stupidity every time…that Kelly, burst into tears.

I came pretty close myself.

CHAPTER NINE

—————

We drove home in silence. Kelly and I were feeling pretty damned guilty. We felt bad about the way we'd treated Lana. But what could we say? Sorry didn't seem to cut it. And then there were all the things we'd been *thinking*. I felt terrible about that too.

Lana didn't seem to notice. She hummed along with the radio and had her arm outside the car, dangling in the breeze. She really surprised me. I guess I'd been a little wrong about her. I should've given her more of a chance. I didn't say these things because I didn't really think I could dig myself out of the crappy hole I'd made. So I sat there in silence, listening to Lana humming.

Kelly parked the car in the garage. When we got out, she led us to her backyard, where we'd sneak home. Then she threw her arms around Lana. Without a word, she turned and walked into her house, closing the sliding glass door behind her.

Lana smiled. "Kelleeee likes me!" I stumbled in shock as I walked and Lana skipped, back to my back door.

My cell rang as soon as I got in. Lana giggled and decided to take a shower. I heard the door close behind her. She had to be spent. I was, and I'd hardly done anything.

"This is Merry," I answered. I didn't want to talk to anyone. I needed to take a shower and just collapse. My whole day had turned upside down, even if it was for the better. There's nothing like a shame spiral to make you want a shower and a nap.

"Ms. Wrath…" The unmistakably handsome voice of Detective Rex sent a jolt of energy through me. "Do you have a moment? Could I stop by?"

I looked out the window. All of the press had cleared out. When did that happen? How did that happen? Maybe Riley finally got them going on a wild goose chase. At any rate, the coast was clear.

But the most important thing was that Rex wanted to come over here, to my house! Clearly he wanted to propose, I thought. "Sure. Give me a minute to…uh…pick up a little. Ten minutes okay?"

"Perfect." I thought I could detect a smile in his voice. "See you in a few."

Rex was coming over! To my house! To see me! Okay, so it could be about the investigation, but technically, he *was* coming over to my house, and he *was* going to see me.

I raced like a whirlwind through the house. Not that it was very messy—it wasn't. But there was dust on the furniture. I didn't have time to find a towel, so I used my hands to dust. I was just wiping off the TV with my fingers, when the doorbell rang.

I looked down at my hands. They were filthy and sadly sweaty. The doorbell rang again. I was keeping my future fiancé waiting. Looking around, I spotted the Dora the Explorer sheets and wiped my hands on them quickly before answering the door.

Rex stood on my front porch like some hero on the cover of a romance novel. He was wearing a suit, and it looked amazing on him. Everything about him looked wonderful. He smiled at me. And I lost the ability to speak.

"Ms. Wrath," he said, "thanks for taking the time to see me. I'm sorry about the short notice." He smiled again.

"Um, no problem!" I said perhaps a tad too enthusiastically. "Come in!"

Rex stepped inside, and I closed the door. He smelled like soap and fresh linen. I wondered if it would be out of line to bury my face in his neck. Would that seem weird?

"Sit down!" I ordered. The demand in my voice made me jump. "Sorry, I meant, would you like to sit down?" That sounded better. Was I an idiot or what?

"Thanks." Rex sat on the green couch. Since there were no other chairs in the room, I had to sit next to him. Mental note—do not get more chairs for the living room.

"You smell like you've been in a fire, Ms. Wrath. Is everything okay?" He looked concerned. I loved him for that.

"Er...no...I just had a meeting with my Girl Scout troop," I babbled. "We were setting fires. I mean, we were learning how to start fires." That sounded bad. Like I was training an army of seven year old pyromaniacs.

He gave me a strange look that faded into a smile. Then he saw the curtains. The curtains that were actually Dora the Explorer bed sheets. The curtains with two, long, smeary handprints on them. It looked like I had killed somebody who was filthy and they died, clinging to the sheets as they slid to the floor.

"Sorry!" I said again. "I...um...have a roommate. She's very dirty." I added. What the hell? I was making it worse.

"Um...okay?" He looked confused.

"Like Pigpen...from the Charlie Brown cartoons?" I added. "She must've wiped her hands on the curtains."

Rex looked at me for a moment like I was completely insane. To be completely fair, I was starting to wonder that myself.

"Tea? A glass of wine? Shot of vodka?" I said out loud as I mentally went through the drinks I had on hand. Then I realized I'd just offered the man shots.

I said nothing more. It was my only defense, really.

"No thanks," the future love of my life said very slowly as if he was trying to figure out if he should run. "I'm actually on duty."

"Oh. Right," I said, wondering why I'd just tried to bribe a cop with booze. Was that a thing? I wasn't sure. It had worked on the Eastern Europeans I'd spied on, and some

of them drank antifreeze for a buzz. Not here so much, I guessed.

"I just had a few more questions. About Ahmed Maloof and Carlos the Armadillo."

Great. Just when things were getting romantic.

"I'm sorry." I faked my most sincere voice. "I can't really help other than what I've already told you."

Rex nodded. "I know you said that. It's just that something is bothering me about you."

"Me?" My eyes grew wide, and my mouth dropped open. That did not sound good.

"Yes. You see, I've been trying to research you. And I'm not coming up with anything."

I waved him off. "Oh that. Well, I don't really have a presence online. No Facebook, Twitter, none of that stuff."

He shook his head. "It's not just that—I can't find *anything* about you. No birth certificate…no record of where you've lived, where you went to school, nothing. It's like you don't exist."

I must've been staring because he added, "Well, I mean, you do exist, obviously. You're sitting right here. But on paper there is no evidence of a Merry Wrath. Nothing."

My skin itched, and my arms and legs grew cold. This wasn't good. I'd been a non-person many times in my life, with many different aliases and backstories. They had a whole wing at Langley that just answered calls about our backstories, pretending to be the companies we worked for, etc. I didn't have that anymore. No one had even offered. Not even the Federal Witness Protection Program. I'd developed this persona—Merrygold Wrath, on my own. Which meant I had to figure this out and back it up on my own. Which sucked.

I frowned. "I don't know how that's possible…" My eyes went up to the left, a sign I knew implied that I was wrestling with what I thought was impossible. If I'd gone to the right, it alerted people that I was accessing the right side…the creative side, the lying part of my brain. Any FBI agent or CIA agent would know that, and so, I assumed, would a detective.

"I grew up here. How could you not find any record of that?" I asked while my brain furiously worked on a solution.

Rex shook his head, "I don't know. I thought maybe you could explain it." He looked at me with eyes that challenged me with *go ahead smart girl—make something up.*

"You met my cousin, Riley, last time you were here," I challenged.

"Just because you say he's your cousin doesn't mean anything," Rex answered. "Besides, he looked more like a Fed to me."

I suppressed a laugh. Riley would hate that Rex thought he looked like FBI. He hated the FBI. It was beyond the usual intergovernmental agency mutual loathing. The Feds once blew Riley's cover in a sting operation. He was stuck with an incontinent chimpanzee for four weeks as a result.

"Why wouldn't his testimony work?" I asked.

"Because he's just a cousin. And I didn't find any evidence of him living here either."

Damn. Rex had really looked into this. I should've seen it coming—it's tradecraft 101. And yet, I didn't. Riley didn't either. We were so absorbed with the dead terrorist thing, we'd forgotten that a smart detective would check us out.

So what to do? I couldn't say my dad grew up here, because I couldn't say who my father actually was, and Rex would look up whatever name I gave him. Even saying I was an orphan was out because obituaries were easy to find.

I snapped my fingers. "Kelly Albers!"

His eyes narrowed. "Kelly Albers? I'm sorry, I don't follow."

"Kelly is my best friend! She lives here and grew up with me. She'll tell you!" Without waiting for him to respond, I called Kelly on my cell and demanded that she come over.

"I've already told you I need more than just testimony," Rex said. "And unless this Kelly Albers has

copies of your birth certificate and college transcripts…which I doubt…she's no good to me."

"Well…" I shrugged, stalling for time. "Maybe she can help us think of something. Like I said, we grew up together. Here. In this very town."

"I'm not convinced she can help, Ms. Wrath. And these are fairly easy things to get. You just have to go down to the county courthouse and ask for your birth certificate. In fact, I could drive you."

I did want him to drive me. But I did not want him anywhere near official records that proved I was really someone else.

"Why would you need to take me? I'm perfectly capable of driving myself."

Rex cocked his head to one side. "I just thought with your car damaged from the accident that maybe it wasn't driveable. I don't have to drive you."

"Is it really important for you to have these things?" I asked. "I mean, I can get them. There's no doubt about that." I totally doubted that. "But why would they be important to the investigation?"

"Because it would satisfy my curiosity, Ms. Wrath," Rex answered. It seemed like he was getting mad at me.

I sighed, as if it was the most inconvenient request ever asked of anyone. "Fine. I'll make sure to get you my birth certificate."

The detective was silent. He was smart (which was good because it meant our children would be smart). Rex was waiting for me to fill the silence nervously and slip up. But I wasn't going to. Not this time.

Kelly just walked in. It's what we did. I was kind of surprised about that because now with people showing up dead in my kitchen, it probably wasn't a good idea to leave doors unlocked.

"Hey Merry," Kelly said naturally. "What's up?"

Her eyes caught sight of Rex, and she smiled. How could she not?

"Kelly, this is our new neighbor—Detective Rex Ferguson. And he doesn't believe I grew up here."

"That's not what I..." Rex started to say.

Kelly cut him off. She was a real pro. "New neighbor? Where did you move in?"

"Across the street. But that's not what I..." He tried to change the subject.

Kelly smiled. "In the old cougar's house?" She walked over to the window and looked out.

"Well, yes. Wait, did you say cougar?" Rex looked puzzled.

Kelly nodded. "Oh yeah. The old lady who mowed the yard in a bikini. I never thought she'd leave." She turned to me. "Remember how she did that when we were kids?"

I nodded, taking the cue. "She was always on the prowl." I looked at Rex. "Did she leave anything weird behind?"

"I've never even been inside that house," Kelly said before he could answer. "You'll have to have us over when you're all moved in."

"Kelly can bring you a tuna noodle casserole," I added quickly.

Kelly smiled. "I make a mean tuna noodle casserole, Detective."

Rex looked from one of us to the other. "Okay, so you grew up here. But that doesn't explain why I can't find any record of you anywhere."

I frowned. "Yeah. I don't get that either. I'll have to look and see if I can find my old report cards or yearbooks or something."

"I probably have a yearbook," Kelly said, her eyes going up and to the left as she thought. She would've made a good agent. "It'll take some time to dig those out. But I'll bring them over when I do."

Detective Ferguson looked at me. He knew he was beat. Which made me a little sad. I really liked him. But my cover came first. We could plan the wedding later. And obviously, Kelly would be my maid of honor.

"Fine," he said. He looked pissed. "Let me know when you've got something."

I held the front door open for him. "Will do. Thanks for stopping by."

I watched him walk across the street to his house and go inside. A few minutes later, I watched as the SUV backed out of the driveway and he drove away. I let out a huge breath and collapsed on the couch.

"What was that all about?" Kelly sat down next to me.

"Me not being prepared," I said morosely.

Kelly got up and walked to the door. "A Girl Scout should always be prepared, Merry."

I gave her a look. "Just see if you can find one of the yearbooks. I'll fix it."

With a nod and a wink, Kelly left. I dialed Riley.

"We might have a small problem," I said.

CHAPTER TEN

———

Riley promised to have someone at Langley work on inserting me into the system. It was sloppy and late, and it wouldn't fool Rex. He'd know the documents weren't there when he looked for them earlier, but he'd have a hard time proving that. Which meant he'd be discredited if he brought it up to anyone in his department.

That was sad. I didn't like hurting his career. I'd done that to other people before. A few of the people I'd turned to give me information—their careers were damaged when I'd left that country. But I didn't care then. All I'd cared about was getting sensitive information out of them and using it to my country's advantage.

I wondered how many people were ruined because of me. It was all just part of the job—I knew that. And some of them were either bad guys or spies themselves. But what about the others? The businessmen, the secretaries to important officials, the people who had to stay behind when I left. The people who had to keep hidden what they'd done. The people who would be punished if they were ever found out. What happened to them?

Some may have lost their jobs. Others might have lost much more. That idea was chilling. You can justify a lot when you think what you're doing is necessary for serving your country. I'd never really thought about that. Probably because I didn't want to think about that.

But now I did. Because now I lived across the street from the person I was screwing over. And for what? To cover my ass because I wanted to keep living here?

I wanted to keep living here. Wow. That's it. I wanted to stay somewhere for once in my life. And Rex was

in my way. And I was doing to him what I'd done so easily to others all over the world. It just came so naturally that I felt guilty about it. Would it be possible to look into things…to see if I could help anyone I'd hurt? There was something in that idea that made me feel a little better.

Kelly eventually dropped off one of our yearbooks, and I sat down with it in the kitchen. It was from middle school. There I was, with glasses and braces, grinning like an idiot at the camera, my arm around Kelly. Back when I thought being teased for having braces was the worst life had to offer (because I didn't yet know that the worst is being stabbed by an agent you thought you'd turned, in a dirty alley in Krakow at four a.m.).

Unfortunately, the yearbook listed me as Finn Czrygy. They couldn't fit Fionnaghuala on the page, but everyone had just called me Finn since kindergarten. I wasn't involved in much, just yearbook committee and the school newspaper. My picture was only in the yearbook four times. Each time my real name was mentioned. I'd have to fix that.

The agency would take care of faking my birth certificate, school records, etc. But I'd promised Rex a yearbook, so I'd have to do that myself. I was hoping to drop it off and offer some sort of apology. Something like, *Sorry to mess with you, and you were right, but I can't have my cover blown, and will you whisk me away someplace romantic?* Okay, not that, but something like that.

"Lana!" I shouted back toward her bedroom, "I'm going out to run a couple of errands." She shouted back a mumbled okay from her bedroom. I'd heard a blow dryer running earlier. I guessed she'd spend a few hours on her hair.

I backed my dented car out of the garage and headed for the nearest art supply store. I was pretty good at forgery. It takes patience and a lot of time to get it right, but there was something satisfying in it. Maybe this could be my hobby? But what would I forge now that I'm retired? Receipts for Oreos? Wait…that wasn't a bad idea…

Half an hour later I was back home. I dumped the contents of my bag on the breakfast bar. One Exacto knife,

some large, glossy photo paper, glue, and thread gave me all I needed to try to reproduce the four pages I needed to replace in the book. I also bought a printer/scanner. It took a few annoying moments to upload the software to my laptop. But once it was done, the rest was pretty easy.

All this stuff can be pretty much done with Photoshop. It's not hard after you've had one thousand hours of training, just time-consuming. I had to make the new pages identical to the old pages. Kelly's book was old, and the pages were turning light brown. I'd use tea to age the new pages once I'd done all the scanning, cutting and pasting, and matching the font to retype "Merry Wrath" every time there was a "Finn Czrygy."

The hard part was making the photos on the page look the same as the others in the book. Scanning kind of made them look lighter. But I'd done a lot of work with the graphic software once on assignment in the Andes. It had been freezing, and I didn't have Wi-Fi. So I spent my time learning Photoshop. It took forever. But my main job was listening in on transmissions, so I had lots of time. I was a graphic design pro by the time I moved on, and my Spanish improved dramatically.

"What are you doing?" Lana's voice was right next to me, and I jumped backward.

"You scared the hell out of me!" I snarled. I hadn't even heard her in the hallway.

"Sorry." Lana pouted like a poodle who thought it could get away with something.

I shook my head. "It's okay. I was working on my backstory." I looked at her for a long time. I guess if she was going to live here and know about everything else, I should probably bring her up to speed. So I filled her in on the visit from Detective Hottie and my attempts to fix things.

Lana studied the yearbook. I was still working with the pages, so I didn't care if she had it. Soon, I'd need to sew the new pages into the binding. But for now, what the hell. She probably didn't have a yearbook back in the orphanage.

"This is you and Kelleeeee?" She pointed at the photo of us together.

I nodded. "Yup. Seventh grade at Herbert Hoover Middle School."

"You look happy," she said. "So you are going to try to make Rex think this proves you grew up here?"

I looked up at her. Something in her voice got my attention. "What, you don't think it'll work?"

She closed the yearbook and handed it back to me. "I don't know. Maybe. He might let it work because he likes you."

I dropped my wireless mouse on the floor. "You think he likes me?" I tried to think when Lana had met Rex. I couldn't come up with anything.

"I don't know." Lana shrugged. "I see him looking at the house a lot."

"That's it? That's all you've got to go on?" I shook my head. "He's probably just keeping an eye on me."

"Maybe. But it looks to me like he likes you."

"How could you possibly know that from seeing him look at the house?"

"I have always had knack for knowing how men think. It's what made me good as a spy."

I sat there, thinking. I really hoped she was right. But then, it made me feel worse for lying to him.

"How did you justify lying to people, back when you were in the business?" I asked. "Did you ever wonder what happened to the people you used?"

Lana shrugged. "I liked being a spy. And people only gave up information because they thought they were using me. That made it okay."

"Using you?"

She grinned. "They thought they would have sex with me if they told me what I wanted. That's how they used me."

"And did you have sex with them when they told you what they wanted?" It was rude to ask, but I was curious.

Lana shook her head. "No. Most of the time I didn't have to. Most were happy just to be seen in public with me. Others needed a little cuddling and kissing."

"Most?" I asked, feeling a little ashamed for pressing the matter.

"There were a few times..." Her voice trailed off, and her eyes grew dark. "But that doesn't matter anymore. I'm not a spy now."

"No one ever asked me to have sex with them in exchange for secrets," I mused out loud. "They just wanted money or stuff." I felt kind of bad about that. Why didn't they want to have sex with me? I wasn't repulsive. I was pretty damned close to *better-than-okay*.

Lana patted me on the shoulder. "That's a good thing, Finn...I mean Merry. You should not feel bad about that."

I watched her walk back down the hall and wondered. Did Lana feel bad about it? Why did she do it then? But then I thought about the orphanage. I'd do anything for a better life too. I shoved these thoughts aside and went back to my work.

Two hours later I was done. I had to admit—it looked pretty damn good. I'd marry me after seeing this. All I had to do was take it over.

My phone buzzed. I answered it.

"Wrath," Riley said quietly, "we have a little problem."

CHAPTER ELEVEN

———

I walked into the tavern downtown, looking for my former boss. It was packed with the dinner crowd. A mom-and-pop place, it was dark with dull décor, but it had the best burgers in the state. I wondered if Riley knew that. He didn't seem like a burger guy to me, unless it was made of tofu. The thought of tofu burgers made me shudder. I was an Iowan. Burgers made of plant matter didn't exist on my radar—something I was very grateful for.

Riley was seated in a booth in the back. He was facing the rest of the interior, including the door. Damn. I wanted that spot. It was ingrained in spies to pick the spot where we could see everything. You never wanted your back to the door.

I sat down opposite him and felt uncomfortable. But with two spooks, what could you do? Someone had to sit with his back to the door. In this case, it was me.

"I ordered for both of us, something called a Reuben Burger," Riley said with a frown. Uh-oh. It must be bad news if he's eating real food.

A frazzled looking waitress chewing gum stopped by just long enough to drop off two bottles of beer. She was busy and probably wouldn't even remember that we were here. That's why Riley had picked this place. We'd stand out in a salad joint—mainly because I would be dramatically crawling across the floor, begging for greasy food.

"The Reuben Burger is famous here. They make their bread fresh every morning." I took a long drink of beer. It was nice and cold.

"Just trying to fit in," Riley said. He looked worried. Something bothered him enough to go all undercovery on me.

"So what's up?" I asked, taking another drink.

"You know, I've been in shitholes all over the world. It always amazes me when I find them here in the U.S.," Riley snarled.

Wow. It must be worse than I thought.

"This is a good place," I said defensively. "The owners have had it all their lives, and their kids work here." I indicated the two young men working the bar. "It's clean, and the food is great. So give it a break, Andrews. Why am I here?"

Just then the waitress dumped two baskets full of beer-battered French fries and the biggest burgers Riley had probably ever seen. The Reuben Burger truly is a work of art. Half a pound of corn-fed Iowa beef, piled high with corned beef, smothered in melted Swiss cheese, and topped off with fresh, authentic German sauerkraut. The buns were made of rye bread. I took a huge bite and savored it.

Riley watched me, bug-eyed, before picking up the bun and staring at what was underneath. I went up to the bar and grabbed a small plate, which I brought back and filled with ketchup. I dipped a couple of fries, ate, and washed it all down with beer. Heaven.

"I'm not going to talk to you until you at least take a bite," I said. His snobbery was bothering me. He'd picked the place, after all. What did he expect them to serve? Bean sprouts? I was pretty sure they still tarred and feathered you here if you asked for that.

Riley shot me a look before lifting the huge burger to his mouth and taking a fairly plausible bite. His expression changed from horror to surprise. He chewed, swallowed, then ate a couple of fries.

"That's pretty good," he said. "I owe you an apology."

"Whatever." I rolled my eyes. "What's wrong?"

Riley held up two fingers. "Two things. First, the Middle East office picked up some chatter about you. Al-Qaeda's considering a jihad against you for Ahmed's death."

"What?" I wasn't quite sure I heard that right. "For a moment there I thought you'd said Ahmed's friends have called for a holy war against me."

"They're just considering it. I thought you should know," he added.

"Okay…" I said slowly as I tried to digest this information, "next you'll be telling me the Colombian Cartel is coming after me."

There was a brief pause as Riley smiled weakly, "Actually…"

"Oh come on! Really?" I slapped my hand on the table. I was more angry than anything. If I was smart, I would've been terrified. But I wasn't. Smart, that is.

He nodded. "We're on top of it. We have some inside guys trying to spread misinformation. Hopefully, they'll give up on the idea before they start auditioning hit men."

"Hopefully?" I just stared at him. "We can't get a little more concrete on that? Like maybe *definitely* or *absolutely*?"

"I'm working on it. I don't want you to worry about it. Think of it as something that's being taken care of."

I grumbled, "I'd rather think of it as something that didn't happen at all." Great. Now I also ran the risk of being hunted by two different kinds of terrorists. Which is fine if you're actually still an employee of the CIA, but not so great if you are retired. Maybe instead of getting a cat, I should get an attack dog. Or two.

"What's the other thing?" I asked. "You said there were two things you had to tell me. I'm hoping this won't be as bad as having al-Qaeda and the Colombians after me."

Riley sighed. "I don't think you're the target," he said, looking at me as if that piece of news would upset me.

"Oh good. So this will all blow over and go away then," I said, taking another bite of burger.

He shook his head. "It won't. Not as long as Lana's at your house."

I dropped the burger into the basket. "What? You think Lana's the target? But that's ridiculous. She showed up after Ahmed and Carlos. Whoever is doing this didn't even know she was coming here."

"I've found several connections between Lana and all three dead guys." He shrugged. "Several," he repeated—which was unnecessary since I'd heard him the first time. "I haven't found a secure connection on all three to you."

I frowned. "It still doesn't make sense. Why make it look like they are targeting me?"

"Red herring," he said.

"You know, you use that phrase too much." I pointed a fry at him before eating it. I thought about asking the waitress to bring me some mayonnaise. I liked dipping my fries in mayo. But that would probably give Riley an empathetic heart attack.

"The bad guys—let's call them *X*— wanted us to think of you as the target. They wanted us to worry about and fuss over you. Then, while we were focused on that, they'd go after Lana."

I shook my head. "No. I still come back to the fact that Ahmed showed up dead at the camp, where Mr. X knew I'd be. Then he threw Carlos in front of my car. Lana didn't even come into play until after that."

"Mr. X?" Riley asked.

I shrugged. "It's more sinister than just *X*, don't you think? Or *Dr. X*. That might be better."

He rolled his eyes. "I don't understand how the murders of Ahmed and Carlos are involved either," Riley said. Half of his fries were gone now. "But the connections are there, and they are hard to refute."

I sighed. "Okay, what are the connections?" I didn't really think this Monsieur X (kind of a French twist to that one) was after Lana. But Riley must've felt he was being ignored, so I'd hear him out. I hoped this didn't mean I wasn't still getting a forged backstory from the CIA. I was kind of looking forward to that.

Riley held up one finger. "Number one, Lana had a connection to Ahmed. The Russian mob had sent her to the Middle East on two separate occasions to serve as a liaison. We don't know what she did there, but in each case she entered Ahmed's safe house and left a couple of hours later."

I nodded. "Okay, so that makes sense. The Arabs love blonde, blue-eyed bimbos. I can see where that might work. But maybe she didn't even meet with Ahmed. They wouldn't risk exposing him like that. Chances are she met with underlings."

Riley shook his head. His fries were gone, and he was now eating mine. I pretended I didn't see that. "Ahmed's always had a thing for blondes. He went through a slew of European prostitutes over the years. Hell, I almost bleached your hair and sent you in there once."

"What? You almost what?" I stared at him. Part of me thought, *Well, you wished you'd been hot enough to be used for sex*, but the other part of me wanted to strangle my former handler with a bar rag. A dirty, greasy one.

"I didn't *do* it." Riley waved me off like this was no big deal. "I just said I thought about it." Like that was okay.

"I told you," I growled through clenched teeth, "that I didn't do stuff like that. Don't you remember that I specifically told you the 'sex-for-secrets' thing was a total no-go?" I was pissed. I'd always thought of our working relationship as a partnership. I had no idea he thought he could dress me up and whore me out anytime he wanted.

"I didn't do it, Merry." He rolled his eyes like he didn't know what the big deal was. "It's a non-issue."

I glared at him for a few moments. Toyed with the thought of killing him with a straw right here. Straws make excellent weapons. You just need to put your thumb over one end and it'll go through an eyeball like nothing.

"It's not a non-issue," I hissed.

"Fine. Whatever," he said, throwing his hands up in the air. "We can argue about that later. The important thing is that Lana met with him, and may have had sex with him, on two occasions."

"You thought you controlled me so thoroughly that you could just send me out to sleep with anyone." He reached out for one of my fries, and I yanked the basket out of reach.

Riley sighed. "I didn't do it, Wrath. I thought of it for, like, about one second, but I didn't act on it."

I folded my arms across my chest. "The fact you thought about it is bad enough."

"Let's deal with this later. We need to focus on the task at hand."

"Which is? That Herr X (German was definitely more sinister) is after Lana? You still haven't proved your point," I said with a hint of total hostility. I wasn't going to let him off the hook, but we needed go over whatever it was he thought he had.

"Wait for it." He held up two fingers. "Number two—I found flight records showing Lana made six different trips to Medellín over the last two years."

"That doesn't necessarily mean she met Carlos the Armadillo. Maybe she was on vacation." I said that, but to be honest, now I was starting to wonder. I mean, who goes to Medellín on vacation?

Riley nodded. "Yes, but each time, she took the same taxi out to the country—to the same location as Carlos' third home. The place where he goes with his mistresses." He sat back in the booth and loosened his tie a little. "I had Espinoza, our South American guy, check into it. Lana always used the same cab driver from the same cab company. Always." What was with him repeating things to me? Did he think I was an idiot? I needed to talk to him about that.

"Espinoza is good…" I murmured. He was used for everything down there. "But why would Lana be so stupid as to use the same cab and driver every time?" I felt a small nibble of doubt in my stomach. Until just recently I'd thought Lana stupid enough to do something like that.

Riley ignored me. "And the third thing is that we found a connection between Lana and Midori."

My head snapped up at that. "Lana told me that Midori was a real bitch. She didn't say anything more. I chalked it up to those rumors we'd heard about the Russian mob and the Yakuza."

He nodded. "They had the closest connection of all. Lana was holed up with a highly-placed Russian official back in 2012, for about nine months. Midori was his aunt."

My eyes grew wide. "What? Are you serious? Midori had family? I'd heard that she ate her young."

"So you see—we have a bit of a problem here." Riley sat back, ignoring my jab. His basket was completely empty. He'd eaten all of it. I thought of warning him that he should get some antacid for tonight but changed my mind.

"Lana!" I cried.

"What is it?" Riley asked.

"I left her at home. Alone!"

CHAPTER TWELVE

———

Riley threw money on the table, and we ran out to his SUV and climbed in. His car was faster, and I had the keys to the house. I dialed the cell Riley had bought Lana before he'd dumped her at my place, but there was no answer.

"If she's the target, I left her alone...practically gift-wrapped!" I shouted. How could I be so stupid? I dialed again. No answer.

"We weren't gone that long," Riley said. "She's probably just in the shower or something." But he didn't sound like he believed that.

It took six minutes to reach the house. We roared up into the driveway and ran to the front door. I fumbled with the keys until I got the right one. Then we burst into the house.

"Lana!" I shouted as I ran back to the bedrooms. Riley went into the kitchen. We met in the hallway.

"She's not here!" I said. Riley nodded. The house wasn't that big. If she was there, we'd have found her.

"I'll search her room. You try her phone," I said over my shoulder as I took off down the hall.

Her door was open. All of her stuff was still inside. There was no sign of a struggle. It looked like she'd just gone for a walk with every intention of coming back.

I called Kelly. It was a slim chance, but maybe, for some inexplicable reason, Lana had gone off to visit with her new friend. Kelly answered and told me she was at work. Robert wouldn't be home either. It was a dead end.

"Any luck?" Riley stuck his head in the room.

"No. You?" There was a slight hint of panic in my voice.

"Nothing."

"This is all my fault." I looked around the room again. "I should never have left her alone. I should've brought her with me."

Riley put his hands on my shoulders and looked me in the eye. "This is not your fault. And I didn't want you to bring her with you. I needed to bounce these ideas off of you before approaching Lana."

"Yes, but you should've given me a hint, and I could've parked her at Kelly's or something." I wasn't really mad at Riley. I was mad at myself. And a little surprised. A few days ago I would've done anything to get rid of the Russian. Now I was worried about her and wanted her back. Did that make sense? Yes, because she's great with my Girl Scouts, and I kinda sorta enjoyed having her around a little bit. Believe it—no one's more surprised about this than me.

"Who else did she meet here?" Riley asked. "Besides Kelly?"

I felt a twinge as he said my best friend's name, but I ignored it. "Well, she helped with my Girl Scout troop today. The girls loved her. But I don't think we should put second-graders on the watch list."

"Has she called anyone? Acted weird?" Riley asked.

"I have no idea. She's in her room a lot. She takes really long showers and spends an hour on her hair afterwards. As for weird, I don't think so. Do you think maybe she thought of this too and fled? Would she do that?" I asked.

Riley shook his head. "I don't think so. You don't seem to think any of her stuff is missing." His gaze swept the room, taking in clothes, the air mattress, cosmetics. "How did she go from a woman with nothing but a dress and stilettos to having so much stuff?"

"I took her shopping." I said. "You'll be getting a bill." Everything seemed to be there—I didn't see anything missing.

Where did she go? And how long had she been gone? I was really worried about her. Now that Riley thought she was the target of Overlord X (Yes! That's the one!), all I could think about was making sure she was alright. I would never forgive myself if anything happened to Lana.

The front door slammed. Riley and I raced down the hall to find one giggly blonde with none other than *my* Detective. Lana had her arm looped over his, and Rex was clearly enjoying her company.

Now I wanted her gone. All concern for her safety flew right out the window. She'd taken things too far.

"Where have you been?" I asked, my voice probably showing more anger than I would've liked.

Lana's eyes grew wide as she saw the two of us. "Oh! Merry! Riley! I didn't know you were back! How is Grandmother?" Ah. The old grandmother routine. I'd played this game before.

Riley didn't miss a beat, "She's fine. She asked about you."

"We came back to get you. Riley thought seeing you would cheer her up." I tried very hard to keep the malice out of my voice. I failed miserably.

"Sorry Ms. Wrath," Rex said. "Your cousin came over to borrow some sugar."

I'll just bet she did.

"I don't have any," Rex continued, "but she told me all about your family. I guess I didn't realize you were Russian on your mother's side." He looked at Lana. "Second generation, was it?"

Lana nodded. "You are so smart to remember that!" Her flirtation was off the charts. Funny how not two hours ago she was saying to my face that Rex liked me. I guess you can't change a zebra's stripes. Lana was going to hit on any man unless you dangled cute little girls in front of her. I remembered that Kelly said she had been snuggling up to her husband.

"Thanks for walking her back," I said tightly, "but we need to have a family discussion."

"About Grandma's end-of-life plan," Riley said smoothly. What, Fake Grandma was dying now?

He held out his hand, and Rex shook it. "Nice to see you again, Detective Ferguson."

"No problem." He turned and opened the front door. "And thanks for the yearbook, Lana. I thought Ms. Wrath was going to bring it over, but it gave me the opportunity to meet you." He shut the door behind him and was gone. I waited for him to cross the street before yelling.

"*You* gave him the yearbook???" I growled. "*I* was going to give him the yearbook!"

Lana looked upset. "Did I not do the right thing?"

Riley looked at her levelly, "Lana—you can't go off and talk to the police. They're investigating Merry. And now you've invented a whole family you'll have to brief us on."

I thought about that. A family where I was related to Riley and Lana. Seemed kind of like a nightmare. Especially now that Lana was flirting with my "boyfriend."

"I worked on that thing forever! It was my excuse to go over there!" I pouted.

Riley turned to me with a strange look in his eyes. "Why did you want to go see the Detective?" Hmmmm…either he was worried I'd botch everything, or he was jealous that I liked him. I didn't know whether to be insulted or happy.

"Doesn't really matter, now, does it? Especially now that Lana has her sights set on him."

Lana looked at me in surprise. "But Merry! I…"

Riley held his hand up. "Save it. You know, maybe that's not a bad idea…Lana could seduce Rex and keep an eye on his investigation. She could firm up the family thing which would defuse his quest to find out if Merry is local and maybe throw a few red herrings into the investigation."

He really needed to quit saying *red herring*. I made a mental note to buy him a thesaurus and shove it down his throat. That was, after I killed Lana for going after my soon-to-be spouse.

Lana shook her head. "Those days are over. I don't want to seduce anyone for secrets."

I glared at her. So her interest in Rex wasn't professional. She just had the hots for him. Which was much worse. I was an idiot to think Lana and I could be friends. The minute I meet a guy, she moves in with her blonde hair and boobs.

This was getting out of hand. "Lana has to go," I said.

Both of them stared at me.

"This isn't working out. And now she's messing with the local police. I think it's time for my 'cousin' to go back to Russia."

I should've said I didn't like her going after Rex. I should've stepped on her neck and held her down until she explained herself. Hell, in the first place I should've refused to take her in. But I was too pissed off for a discussion that would basically turn into me screaming incoherently. She'd only make some excuse or lie to me anyway.

Lana burst into tears and ran down the hall to her room, slamming the door behind her.

Riley stepped closer to me. He was frowning. "Look, I know she complicated things just now, but Lana stays."

I shook my head. "The Slutty Roommate goes. It's my house. And I don't work for you anymore."

"You can't do that," Riley said. "You're being investigated by the CIA and the Feds. This local thing is just the tip of the iceberg. The media gave up, but the two government agencies won't. You're in it whether you like it or not, and you need my help. Lana stays."

"You can't be serious," I said, arms folded across my chest to form a barrier between us. He was standing pretty close to me. "You can't tell me what to do."

"What are you going to do? Go and confess to the cop? Confess to the world? It won't help you. You'll have to move, and you'll try to start over, but it'll be worse because you'll never feel safe. I'm trying to help you."

Riley put his hands on my shoulders. He looked deep into my eyes. I wanted to believe him. I wanted to think he could just make this go away. And for some reason, I wanted to think he was jealous of Rex.

Wait…did I just think that? Why would I care what Riley thought? I held his gaze. There was something else in his eyes…other than professional concern. Or was I just hoping to see that in there?

He was handsome. He was smart. And he smelled wonderful. I felt the tug of his sex appeal drawing me toward him.

"But…but…" I floundered, grasping for a counter-argument.

Riley put his index finger on my lips. His voice softened. "But nothing. I just want to help you, Merry. Let me help you."

And then he kissed me. On the lips. His mouth was completely on mine. I didn't think there'd be fireworks like that, but in my head I heard them explode over and over. The sensation was tingly and zapped me all the way to my core. Just as I was about to climb him like a tree, he pushed himself away.

"Sorry." He ran a hand through his hair and looked a little shaken. "I don't know what came over me."

I just stood there, blinking like an idiot.

Riley cleared his voice and straightened his tie. He walked to the door and opened it. "Lana stays, Wrath. End of discussion." And out the door he went.

CHAPTER THIRTEEN

———

I stood there for I don't know how long, staring at the doorway. Riley had kissed me. And I liked it. Really, *really* liked it. What the hell was going on? Hey! He walked out on me! I continued to stand, staring out the door, replaying things in my head. Riley Andrews of the CIA had kissed me. And I hadn't been kissed like that since…well, it's been a really long time. In fact, I don't think anyone had ever kissed me like that.

That was a depressing thought. It snapped me out of my trance. I locked the door and turned out the lights.

I got ready for bed, ignoring the sobbing Russian in the next room. A tiny, obnoxious voice inside said I should try to talk to her. Make her explain herself. But did I really want to hear it? No. She should think about what she'd done and stew over it a while. If I still felt like I needed answers—I'd ask them while she was packing her stuff in the morning.

I shoved the thoughts of Lana's betrayal out of my mind and started thinking about the kiss. Riley's kiss. I couldn't fall asleep, wondering what it meant. Was Riley attracted to me? Or did he kiss me to shut me up and get his way? I couldn't tell. I'd worked with him for years and always assumed he was on the take where women were concerned.

Had he ever had a serious relationship? I couldn't think of any. But then, I didn't know how he spent his personal time. I guess I always thought he went surfing and overused words like *red herring*. Of course, in his down time he'd have tons of lady friends. Even in the future I saw him

as the guy in the nursing home who had a different girlfriend for each night of the week.

There'd been soooooooo many women. It was impossible to count. In fact, I couldn't attach a name to any one of them. Thinking of Lana, I wondered if Riley had seduced those women purely to get intel. Is that why he did it? I'd written him off a long time ago as just a Casanova—a handsome guy who slept with women because he could. But was that accurate?

And was I just another woman falling for it? I hated to think that was true. I'd avoided using sex as a tradecraft tool, but maybe that was Riley's thing. Like Lana.

I was seriously pissed at her, and a little hurt. She'd used whoring to get what she wanted her whole life. In fact, she lied for her living. It was possible she'd lied to Kelly and me about the orphanage thing. Now I was even angrier. She'd manipulated us completely, making us feel sorry for her! And we'd fallen for it. Kelly—forgiving her for sleazing up to her husband, and me for, well, everything. The fact that I'd believed her was the worst. I'd been a good spook. I saw through cover stories and lies. How had I missed this?

Grumbling, I got up and started pacing the room. Great, now I couldn't sleep. I glared at the door. The sobbing had ended. Maybe the boyfriend-who-wasn't-really-my-boyfriend-yet stealer was asleep. She'd better sleep well because tomorrow, I was moving her ass out, and the CIA was getting a huge, obviously inflated bill from me.

As soon as she was gone I'd figure out what to do. Hell, if Riley was right and she'd been the target all along, maybe the trail of dead terrorists would follow her, and everything could go right back to the way it was.

I felt a small pang at the thought of Riley leaving. Of him going back to Langley. Maybe it was for the best. Falling for someone like Riley was out of the question. Rex was a much better bet. A nice guy. More stable. And he lived here.

Rex. Why wasn't I angry with him for getting all gooey around Lana? It was clear he couldn't help himself—a

knockout blonde fawning over him—who could resist that? Then I realized that's what Riley had done to me.

No, Rex was a safe bet. And I was attracted to him. Why had Lana done it? Why did she take the yearbook over? She knew that I wanted to do that. Clearly she couldn't resist. I didn't need someone like that in my life. In my house.

I had to shake off this investigation if I wanted Rex to think of me as something other than a suspect. But if Riley was right, and this was about Lana—her moving out of here would take care of that.

Riley's theory barged its way into my brain. It was out there, for sure. It was hard to believe that all of this was for Lana. She did have the connections though. But so did I—to Ahmed and Carlos at least. Not to Midori. Lana had the connection to Midori.

That was the only thing that kept me from dismissing the idea outright. The Agency had proof that Lana had been personally connected to these three baddies. It was possible that someone found out the CIA was going to set me up as her babysitter. There'd been leaks to information like this before. Why not now?

If that were true, then I was really pissed. The CIA was dragging me…an employee they'd let go, into their bullshit. Making my life…a life that was just starting to get interesting…a nightmare. I didn't deserve that. I'd given up a personal life when I'd worked for them. I'd sacrificed everything just to do their bidding. Now I had a chance to make up for my lack of, well, any life, and they wanted to drag me in again. Talk about unfair.

And yet the tremor of doubt remained. I just couldn't shake it—no matter how beneficial it was for me. Something wasn't right about Riley's theory of Lana being the target. I just couldn't put my finger on it. I toyed with the possible connections until I finally climbed back into bed and fell asleep.

* * *

THUNK. THUNK. A sound roused me from sleep.
THUNK. There it was again. What was that? I opened my
eyes and lay very still in my bed. A few minutes passed, and
I heard nothing else. Probably Lana's foot hitting the wall
while she slept. Stupid big-foot bimbo.

THUNK. I sat up this time. It kind of sounded like
someone throwing a baseball at the side of the house.
THUNK. What the hell was that? I looked at the alarm
clock—three a.m. Without turning the lights on, I got up and
put on some shoes.

THUNK. THUNK. THUNK. The sound was always
the same. It hadn't changed in volume. Maybe a branch was
hitting the house. I listened. It was windy outside.

THUNK. Well if it was a branch, then I needed to
make it stop. There was no way I'd be able to sleep. I opened
the door and moved down the hall.

Thunk. Thunk. The sound grew softer. It must be
right outside my bedroom, but I had no windows on that wall
to check it out. There was an old oak tree right next to the
house. That had to be it.

I opened the front door and stepped outside. It was
damp. Humid. We'd had some rain. I must've slept through
it. Maybe a storm had knocked that branch loose. I moved
into the wet grass and walked around to the side of the
house. A huge pine tree stood between me and the oak, and I
made my way carefully around it. My bedroom wall faced
the street, but there was no traffic at this hour, which was
good since I was wearing Dora the Explorer jammies. I
rounded the big pine and stopped dead in my tracks at the
foot of the oak.

It wasn't a branch banging against the side of the
house. It was a body. And it was still alive. A piece of cloth
was wrapped around the head and covered the body down to
the ankles. The rope looped around the head and arms so
they were unable to move much. Legs kicked and flailed,
occasionally hitting the house. That's where the sound came
from. No other noise came from the victim—they must've
been gagged.

I ran up to the body, wrapped my arms around the legs, and lifted, supporting them with my weight so the rope wouldn't strangle him anymore. Whoever it was immediately stopped kicking. Either they were afraid that the assailant was back, or they knew I was trying to help them.

"It's going to be okay!" I shouted. They didn't respond. By now, I was pretty sure it was a woman. The legs had that shape to them that I could feel through the blanket.

I stood there, holding the body up and looking around for something to help me. A ladder would've been nice, but I thoughtlessly didn't think to put one out before going to bed, probably because I didn't own one. The body was getting heavier. Or my adrenaline was running out. I needed to do something fast.

I wondered if I could flag down a passing car. But there was no traffic. None at all. That was strange. Any car would be able to see me very clearly from the road. It was a fairly busy street—even at three a.m. there'd be a car every now and then.

If I screamed, I wasn't sure anyone would hear me. It was summer. Air conditioners were humming all over the neighborhood. No one would hear anything.

Where were the cars?

I looked up at the tree branch. The rope was just slung over it, tied to the trunk. Knots. Why did it have to be knots?

If I couldn't find something to prop the person on, I'd have to get up there and untie the knot. I looked at the rope around the body. One knot in the tree. Six knots on the victim. My best bet was the tree.

Okay, so I had to let go and work fast. I wasn't entirely sure I could do that. But there were no other options. In the time it took me to go into the house, then the garage, and come back out with something to cut the rope or put under this person, they would strangle to death.

"I'm going to have to let you go," I said. "Just for a few seconds, so I can untie the rope."

Whoever it was barely moved. I took that for approval. It must be another bad guy. The only difference was, this one was still alive.

"I want you to tighten the muscles in your neck as hard as you can. On the count of three." The body didn't move. "One, two," I paused for a second. "Three!"

I gently lowered her, and the second I let go, I scaled the tree. The knot was in a V-formation where the trunk split off into two huge branches. It was tight.

The victim started to kick a little. I'm sure the noose was starting to cut off her air. I pulled at the huge knot, but it wouldn't budge. Damn it! Did I make the wrong choice? Should I have gone inside? My stomach was around my knees, and I felt like throwing up.

"Hold on!" I shouted down, my fingers were numb as they twisted the stiff rope. I got the knot a little loose. But by now the hanging victim was really kicking. I had to make a decision quick. I dug my fingers into the little space in the knot, but the body's weight was not helping. I wasn't going to make it. This lady—whoever she was, was going to die. Right here. Right now. And there wasn't much I could do about it.

"Ms. Wrath!" A startled Rex Ferguson was running toward me. He grabbed the hanging body by the legs and held it up.

"Keep her supported! I'm trying to untie the knot!" I yelled, breathing a little more regularly. I was so grateful that Rex had showed up, I didn't have time to realize that this would only hurt the investigation.

The rope began to budge now that there was no weight on it, and with one more pull, the knot came undone. The body fell forward, and Rex caught her. The cloaked woman lay limply in his arms. Were we too late?

"Let's get her inside!" I said, and Rex followed me into my house.

We laid the person on the couch, and together we untied all the knots. When the noose was removed, I lifted the blanket off.

"Lana!" I cried. She looked bad. There were bruises on her face and an angry, red line around her neck where she'd been strangled. She was unconscious but breathing.

"We should get her to the hospital," Rex said.

I'd already dialed Kelly. She arrived in seconds and began to look Lana over.

Rex and I stood back, watching her as she listened to Lana's heartbeat and lungs.

The detective turned to me. "What is it with you and that cartoon character?" he asked, indicating the curtains.

"I like Dora..." I said absently.

Suddenly, it all seemed so ridiculous. My anger at Lana seemed totally unfair. "Is she going to be alright?" I asked Kelly.

Kelly stood and turned to us. "She's going to be okay. I don't think she needs to go to the hospital. The bruises on her face seem superficial, and there's no real damage to the throat. She's breathing normally."

Rex frowned. "Maybe we should take her to the hospital just in case?"

Kelly shrugged. "You can, certainly. But it isn't totally necessary."

I knew what she was doing. Kelly was deflecting. She knew Lana probably didn't have any insurance and that the scrutiny she'd receive in the hospital would throw more unwanted attention on me.

"I need to interview her," Rex said. "Someone tried to kill her. We need to see if she remembers anything."

"I should call Riley," I said. "He'd want to know."

Kelly smiled as I heard the sound of a car door slamming outside. "I already did. On my way here—he'll be right over." Huh. Now Kelly was calling Riley. On his personal cell. I shouldn't be weird about that. Right?

Riley came in—the door was unlocked. I thought that looked good—like he knew he was family and could do so. On the other hand, the CIA was being pretty forward with my house. I'd have to do something about that.

"Is she okay? What happened?" Riley asked. He was in a full suit, neatly pressed. He must've jumped right into it.

I thought it was best to explain exactly what happened—leaving out any CIA bits, of course. We left Kelly in the living room with Lana and went into the kitchen. I made tea. Then I told them both the whole story, from the noise outside my bedroom to Rex coming to the rescue.

"What made you come over?" Riley asked Rex. He was sizing the detective up, looking for something that screamed *fraud*.

"I thought I heard someone shouting outside," he said as he sipped his tea.

I frowned. "You heard that over the air conditioner?"

Rex shook his head. "I didn't have it on. I sleep with the windows open." He set down his cup. "I heard you shouting and looked out my window. I saw you holding Lana up. By the time I got here, you were up the tree."

Riley and I looked at each other. It sounded feasible. I did shout. And I was glad he heard me. I needed the help.

"Thank you," Riley said, "for helping my cousins."

"Are you going to tell me what's really going on?" Rex asked.

I held my breath and waited. It was up to Riley. I didn't want to bring down the wrath of the CIA on me by saying anything that could send me to prison. Or worse.

"I'm not really sure myself," Riley said smoothly. "Did you check how they got Lana out of her room in the middle of the night?"

He was changing the subject, forcing Rex to investigate. It was a good idea. The three of us ran to Lana's room.

The window was open. She'd left it unlocked. Why did she do that? A wet, muddy smear came up over the windowsill and down the wall. Someone came in from the outside. There were signs of a struggle. How did I miss hearing it? Rex walked around the room, surveying the scene.

I studied my neighbor. He was wearing a T-shirt and pajama bottoms. No cartoon characters. They were just plaid. He had slippers on his feet. They were soaked from

the wet grass. He smelled like rain and fresh air. I know I should be worrying about Lana, but I couldn't take my eyes off of Rex.

Neither could Riley. The blonde hunk was scrutinizing the brunette hunk. Trying to decide how much to tell him. Riley's eyes weren't on the room. They were on the man. They were sizing up the threat.

Kelly stuck her head in. "She's come to."

We followed her down the hallway to where Lana was sitting up. She looked like hell. Kelly had wrapped a comforter around her and had given her some tea. Lana held the cup in shaky hands. She looked at us. The bruising around her eyes was more pronounced.

Rex knelt in front of her. "Miss...Miss..." He looked at us.

"Babikova," I said. I left out the Svetlana part.

"Miss Babikova, can you tell us what happened?" His voice was so gentle. It wasn't pushy or prodding. Just asking for the facts and sort of saying it was alright if she couldn't give them.

Lana looked at me, then Riley. The fear in her eyes was agonizing. I felt horrible. I'd been so mean to her, and then I didn't even wake up during the assault. Hell, it probably looked to her like I'd let her attackers in and pointed her out.

Riley nodded, almost imperceptibly. Rex didn't see it, or he would've known something was up.

"I...I didn't see much...the light was off." She hugged the comforter around her. "I woke up to someone punching me over and over in the face." She flinched. It must've hurt. "I think I was unconscious when they hung me in the tree."

"Did your assailant speak? Was there more than one?" Rex asked.

Lana shook her head. "He didn't speak. I think there was only one, but I'm not sure." She didn't add anything to that. She was a good spy. She knew what to offer and what to withhold...if she was withholding that is.

Rex stood up and nodded. "I'm going to have to call this in. The crime scene guys will be here. They'll want to take pictures of your injuries." He looked down at his pajamas and slippers. "I'll run home and change while we're waiting."

Lana nodded. I did too. Riley said nothing. I watched as Rex excused himself. I wondered if I shouldn't go with him and maybe help with his shirt or something. I could use a distraction right now.

"Anything else, Lana?" Riley asked. "Before the detective comes back?" He put emphasis on the word detective. He didn't want us to forget that Rex was a cop and that this would make things harder for us.

"Maybe we should come clean?" I interrupted. I wanted to buy Lana some time before she told Riley anything more. "I mean, we all work for the government. Us, the CIA, the Feds, the local cops. We're all the good guys."

Riley shook his head. "I'm under strict orders from Langley not to let the locals handle this. They think it's a matter of national security."

Something about that sentence wasn't right. "Okay…then why aren't there more officials here? Why just you?" I asked. It was a valid question. Why was Riley the only one handling this if it was considered a threat to national security?

Riley frowned and shot me a look. "Not now. We need to get any info out of Lana before Rex comes back."

"I did see something. Something else," Lana said as her eyes darted to the door. "The guy who beat me up had a ring on. It's a very specific ring." She swallowed hard.

"You'd seen it before?" Riley asked.

Lana nodded. "I've seen rings like that many times. It was given to FSB members only."

Riley frowned.

"The former KGB," I whispered. "Crap."

CHAPTER FOURTEEN

———

I got dressed while a forensics team crawled all over Lana's bedroom and the side of the house. It's a small thing, but I didn't want them to see me in my Dora jammies. Instead, I slipped on a white T-shirt and pair of shorts. Kelly stayed with Lana. I think she felt a little protective of her.

We watched in silence as the team worked. Rex and I gave them our shoes so they could distinguish our footprints outside from the kidnappers'. Riley said nothing. Kelly stayed to answer questions on her involvement. One by one we were interviewed. It was all standard operating procedure. Nothing out of the ordinary.

My mind was racing. FSB. The Russian Foreign Intelligence Service. It was them? Riley was right? I'm sure he thought so. And it made sense that the FSB would come after Lana—after all she did spy on them…for me.

But why involve Ahmed, Carlos, and Midori? If they were going to kill Lana—and wear a ring that broadcast who they were—why kill the other three? What purpose did that serve? Was it all to frame me? To cover up that the real target was Lana?

The ring. Why wear the ring, letting us know who they were? Maybe they thought she'd be too terrified to tell us.

I needed to talk to Riley, but that would be impossible until everyone else had left. I wondered if the FSB still had agents in the area. They were probably watching the house. I would. I'd want to make sure my victim died before leaving if I were them.

If they were watching, then they would know, if they hadn't figured it out already, that Lana had survived. And if they came all this way and went to all this trouble, they'd stay until they were sure she was dead. It was how they worked. They'd come too far and wasted too many resources to fail.

The police took photos of Lana's bruises. It must've been the only time in her life she'd taken a bad photo—and even then she looked gorgeous. She also looked scared. She'd worked with FSB and knew what they were capable of.

Rex approached. He was in a suit, just like Riley. How did men throw on a suit like that and look so good doing it?

"They found construction barricades across the street a few blocks in both directions. That's why there wasn't any traffic going by when this happened," Rex said.

"I wondered about that," I said. Obviously, the FSB didn't want anyone driving by, attempting to save Lana. They wanted her dead, like Ahmed and the others. Thankfully, she was smart enough to kick my bedroom wall.

Rex added, "We're not going to *insist* that Ms. Babikova go to the hospital, but I think she should." He watched as Riley shook his head. "Alright. Well, we are going to put the house under surveillance for a couple of days, just in case whoever did this comes back. I'll come back over in the afternoon to see if there's anything else Ms. Babikova remembers later."

He could rim the perimeter with land mines and rabid Dobermans—it wouldn't matter. This wasn't some random murderer. These were trained professional killers hiding beneath a government flag. A Russian flag. It seemed unfair to let Rex think it was just a simple, Midwestern murder attempt. But then, maybe he wasn't thinking that.

Rex handed me a card. "My cell number. That's the best way to reach me. If anything, and I mean *anything* happens, don't hesitate to call."

Oooh! He gave me his cell number! That's got to mean something, right? Like he's *interested*. Right? My

stomach dropped a little when I thought how he'd seemed interested in Lana yesterday. *No*, I shook my head—which probably looked ridiculous to those around me who were watching. *Rex was just being polite*. He didn't really flirt back. He probably didn't know what to do with the blonde bangle dangling from his arm. Yes, that was it, I told myself, and went back to being excited about getting his number.

The forensics team had packed up and were heading for their vehicles. It was dawn, and everything that had been dark as pitch was now bathed in lavender light. Somewhere in this neighborhood, assassins were hiding. Watching. It was better motivation for staying awake than any form of caffeine.

Riley saw Rex to the door. He shook his hand. "Thanks for everything Detective. I really appreciate it."

Rex nodded at him, then turned to look at me. "You did great, Ms. Wrath. Nice job."

I blushed. "You can call me Merry, Detective. We're neighbors too."

Rex smiled. It was the kind of smile you wanted to curl up inside of. "Then you should definitely call me Rex." He winked. I melted. He left.

I made Lana some eggs for breakfast. I at least knew how to do that. Riley sat with her in the other room. I thought about what I should do next. Lana needed to know, if she hadn't figured it out already, that FSB may have been behind this all along. Riley should move her to a safer place. I needed to go on a vacation. Under an assumed name. To a country I'd never been to before. Which was a very short list that was unfortunately made up of only Greenland and Papua New Guinea.

"Here you go." I handed Lana a plate of scrambled eggs, toast, and a fork. "Do you feel like eating?"

Lana nodded and took a few bites. She swallowed some more tea. Riley and I watched her as she ate the whole thing. I could bet that her mind was racing like ours was. Interesting how you could put three spies in the same room and know, without them talking, that they were all thinking

completely different things about the same problem. It was just a given.

"Lana," Riley said quietly, "can you remember anything else?"

She looked at Riley. Then she looked at me. She held my gaze so long I had to look away. Did she wonder why I didn't come to help her last night?

"I didn't hear anything, Lana. I swear! I had no idea until you woke me up kicking the side of the house." I felt terrible. Horrible. Worse than horrible. Horriblester.

"It's okay, Merry," she said. "It happened pretty fast. I didn't have much opportunity to fight back." Her words hit me like arrows. Arrows tipped in curare and lemon juice.

"Sorry," I said softly.

"Lana..." Riley turned her attention back to himself. "Have you seen any FSB around? Was there any sign they were in town?"

I stifled a laugh. The idea of Russian spies trying to blend in, in small town Iowa, was ridiculous. If they'd been there, we would've noticed.

Lana's eyes went up and to...the right. "No. I never saw anything."

She was lying. The woman was obviously terrified. Their intimidation had worked on her. If I'd been a better friend, maybe she would've confided in me.

Riley stood up. "All right. I need to call this in." He looked out the window. "Looks like Rex moves fast."

I joined him at the window to see a black and white sitting at the curb. Subtle.

"Small town cops won't scare off the FSB," I said.

Riley raised an eyebrow and studied me. "I'll only be gone a couple of hours. I need to get back to the hotel and make a few calls. Then I'll be back." He grabbed my hands in his and winked. "You'll be okay until then."

I watched as he walked out the door. Two winks in one day by two gorgeous men. It may not sound like much, but it's been a bit of a dry spell for me this past...well...lifetime. I'd take what I can get.

"Merry?" Lana's voice sounded pitiful behind me. I joined her on the couch.

"I didn't mean to upset you yesterday." Her eyes grew watery, and her lower lip was quivering. Remember how I said I couldn't handle it when my Girl Scouts did this? Same was true for Lana.

I hugged her, gently of course. "It's okay. I know that now." I still thought a little bit that she was on the make with Rex, but I could overlook that. What I really wanted to know was why she was lying to us about having no clue Russian assassins were in town. But I still felt guilty about not being there for her, and she needed some rest. I could interrogate her later.

"You can sleep in my room," I said. "I'll call Rex and see if I can go ahead and clean up yours."

"Okay," she said in a small voice. I watched as she stood up and handed me her plate and tea cup. Then she walked down the hall to my room and closed the door.

I sat back on the couch. From where I was, I could see the police car in front of the house. The cop inside was drinking coffee. I was tired just looking at him. Yawning, I realized I hadn't gotten much sleep either. But with Lana out and the Russians probably watching the house, I needed to stay awake.

I'd only ever dealt with the Russian Foreign Intelligence Agency through Lana. I'd been stationed in Kiev and made only a dozen trips across the border to meet with her in Moscow and St. Petersburg. I knew what the agents looked like but had no up-close experience with them. They tended to wear expensive Italian suits and shoes, which would stand out like a neon yellow sperm whale in a public fountain here.

I wished I had a dog. Walking a dog was the perfect way to do surveillance of a neighborhood. Going jogging was out—I couldn't run ten feet without quitting. And if they've been watching the house, they'd know that I never so much as walked around for exercise.

But I'd feel better if I did some recon, just to play Spot-the-Spies so I'd know how many were out there. On the

other hand, if I left, they might move in. These guys weren't afraid of a local cop. They'd probably kill him. No, if they saw I was gone, they'd definitely try to finish what they'd started last night.

Chances were they'd strike after dark. Making a spectacle of themselves was not in their modus operandi. They'd hit us hard at night, then get clear of town before dawn. They broke in last night and did everything they could to keep it covert. Clearly they wouldn't launch a full scale attack in broad daylight.

They tried to avoid me last night—maybe they were setting me up for the fall, thinking I'd be blamed for Lana's death. Maybe they were after both of us. After all—I'd been Lana's handler.

Another thought crossed my mind. Why didn't they kill Lana outright? Why leave her dangling and alive? Seemed to me they'd just as easily have slit her throat and leave. But they didn't. Why not? Were they worried about being seen and decided to make a break for it?

Ahmed and Midori were dead when I stumbled upon them. But Carlos was still alive. This was getting me no where. Maybe I was overthinking it.

I should just wait for Riley to get back. It really was up to him to figure this out and come up with the plan. He was the professional now, not me. I needed to let him handle this. But the urge to get involved was kind of tough. Old habits, especially the ones you liked, die hard. I didn't want to retire. My own government made me.

Rubbing my eyes, I went into the kitchen to make a very strong pot of tea. The caffeine would do me some good. I drank two cups before I remembered: *the suitcase.* I smiled. Maybe I wasn't so out of it after all. But first, I needed to talk to Rex.

"Detective…I mean, Rex?" I asked as he answered his cell on the first ring. I got a little thrill when he answered. After all—this was our first private phone call together. Clearly it was time for me to consider bridesmaids dresses.

"Ms. Wrath?" Of course he answered that way. He was in the office and on duty. "Has something happened?" Rex sounded alert, ready to pounce. It was hot.

"I just wanted to know if I can clean up Lana's room. She's sleeping in my bedroom. I thought I'd put everything back so she isn't traumatized when she wakes up."

"Go ahead. We took photos and had everyone in there. It's pretty obvious what happened. You can clean it up."

"Thanks. I'll talk to you later then," I said.

I heard a smile in his voice. The same one he'd given me earlier. "You're welcome. Looking forward to it."

Ooooh! He was looking forward to it! I tried to hide my glee as I went down into the basement. First things first. Secure the perimeter, clean up Lana's room, *then* date the detective.

I only used the basement for storage. My washer and dryer were in the upstairs bathroom in a closet, so I never needed to go down there. It was an unfinished basement—all cement and spiderwebs and visible beams. I switched on the bare, exposed light bulb and went to the corner shelves. Pulling out a bunch of old paint cans, I felt for the case. I found it and carried it back upstairs.

It was dusty, and I thought I spotted some mouse droppings. I guess I really did need a cat. I set it on the breakfast bar and wiped it down. It was a small, leather case from the '50's I'd gotten at a thrift shop for five dollars on my first week on the job. The leather creaked as I opened it.

Perfect.

Some people bought souvenirs of all the places they traveled to. I collected all the tools I'd used. The ear piece I'd used in Malaysia…the pack of tampons that held a hidden camera from Brazil…the tiny bobby pins that doubled as extra secure door locks that I'd used in Qatar…and much more. These were my souvenirs.

By the way—the box of tampons with the hidden camera was one of my favorites. I've never met a man who would touch it—so it always went uninvestigated. In fact, I think we need more spy stuff disguised as feminine hygiene

products. I think a douche box with a hidden gun inside would be perfect. Of course, that would only work for a female spy…

Oh sure, I was supposed to turn stuff like this in when I left the agency. That's why I didn't use the agency's Halliburton metal briefcases. They would've confiscated that. No one ever touched this suitcase that I told them had been my grandmother's when she went to boarding school at the convent. (*Pssst*—my grandmother never went to a boarding school, and if she had ever been in a convent I was pretty sure she'd have burst into flame. Grandma had some authority issues.)

Why did I keep it if I was never planning to use this stuff again? Sentimental value mostly. I thought that someday I'd buy one of those display pieces, the ones people use for those weird little porcelain statues or china, and put this stuff in there. That reminded me—I needed to buy a display case—in addition to getting a cat.

When I did get a house, I thought people might find it weird to see I kept things like bobby pins and tampon boxes in a glass display case—so until I had a better idea, the case was hidden in the basement. Among the spiders and mice. My argument for getting a cat was definitely shaping up to be a good one.

I picked carefully through everything, the laser sights that looked like a contact lens case, the can of Diet Coke that took pictures when you tilted it up to drink, my disguise kit…until I found the security alarm system. The orange iPod Nano and its docking station were one of the best inventions Langley put out. Most travelers brought mp3 players with them to make cold, impersonal hotel rooms seem more like home. No one ever suspected it, especially when teamed up with a set of earbuds and the speaker you docked the iPod on.

It worked wirelessly. When you plugged the iPod into the speaker, it cast a five thousand square foot perimeter that alerted you to intruders, based on music selections. For example, if a raccoon or anything crawling on all fours entered, "Rocky Raccoon" by The Beatles played. For the

two-legged animals that wanted to kill you in your sleep, you got "Brahms' Lullaby."

I never figured out how to change the music. It was weird that classical played when a human approached. But maybe the lab thought an intruder would dismiss classical music. It didn't really matter, because it worked. Saved my life once in Budapest. An assassin tried to slip into my hotel room. I'd heard the Brahms' and took him out with a salad fork before he even saw me. Fortunately, room service hadn't come up to claim my dishes yet.

I picked through the case and found one or two other things I might need, set them on the counter, and closed the case. Time to get to work. With a little bit of luck, some extra batteries, and a screwdriver—no one would get to us today.

CHAPTER FIFTEEN

———

I spent the morning setting up the equipment. Bobby pins were inserted into every window as extra locks, and the iPod was set up to alarm the house a few feet into the yard in all directions.

Now I just needed weapons. I didn't have anything but a steak knife. One steak knife. I hadn't really thought I'd need lethal weapons once I retired. I'm pretty damn good in a fist fight and have a few martial arts moves they taught me at the academy. But I'm even better with a pistol.

The only problem was the waiting period. You needed to go and buy the gun, fill out the paperwork, and come back three days later to fill out more paperwork before you could pick it up. I didn't have that kind of time. If I were to hazard a guess, I'd say the Russians would be back tonight to finish what they started. And they wouldn't take the time to frame me for it. This job was supposed to have been done yesterday, so they'd most likely break down the door and shoot us in our beds. It was messy, but they couldn't afford another mistake.

Kelly was the only other person I really knew in town, and she didn't have so much as a shotgun, which was weird with her living in Iowa and all. I was pretty sure neither Riley nor Rex would lend me their service pieces. Riley knew I could handle it, but Rex had no idea about my past. He'd think it was an impulse thing, and he'd assume I had no training. Asking him wouldn't work.

And until Riley got back, I couldn't leave the house. I was all that stood between Lana and the FSB. It wasn't enough. Driving to Weapons R Us (if it existed, which by the way would be very cool) or anywhere else and leaving Lana alone was out of the question. I couldn't count on the cop outside to be the first and only line of defense.

Which meant I'd have to come up with something lethal from whatever I had. Theoretically, I could kill the first guy through the door and use his gun on the others. But that was a crapshoot if I wasn't able to take him out. I didn't like crapshoots.

I checked the garage first. A bunch of tools came with the house when I'd bought it. I thought nothing of it at the time, since I could afford to hire people to fix stuff for me. But since I needed something, I figured this would be a good time to go through things and see what I had.

The old man who'd lived here before had taken a lot of care of his tools before he died. He'd had no family, so they stayed with the house. There was a workbench along the back wall with all kinds of shelves. I started there.

The first thing I found was a giant wrench. It was extremely heavy and the length of my arm. Perfect for bashing a man's skull in. I set it aside as a *yes*. Hanging on the wall were two hammers—a large sledge and a small claw hammer. I took both of those too. I sorted through boxes of nails, screws, and washers till I found a case filled with screw drivers. I took the medium sized flat-tip and put it with the hammers and wrench. On a good piece of luck, I found a whetstone and put it with the screwdriver. So far so good, but I needed something I could use from a distance.

I'd gone through almost everything before I found it…a nail gun. I'd never used one before, but how hard could it be? I pulled it from the box, and after finding the right sized nails, I plugged it in. There was an old block of wood in the corner on the floor. I picked that up and aiming the nail gun at it, fired.

I'd need to be fairly close. The nail went in but it didn't shoot a projectile like a bullet from a gun. And it had to be plugged in. That might be a problem. But I felt a little

bit better having something with the word *gun* in the name, so I decided to add it.

Carrying everything into the house and kitchen, I dumped the stuff on the counter. I'd have to stash each of these in just the right place. The points of entry were the garage door to the house, the kitchen door, and the front door. No matter what I did, those could all be kicked in fairly easily. There was no time to buy ironwork for them— and that kind of thing, while at home in a bad neighborhood in L.A., looked weirdly out of place here.

I also had to consider the windows in each bedroom, the living room, and kitchen. I was pretty sure even I couldn't get through the basement windows, so I'd leave those for now. I got some paper and a pencil and drew a sketch of the house.

It was nice getting to do this again. Well, nice and scary, because some big nasty bad guys were going to attack and try to kill us. But nice nonetheless. It was also nice to be busy with something to do. This past year had been pretty dull.

I put the nail gun in the living room. The outlet was on the wall near the front door, but it could also cover the kitchen entrance into the hallway and the garage entrance through the kitchen. Since I could fire multiple nails, that was the best location for staving off attacks from the three entrances.

I put the steak knife…the one steak knife…on the counter in the kitchen, under a dishtowel. It would look more natural there, and I'd have quick access. The large sledge would be a problem. It would have to go someplace where I could swing it. My house was small. The living room and kitchen were the only places large enough. I thought about taking it back out to the garage but then realized if they came in through the back door there, they could use it to break down the door to the kitchen.

I set it in the hallway, within reach of both rooms. It still worried me, because I didn't want it used against us. But in a bad situation I'd need it, so I left it. That left me with the big wrench, claw hammer, and the flat-tipped screwdriver. I

wetted the whetstone and started sharpening the screwdriver while I thought about this.

I needed to put something in each bedroom. The windows had been locked down, backed up by the bobby pins. But the bad guys could just smash through the glass. It would make noise and possibly alert Rex across the street, but they were probably desperate. If they'd be thoughtful enough to provide us with a schedule, I'd know exactly when they'd attack, and I could stash Lana in the bathroom. There were no windows there, and she could lie in the tub with some protection against bullets.

But sadly, FSB couldn't be counted on to call me and make an appointment, so I'd have to figure this out on my own. I looked down at my hands, and butterflies flew around my stomach. A screwdriver, wrench, and two hammers. That was all I had for the bedrooms. What was I thinking? I set the tools on the floor in the hall between the two bedrooms.

I still needed to clean up Lana's room. The solution might come to me while cleaning, and Riley would probably show up before I had to decide. I got some rags and solvent and went into her room.

The police had shut and locked the window, but the curtain was open and the mud was still there. My rattled nerves were replaced by guilt. I'd been so tired when I crashed that I didn't hear the struggle in the next room. But then, there was a closet, hallway, and two walls between us, and they'd muffled the sound. The glass hadn't broken, so I didn't hear that. And there was no window on the side where they hung Lana. The logic that I wouldn't have heard anything was sound, but it didn't help.

I scrubbed the mud off the wall under the window. That made me feel a little better. It was like washing away what had happened. I got the muddy footprints out of the carpet next and then made Lana's bed. As I did I noticed a little stuffed bear no larger than my hand. It had fallen on the floor. I picked it up. The label was in Russian. The dark brown fur was worn, and it was missing an ear. She'd had this a long time. Maybe since the orphanage.

Where had it come from? She showed up in a skin tight dress and a pair of shoes. Maybe she'd had a purse. No, I'd remember that. Hell, she probably hid it between those huge boobs of hers. I could imagine she didn't want anyone to see it.

I was just about to set it down when my spy sensor went off in my brain. Why wasn't I more suspicious here? I was getting too lazy. The bear could've come from anywhere. I'd never seen it before. Did the FSB drop it to spy on us? It would be just like them to do that.

I turned it over in my hands but couldn't find a zipper. I found a little scam at the bear's neck. Aha! They thought they were really getting one over on me. I slipped out of my room and took the bear to the kitchen for a pair of scissors. At the kitchen counter, I carefully snipped the dark brown threads until I could pull the head completely off. Sawdust spilled out onto the counter as I shook the now limp stuffed animal to see what fell out. Nothing. Wait! I saw a little something stuck in one of the arms. I reached in with my fingers and pulled it out.

A yellowed piece of paper, folded several times, lay in the palm of my hand. I looked around to make sure Lana hadn't snuck up on me. Very carefully, I unfolded it. In Russian, in a crude, child's hand, it said, *Mr. Booboo belongs to Svetlana.* Uh-oh.

I heard a sound and tiptoed down the hall to my room. Very quietly, I opened the door. Lana laid there, sound asleep.

"Mr. Booboo?" she asked as she blindly pawed the sheets as if looking for him in her dreams. She finally stopped moving—which was good because it was killing me to see her like that. I closed the door and made my way back to the kitchen.

The bear was Lana's. And it meant a lot to her. And I'd decapitated and gutted it. I'd have to fix it. I re-folded the note and shoved it back inside, but now I had a problem.

The neck of the bear was only about two inches wide. How could I get all that sawdust back in there? At first, I tried picking up small amounts with my fingers, but

that only made more of a mess. An idea popped into my head, and I dug through the drawers to find my funnel.

I don't know why I had a funnel. But it wasn't worth questioning now. Sticking the narrow end into the bear's neck, I held the top part level with the counter by wrapping my fingers around the necks of the bear and funnel. Using my other hand, I carefully scraped the sawdust off the counter and into the bear.

Okay, the bear was now full again. Which brought me to the next problem—how to get the head back on? The funnel was lucky, but I couldn't find the needle and thread I'd used on the yearbook. I looked everywhere, but it was gone. Apparently my mind wasn't the only thing I was losing. So what could I use? The head had to be sewed back on so it looked like it hadn't been eviscerated by a paranoid idiotic former CIA agent.

It was getting late. Lana could wake up at any time. I was starting to panic. Maybe I could convince her that the FSB took it? But then she'd be upset, and I'd get the pouty lips and tear-filled eyes. That seemed far more horrifying.

Kelly! She might have stuff like that. I called her and gave a silent thanks when she answered.

"You need what?" she asked on the other end, as if I'd asked for something weird like a cup of sugar.

"I need a needle and dark brown thread," I whispered. "Do you have any?"

"I'll be right there." Kelly sighed. She arrived in minutes with both.

I told her what I'd done. You can't keep stuff like that from your best friend. They always know when you're lying. Kelly frowned and said something to the effect that I was a moron, and I agreed. And then she sewed the bear's head back onto its body without being asked.

"I have no idea what kind of stitch originally held it together," she said when she was through. "She'll probably figure it out if she's had it since she was little."

"I'll think of something," I said as I shoved her out the front door, locking it behind her.

Okay, so now I had to think of something. Well, the main thing was to hide the stitching, right? A ribbon! I could say I found the bear on the floor when cleaning her room and tied a ribbon onto it—like I was sentimental and compassionate or something.

Ribbon…ribbon…where would I find a ribbon? I had garrotes, but as far as I knew, no ribbon. What to do…

The ropes we used for the Girl Scout knot-tying class! I could tell her I used that so she'd always have a reminder of that happy day. It was weak, but it just might work. I found the rope and cut a length and tied a clumsy bow around Mr. Booboo's neck. Perfect.

I placed the bear on top of the pillow on the air mattress, let out a huge sigh of relief, and moved on. I still had a lot to do. I hung up clothes and stacked what was left on the closet shelf. At least the room looked a lot better.

Crossing the hall, I quietly opened the door to my room and looked in. Lana was out cold. Good. At least she was sleeping.

The front door creaked. Someone was coming in. That was fast. Apparently the FSB wanted to finish Lana off and get it over with. I silently closed the door to Lana's room and spotted the nail gun on the floor in the hall. I ran for it, plugging it into the outlet and dropping to my stomach. I saw the flash of black shoes and fired.

There was a great roar, followed by, "Dammit Wrath!"

I looked around the corner and saw Riley standing there. He'd showered. The tips of his hair were still wet, and he was freshly shaved. A snug, black T-shirt showed off his lean muscles and topped off dark denim blue jeans that fit like they were sculpted onto his body. Riley was dressed for action, and he looked amazing.

Well, except for the nail sticking out of his shoe. That kind of ruined his look.

"Sorry," I mumbled as I got to my feet, "I thought you were the baddies."

Riley grimaced as he reached down and pulled the nail out of his shoe. There wasn't any blood on the nail. Huh. I must've missed. I'd need to work on my accuracy.

"What the hell is this?" Riley held the nail out to me.

I took it, slipping into my pocket. "It's a nail."

He stared at me. "I know it's a nail, Wrath. What's it doing in my foot?"

I rolled my eyes. "It didn't go into your foot—there's no blood on it, you big baby."

"I'm not a big baby!" Riley cursed. "I just don't like having hardware embedded in my body."

"But it wasn't embedded. I missed," I said as I turned to go into the kitchen.

"You haven't answered my question," Riley said behind me.

"Oh," I said, "that's my home defense system."

Riley followed me into the kitchen and sat at the breakfast bar.

His eyes ran over the suitcase on the counter. Damn. I should've put that away.

"A nail gun is your home defense system?" He looked amused now.

"It's all I have to work with," I said. "Lana's sleeping. I cleaned up her room and put some security measures in place."

Riley nodded as he rubbed his now perforated shoe. "I'm staying. It looks like you'll need my help." He pulled his gun from his belt. "And my gun."

It was then I noticed he had a duffle bag with him.

"I parked in the driveway," he added. "I'm hoping that will be a deterrent to anyone watching the house. It isn't much, but I made a slow demonstration of getting out of the car and walking up to the house. They'll know I'm here and staying."

The image of Riley casually stepping out of the car—of his slow, confident swagger as he walked to the door turned me on a little. And he was sleeping over.

"What's this?" Riley indicated the suitcase.

There wasn't any point in hiding this from him. If he confiscated the equipment when it was all over, there was nothing I could do about it. I was too tired to argue anyhow.

"Come on. I'll show you," I said. I led him through the house, showing him what I'd done and the weapons I'd selected. We ended in the living room.

Riley picked up the nail gun in the hallway, weighing it in his hands. "I should get you a gun," he said.

"Can you?" I asked.

He shook his head. "Well, you have mine and me. But I don't know how I'd get you your own. There's no one from the agency within driving distance who could loan you theirs."

"Come on. You're the CIA. Surely there's something…"

"I don't think so. Sorry," he said. I could tell he meant it. But that didn't help.

"Why are you the only agent here?" I asked.

Riley frowned. "What?"

I repeated the question. "Why is it just you here, handling this? If it's what you said—that this is a matter of national security, why not send you some help?"

Riley looked out the window. "That's classified."

I threw my hands up. "Classified? You can't be serious! How is having the entire encyclopedia of news networks on my front lawn something that's classified? How is having the FSB in my house, uninvited I might add, classified? The secret's out, Riley. The whole world knows what's happened here."

"I'm aware of that, Merry," he said slowly, "but it's still classified. Which means I can't tell you. Which means you should stop asking."

I thought about what we still needed to do and about the uninvited guests who would soon be knocking at the door or smashing in the windows.

"I will…for now. But you can't stop me from thinking about it. And I will bring this up later." I knew I had a valid question. And I knew he was evading. But maybe this wasn't the right time. I wasn't going to give up though.

Riley smiled and nodded. He was probably trying to figure out how he could blow me off later. Good luck with that, I thought.

"I brought lunch." From his duffle bag he produced a large, plastic bucket with a lid and two, long loaves of bread wrapped in foil. I knew what it was before I smelled it.

"Oh thank God," I said as I took the food and unwrapped it. Tortellini in red meat sauce and garlic bread. "I must be a good influence on you. You're starting to eat like a normal person."

He smirked. "My eating habits are not up for debate. Accept your victory gracefully, or it's tofu and veggies from here on out."

I held up my hands in surrender. "You got it. No complaints from me."

I pulled out plates and forks, sliced the bread, and served the pasta. Riley and I sat side by side at the breakfast bar.

"Oh..." I moaned. "This is sooooo good." I took another bite of tortellini and moaned again.

Riley looked at me, one eyebrow arched. "You really enjoy your food, don't you?"

I nodded. "Of course. It's one of the great pleasures in life that you get to do three times a day. Well, I can see how you don't enjoy your food, what with your weird health habits and all."

He frowned. "Hey! I'm not that bad."

"Oh really? Are you saying you don't savor carrot sticks and low-fat salad dressing?"

"No. Not really." He looked at the Italian feast on his plate. "You may be onto something there. But remember, I'm from California. I grew up eating like that."

"And I grew up here, eating meat with potatoes almost every night."

"That's a bit revolting," Riley said, biting his lower lip. He looked adorable doing that.

"Don't judge," I said as I got up to put the leftovers away. "You haven't been shying away from food here."

"I'm not totally reformed. Yet." He smiled and got up, went over to the sink, and started washing the dishes.

"What are you doing?" I asked, trying to keep my eyeballs from popping out of my head. Over the years, I'd imagined Riley doing many things, but this wasn't one of them.

"The dishes. I *can* do dishes, Wrath. Most people can."

"You are welcome to do them anytime," I said.

We finished cleaning up. I put a plate for Lana in the oven, and we went to the couch.

"I owe you an apology," I started

He frowned. "What for?"

"Lana. You were right about her being the target. I still have some doubts and questions, but they very obviously went after her."

Riley nodded. "I talked to Langley this morning about the whole thing. They alerted the Feds to the appearance of the FSB. I don't like your house being Ground Zero."

"Nothing we can do about that." I looked around my living room and thought that it might be in ruins before the night is out. I mean, maybe we could get lucky and they'd move on, but after seeing Lana dangling from that tree, I kind of doubted it.

"Is there any other place we could lure them to?" Riley asked.

I perked up. "That's a good idea. We walk out in broad daylight with Lana and a suitcase and maybe they'll follow us."

"Okay, so where? This is your turf, Wrath. I don't know my way around like you do."

I thought about this. Taking the fight elsewhere would mean innocent people wouldn't get hurt. It also meant we might be able to keep Rex and the police out of it. But would they fall for it? Would they take the bait?

And then I had it. I knew exactly where to go.

Riley looked at me, amused. "You have an idea."

I nodded. "I have an idea."

CHAPTER SIXTEEN

———

About half a mile out of town was an elementary school. It had been there since the 1930's (nothing screams Depression Era Architecture like a big, brick block.) and was slated to be demolished at the end of the summer. Normally it wouldn't be very convenient to have a school on the outskirts of town, but eighty years ago, a farmer gave some of his land to the city, and the city jumped on the freebie to replace a crumbling school in the center of town.

Kids attended there up until this past May, while they built a new school, ironically, on the land where the original school had been. As far as I knew, the school would be completely empty. And being outside of town—a skirmish there wouldn't attract undue attention. At least, not for a little while. Also, there'd be no innocent civilians to get in the way or to grab as human shields, and a hottie detective didn't live across the street.

Riley liked the plan. We decided to go about six p.m. That would give us a little time to prepare for them.

"And you know the building well?" Riley asked.

"I should. I went there from kindergarten to sixth grade." And I had. The only real differences might be educational décor, but the building would be the same essentially. I drew out a diagram for Riley.

"It's a big square," I said as I pointed to what actually looked like a trapezoid with wavy lines, because I can't draw worth a damn "Classrooms are lined up along the outer walls, leaving one, square hallway that loops around a gym that sits right in the center of the building."

"How many ways into the gym?" Riley asked.

"Three," I indicated by drawing lines to indicate doorways. "One on each side opposite each other and one at the back where the kitchen is." Memories of pigs in a blanket and Tater Tots filled my head and made me realize I was still hungry. We needed to eat before we went to our shootout.

"Is the school only one story?" Riley looked a little concerned.

I shook my head with a smile. "No. It looks like it is only one story from the outside. But there's a basement, where the boiler is, and a hidden attic over the office. You can't see it from the outside. You wouldn't know it's even there until you're in the office, and only if you happen to open the principal's closet to see a trapdoor in the ceiling. It hasn't been used in years. That's where I think we should stash Lana."

"Not bad." Riley looked at the drawing. "Are there adjoining doors between classrooms?"

I nodded. "Yes. It's obvious, but it's still an advantage, for a few seconds really." Anyone could come barging through the hallway door into a classroom, but it would take a second for them to register that you'd gone out the adjoining door to the next room. When headed for a standoff with an unknown number of bad guys, every second would be an advantage, and you take what you can get in this line of work.

"We'll have to either get past the cop out front or give him a plausible story as to why we're leaving," I said.

"Since we want the FSB to see us leaving, we'll have to give the policeman an excuse. Otherwise he'll call it in, and then we'll have locals following us to a showdown they're not equipped for."

"I don't know," I said slowly. "Maybe we should rethink that. After all, their mission is to protect the public. Maybe we should involve them or the Feds."

Riley shook his head. "Absolutely not. The Agency doesn't want anyone else involved."

That kind of pissed me off. "But why? It doesn't make sense. Why just have two people take on who knows how many FSB? It's suicide."

"I think it's probably two or three FSB at most." Riley gave me his mind-control smile. I recognized it from when we worked together. That smile could get almost anything and had loosened the underwear of many an unsuspecting woman. "Do we really want to start an international incident between two governments?" he added.

I narrowed my eyes at him. This *was* how the CIA operated. Keep it simple, and keep it quiet. A full-scale high-noon shootout between a U.S. agency that wasn't supposed to operate on American soil and our former number one villain would make headlines the world over and cause endless government investigations. I'd already been involved in one such investigation, and Riley knew I didn't want to go through that again.

"We'd better get all of them, then. There's no margin for error if that's how we're going to play it out," I said.

Riley nodded. And that was the end of that.

We woke Lana up, and I made dinner (Sadly, I didn't have pigs in a blanket or Tater Tots.) while she showered and got dressed. We briefed her while we ate.

"But why hide me away?" she protested. "I'm an agent, like you. I can fight."

Riley shook his head. "No. You're the target, and I don't want to give them easy access. It's out of the question."

"Riley's right," I said. "If they found you, they'd shoot you and leave. I'd personally rather catch one of those bastards or take them out entirely."

"What about weapons?" Lana asked. "Only Riley has a gun."

She had me there. I didn't want to get too close to these guys when they'd have guns and I didn't. I looked at Riley meaningfully.

"Let me make a couple of calls," he said grudgingly. Apparently, he *did* have access to guns but didn't want to lose any favors just because *my* life was on the line. I wanted to punch him, but I didn't. Instead, I kicked him out the kitchen door to the garage with what I hoped was a *you'd better get more guns, or I'm taking yours* look.

"And the policeman out front?" Lana bit her lip. "What do we say to him?"

I thought about that for a moment. He wasn't going to buy just any line we gave him. And he might call Rex.

Riley came back in. "There'll be a black bag drop at the school by six."

I glared at him. "Really? You were going to make me use this?" I held up the nail gun and toyed with aiming it at his balls.

He smiled. "I just wanted to see if you could."

We didn't have time for this. "Give me your secret phone."

Riley's eyebrows rose. "I don't have a secret phone."

I crossed my arms over my chest. "Yes you do. You always have an untraceable blank cell phone." I aimed the nail gun at his groin. "And you have two seconds to give it to me before I shoot you."

"Fine." Riley sighed and reached into his bag and pulled out the phone. "What are you going to do with it?"

I held up my hand to tell him and Lana to shut up. Then I dialed.

A bored dispatcher answered. It's a small community with very little happening. I was counting on her not being busy.

I adopted a Southern accent. "Help! I'm at the grocery store on Main! There are two armed men here, and they're holding a bunch of people hostage!" I hung up and then went to the window.

It only took a few seconds before the black and white out front turned on its siren and roared off. There weren't that many police officers in this town. And for a holdup at a grocery store with hostages—well, they'd need every one of them. Excellent.

Riley and Lana applauded. (I deserved it, of course.) Then we got our stuff together and left the house.

Lana limped and moaned with great exaggeration all the way to the car. Loudly. Riley and I took our time throwing the bag in the back and getting into the car. As we pulled out in Riley's SUV, Lana crouched down on the back

seat so whoever followed us wouldn't shoot her on the way
there.

We got a few blocks before I spotted the tail. It was
one huge guy in sunglasses, a black muscle shirt with a huge
gold chain around his neck. He was crammed into a black
Volkswagen Beetle. Rental cars are slim pickings in these
parts.

"That him?" I asked.

Riley glanced in the rearview mirror and burst out
laughing. "Yeah. That's him. I wish I could take a picture of
him squeezed into that tiny car. It would be worth circulating
to Interpol."

"It's only one. That's good," I said. And it was. It
meant he had to go back and get the other guys. That bought
us a little time.

I gave Riley directions to the outskirts of town, and
he drove slowly, even taking a few unnecessary left turns
just to confirm we had a shadow. The muscle-head in the
Volkswagen never strayed from his position.

"They used to be better at that," I said, looking in the
side mirror. "But I guess things change."

Riley answered, never taking his eyes off the road.
"The end of the Cold War changed all that. Now they barely
train them."

"Well," I said, "that's good for us."

We arrived at the school. There were several tractors
around it, like they were thinking about working on the
school but hadn't really gotten around to it just yet. Riley
drove the perimeter to see if there were any construction
workers, but we didn't see any. He parked the car in the back
lot, and after putting on black latex gloves, we helped Lana
get out. The black Beetle slowed to a stop and then roared
off.

"Subtle," I murmured as I picked the padlock that
held the chains to the door. Padlocks. I mean really. If you
want to keep people out, you have to do better than padlocks.
They're so easy to pick it's ridiculous. But then, the
construction crew could never have foreseen a gunfight
between CIA and FSB on the premises.

The lock and chains fell to the ground, and we entered the old school through a door that creaked loudly. Riley did a light jog around the hallway loop to get a lay of the land and to make sure there wasn't anyone inside. I must admit—he looked just as good jogging away from me as he did minutes later jogging up to me.

"All clear." He was holding a black satchel as he joined us. "Here are the guns."

Lana got a Browning High Power nine millimeter with two magazines. I got a Colt Gold Cup .45 with one extra mag. I stuffed it into the back of my shorts and led the two to the office.

Herbert Hoover Elementary looked like the kids had just left hours ago. There were trophies in the display case, children's artwork on the walls, and a huge composite photo of all the students and teachers. It seemed a little sad to wreck it all, but then, why did they leave this stuff?

I gave a silent thanks when I found the principal's closet empty. We gave Lana instructions and shoved her up into the small space.

"It's hot up here!" she shouted. But she didn't try to get down.

"We'll get you out as soon as we can," Riley shouted back.

I gave Riley a more detailed tour of the school that took about ten minutes. It was so weird being back here. I thought about Kelly and me as pigtailed little kids running through the hallway. If only I'd known then what I knew now. Bullies would most likely leave you alone when they realize you know how to waterboard them.

"Are you sure they aren't still using this school?" Riley frowned as he saw the volleyball net up in the gym.

I nodded. "Positive. They did a huge story on it for the news. Didn't you see the construction stuff outside?" I stared at two rubber balls on the floor. "I don't know why this stuff is still here."

He shrugged. "Okay then. Let's head back to the office."

The front room of the office had a view of the street and the one and only entrance to the school parking lot. From there we'd be able to see the Russians as they drove in. They could arrive at any time, and we wanted to be ready.

"Not bad, Wrath," Riley said as we sat on the secretary's desk. "This could work."

"Um…thanks?" I said sarcastically. "You know, I was an agent. On my own. In foreign countries. And I did pretty well."

He nodded. "Yes you were." He gave me a strange look. "You know, I've missed you."

I gulped, and my eyes went wide. "Seriously? You missed me?" I felt that little flutter in my stomach. The same flutter I'd felt just before he'd kissed me.

Riley nodded. "I really did. You were always good at thinking on your feet."

"Oh. Right." I hoped I didn't sound too disappointed. "Like I told you, I was a great agent."

He reached out and tucked a stray curl behind my ear. His touch was so soft, it felt like a whisper. And it made my skin feel all tingly. I watched as Riley stepped closer to me, his eyes on mine. Was he going to kiss me again?

I closed my eyes in anticipation and parted my lips.

And then, Riley laughed. Hysterically. I opened my eyes, furious at him for making me feel like an idiot. I was just considering whether to shoot him or not when I realized he was looking over my shoulder out the window. I turned to see the black VW pulling in with three large guys barely stuffed inside. Okay, so that was pretty funny.

"Let's go." Riley ran out of the room to the gym. I took up my position in the third classroom near the door where we'd broken in. I crouched down behind the heavy, wood teacher's desk and thought about Riley, hidden behind the curtain on the stage in the gym. If they went straight to the gym, they were Riley's. If they decided to check the classrooms first, I was supposed to take out the first guy and lead the other two to the gym for a final standoff.

This will work. I told myself. *It's a good plan.*

The door to the school opened with a creak. I stifled a grin. They fell into the first trap—locating the spot where we'd broken in as the easiest point of entry. So lazy. And the door creaked, just like it had for us.

CREEEEEEEEEEEEEAAAAAAAK.

I tried not to laugh out loud. They were trying to open the door more, but it only creaked louder.

CREEEEEEEEEEEEEEEEEAAAAAAAAAAAAAAAAA AK.

I heard a lot of Russian swearing. They were in. And they knew they'd been heard. I figured they'd take up positions in the hallway for a moment, to see if anyone came at them. But no one would. That wasn't the plan.

You can't rush these things. Agents who have no patience never survive long in this business. In the military they have a saying: *hurry up and wait.* Well, it's pretty much the same for us too. Many an agent has died because they had the attention span of a caffeinated gnat.

I heard some hushed arguing. They realized now that they had to come to us, and they were trying to figure out how to do that successfully. I understood Russian enough to know that the three FSB guys were named Vladimir, Aleksei, and Yevgeny. They couldn't decide whether to stay together or separate.

I stayed put. No point in jumping out too soon. Besides I wanted to drop them in the school. I didn't want to give them the opportunity to escape, or worse, kill me.

Riley had almost kissed me in the office. I was sure of it. He liked me. And clearly, I liked him, or I wouldn't have felt all squishy when he tucked my hair behind my ear. But what did it mean? I didn't fully trust him. There was still a lot he wasn't saying. And that bothered me.

I heard footsteps in the hall and closed my eyes to focus on the sound. One guy had entered the first classroom. The other two were going down the hallway, one on either side of the gym. I thought they'd do that.

I heard another door swing open. My guy was done with the first classroom and entering the second one. Pretty soon he'd come through one of the doors into my room. He

wouldn't be able to see me from either doorway. The desk was huge. It didn't matter which door he came through, I was ready for him.

The door to the hallway swung open. So that's the one. Footsteps moved quickly toward me. I knew he'd check the desk—it was the only hiding place in the room. Still no sound from the others, so they hadn't gotten Riley or Lana.

The footsteps came closer. We'd decided to try to take these guys out silently if possible. Most people are afraid of the unknown. It was a knee-jerk reaction. As the Russians disappeared, the remaining one or two would panic.

I was going to go for a chokehold. If that didn't work, I'd shoot him. I didn't have time to screw around.

The footsteps stopped just in front of the desk. My leg shot out and swept him off his feet. Just as he hit the ground, I reached out and grabbed him, my arm around his neck and dragged him halfway under the desk.

There was only a one and a half foot gap between the floor and the desk. The guy's head and shoulders were underneath on my side, but his forearms, hands and the rest of him were on the other side and there was no room for him to bring his arms up. He was pinned down by the heavy, oak desk.

He was big. I held on and kept up the pressure, squeezing as hard as I could. The Russian kicked and tried to get free, but his chest was trapped under the desk with me. Even if he managed to free himself, he wouldn't get away from me easily.

I'm not a big person. Strangling a big guy with a thick neck was not easy. My arms were burning and my shoulders strained, but I held on because the alternative would not be good for me.

The man struggled less now. He was out of air and soon would lose consciousness. I wished it would happen quickly because I was wiped out. Finally, the body went limp. You'd think I could've let go then, wouldn't you? Oh no. I hung on for at least another minute. Most people make the mistake of letting go when the victim passes out. But

that's a huge mistake. The guy could come to and take you out. You had to hold on until you were sure they were dead.

I eventually let go, my muscles screaming in protest. Okay, I'm just going to shoot the next guy. There were two left. Riley could take out the other one.

I dragged the dead Russian all the way under the desk. He'd stay hidden for a little while. I took his gun—an H&K nine millimeter. Nice. I stuck it into my waistband and pulled out the Colt. A nine millimeter pistol was nice and all, and the H&K was an expensive gun, but these were big guys. The .45 had more stopping power.

Staying low, I held the Colt in front of me and crept to the adjoining door. I listened for a moment before opening it really slowly and moving into the second classroom. Doubling back is always a good move. They don't usually see it coming.

Someone was running down the hall in my direction. Ah. Dress shoes. Riley was wearing tennis shoes. Much different sound. And unless Riley had decided to trade shoes somewhere between the car and the gym, I was pretty sure this was another Russian.

"Vlad!" A loud whisper came from the hallway. What idiots. Who trained these guys?

The guy stepped into the room with me. I was behind the door. The minute he stepped out of the doorway, I was going to shoot him.

The Russian smacked his fist against the door, apparently angry that Vlad wasn't answering. Unfortunately, that drove the door and the doorknob into my body. I gasped involuntarily. I couldn't help it.

A giant, beefy hand grabbed the edge of the door and yanked it away. As I tried to regain my breath, a big ugly man inconsiderately wrapped his big paws around my throat. It seemed kind of ironic, since I'd taken Vlad out that way.

As I choked and sputtered, the guy lifted me off the floor and laughed. He thought he'd hit the lottery by getting a tiny woman for an opponent. He squeezed his fingers as I brought up the Colt and squeezed the trigger. I fired two

shots directly into his gut, and he let go and staggered back with a look of shock on his face. Clearly, this guy didn't lose very often.

He started yelling. Now that, I couldn't have. The sound of gunshots would've echoed in the big school. But yelling would tell his partner where he was. I didn't want to risk a third shot. I had to find something to render him unconscious.

I smashed the first thing I could find into his head. The globe broke in two, and I looked at the hollow half shells. Vlad was still conscious. Huh. I thought the globe would be, I don't know, sturdier than that. Oh well. Lesson learned. I kicked him in the side of the head. That seemed to do the trick.

Using the cord from the window blinds, I tied him up. He was gutshot, but I've seen guys get up after being shot and fight on until they bled out. No way I was going to let that happen. I took his gun, another H&K, and stuffed it into my shorts. Now I had three guns. No waiting periods now for this girl.

I got low to the floor, peeking out into the hallway only a foot off the ground. People tend to aim higher, expecting a target to walk out of the room. They aren't used to seeing someone low to the ground. Like I said, every extra second is an advantage in your favor.

The hallway was empty. I heard nothing. That was weird. I'd have thought the bad guy would've found Riley by now. Or at least would have come running at the sound of my two gunshots. Unless he's waiting to ambush me.

I withdrew back into the classroom, kicking the tied up Russian in the head again, just to make sure he stayed out. He was still breathing, but raggedly. It wouldn't be long. I slipped over to the adjoining door to the other classroom and passed through it.

Making my way slowly, from classroom to classroom, I couldn't stop wondering why I hadn't heard any encounter Riley had with the last guy. Maybe it happened while I was shooting the second assailant? But then, why

hadn't either Riley or the Russian come running to help or kill me?

A chilling thought froze me in my tracks. Could they have killed each other? Maybe they fired at the same time, during my little one-sided gunfight? Maybe Riley was bleeding out somewhere? My pulse quickened. I had to check it out.

I was halfway down the hallway, still in a classroom, when I realized I was even with the side door to the gym. I hesitated, straining to listen. But I heard nothing. Absolutely nothing. What was going on? None of this seemed right.

"Merry!" I turned to see Lana whispering at me as she slunk through the door to the next classroom. Her gun was in her right hand. She looked spooked. I motioned for her to join me.

"What are you doing here?" I hissed. "I told you to stay put until we came to get you!"

"I heard two gunshots. I got worried," she said. That meant she'd only heard me firing twice into Russian number two. Which meant that if there was a scuffle in the gym, she didn't hear it.

"You didn't hear anything else?" I asked. Lana had been way closer to the gym. I'd been on the opposite end of the building from her.

Lana shook her head. Riley and Russian number three were unaccounted for. One thing was certain—I needed a new plan.

"I took out the other two," I said quietly, "which with you, now makes it three against one."

"So you are letting me fight?" Lana asked.

"Might as well," I answered as I held a gun in each hand. "We'd better go see what's going on in the gym."

Lana nodded and followed me into the hallway, sweeping her gun to the left while I checked the right. Nothing. The gym entrance was right across from me. I motioned to Lana that she should stay here, where it was clear, while I went around to the entrance on the opposite side of the gym.

"Be careful," I whispered. "I have no idea where the third guy is. Keep an eye on the doorway. Enter only when I signal you."

I slipped quietly along the wall, visually checking each classroom opposite me as I went. This wasn't working out exactly as I'd hoped. We'd set everything up so that the FSB had to come to us. Now we were in the position of finding the third guy, who was probably laying in wait to ambush us. And where the hell was Riley?

I turned the corner and made my way halfway down the hall toward the entrance to the gym by the kitchen. I needed to take a quick look before moving to the door opposite Lana. Once again, I got low and looked in.

I couldn't see anything. Not Riley, not the Russian. There appeared to be no sign of struggle. I got back up, and after clearing the hall behind me, made my way around the next corner to the opposite end of the gym, clearing the classrooms as I went.

Once I got to the doorway, I signaled to Lana to go in, sweeping on her right, while I would do the same sweep on my right. She nodded. I held up three fingers and counted down…3…2…1.

We both jumped into the gym at the same time. My end of the gym, which included the stage where Riley was supposed to be hiding, was empty. Lana nodded that her end was clear too. Together, we silently slid along the wall, walking toward the stage.

I had a bad feeling about this. Riley would've let us know if he'd taken care of his guy. But he didn't. That could mean the third Russian had hurt or killed Riley and was just waiting for the rest of us to show up.

I'd been in these kinds of standoffs before. But it never failed to scare the crap out of me. My mouth was dry, palms wet. My stomach churned, and I was listening so hard my ears hurt. Robots would have it much easier. The CIA definitely needed robots.

We were both on either side of the stage now. Lana stopped and waited for me to indicate what to do next. I held up my hand in the universal signal for *stop* and closed my

eyes. I strained to hear anything. A footfall. The sound of a creaking rope. Human breathing. This was the part I hated most. A decision needed to be made. Do we go forward? We couldn't stay here.

Lana had a determined look on her face, so obviously she was in. I knew what the answer was. We had to clear the stage before searching the rest of the school. There was one guy left, and he couldn't be allowed to flee. But more importantly, we had to find Riley.

If he was waiting behind this curtain, I was going to kill him. I know, if he was, he probably heard me and Lana and thought maybe we were the FSB. On the other hand, he had to have heard the two shots I fired and wondered what that was. Why hadn't he come to my rescue? Why did I have to take out two guys when he only had one? Seemed a bit unfair and was definitely something I was going to take up with him after I rescued him *or* gunned him down by accident.

I signaled Lana. We were going to jump up on the stage and clear it as fast as we could. She'd take the left side, and I'd take the right. I counted down again, and we both leaped onto the stage and swung around our assigned curtain.

There was no one there. What the hell? Where was the guy who was supposed to be dead by now? And where was Riley?

CHAPTER SEVENTEEN

"What do we do?" Lana asked.

"We're going to have to search the whole school," I answered. What else could we do? We had to find Riley, and wo had to find the third guy. One of them I wanted to strangle— the other one I wanted to kill.

Together we wordlessly made our way to the office. After a quick examination, we decided to split up. I didn't want to. That exposed Lana to the last Russian. But the odds were better one-on-one, and Lana had a gun.

"I will go this way." Lana pointed to the hallway on her right. That's where I'd taken out the first two FSB guys.

I nodded. "Okay. Clear each room carefully. You'll need to go through the adjoining doors too. I'll meet you in the third and fourth rooms. Where I left the bodies."

Lana nodded and took off, I went left. Memories of going to school here as a kid washed over me as I looked at walls filled with kid art and posters. As a fourth grader, I never would've imagined I'd be roaming these halls as an adult. Or that I'd kill two FSB agents here.

I took the first room quickly. There was only one adjoining door in here because it was on the end. Once inside the doorway, I bent down to look under the desk. Nothing was there. I slipped along the wall to it anyway, just to make sure. Although I don't know what I expected to find. Did I think there'd be a three-hundred-pound man hovering a foot off the ground and crouched in a way that would guarantee he'd never have children? It didn't matter because I had to clear it.

When I found nothing, I made my way back to the hall door and peeked out. Empty. It wasn't going to be easy doing it this way. But I had to make sure that Riley wasn't a prisoner in these rooms and that the other agent couldn't get away.

I charged into the next room through the adjoining door and crouched to look under the desk again. It was hot in the school. Sweat trickled down the sides of my face and neck, annoying me. But I kept both hands on the gun. No point in getting shot just because I wanted to wipe sweat away. That would be a stupid way to die. Riley would think it was funny. Hell, he'd go back to Langley and tell everyone I was murdered because I couldn't take the heat. Death by perspiration, he'd say. Then they'd all laugh, and I'd come back to haunt the crap out of them. Ghosts don't like being teased any more than the living.

I cleared the second, third, and fourth rooms the same way. It seemed strange to me that I never heard another sound. No footsteps. No sounds of a struggle. Nothing. On the one hand, that was good. It meant Lana was still safe. On the other hand, it meant that guy number three was lying in wait for me, levitating behind a desk somewhere.

Once I got to the classroom on the other side of the gym door, I tiptoed across the hallway. I'd feel pretty stupid if the bad guy went back in there to hide and I hadn't checked. Very slowly I cleared the gym for a second time. Where in hell were they, dammit? You'd think Riley would at least make some noise…rock his chair back and forth or grunt, whatever.

I went back across the hall and into the fourth room again. Just for good measure, I ran quickly through the previous three rooms but still found nothing. I was running out of rooms. That was good in that no one had tried to kill me yet. But bad in that my prey was still missing. Eventually, I'd run out of rooms and run into him.

There was no sound from Lana on the other side of the building. I prayed silently that she was still okay. But maybe the FSB guy got her too. Dragged her out to his Volkswagen Beetle and stuffed her in the trunk while I was

clearing the other side. The idea freaked me out, and I started sweating even more.

Had I just given the guy the opportunity to get what he wanted by letting Lana go alone? Why didn't I insist that she stay with me? This Russian could have both Lana and Riley trussed up somewhere. Then it would be down to just him and me.

Those odds didn't bother me. I'd faced them before. The problem was that I didn't know where Riley and Lana were. I toyed with the idea of calling out to her as I turned the corner to clear the last three rooms. Should I run the perimeter, find Lana, and make her stick with me?

No. We had to keep going the way we were. I was almost done, which meant that Lana, if she was still here, was almost done too. I raced through the last three rooms rather sloppily. My spy brain was screaming that something might be wrong. I'd always had an overactive imagination. That's a bad thing for a spy. You need a cool, level head for that job. Otherwise you could imagine all sorts of things.

When the last room was done, I stepped into the hall and let out a breath. Lana was up against the wall, gun drawn. She was alone and she was okay. I nodded at her, and she nodded back. Now we just had the classrooms by the entrance— two of which held dead bodies.

I stepped into the third classroom, where I'd killed Vlad. The only thing we could do was grab the bodies and dump them somewhere they wouldn't be found. I didn't need any more dead foreign spies in my hometown.

"What the...?" I stood behind the desk, blinking. Vlad was gone. How had that happened?

I ran to the next room and looked for the second guy, the guy I'd let bleed out on the floor. The puddle of blood was all that remained of him.

"I thought you said you took two of them out, Merry," Lana said softly.

I nodded, staring at the blood. "I did. I strangled the first guy, then shot this guy twice and tied him up. They couldn't have walked out of here on their own." *Could they?*

No, I'd checked the first guy's pulse before I left the previous room. He'd been dead alright. And this guy was hogtied and close to death when I left him. Unless they were zombies, they should be here, waiting for a little chalk outline to be made around them.

The third guy. He must've come back and gotten them when we were in the gym. But how? There wasn't even a trail of blood to follow.

I ran to the door with Lana hot on my heels and pushed through it, ignoring the creaking. My eyes scanned the parking lot, and I swore softly. The Black Volkswagen was gone. But the SUV we drove was still there.

I reattached the chain and padlock as Lana took our guns and climbed into Riley's SUV. Riley, wherever he was, had the keys. I tore open the console to hotwire the car. I hate new cars. They totally suck to do. It's not entirely impossible to hotwire a car these days, but it is much, much harder. My mind rolled back to my training. It took a while, but I eventually made it work. Of course the console was a mess, and the SUV would be undriveable after we got home. When you hotwire a car, you have to kind of destroy it. There's no way I'd get it going again. It was going to be expensive for the rental place too. Stupid modern cars. That was the great thing about working in third world countries— the cars were a lot older.

Neither Lana nor I spoke as I put the car into gear and drove us out of the parking lot and back into town. Lana watched for a tail, but there wasn't one this time. I did several left-hand turns to make sure before finally pulling into a fast food parking lot. It was getting dark out. My stomach rumbled.

I reached into the glove box and pulled out my wallet. Lana had to stay in the car. She still had two black eyes, and I wanted to keep her out of sight. She moved to the driver's side, ready to peel out of here if there was any sign of danger.

I ran into the restaurant and ordered two double cheeseburgers, fries, and iced tea. It felt a little silly hitting a

fast food franchise after killing two men. But they were big guys, and I'd expended a lot of energy. I needed to eat.

I used to travel with a box of macaroni and cheese. After anything like what happened at the school, I'd go back to whatever hole in the wall I lived in, and I'd make macaroni and cheese. I don't know why, but it always helped.

Fast food would have to do in this case. I paid up and noticed the pimply teenager behind the counter staring at my shirt. Really? Sexism *now*? It really wasn't the time or place for some stupid boy to stare at my chest. I looked down. Oh shit.

There was a spray pattern of blood that basically announced that I'd been shooting people. How did I not check that? Why didn't Lana mention it before I went in? It's like telling a friend she has broccoli in her teeth. Only with spies, you always mentioned when they had blood on their clothes and were about to go out in public.

"I was painting my barn," I said lamely. It was all I could think of. Barns are red, right? And there were a lot of farms outside of town.

The kid nodded and said, "Whatever." I fled.

Lana was still there, unlike Riley—who was still missing. She unlocked the doors, and I climbed into the passenger seat. I gave her directions, and she drove us to a very well-lit parking lot in the center of town where the teens cruised and hung out. We parked next to a group of kids who were goofing around. They eyed us suspiciously. It was a good spot to hide. Adults avoided places like these for a reason. Anyone looking for us would see dozens of obnoxious teens and most likely would flee.

I unwrapped a cheeseburger and handed it to her. We ate for a few moments in silence while the kids around the car tried to decide if we were cops or just weird old ladies. Eventually, they ignored us and went back to acting like idiots.

"What happened to Rilee?" Lana asked after she'd polished off the burger and fries in record time. With that

body, I don't know how she ate junk and never gained an ounce. I'd never once seen her exercise. It just wasn't fair.

"No idea," I said as I sucked the rest of my drink down. "Best guess—the remaining FSB guy, Aleksei, took him and the bodies with him."

"His name was Aleksei?" Lana frowned.

I threw my hands up in the air. "I don't know. That was one of their names, and I know the first guy I killed was named Vlad. It just helps having a name for him so between Yevgeny and Aleksei, I picked the easiest one to say."

"I guess Riley couldn't have been dead." Lana stared off into the sea of writhing, howling teenagers. "Aleksei needed him to help carry the bodies out. He couldn't have carried all three without us catching him."

I nodded. "That's what I was thinking too." Riley was most likely alive. For now. What I didn't say was that the only reason Aleksei would've kept him alive is to trade. For Lana. It was only a matter of time before the message was delivered.

"He'll want to trade Rileee for me, won't he?" Lana said. Of course she came up with that. How many times did I need to remind myself that she'd been a trained spy?

"Yes," I said. No point in sugar-coating the truth. "My guess is they'll call me using Riley's cell phone."

Lana nodded. She didn't say anything more. Maybe she was wondering if I'd do it. If I'd agree to trade her. I was wondering that myself. As much as a pain in the ass as she'd been when she first arrived—Lana was kind of growing on me.

"Come on," I said as I balled up the garbage and threw it into the back of the SUV. I thought for a moment that I wished Riley would be able to see the junk food bag in his car and freak out. "Let's head home."

Lana caused a bit of a stir with the high school boys when she got out of the car to switch places with me. Even with two black eyes, she still made men drool. I ignored it, got into the driver's seat, and drove us out of there.

The black and white police car was out front as we pulled into the driveway. And sitting on the porch was

Detective Rex Ferguson. I felt a little shiver of excitement at seeing him there, waiting for me. But then I realized why he was waiting for me, and my heart sank.

I shoved the guns under the seat and grabbed the fast food bag from the back before getting out of the car. Lana waited until I walked around to her side. She obviously got my cue because she stepped out holding the two drinks.

The officer in the squad car looked embarrassed. He probably got reamed out for leaving, and I felt a little bad about that.

"Ms. Wrath." Rex got to his feet. He wasn't smiling. "Ms. Babikova." He motioned towards the door. "May I have a word with you, please?" Awwww. He was polite. That was a good characteristic in a future fiancé.

I nodded and unlocked the door as Lana and Rex followed me into the house and into the kitchen. He sat down at the breakfast bar as Lana and I stood on the other side like a couple of naughty kids in front of the principal. I plunked down the bag and drinks and tried to look sheepish.

"You left," he said with a frown. "You took advantage of the fact that the officer out front had been called away, and you left."

"How did you know we were gone?" I asked.

"I had the officer check the house when he got back. You didn't answer," Rex replied.

"Sorry," I said, trying to blush. "We were hungry, and Lana just wanted to get out of here to get some air."

Lana nodded. "I felt uncomfortable here after what happened in my room." She was a good actress, better than I'd originally thought. I smiled at her, only to see her looking meaningfully at my T-shirt. My blood-splattered T-shirt. That I was still wearing. Oh damn.

Rex caught it right away, of course, because he's a brilliant detective. "You have something on your shirt."

I did the only thing I could think of. I pulled the shirt up over my head and took it off. That's right. I stood before Rex and Lana wearing nothing more than a bra (which sadly, was not lacy or even remotely interesting). Rex was so

shocked he didn't say anything as I balled the shirt up and held it in my fist.

"Sorry. I had an accident with a Slurpee machine." I shrugged.

Rex regained his composure quickly. Too quickly, dammit. He stared at the fast food garbage and then at me. "They don't have Slurpees there." He pointed to the logo.

I nodded. "Lana wanted something cold to hold against her face. We stopped at the gas station first." I was a very good liar. "But after my cherry Slurpee exploded on me, she decided she was hungry, so we left."

Lana tore her eyes away from my bra and nodded at Rex. "The red dye freaked me out." She pouted adorably.

Rex looked from me to Lana. I tried to stand there as naturally as a lying, topless woman can in front of a police detective she finds attractive. I tried to look embarrassed and apologetic, and like fiancé material all at the same time. Not sure if I pulled it off.

"I'm just going to run to the bedroom and put on a clean shirt," I said as I made my way around the breakfast bar with the balled up blood shirt in my hand. Before he could object, I ran down the hallway, stuffed the shirt under the bed, and put another one on. I was going to have to get rid of that shirt as soon as Rex left.

"…I can't stress that enough," Rex was saying to a petulant Lana when I rejoined them.

"What's that?" I asked with a smile.

"I was just telling Ms. Babikova that we are using considerable resources to guarantee her safety. She needs to understand that we are doing this for her own protection." He turned to me. "That means you two need to stay here. At least for another day or two until we decide the threat is over."

The threat is over, I thought. *Mostly.*

"Where's your cousin? Riley?" Rex asked me. "I thought he'd be here with you tonight."

"He will," I said rather quickly. "He had to make some arrangements for work…because he's going to take some leave time. Then he'll be here."

Rex frowned. "But isn't that his car you drove up in?"

Dammit. He was smart. Normally, I'd rejoice in that fact—I mean, who wants a stupid boyfriend? But now, well, this was inconvenient to say the least.

I was at a loss. Normally lies trip off the tip of my tongue like a bi-polar psychopath at a schizophrenia convention.

"He loaned us his car," Lana spoke up. "Merry's car isn't running well since her accident. He said he was going to get a rental." She tossed in a one-hundred-kilowatt smile, just for good measure. Which, I should probably admit, made me a little jealous.

Rex looked thoughtful. I had no idea if he'd bought it, but he seemed to be willing to drop it for now.

"I'll check in on you in the morning then." He held up his cell. "Call me if you see anything out of the ordinary. I'm just across the street."

He got up and headed for the door. I followed him and gave him my best, apologetic smile. "Thank you for looking after us. I'm sorry we left. We won't do that again."

"Good-night, ladies," he said with a slight smile as he walked out the door.

I leaned against the door and let out a huge sigh. Lying to Rex was exhausting. But I had to do it one more time. I'd have to leave the house, probably in the next couple of hours, to rescue Riley.

CHAPTER EIGHTEEN

"So what happens now?" Lana asked as I joined her in the kitchen.

"I guess we wait until Aleksei calls us." I chewed on my lip. "What else can we do?"

What else could we do? The only good thing about this mess was that Riley was most likely still alive and two of the three Russians were dead. In fact, it was better than that because it was on Aleksei to dispose of Vlad and Yevgeny. We didn't have to drive around with two corpses in the trunk, trying to find a good place to dump them. He'd do a good job, too. He wouldn't want them found any more than we did.

Unfortunately, Aleksei was in charge of what happened next. Since he had Riley, he called the shots. He could call tonight or in three days. I could call Riley's cell, but I didn't want to make Aleksei jumpy. Jumpy spies tend to kill their hostages and run.

Once he did call, though, we'd need a plan and quickly. I was tired and out of ideas. The school shootout was good, but it left me pretty spent in the idea department. The Russian would decide the time and place. I'd have to adapt very quickly to that and very carefully to make sure Lana and Riley didn't get killed in the process.

That's right. I wasn't going to hand Lana over. I'd let the FSB *think* that. But it wasn't going to happen. And Riley would be pissed if I did that. He'd charged me with her safety and trusted me to do the right thing.

Riley had been a spy for a long time. He knew the risks. And he was probably thinking up a plan of his own

right now. How had he let himself get taken? He was too good for that to happen.

Live to fight another day was kind of our motto at the Agency. When things went south, you got out of there, found a safe house, and regrouped. Riley must have decided it would be better to leave with Aleksei than engage him. Or maybe he was doing it to protect us.

I turned that thought around in my head for a moment. It was possible that the Russian had a bead on either me or Lana back in the gym. Riley probably saw that and decided to go with Aleksei to spare us. Awww, that gave me more fuzzy feelings toward Riley. I remembered that he'd almost kissed me in the office. Was Riley protecting me? Did Riley have feelings for me?

I shook it off. No, I had to keep my focus on the task at hand. I was guessing too much. Making up stuff that I had no idea was true. *Stick to the facts, Wrath.* What did we know?

Number one—we knew that Riley was gone. Aleksei and the bodies were gone. The black Beetle they drove in was gone. Riley's SUV was still there. Either Riley was dead somewhere in the school, and we somehow missed him, or he went with the Russian.

My conclusion was that Riley was with Aleksei. Lana and I scoured that school. And if Riley was dead, and his two buddies were dead, Aleksei would've stayed until he'd finished the job. And, he needed Riley to help him carry off Vlad and Yevgeny. Otherwise, the time it would've taken him to drag two huge guys out to the car would've doubled. And if it was doubled, we would've caught him. So Riley must be alive.

Number two—Yevgeny and Vlad were dead. There was no doubt about this in my mind. When I'd left him, Vlad wasn't breathing and had no heartbeat. Unless an EMT with a defibrillator had accidentally happened by, Vlad was still dead. Yevgeny was very close to death when I'd left him. I'd shot him twice at close range in the stomach. He'd dropped me immediately, which meant he was too weak to hold onto me anymore. I knew this because I've shot guys before, and

they still kept coming—mainly because I hadn't hit anything important.

I probably hit his spine, which would've permanently immobilized him. He dropped me and fell to the floor pretty quickly. And I'd tied him up without a fight. That was something, in spite of my knot disability, I knew I'd done well. (Hint—it's all in the wrist.) No...Yevgeny didn't leave that school alive. I was convinced of that.

Number three—Aleksei took Riley. He made Riley go with him, because he still wanted Lana. He didn't have to take the other bodies. He could've left them there and run off. But he didn't. That meant he wasn't giving up. I wondered how he got the drop on Riley. My former handler was a pro. It wouldn't have been easy. Oh well—I could figure that out later.

Number four—we had some time. Aleksei needed time to secure Riley and get rid of two bodies in a way that they'd never be found. He didn't seem all that bright, but he was probably the smartest of the three FSB agents since he'd made it out of there with two bodies and a hostage. On top of that, he'd need time to come up with a plan. There were two of us, Lana and myself, against him. And he had to know we'd be armed. If Riley had gone with him to spare us, the Russian would also know we weren't about to give Lana up without a fight.

I closed my eyes and rubbed my forehead. I was tired, but I needed to take advantage of this time to come up with something that would get Riley out alive, spare Lana, and make Aleksei dead.

I heard shouting outside and ran to the front door.

"Back off Kevin Dooley, or I'll tell your mom!" Kelly's voice came from the other side of the door. Kevin Dooley? Who was that? Rusty gears squeaked inside my head, and I remembered. Kevin Dooley was the geeky guy in high school who made fun of Kelly and me. What was he doing outside my door this late at night?

"Just get back into your car. I'm not a threat," Kelly growled.

Ah. He must be the cop out front. I opened the door and grinned. Kelly stood there with another casserole. She pushed past me and headed for the kitchen. I locked the door behind her and joined her and Lana.

"I came to check on the patient and bring you dinner," Kelly said.

"It's like eleven o'clock at night!" I protested. But only half-heartedly because it was a casserole, after all. Spies never, ever turn down free home cooking.

"I only saw you and Lana get out of the SUV. Riley wasn't with you." Kelly folded her arms over her chest. "Do you want to tell me what's going on?"

"How did you see us?" I asked. "You live a block away!"

Kelly rolled her eyes. "I was driving home from my shift."

Oh. Right. The hospital. "And how did you make a casserole in that amount of time?" I asked. Not that I was complaining. This one smelled like a Tater Tot casserole. Nope, not complaining at all.

She shrugged, "I had one in the freezer. I heated it up. It still needs about twenty minutes." Kelly marched toward the kitchen and popped it into the oven. We followed her.

The three of us set the breakfast bar, and I made some tea. I needed the caffeine because eating one-third of a Tater Tot casserole would most likely make me sleepy.

"All right," Kelly said minutes later as she spooned the casserole onto our plates. "Spill it."

"What do you mean?" I feinted before shoving a fork into my mouth to stall. Oh my God. This was so good. I tell you, if you want to know fifty different ways (and all delicious) to cook with Tater Tots, come to Iowa. It's a point of pride here.

Lana nodded, and I realized she hadn't said much since we got home. She was probably traumatized.

"Knock it off, Merry." Kelly narrowed her eyes. "Something's going on. And by the guilty looks on your faces, I can tell it's not good."

I sighed. "Fine." I was exhausted and sick of lying to everyone. I told her everything. About us going to the school, stuffing Lana in the ceiling of the principal's office, the shootout, and the surprise absence of Riley. I even told her about Rex waiting for us. When I finished, I went back to eating.

Kelly processed this for a moment. She did not look happy. "Did you try calling Riley's cell?"

I shook my head. "Not yet. I didn't want to force Aleksei's hand. Riley's still alive. I'm sure of it. The Russian will call when he's ready. Hopefully then we'll be ready too."

"For what? How?" Kelly threw her hands up in the air. "It'll all be on his terms. You have no idea how to prepare for that!"

"Um, excuse me!" I put my hands on my hips. "I *was* a spy. We're used to this kind of stuff! I'm better prepared than you would be!" I was deeply offended. I didn't go to the hospital and stand over Kelly and ask her what her plan was for a sucking chest wound. Okay, so maybe they do actually have a plan for that, but the point is, I don't tell her how to do her job. Of course now, I wondered what the plan was for a sucking chest wound. My mind wanders when I'm tired.

"This is all my fault!" Lana burst into tears. "They wanted me, not Riley. And now you two are fighting! I'm so sorry!"

Kelly immediately started consoling the blonde bombshell with intermittent glares at me that said, *This is all your fault, and what are you going to do about it?*

"Look, Lana," I started, "it's not your fault. It's just part of the job."

"Do you think the KGB, or whatever you called them, killed Carlos, Ahmed, and Midori?" Kelly changed the subject to make Lana feel better.

I thought about this. "It kind of looks like it…"

Lana interrupted me. "Of course they did it! The FSB is behind it all!"

"I don't know," I said. And I didn't. With everything going on, I hadn't taken two minutes to examine this clearly.

"I mean, on the surface, yeah, I'd say they did it. And I'd like to think that because once I kill Aleksei, it's all over."

"But?" Kelly searched my face. She knew I wasn't convinced.

I shrugged. "But what's the motive? If Lana was the endgame, why not just come and get her?"

Lana frowned. "They wanted to blame you, maybe? Because you are the one who recruited me to spy on them?"

I nodded slowly. "Yeah, I guess I could see that. But why *those* three terrorists? Why go to all that trouble of bringing them here alive? It's a LOT of work to go to. Why not just kill me too?"

"By framing you," Kelly said slowly, "they get the Yakuza, Colombian drug cartels, and al-Qaeda angry. Wouldn't it be worse to be hunted by three different terrorist groups?"

I smiled. Of the two of us, Kelly was the smart one. "That makes a little more sense," I said, "but it still seems like a reach…"

Kelly rolled her eyes. "Why does it have to be more complicated than that? I think you're overthinking it."

Lana nodded. "Maybe they were behind you being outed and forcibly retired?"

That stopped me. Was that what happened? "So you think they leaked the information on me?" I remembered the hell I'd been through to get back to the U.S. when it had happened. Especially that armed chicken. I'll never forget *that*.

"Maybe they thought I'd be killed on the spot. That I wouldn't make it home alive?" That was possible.

We sat there in silence, thinking. Of course, we also had another serving of the casserole. It helped—believe me.

"I don't know," I said finally. "I mean, it could've happened that way, but it seems like a pretty elaborate conspiracy just because I turned Lana."

"I think it's a good explanation," Kelly said.

"Yes, but you're not a spy," I countered. "And besides, how do you explain the Congressional commission finding that the Vice President was behind the betrayal?"

"He denied it all the way," Kelly said. "Maybe the commission was wrong."

I could tell she really liked this idea. Lana seemed to be backing her up, because her head was nodding like a bobblehead that mainlined a pound of speed. Why was I so unsure? It just seemed too fantastic. Too bizarre. But then, the FSB weren't quite the agency they were in the Cold War.

"I'll have to worry about that later," I said finally. "Our main objective right now is to get Riley back alive." I pulled a plastic grocery bag from under the counter and rolled some dishtowels up inside of it.

"What are you doing?" Kelly asked.

I went to the front door. "I have to get our guns out of the car. I couldn't bring them in when Rex was here. And if Aleksei comes here tonight, I want to be ready."

I was out the door before they could say anything. I squinted at the patrol car. It really was Kevin Dooley in there.

"Hey Kevin!" I waved. "I have to get some things out of the car. I'll just be a minute!"

He nodded, then went back to staring into space. Since I found out that I knew him, I felt a little guilty about betraying him by leaving. Even if he was a jerk to me in middle school.

I climbed into the driver's side of the SUV and shut the door. The console was a mess as a result of me hotwiring the car. Damn. Riley wasn't going to get his deposit back on this rental, and I wasn't going to get this thing started again. I wonder if Kelly would let me use her car to go rescue Riley.

The guns were under the seat, so I grabbed all three and wrapped them in the towels before putting them in the bag. I reached up to adjust the rearview mirror to look at Rex's house. It would probably suck if he came over and caught me with three unregistered handguns in a grocery bag.

My hand bumped the visor, and a set of keys fell into my lap. Really? They were there the whole damn time? Perfect. I shoved them into the bag too and got out of the

SUV. I held up the bag to Kevin as I walked by. He nodded, and I went back into the house.

I put the two H&K's and the Colt Gold Cup on the kitchen counter. Well, at least we had weapons. That made me feel a little better. I couldn't imagine charging into a rescue operation wielding a nail gun that required an extension cord.

"Why do you have tools lying all over the house?" Kelly asked me as she carried the giant wrench into the kitchen.

"It made sense at the time," I said irritably. Why was everyone criticizing my homemade weapons system? First Riley, now Kelly. I'd like to see them do better. "It's all I had to work with."

Kelly dropped the wrench on the counter with a loud clank. "You thought they'd come back, didn't you?"

I nodded. "Yup. Only we didn't have to do that. And now we have these!" I held up the Colt.

We sent Kelly home with a clean casserole pan. Lana and I unloaded each of the guns and checked the magazines. They were in good working order. We re-loaded the magazines and racked the slides to chamber a round before putting the safety on. I plugged my cell into the charger. We were kind of, sort of ready.

Now all we had to do was wait.

CHAPTER NINETEEN

I woke up to the sound of someone banging on the door. I was face down on the breakfast bar, with a pistol for a pillow under my check. Daylight streamed through the kitchen window. What time was it?

I got up, somewhat unsteadily and looked around. There was no one else in the kitchen. Lana must've gone to bed. I ran cold water over my face in the sink, ignoring the continued pounding on the door. The clock on the stove said it was eight o'clock in the morning. Great.

And who the hell was beating on my door? I swept the gun off the counter and into a drawer. After running my hands through my hair, I straightened my shirt and answered the door.

Rex stood there wearing a suit and a smile.

"Yes?" I asked a bit irritably.

Rex looked at me for a second, like a dog looks at you when it doesn't understand what you've just said. He pointed at my cheek. "You've got the word *Colt* imprinted on your face."

I rubbed my cheek vigorously. "Why are you here, Rex?"

"I just wanted to check on you and Ms. Babikova," he said, his smile never fading. "Before I go into the office."

"Oh. Right," I said. "We're okay. I fell asleep watching TV. I should probably take a nap." I didn't really want him to go. But I needed to brush my teeth and wake up Lana. Why didn't she hear the door?

Rex sighed. "You know, Merry," he said softly, "I'm just doing my job."

For reasons I couldn't really explain, that just pissed me off. "Just doing your job? Well, if you're just doing your job, you know that we're okay so you can go now, Detective."

"Well, it's more than that, really." His blue eyes studied me. Like he was sizing me up. Like he wanted to tell me something.

"Yeah?" I snapped. "Well, it's starting to feel like harassment." I hated myself a little just then. He was a great guy. A good neighbor and a cop just trying to help people. But I needed him to go. My cell could ring any time now, and I didn't want him there when Aleksei called

He nodded. "Sorry to bother you." I watched in agony as he turned and walked a few steps away. Then he turned back to me. "You know, Merry, you really need to let someone help you every now and then. I'm not a bad guy. I'm not the enemy." With a half smile that seemed a little sad, Detective Rex Ferguson turned and walked away.

I stood there, on my stoop, and watched as he walked across the street, got into his car, and drove away. I noticed the officer in front of the house was staring at me.

"Go *away*, Kevin!" I shouted as I turned and went into my house. Like I needed judgment from *him*.

When this was all over I needed to take Rex a cake or something to apologize for being such a jerk. Maybe Kelly would help me. Or maybe she'd just make it for me. But that would have to wait until after I'd killed Aleksei, Riley was rescued, and Lana was safe from threat. Then I could get my car fixed, buy real curtains, and start acting like a normal person—or at least a person who doesn't get into shootouts with terrorists. Now that I think of it—that seems like a pretty long list. Maybe I could take him a cake before I get curtains. Something to think about.

As if on cue, my cell began to ring. I ran to it and grabbed a pen and paper. You know how in those spy movies, the villain calls and gives detailed instructions to James Bond, and he memorizes it—addresses, names, etc. without any problem at all? Well, that's not me. That's

actually not any spy I know. It's just a movie. I needed paper and pen.

"Hello?" I answered. "Riley?" I asked hopefully.

"No." A thick, Russian accent said. "If you want to see Riley alive ever again, you need to do exactly as I say."

Ugh. What a cliché! I swear, some of these foreign agents learn English from bad TV shows.

"What do you want?"

"I want you to meet me at noon at the school," he said. Clearly he didn't have an original bone in his body. We'd already done the school. Oh well.

"Fine. Is that all?" I asked. But he'd hung up.

"Lana!" I ran down the hall to her bedroom. "Lana!" I knocked on the door as I opened it. "We've got our instructions!" I said as the door swung open on an empty room.

Oh, right. Of course. She must've spent the night in my room. It's probably still scary to be in hers.

"Lana!" I called as I crossed the hall and opened my door. The bed was made. Lana wasn't there. I ran through the house calling for her, but she never answered. I checked the basement, the garage, and the backyard. I looked in every closet. But Lana was gone.

I pulled my gun out of the drawer and looked around. That's when I realized that the other two guns were missing. And after that, I realized that during the phone call with Aleksei, he never mentioned Lana during our conversation. Not even once.

I sat on the couch with the gun in my hand and thought about it. If this was about Lana, Aleksei would've asked me to bring her. But he didn't. He just asked for me. Either he was really bad at this and didn't realize he'd made a mistake, or he wasn't after Lana to begin with.

Damn.

* * *

An hour later, I was no closer to any ideas than I'd been before. I was tired. Exhausted. I couldn't remember

ever being this tired before. More than a year ago, I would've loved something like this. But that all changed when I went civilian. I didn't really want this anymore. Granted, I had no idea what I wanted...but I knew it wasn't this.

I was in way over my head here. The only other person who knew about this was Kelly, and there was no way I was dragging her into a showdown. And if she knew Aleksei had taken Lana too, well, there'd be no way I could stop her from coming.

Was that what happened? Aleksei showed up and took Lana at gunpoint? I rolled that idea around in my head. When would he have been able to do that? Sure, I'd fallen asleep, but I was pretty sure that something like a huge Russian busting down the door and dragging Lana off would've woke me up. I wasn't that sound a sleeper.

Maybe he called her, on her cell phone? Maybe he told her he'd kill Riley if she didn't come. That made more sense. Lana would sneak out in order to get him to leave me alone. But that idea didn't jive with the fact that Aleksei still wanted *me* there. So why didn't he take both of us if he'd been here to take Lana? My head was spinning. Both theories had good and bad points about them. In fact, there really wasn't any way I could know what had happened until I showed up at the school at noon.

All I had was one gun. Aleksei or Lana didn't take it because I was lying on top of it, hiding it with my face.

With no handler to help me out—no headquarters to back me up—I was screwed. I thought about that for a moment. Why not call Langley? Riley still worked for them, and really, this was their problem, not mine.

But who would I call? I had no idea who Riley's chain of command was. What was I going to do? Call the receptionist and say, *Hey, do you know who Riley Andrews' boss is? He's been kidnapped, and I need some backup.* I couldn't do that. And there were—actually, that's classified—but let's just say there were a LOT of staff personnel in the Black Box. How was I supposed to know whose extension I wanted?

Dammit! Riley had never included me in his connections with the agency. I should've forced him to tell me more. But it never occurred to me that I'd need the name and phone number of his supervisor. Riley was just always there. And he kept saying that this was too classified to have other agents there. Too classified for me to know anything more about it. Too classified...

Why did he have to leave me out of the loop? I know I wasn't an agent anymore, but I was involved. So it was stupid not to fill me in. It's not like I was a stranger to covert ops. I would think his little cabal at the agency wouldn't mind me knowing what I was up against. It seemed kind of stupid really. But then, I'd never really pressed Riley to tell me either.

In fact, I couldn't think of a single time in the past when he'd been so secretive. We'd always been upfront with each other. I get that this was different, but he should've clued me in. My brain kept coming back to that. The more I asked myself these questions, the weirder it seemed. Riley's mistake of keeping me in the dark only made things easier for the FSB. And it was rare for Riley to even make such a mistake in the first place. It's like he was...like he was...uh-oh.

Was Riley behind all this? Gears started rolling in my head. Riley. It couldn't be. No. No, no, no, no. That was impossible. What was I thinking? Riley worked for the Agency way longer than I had. He started right out of college and never worked anywhere else. I couldn't think of one single instance when he'd so much as *criticized* the CIA.

Why would he risk everything to betray his country? No. That was ridiculous. I was kind of pissed that my brain introduced the idea. Bad, stupid, naughty brain! Riley would never go rogue. He was married to the job.

I felt a little flustered thinking of him. There were definitely some feelings there that I couldn't ignore. And he'd kissed me. There was an attraction on his side too. After all, I hadn't initiated that. He liked me. Right?

And yet, my mind kept coming back to that little seed of doubt. I couldn't convince myself entirely that Riley

was completely innocent. Why was that? I'd always been big on trusting my instincts. They'd never failed me. Not even when all the signs pointed to something different.

Once in a Caribbean country that shall remain nameless (It's still classified.), the agent I was working with assured me that he was on my side. There wasn't even the slightest shred of an idea that Paolo was selling me out. Everything he did and said pointed to his loyalty. I'd even followed him several nights after he'd left me and found nothing even remotely disingenuous.

But I never could get rid of that sick feeling in my stomach that something was wrong. So, I kept surveilling him, even though I felt like an idiot doing so. Day after day, week after week, I double-checked all the information he gave me. It was completely solid. There were no holes in the intelligence he gave me.

And yet, I still felt weird. So I kept following him and checking up (and feeling a little like an ass). It wasn't until two months later that I caught him selling me out to that nation's government. I was behind a barrel in a warehouse down by the docks (I know, total cliché, right?) when I overheard him telling *his* handler all about what I looked like and how to find me. Of course, he didn't really know how to find me because like I said, at that moment, I was hiding behind a rather rancid barrel of fish.

Of course, I left the country immediately. You don't stick around once you've been made. And I kicked myself for trusting him. But on the other hand, I'd been right. My instincts had gotten me out of the jam. And I've trusted them ever since.

And those instincts told me that something was wrong here. And my thoughts kept turning to Riley. Every time.

After all—Riley could've found a way to get Ahmed, Carlos, and Midori here. Riley showed up on my doorstep out of the blue—saying the agency was worried about my involvement. Riley brought Lana here. It was Riley who got me out of the house to tell me he thought Lana was the target. Lana would've trusted Riley. She would've gone with

him this morning if he'd showed up and asked her to, without a second thought.

She'd been so convinced that she'd put me in danger—she would've left with him no problem if he'd showed up in the middle of the night and asked her to help him take out Aleksei. Riley couldn't get me a gun until I insisted. Riley wouldn't call for back up.

Because the CIA didn't know Riley was here. Or, they knew he was here and didn't come because he said he'd handle it. There was no involving the agency at this point because they'd think I was an idiot if I called. Because it was more than likely that Riley was behind it all.

And I was going to kill him.

After I got Lana back, that is.

The memory of Riley kissing me—that was all subterfuge. He was trying to sort of seduce me to keep me from suspecting anything. And it worked. Dammit! To say that I was upset would be like saying the ocean was made of water. It hurt. It really hurt. I was starting to develop feelings for the guy! And it had been a long, long, time since that had happened. How did I get sucked in so easily? Was I that desperate for a kiss?

I felt pathetic. Mainly because I should've known better. Like I said, I've experienced betrayal before. Granted, some of it was more blatant than what happened with Paolo. There was the kid in the Rio slums who sold me out to a gang for a soccer ball and a jar of pickled herring. (It's a novelty there—and it's something that should never be a novelty *anywhere*.) Then in Shanghai, my interpreter informed on me to the police for three and a half squid— which made no sense to me because what do you only want half a squid for? Why not go for another whole squid? Well, anyway, you get the picture.

I swallowed my pride and shook my head to clear the emotions away. There was no time for this. I needed to get my act together and focus on the facts. Emotion was deadly to espionage. I couldn't let Riley think he'd gotten the better of me. The bastard.

So I focused on what I could deal with. Aleksei worked for Riley. And in a couple of hours, Riley and Aleksei would be at the school with Lana tied up as bait—waiting for me to show up.

But why? Why did Riley hate me enough to set this whole elaborate scheme up? What had I done to make him want to target me? Maybe he always hated me? Was he behind me being outted…being retired early?

You know, those kisses weren't really all that passionate. If he hated me, I could understand why he only kissed me twice. And that was as far as it got.

That pissed me off. Riley had used me this whole time. Used me to set me up and to most likely kill me. Who knows what his motivation was? It could be anything. He was crazy. Crazy enough to hate me for no reason whatsoever (I was a *model* employee.) and crazy enough to drag Lana and three terrorists into it.

There was no point thinking about it anymore. He'd probably monologue like a James Bond villain once I got there anyway. I'd find out then. For now, I needed some sort of plan. I needed help. With a heavy sigh, I picked up my cell and dialed. No point in keeping secrets anymore. It was time to call in some backup.

CHAPTER TWENTY

———

Rex blinked at me from my living room couch. He said nothing, which made me a little uncomfortable. Maybe it was because I was decked out in full tactical gear. I looked a little like a grown up Kim Possible with my combat boots, green cargo pants, and black T-shirt. The holstered Colt probably only added to my looking like someone from a bad action movie. Or maybe it was because I'd just told him a story of espionage, Russian spies, KGB spooks, and one rogue CIA agent who was setting me up.

I was taking a risk here—involving the local police. There was always the possibility Rex wouldn't buy it and would arrest me for having an unlicensed gun and for being completely crazy. (Which I'm not sure is a real crime—but he'd probably make it become one, just because.) Why should he believe me? I'm not sure *I* would believe me at this point. Even Kevin out in his squad car would have a hard time buying my story. *Blasted Kevin.*

But Rex was all I had. I needed help. And I no longer cared if the CIA got a black eye in all of this—the bastards. They should've known Riley had gone off the grid. They were responsible for not picking up on that. And if I survived this—I was going to sue the crap out of them.

"Okay," Rex said finally.

"Okay? Okay as in, you believe me—or okay as in, you think I'm nuts and should be committed?"

Rex shook his head. "Okay, as in I believe you."

"Really?" I felt a little surge of adrenaline. Or maybe that was the three energy drinks I'd just slammed. Lana had bought them on our shopping trip. I didn't think she'd mind.

He put his hands on his knees and stood up. "I knew something was weird the moment I met you, Merry."

Well that didn't sound good. He'd thought I was weird. On the other hand, that's what made him a good detective. There were benefits to that.

"What convinces you that my story is true?" Actually, I just wanted to make sure he did believe me and that there wouldn't be an ambulance secretly waiting outside to take me to an asylum.

He sighed. "Number one—you basically don't exist on paper or online. That isn't unusual. It's impossible. Number two—your "cousin" Riley didn't seem as much a family member as a supervisor. It was obvious that he was controlling the situation. Number three—you and Lana couldn't possibly be related. You don't look even remotely alike. Also—neither Lana nor Riley had a presence on paper or online. How could all three of you be off the grid?"

"Why didn't you say anything?" I asked. Why did we think it would be so easy to fool Rex? He wasn't some third world cop who happily looked the other way. And yet, we'd treated him like that. I kind of felt a little stupid now.

"I figured it would play out eventually. And you were entertaining to watch."

Oh great. "Well that doesn't sound very flattering."

Rex looked me right in the eye. "And it's flattering to me that you guys thought you could play me like shuffleboard? At least now I get to say *I told you so.*"

Shuffleboard? What was he, an old man in a hot, young body? I'd really have to get past that when we started dating.

"This is serious, Rex. People's lives are in danger here. My friend Lana is one of them."

"Our lives included," Rex said with a frown. "I don't like going into this with no time to prepare properly. This is not how a police force operates."

I shrugged. "It's exactly how the CIA operates. In those circumstances, you have only yourself and possibly one other agent. And you have to act immediately. Time is not on your side."

He didn't say anything for a moment. This was a big deal. He barely knew me, and here I was asking him for something impossible. I wasn't entirely certain that he wouldn't just put me in the back of Kevin's squad car and call in the National Guard. On the other hand, trusting me would be like taking a huge step forward in our future relationship.

"I'll do it." Rex sighed. "But on my terms."

I frowned. "What terms? *I* have to go. This is *my* fight. Not yours. I'm involving you as backup."

He shook his head. "It's not just about you. You're involving the community, even if it is outside of town. And my job is to 'Serve & Protect'…just in case you didn't see that on the black and white outside."

Jeez! Did he really talk like that? *Shuffleboard* and *black and white*? We'd have to work on that before we officially started dating. I had some standards after all.

"Fine," I said grudgingly. I don't know what bothered me more—that he was taking over what was really my problem, or the fact that he seemed to be more interested in protecting the public than worrying about me. Yes, I know that's selfish. I never said I wasn't selfish.

Rex walked toward the door. "I'm going to need to change before we go. You'll have to come with me. I don't want you running off without me."

He wanted me to go with him! To his house! Where he was sometimes naked! Okay! If I died today, at least I was able to see inside Rex's house, and who knows, maybe I'd get to watch him change. Kind of like the last meal for a convict on death row.

I followed him across the street to his house. Kevin looked up and stared at me. I flipped him off, but secretly, so Rex couldn't see. He led the way into his house, and I followed, shutting the door behind me.

Whoa. Rex had a nice house. It didn't look like a bachelor had just moved in there either. There wasn't a single box. The living room was completely set up as if he'd always lived there.

"Stay here," he said. "I'm going to go change."

Damn. "Okay," I said a little grumpily.

While he was upstairs, I snooped around his house. It was pretty impressive. His living room furniture, rugs, and drapes all matched. The hardwood floors gleamed and there was a piano in the corner. A piano? Did Rex play the piano? Maybe it was just for show. Maybe I should get a huge harp or something.

The dining room was just off the living room. A gorgeous, dark wood table was surrounded by six matching chairs. There was some sort of bronze sculpture in the middle of the table. I picked it up and examined it. There were moving parts, and one of them broke off in my hand. Uh-oh. The man lets me into his house, where he's sometimes naked, and I break his weird little sculpture before I'm here five minutes! I carefully put the sculpture back, leaning the broken piece against it in the back where it wouldn't be spotted right away. If I survived what was coming—I'd make sure to fix or replace it first thing.

The kitchen was off the dining room. It was pretty basic. Bright white cupboards and countertops. And it was clean. Did Rex even live here? *Knock it off, Wrath! He's just a neat and organized guy.* I heard him coming down the stairs and raced back into the living room, draping myself casually on a leather chair. My holstered gun dug into my side, but I acted as if it didn't.

Rex made his way downstairs, and I gasped. That man was way too attractive to be a cop. He had on a black T-shirt, one that fit him like it was sprayed onto his very nice, leanly muscled torso, dark green pants, and black boots. In fact, we kind of matched. I didn't know whether to be excited or freaked out by this. He was in the process of putting on a belt with a holster. It looked like he had a Glock .45. Nice.

"I called in backup," he said. I opened my mouth to protest, but he held his hands out to stop me. "This is non-negotiable. I would like us to both survive this situation."

My mouth dropped open. "You would?" In hindsight—this was kind of a stupid question. Who didn't want to survive a gunfight?

Rex nodded. "And if we do, I'd like to take you out to dinner."

Wait. What?

"Okay," I said, a little dazed. It felt like the room was spinning a bit. Actually, for someone who'd been obsessing about dating Rex, it was a ridiculous reaction. But then, I'd never really thought I could coax a date out of him. So this was nice. Really, really nice.

"…it's just SWAT and a tactical team," Rex was saying. Had he been talking? He was grinning at me—which I guess meant he was amused by me. That was okay.

"They have to be hidden. If Aleksei and Riley see them, they might go ahead and kill Lana, not to mention try to escape." I had to get Lana back safe. That was the most important thing. I felt as though I'd let her down. Besides, my Girl Scout troop would never forgive me if something happened to her. I think I was more afraid of facing them.

"They will be out of sight. And they won't move until I give the signal," Rex assured. "But I'm going in with you."

I shook my head. "I'm supposed to come alone. You have to come in *after* I go in."

Rex frowned. "I'm going in with you. You can argue all you want, but that's what's going to happen."

I had to think for a moment. Would Riley and Aleksei react badly to Rex's presence? I could sneak him in through the classrooms. I was pretty sure the showdown would be in the gym. It was large and centrally located. Riley would know I'd head straight for that. He wouldn't want to waste time having me search all of the classrooms.

"Fine. But you have to stay out of sight until I call you in."

"If I hear shooting or a prelude to shooting—I'm coming in hot," Rex insisted. Damn straight he was. He couldn't come in any other way dressed like that.

I nodded. "Okay." I looked at my watch. It was a quarter till. We had to get going.

I drove my crappy, damaged car. Riley had used the office to watch for the Russians earlier, and I was pretty sure

he'd do it again. If he saw Rex's car, he'd know something was up. Something actually was up, but I didn't want him to know that just yet.

Rex ducked down once we were a few minutes out, and I drove carefully into the school parking lot and parked where we had earlier. I took a deep breath and let it out. I was nervous. More than I'd been when we were going to take on the Russians yesterday. It was probably because I knew they wanted to kill me. No one has wanted to kill me in a long, long time. You never really get used to that feeling.

I waited a few minutes to give Riley and Aleksei time to move to the gym. Rex and I got out of the car. I motioned to the unlocked door and signaled him to wait a few minutes to enter. I'd already briefed him on the layout of the school on the way. He was going to do what I did—use the interconnecting classrooms to get to one of the gym entrances.

"See you soon," Rex whispered.

I entered the school noisily. They knew I was coming. My guess was they wanted something dramatic. They weren't going to shoot me down in the hallway. And Riley would of course want to give a speech on how he'd fooled me and why he'd done it. I had no doubt about that.

I headed down the hallway and entered the gym through the side door. The room looked empty.

"Здравствуйте." A Russian voice welcomed me from the stage. I turned to see Aleksei standing in the middle of it with spotlights directly on him. Apparently, we were going for full-on drama.

"Пошел на хуй! I swore back at him—I told him to eff off. I'd wanted to make an impact.

And I did. Aleksei's face darkened. I didn't give him a chance to respond.

"Где Светлана?" I shouted the question, shaking with building fury. I switched to English. "I'd like to see her first! She needs to go free before whatever you're planning happens!"

A strange look crossed the Russian's face. I couldn't decipher it. Maybe because he was so ugly. He switched to a wicked leer.

"Aren't you worried about Riley, Miss Wrath?" He asked in heavily accented English. "Or should I say, Miss Fionnaghuala Czrygy."

I shrugged. "So you know my name. Big deal, Aleksei." I wasn't going to tell him I was impressed that he pronounced it correctly. He didn't deserve it.

A look of shock crossed his face. "How did you know my name?" Ah. So I was right about that.

I smiled. "Tradecraft. I was a pretty good spy, you know." My goal was to make him think I wasn't afraid of him. In the back of my head, I was straining to hear if Rex was moving through the school. I heard nothing. I'd have to take it on faith that he was there.

The Russian regained his composure. "Does not matter. I will soon wipe smug look off your face."

Threats. Well, that's what I was here for, wasn't I? To put myself in danger so Lana would be released. I wondered, with an internalized shudder, what he and Riley had planned for me. It wouldn't be good. I was pretty sure of that.

"I don't want to talk to you, Aleksei. I'd rather talk to your puppet-master. You're just the hired thug." My voice projected confidence, but inside I was worried.

"What does this mean?" Aleksei frowned. "This puppet-master?"

I sighed. He wasn't totally proficient in English then. Fine. "The guy who's manipulating your strings. That's the puppet-master."

He cocked his head to one side. "Puppet." He thought about the word for a moment, and I let him because I wasn't in any hurry to march into my own death. "Puppet?"

Great. He was a total idiot. I held up my hand and formed a puppet with my fingers. I opened and closed the fingers like it was talking. "Puppet. A sort of doll you put on your hand."

A look of understanding crossed his face. "Ah. Like the Muppets! I love Miss Piggy." Then he frowned. "But no strings on Muppets."

Oh my God. This could drag on for hours. I held up both hands, palms down and mimed holding marionette strings. "It's a different kind. The ones that don't talk but you can manipulate their bodies."

"Oh," Aleksei said simply, "are you calling me a Muppet?"

Okay, so that took the sting out of my earlier request. And I'd thought it was a good line. Oh well. Time to move on.

"Where's Riley?" I asked instead. "I know he's here."

The Russian understood this. He walked off stage, and I heard a kind of scraping sound before Aleksei came into view, dragging Riley, who was tied to a chair. Great. So they believed I hadn't yet figured it all out. You know, it was just like Riley to do something like this.

"You can cut the act with me," I growled. "I know who's behind this. What I want to know is why?"

Riley, who was gagged pretty convincingly, gave Aleksei a look. Aleksei returned that look. Clearly they were communicating. It was time for Riley to give it up. I knew too much to be fooled by his being fake-tied-up.

"Why?" Aleksei asked as if he was in the dark about the reason we were all there. He was definitely just muscle.

A look of recognition crossed his face, and he smiled while pulling a piece of paper from his back pocket. Was he going to read a script?

"It is written down so I get this right." Aleksei smiled as he tapped the piece of paper. "I begin now." He kicked a red, rubber ball that was at his feet on the stage. It bounced over to me and stopped a foot away.

"Great," I mumbled. This was too ridiculous for words. What was he going to do? Challenge me to dodgeball to the death now?

"You…" He stopped after one word and pointed to me. "Fionnaghuala Czrygy, are charged with crimes against Russia. I am to take you back to Moskva where you will be

tried and executed for these crimes." He folded up the piece of paper and stuffed it back into his pocket. He smiled, clearly pleased with his speech.

I rolled my eyes. "*That's* what this is about?" So, Riley was working for the Russians now? What turned him? It had to be money. The FSB paid well, and the CIA still used the government pay grade—which basically sucked.

Aleksei nodded, confused. "Of course it is! What did you think this was about?"

Out of the corner of my right eye, I saw Rex standing in the shadows of the doorway. I felt a little better. Two on two were better odds. At any minute now Riley would drop the ropes and pull his gun.

I shrugged. "I just thought it was more complicated than that."

Clearly, Aleksei didn't understand. He once more exchanged glances with Riley, whose act was starting to get on my nerves. I wasn't a particularly fast draw, but maybe I should shoot him before he stood up.

"Ah." Aleksei figured it out. "Because of dead terrorists."

I nodded. "Yes, because of them. If you just wanted me, why go to all this trouble?"

He shrugged. Clearly he was not the mastermind of anything.

"So what now, Aleksei?" I asked. "You won't take me until I see Lana go free." He didn't know Rex was in the hallway or that the building was surreptitiously surrounded by cops. Did he really think it would be this easy?

"And Riley…" I narrowed my eyes at my former boss and until recently—possible candidate for boyfriend. "You can drop the act now. I *know*."

Riley narrowed his eyes at me. Now that was a look I understood. He was pissed that I was smart enough to call his bluff. Seriously—men's egos are so fragile!

"I get that you're still trying to make me think you're a hostage, but I figured it all out." I folded my arms over my chest. "Just how much are they paying you to betray your country, anyway?"

Riley's face was red, and he was shaking with fury. I guess he was still convinced he could play this out.

"Ugh!" I stamped my foot and curled my hands into fists. "You're being a big baby about this. Give up the masquerade already!" Men! I'd about had it with them. I was definitely getting a cat after all this was over. I wondered if Lana would like that. I hoped she wasn't allergic or anything…

A strange sound echoed off the hallway on my left. It was singing! It sounded like a lot of voices. A chill ran through me as I realized who it was. No! It couldn't be!

"Everywhere we go…people want to know…who we are…so we tell them…"

Just then, two rows of my Girl Scout troop, in their uniforms, marched into the gym, singing one of their songs. My jaw dropped open. Why did the SWAT team allow them in? What kind of sick bastard kidnaps little girls? Oh. A sick bastard who didn't want a gun fight. Because I wasn't going to shoot with my troop in the middle of it all.

The girls stopped marching and singing, staring at me as if I'd turned into a rabid hippopotamus. Oh right. I had a holstered gun on my hip. That might've seemed a tad terrifying to them. My heart was pounding as I turned to the stage.

"You don't need them!" I cried out to Aleksei. I brought my hand up to my heart. "I was going to go with you! Send them back outside right now!"

I turned toward the doorway. The last of the girls were marching in now. And right behind them, marching along and singing with them, was Lana.

CHAPTER TWENTY-ONE

"Lana!" I shouted. They must've made her contact the troop and bring them here. "How could you? You should've refused..." my voice drifted off.

Lana was smiling. Lana was holding a gun. And she was aiming it into the two rows of girls. It was Lana who was the puppet-master. Not Riley. Lana.

I turned to Riley whose eyes had grown wide with fear when he saw the kids. "Oops. Sorry Riley," I said weakly. I was starting to feel bad for suspecting him. And for letting Lana live with me. And for letting her near my troop.

Lana. Aleksei worked for Lana. My head was spinning. She was behind all this? How did I not see this coming? For a moment, I thought I would throw up. Danger never bothered me before, but now there were fourteen little girls in the middle of it all.

How could she? I took her in! Fed and clothed her! Hated her, then liked her, then hated her, then felt sorry for her! I was going to rescue her from this! I was literally here to save her life. Well, forget about that now!

Riley gave me a look that said, *We are going to talk about this later!*

"Hey!" I said with a wounded look. "You're the one who brought her into my home! This is your fault. Don't go blaming me!"

Riley looked like he wanted to argue. But he couldn't. Because of the gag. For once during this whole mess, I was a little grateful that he couldn't speak.

I turned to Lana. "What the hell, Lana?" I wanted to say something a little stronger, but the girls were in the room. It's all about being a role model, you know.

Lana threw back her head and laughed. "Stupid, stupid Merry!"

"Hey!" I said, a little hurt. And pissed. Seriously pissed. I'd been nice to this bitch! I took care of her! Now I wanted to kill her. *Please, please give me the opportunity to do so.*

"You fell for the whole thing!" She laughed. "It was so easy to manipulate you! I just had to pull the rubbery lip pout, and you'd have done anything for me!"

"I thought you were an orphan," I snarled.

Lana laughed loudest at this. "Of course not! My father is a very important political man in Moscow."

Great. There's nothing like public humiliation. Maybe Rex wasn't paying any attention out in the hall. It was kind of important to my self esteem that he think I was a good spy.

"Yes. I fell for that. But I've been out of the business for a while…so…" It was weak, but I had to say something.

Lana's eyes were ice cold. I almost didn't recognize her. "That was a problem for me at first. You disappeared. You even got out of Chechnya alive." She shook her head. "When I get back the first thing I'm going to do is eat that damned chicken."

"You tried to kill me then?" I thought back to the armed chicken I'd encountered. First time I'd heard of a chicken as an assassin. I suppressed a shudder. The Chechen Chicken. You know, I don't mind human killers. You can reason with them…stall. But a screaming rooster running at you at top speed with razors strapped to its legs and a small, laser-sighted heat seeking missile mounted on its head is a little different. I don't know how they trained it to set the thing off, and I don't care. Two barns and a haystack and an unfortunately placed fireworks stand were obliterated by the time I got away.

I looked at the girls. They were hypnotized by the whole thing. Which was good, because I didn't want them to

freak out. I was freaking out, but they weren't allowed to. My mission of just coming into a firefight was nowhere near as scary as having to keep these girls from getting hurt. How was I going to get them out of here unscathed?

She nodded. "I've wanted to kill you from the day I'd met you. You stupid Americans think it's so easy to get us to betray Mother Russia! You needed to be taught a lesson." She was working her way up to a full blown tantrum. It sucked to realize I had absolutely no idea how she was going to play this out. I'd been wrong about her so far. Devastatingly wrong. For all I knew, she could just start killing children and think nothing of it.

"But I never had the opportunity. Then poof! You vanished. I had to try something else." Her eyes strayed to the stage, and she wiggled her fingers at Riley. He turned an alarming shade of red.

"So, I contacted Riley and told him I needed asylum. That I'd been found out in Russia. He led me right to you!" Lana laughed. It wasn't that cute, musical little giggle she'd been doing these past few days. It was a hearty, full out, maniacal laugh. It was kind of like listening to the Darth Vader theme.

I needed to stall. Keep her talking so I could figure out what to do next. I looked out into the doorway where Rex was. He was talking into his cell phone. If he brought SWAT in too early, these kids were dead.

I tried to keep my voice steady. "So what was up with the dead terrorists? Why go to all that work?"

Lana shrugged. "I wanted to discredit you. I wanted the CIA to think you were a mole in several organizations. After you were humiliated, I'd kill you."

"Well that's kind of a stupid idea," I said. "Why not just kill me the first time?"

Lana's face turned purple and she brought the gun up level with my chest. I could almost see sparks shooting out of her ears. Okay, so don't piss off the scary blonde. Got it.

"I could have killed you one thousand times over! But I didn't want you to die too soon. I wanted to humiliate you. To fool you. To make you realize what an imbecile you

are. I wanted you to suffer!" she screamed. "I wanted you to know the pain of having everyone hate you! That's why I brought them here and killed them!"

The girls started fidgeting nervously. A couple of the Kaitlynns looked like they were going to faint. So far they weren't losing it. I'd be proud of them if I wasn't so scared about what Lana might do to them.

I waved my pistol at her man. "You think *I'm* an imbecile? You hired these idiots. I bested two of them on my own. Who's the idiot now?"

Lana's eyes grew wild. Whoa. Maybe I'd better reign it in with the insults. There's no point in pissing her off just to soothe my fragile ego. I had to keep her talking without exploding.

"How did you get them into the country?" I looked at Riley, and he nodded. Apparently, I'd asked the question he was thinking all along.

Lana snorted and rolled her eyes. "Too easy. Ahmed was a sex maniac."

"Hey! Keep it clean! There are kids here!" I protested. I thought I heard a couple of giggles from the girls when Lana said *sex*. That's fine—better than them screaming and forcing her to shut them up with bullets.

The Russian acted as if I hadn't said anything. "Ahmed had a thing for blondes. I told him that there was a secret harem of blondes in the States—who would do anything he wanted. Men are so ridiculous. I smuggled him in by declaring him my personal bodyguard. The documents were easy to forge. You Americans suck at that."

I wanted to keep her talking until I could think of a way to get the troop out of here. Well, that, and I wanted to know how it all went down.

"And Carlos?" I asked. She still had the damn gun. I was seriously worried she'd get bored with conversation and start shooting.

"I told him there was a problem with his supply route. Something he'd have to take care of personally. I might have promised him sex too." She stuck her tongue out at me. Clearly, she didn't care about what the girls thought.

That worried me. If she didn't care, she'd have no problem killing them.

"How did you get him into the country?" I was getting nervous. At some point she was going to get tired of my questions.

"Ah," she said with a smile. She really was enjoying herself. "I brought him in using a yacht. He was hidden in a special compartment his organization used to smuggle drugs in. We landed on the island of Catalina and took the ferry to the mainland. No one tried to stop us."

She picked a long blonde hair off her gun and dropped it on the floor before continuing, "In fact, the only real problem was keeping them both here at the same time. But all I had to do was rent two different mansions in the area. I told them I owned the houses. They had no idea what was going on. Or maybe Carlos did when I shoved him from a hedge in front of your car."

Lana narrowed her eyes. I was running out of time.

"And Midori? How did you pull that off?" Of course! She dragged the dead Yakuza leader into the kitchen when I was looking out the window in the living room. She'd gotten to the body before me. Obviously she'd stashed it in the garage until it was time to dump her in my kitchen.

She shrugged. Man, this chick could go from full-blown rage to calm in seconds. Not good. It meant she was mentally unstable, which only made our situation worse.

"No idea. Midori wasn't mine. I was just as surprised to see her there as you were."

What? Was she lying to me? Trying to get me to say...say what? I looked at Riley who looked equally confused. And then I remembered that Rex was listening in the hallway. They didn't know about Midori. They would want to know where the body was. I couldn't deal with that now.

"So my big question is..." I took a deep breath, hoping that looked dramatic. "Why?"

Lana scowled. Even with the bruised eyes, she still looked gorgeous. I hated her a little more for that, and this time I didn't even feel guilty.

"Why? Why? For Mother Russia, of course! To strike a blow to the CIA! To America!"

I was a little flattered that she considered nailing me to be a blow to the CIA, but I wasn't going to tell her that.

"Really?" I asked.

"Yes! Of course, really!" Lana was back to fuming now. "Why?"

I shrugged. "Seems kind of simplistic—the whole Evil America thing."

Lana sneered. "You Americans and your need for elaborate plots and intricate intrigues! You all sicken me! I know it won't mean much, killing one CIA operative. But since you were found out, you became famous. And now you lived off the grid. Taking someone like you out would make me a big hero back home!"

"I'm really not that famous," I said. "And your whole plan was an elaborate plot with intricate intrigues, you hypocritical bimbo!"

Lana started sputtering in Russian. Clearly, she hadn't thought about it. I might be in a bad situation, but at least I nailed her on that. Ha!

"And I have the distinct feeling that you plan to kill *two* agents today." I shot a look at Riley. He sat there in stony silence. Mainly because he couldn't do much else.

"Yes!" Lana's eyes grew wide, and she looked a little deranged. "Yes! I'll kill you and your handler! That was the plan!"

My Girl Scouts looked horrified. They looked from Lana, to me, and then to Riley tied up on the stage. We'd been throwing the word *kill* around a lot. And some of us had guns. I watched as it slowly started to sink in what was really happening here.

Then the screaming and crying started. Have you ever been in an elementary school gym? There's an echo you wouldn't believe. Screams bounced off all the walls and back into our ears in a deafening cacophony of horror.

Lana brought her hands up to her ears. Clearly this caused her some discomfort. Good! She was only about six feet away. I tackled her before she could lower the gun. We

crashed to the floor, wrestling for dominance. Now would've been a really good time for Rex to step in and take out Aleksei.

Lana squeezed a shot off and the noise was unbearable. And the screaming got louder. She hadn't hit anyone, but the hissing and deflating red rubber ball in the corner probably wasn't going to make it.

I pounded her wrist against the gym floor until I heard a satisfying snap. I love going for the wrist. Such a fragile part of the human body. So many tiny little bones to break. The gun went skittering away as Lana howled in pain. With her working hand, she reached for the Colt in my holster. I slapped her hand away and punched her hard in the face. As my hand came away, I noticed something blue on it. Makeup. The black eyes were fake! I was going to give her two real ones as soon as I could.

Lana rolled on top, pushing me to the floor underneath her huge boobs. Well that wasn't great. Once again, she tried for my gun. She landed a punch on my chin with her good hand and it hurt. I reached up and grabbed her hair, pulling viciously. Weirdly, a hank of hair came off in my hands. Extensions. Was anything about this woman real?

It wasn't too hard to keep a one-handed woman from my gun, but it meant *I* had trouble accessing it. Lana was like a stark, raving berserker. I guessed the broken wrist didn't hurt her due to her off the charts adrenaline levels. I reached up and grabbed the dangling wrist, squeezing and twisting it. Lana screamed, her eyes filled with pain and rage.

I heard a scuffle nearby and risked a look in that direction. Rex had Aleksei in a choke hold that made him look *totally* cool and *really* hot all at the same time. Riley struggled against his bonds, looking a little less hot. I felt a little guilty about suspecting him.

Lana punched me hard in the face, and I heard my nose snap. Blood started gushing and the girls' screams turned into *EWWWWWWWWWWWWWWWWWWWW*s. Which didn't make the echo situation any better.

I brought my knee up behind her and hit her in the ass, propelling her over my head and onto the floor. I got to my feet, not wanting to waste any time. I pulled the Colt and held it on her. Lana lay there unconscious, and I wondered if she'd broken her neck when she hit the floor. Honestly, I wouldn't feel too bad if she had.

Rex untied Riley and called the SWAT team in. Boots pounded down the hallway and a group of armed men in black surrounded the Girl Scouts and me. They had their guns trained on Lana as four of them jumped onto the stage to pin Aleksei down.

Riley came over to me and looked down. "Sorry about that. I was completely taken in by her."

"Boobs can blind a man..." I said, "but still, you should've caught that. Maybe it's time you retired."

Riley shook his head and wandered out to the hallway with his cell phone. He'd be calling this in to his people—who used to be my people. I watched as Rex ordered the team to take the girls out to the parking lot. My troop looked up in awe as these big men in tactical gear gently calmed them down.

"I wonder if I'll be able to cuff her with that broken wrist," Rex said.

Lana's hand was bent back in a very unnatural position. It looked like it hurt.

"I guess you won't be teaching knot-tying anytime soon, Lana," I said to her unconscious body. It really sucked that she didn't hear me. I thought it was a pretty good slam.

One of the Katelynns looked at me. "I never liked that lady, Mrs. Wrath."

There was some small satisfaction in that.

CHAPTER TWENTY-TWO

It felt like I'd spent a month at the police station. There were so many questions to be answered. Riley tried to shield me as best as he could, but this was the police's jurisdiction. A couple of older dudes I didn't recognize showed up. They were wearing black suits and blue ties. I was pretty sure they were from the CIA. They didn't acknowledge me but spent a lot of time with Riley.

I felt terrible. And stupid. Yes, I blamed Riley for leading Lana to me, but I should've figured it out before now. Worst of all, I'd endangered the lives of my Girl Scouts. Their parents would never let me lead them now. Maybe Kelly would let me watch meetings from a distance. That would be nice, and probably creepy when the girls spotted me lurking behind trees and rocks.

I'd watched as a doctor set and bandaged Lana's wrist and my nose. Rex had called the doctor to the station. He didn't want an international terrorist in the local hospital. Rex avoided cuffing her on her broken wrist, instead cuffing her to him. I suppressed a flare of jealousy.

Lana glared at me the whole time. She was pretty pissed. Every time she looked at me, I gave her a thumbs up. Some Feds showed up to escort her away. I have no idea where they were taking her, but I do know that even she won't look good in prison orange.

My troop surprised me. The police questioned them, and the kids did an amazing job. They'd stopped crying back at the school, and now each and every one of them was calmly giving their statement. Of course, no two girls told the same story. More than once I heard a girl mention rescue by a magical unicorn/Barbie/Princess Aurora. And a couple

of the girls asked if they could get a puppy when this was over. To their credit, the police didn't even bat an eye at these requests. Sadly, no one brought them puppies.

"Mrs. Wrath?" I looked down to see one of the Kaytlins patting me on the arm.

I slipped out of my thoughts. "What is it, honey?" I said as gently as I could. These girls would need some serious counseling after all was said and done. I felt even worse. They'd been in a gun fight because of me. This was my fault, and no amount of s'mores was going to make it right. Better, maybe, but not right.

"Thanks for the BEST DAY EVER!" Kaytlin shouted. I looked around at the other girls. They were all smiling and nodding. Well how about that? Maybe some of them would grow up to be spies. I'd have to check later to see if there's a merit badge for espionage.

With all this testimony, it wasn't hard to piece together what happened. Turned out that Lana came up with using the girls at the last minute. When she couldn't find my Girl Scout call list, she went over to Kelly's to get it. Kelly was suspicious, so Lana pulled a gun on her and her husband and had Aleksei tie them up. That was this morning. Sigh. Once again, Kelly knows something before I do. I'd never hear the end of that. I was pretty sure that also meant no Tater Tot casseroles for a while. That was tragic.

So, Lana had called all the parents and said they were going to do a service project to clean out the school before demolition. Because parents love nothing more than to have a babysitter offer to take their kids off their hands, and because they all had weird little crushes on Lana, they had no problem dropping them off. Lana had them meet in another parking lot under the guise of the school parking lot was a construction site and insurance wouldn't cover the girls if they got hurt running around.

And why didn't the police intervene? That was Rex's first question. (Mine was *Can I shoot Lana?* But no one answered me.) They didn't react because by the time SWAT realized what was happening, Lana had marched right past their hiding spots. They saw the gun in her hand, and since

she was surrounded by girls, they didn't take the shot. Rex wasn't too happy about that. Neither was I.

I was exhausted. Beyond exhausted. But I stayed and answered questions and did my part. I had to do some serious explaining to a bunch of angry parents. And a couple of the dads were really upset that Lana was no longer part of the troop, in spite of the fact she'd almost killed their daughters. But they'd all get over it. At least I hoped they would.

While I was waiting to be released, I called Kelly.

"Your roommate pulled a gun on me," she said as soon as she answered.

"Yeah. Sorry about that," I apologized.

"You owe me big time, Merry," Kelly said.

"Well, it's actually worse than that," I said. Then I explained how the troop got roped into our showdown.

"But no one got hurt, and they're all okay," I added quickly.

There was a long, martyrish sigh on the other end. I didn't really have any friends in town besides Kelly. I'd thought Lana was a friend, but look how *that* turned out. If I lost Kelly, I'd have to get a whole herd of cats just to stave off loneliness.

"Just promise me no more roommates," Kelly finally said.

"I was thinking about getting a cat..."

"A cat is fine, as long as it can't operate a gun," Kelly insisted.

I thought about that armed chicken. "Maybe I'll wait a little bit on that."

I could almost hear her grinning. "Yeah. That's one relationship you should take slowly."

I remembered what Rex had said about a date. Covering the phone, I whispered, "Rex asked me out!"

"Really?" Kelly expressed some surprise.

"Hey!" I protested. "It's not that weird!"

She laughed. "When are you going on this date?"

"Um. I don't really know. The last thing he said was that it was contingent on our surviving the showdown. And we *did* survive it."

Doubt crept into my mind. It was possible Rex had second thoughts after this whole mess went down. After all, I was completely wrong about Riley and Lana. And my Girl Scout troop had been involved—which was also bad.

"I'm sure he meant it." Kelly seemed to be her old self again. "Call me back when you get home, and I'll come over. I made Rice Krispies Treats."

My stomach rumbled. When had I eaten last? "Sounds great, but I'm beat. How about tomorrow?" I was more tired than hungry. Kelly agreed before hanging up.

I watched Rex and Riley as they worked. Riley's laid-back, surfer vibe was a stark contrast to Rex's dark, all-business manner. But maybe that was unfair. He was at work, after all. Both of them shot me a smile whenever they could. And it seemed like they were both a little interested in me. Right?

A couple of SWAT guys approached Rex, and I studied him while they talked. There was no doubt that Rex was respected here. I'd never really worked in an office full of people, but it seemed like that was a good thing. When talking to the other officers, no matter where they were in the hierarchy, he seemed to have command over the conversation. It was pretty hot.

Riley moved back and forth between the police chief and the old men who'd showed up earlier. They had to be administrative CIA. I was pretty sure they weren't happy with the way things went down. They had that constipated scowl that old men get. Riley didn't seem worried about it. He smiled and laughed easily, coaxing good moods out of everyone he talked to.

These two were about as different as they could be. Which one was my type? Hmmmm… I'd never really thought about having a type before. Maybe that was a good thing. These two men were physically fit and had very nice bodies. But there was no resemblance after that. Rex had black hair cropped close to his head. His eyes were blue and

intense. When he talked to you, you knew you had all of his attention, but it took a little while to get to that point with him.

Riley's longer, thick, wavy blonde hair, smiling blue eyes, and easy smile made him irresistible from the moment he introduced himself. And he'd kissed me. He hadn't asked me out like Rex had, but he'd kissed me.

I closed my eyes. There was no point thinking about this now. It was too early to tell if a relationship with either man was even remotely possible or if I was destined to be a neurotic, multi-cat owner instead. I was too tired to think about these kinds of things. I really wanted to go home and crawl into bed.

"You can go now, Ms. Wrath." Rex spoke, and my eyes flew open. When did he sneak up on me? "If we need anything more, I'll call you." He winked. I guessed that the dinner date thingy was still on the table. Yay!

"I'll take her home, Detective," Riley said as he extended his hand. Rex shook it. "And thanks again." Rex nodded, as another officer approached him with a large file.

"And what are we using for a car?" I asked as we left the station. "Mine's in the garage, and yours is in my driveway." I kind of left out the part that I'd broken his car. I figured that was a discussion that could wait...at least until I was fully armed.

"I had a new rental delivered while you were being questioned." He said as he opened the door to what looked just like the other black SUV.

Riley didn't say a word all the way back to my house, and that seemed like a solid strategy, so I didn't either. He came in with me, and I went straight to the fridge to pour us each a glass of wine.

"Again..." He cleared his throat. "I'm sorry about Lana. I had no idea."

I swallowed the whole glassful like it was a shot and poured another. "Well," I said, "I guess I didn't see it either. So don't worry about it."

My face hurt. I studied my reflection in the microwave door. I should put a mirror in here. Was that weird? Did people have mirrors in kitchens?

There was a fist-shaped bruise on my chin, and my nose had started to swell to the size of a pumpkin. But that didn't hurt as much as the guilt I was feeling.

"I'm sorry too," I said slowly, "for suspecting you, I mean."

Riley frowned. "About that…really? You really thought I'd turned for the Russians?"

"Um…no?" I gave him a weak smile, but I was sure it wouldn't help. Accusing a CIA agent of turning mole was about the worst insult there was. I couldn't take those words back, no matter how much I wanted to.

I changed the subject. "What about Midori? Did the police ask about her?"

Riley shook his head. "I think the good detective forgot about her, or he didn't hear Lana in the first place. We're okay for now."

"So if Lana didn't bring her here, kill her, and plant her in my kitchen, who did?" It was the one loose end that still dangled.

"I don't know. But the agency is concerned. You saw Smith and Johnson at the station?"

My eyes bulged to a size almost on par with my nose. "THAT was Smith and Johnson?" Smith and Johnson were legends at the Agency. Legendary heroes of the Cold War, those guys practically invented the tradecraft we used to this day. They were superstars! No one I knew had ever met them. And here they were, in my hometown, because of me! Wow. I'd rated big enough to get Smith and Johnson!

Oh no…I'd rated big enough to get Smith and Johnson. Now that I thought about it, I was pretty sure that wasn't a good thing. Obviously I was still under suspicion.

"Yes," Riley said, reading my mind, "you are still being investigated." He frowned. "And they're wondering if maybe you did know about Lana."

"WHAT??? I didn't know about Lana!" Shit. This was going to make me the laughingstock of the CIA.

He nodded. "I know, I know. I'm trying to convince them that you had no idea. That you were completely fooled by her."

I grumbled. "Not better. I'm either a traitor or a moron." Somewhere in the Black Box at Langley there was a file with my name on it. And it just got a little bigger. And not in a good way.

Riley drained his glass and got to his feet. He seemed to be staring at my ginormous nose.

"At any rate, I'm sticking around for a while. Just to make sure no more dead bodies show up around you."

My heart skipped a little beat. He was staying? I guess I'd thought he'd be on the first plane to DC once the paperwork was done.

"Lana explained Ahmed and Carlos," I said.

He nodded. "Yes, but not about Midori. And there's no reason I can think of for the head of the Yakuza to show up dead in your kitchen."

He had a point. "So you're staying?" I asked.

"Yes, Wrath. I'm staying." He looked like he was going to say something more but changed his mind. Riley took a step closer to me.

"I'd kiss you," he said softly. "But I'm not sure that's possible just yet." Then he took my hands in his and squeezed them before leaving my house. Yet? There was going to be a *yet?*

That seemed pretty positive that another kiss was impending. I watched as the door swung shut. Was Riley really boyfriend-worthy? I'd have to think about that.

I took a shower and changed into my Dora pajamas. I needed to get more grown up jammies. I wandered into the living room and looked at the Dora sheet. The long, muddy smear was still there. It made me think for a moment about Lana. It was really too bad she hated me. For a short time I'd actually thought we could be friends.

Can't do anything about that, I thought. But I could do something about getting real curtains. *When I talk to Kelly tomorrow, I'll have to ask her to help me measure.* Maybe she'd go with me to the mall to get drapes and pj's.

She was coming over to bring the Rice Krispies Treats. My stomach complained loudly.

I found some bread and made a couple of pieces of toast. As I chewed it occurred to me that more had happened to me in the last few days than in the past year. And I'd liked it. I'd missed it. Going back into the CIA was a no-go. But maybe I could find something here to keep me occupied and give me that same buzz.

Rex stopped by as I was cleaning up. He insisted that my part in all of this was pretty much over.

"The CIA sent some serious guns to bail you out." He smiled.

"Yeah," I said weakly. He looked so good in a suit. "I heard about that."

Rex sat at the breakfast bar and looked at me in a strange way I couldn't dissect. "That was pretty awful, back at the school."

I nodded. "You'll get no argument from me about that."

"You did this kind of thing before? When you worked for the CIA?" He seemed puzzled.

"I did. I spent most of my time gathering intel, but there was a lot of action too." Did he doubt me? What was I thinking? Of course he did. I would've if I were him. This whole screw up made me look like a terrible agent.

"I was good at what I did, Rex," I said. "I know it doesn't seem like that now, but I was a damn good agent."

He pointed at my nose. "That explains why you're not freaking out about that nose. Most women would've screamed the minute they got hit. But not you."

I shook my head. "No. Not me." I thought about giving him a laundry list of my injuries and wounds over the years. But maybe I should save that for our first date.

Rex got to his feet and came over to where I was standing. He reached out and lifted my chin, examining my face. "Not bad. I think you'll heal."

Rex's eyes were really close to mine. We stared at each other for a moment before he let go and stepped back.

In a dazed voice, I asked, "Did you get in trouble? For being part of it without authorization?"

"No." He smiled. "Not much. It might actually work out. The Captain is trying to get some funding from the CIA. When I left it looked like it was a definite possibility."

"They should," I said. "They've got deep pockets. I used to give my informants huge sums of money. The agency never batted an eyelash when I asked for it."

Rex arched his right eyebrow. "You look like you want to ask me something."

I nodded. I was worried about something. "Are you sure you won't get busted down to patrol? This wasn't exactly a good thing for you to be part of."

"I won't get busted." Rex laughed. "I won't get promoted, but I won't get busted." He tucked a strand of my hair behind my ear. "SWAT's pretty pissed at me though."

"Because you called them in?" I asked. I could still feel the warmth of his fingers on my cheek.

He shook his head. "No. Because they didn't get to shoot anyone."

"They could've shot Lana. I wouldn't have minded that very much." I smiled.

"I'll keep that in mind next time I have you and them in an old elementary school gym, surrounded by seven-year-old girls."

There's going to be a next time! Like a date, but with bad acoustics and guns. I didn't care if it included rutabagas and bat guano. Rex was imagining us in the future.

"You know," he said slowly, "it's going to take a few days to get all of this sorted out. But when that's over, I was wondering if you'd still want to take me up on that dinner?"

I smiled. "I'd love to."

Rex opened the door and looked back at me. "Good." He winked at me just before he walked out.

As I closed the door behind him, I leaned against it, the grin still on my face. Two men were interested in me. Two totally hot men. And even though I was out of commission with the CIA, I had a feeling that soon I'd be seeing some interesting action.

ABOUT THE AUTHOR

Leslie Langtry is the *USA Today* bestselling author of the *Greatest Hits Mysteries* series, *Sex, Lies, & Family Vacations*, *The Hanging Tree Tales* as Max Deimos, the *Merry Wrath Mysteries,* and several books she hasn't finished yet, because she's very lazy.

Leslie loves puppies and cake (but she will not share her cake with puppies) and thinks praying mantids make everything better. She lives with her family and assorted animals in the Midwest, where she is currently working on her next book and trying to learn to play the ukulele.

To learn more about Leslie, visit her online at www.leslielangtry.com

Made in the USA
Middletown, DE
18 July 2023

35391002R00118

DEVOTION NOTES

DEVOTION NOTES

DEVOTION NOTES

DEVOTION NOTES

DEVOTION NOTES

DEVOTION NOTES

DEVOTION NOTES

DEVOTION NOTES

DEVOTION NOTES

DEVOTION NOTES

Additional copies of this book and other book titles
from
ALBURY PUBLISHING are available at your local book-
store.

Albury Publishing
P.O. Box 470406
Tulsa, Oklahoma 74147-0406
In Canada books are available from:
Word Alive
P.O. Box 670
Niverville, Manitoba
CANADA ROA 1EO

To contact the Author write:
T.D. Jakes Ministries
P.O. Box 210887
Dallas, Texas 75211